IN AZGARTH'S SHADOW

Cassie Sweet

A NineStar Press Publication

Published by NineStar Press
P.O. Box 91792,
Albuquerque, New Mexico, 87199 USA.
www.ninestarpress.com

In Azgarth's Shadow

Printed in the USA
First Edition
April, 2018

Print ISBN: 978-1-948608-55-8

Also available in eBook, ISBN: 978-1-948608-50-3

When popular artist Nicholas Alexandre is shot and killed in a patron's bedroom and his body dumped in Whitechapel, it is up to the talents of Drs. Mikhail Stanslovich and Dante Savoy to bring him back to life. Since the death of his beloved sister a few months before, Nicholas has lamented his pact with the fae master, Azgarth—for the world of the fae is one of broken promises and terrifying illusions.

Fae agent, Roman Cetanni has spent his tenure as one of Azgarth's representatives trying to shield his charges from the fae master's wrath. But what once seemed a division of worlds has now morphed until the lines between the human and fae world are blurred.

Even as Roman tries to help Nicholas recover from his injuries, a new threat looms. Lately more beings from the fae have invaded the human realm, and Oiredon, another fae master, wishes an alliance with Roman and his charges to aid in overthrowing Azgarth.

In these uncertain times, one thing is for certain: war has come to the fae and the lives of the humans they've touched hang in the balance.

To all the fans who have waited patiently for the next chapter in Azgarth's saga, I thank you from the bottom of my fae-touched heart.

Chapter One

Light caressed Lady Clarissa's bare breasts, creating interesting shadows as supplied by the long dark hair that cascaded over her shoulders in tousled curls. The strands revealed as much as they hid. She lay on the bed, gaze fixed out the window, staring at the moonlight. A pensive expression filled her lovely face. She didn't do pensive well. Pouting and preening were more in line with her nature. Oh, there were the intrigues, instigations, and incidents, but they were solely to amuse.

"How much longer, Nicholas?"

"Not too much, my dear."

Nicholas Alexandre put the finishing touches on the canvas and stepped back from his work. He'd painted her as Tatiana from *A Midsummer Night's Dream*. Most people assumed Shakespeare wrote the play as a fanciful comedy. What they didn't know, or understand, was the fact the Bard wrote it from his experiences of the fae realm.

Lady Clarissa was as much Tatiana as any woman Nicholas had ever known. Petty and jealous, she lived in a world where her needs and desires were met at the cost of those around her. He indulged her because her behavior, though outrageous, amused him. He enjoyed the way her schemes horrified society. These days, it was the only thing that lifted his grief.

He studied the details of the painting, not quite satisfied with the illumination. Not to worry, he'd add flourishes later. For now, he was exhausted and wanted only to pack up his paints and—

The door burst open and banged against the wall.

"You wretched whore!"

Lady Clarissa screamed and grabbed at a sheet to shield her naked torso from her enraged husband. "My heart, it's not what you think."

Sir Rodderick Danworth laughed and held the dueling pistol pointed at Nicholas's stomach. "You expect me to believe that? In my own bedroom?"

Nicholas wiped paint from his brush, unperturbed that the angry husband threatened his life. "As you see, I came here to work. I'm nothing more than a humble painter."

The laugh this time came out bitter, pained. "There is nothing humble about you. Do your promises mean nothing?"

A prick of conscience and a slight brush of regret. "My word is still good, but my purse is not subject to the whims of honor. I still need to eat and live. I have a grieving mother to support."

The fact his mother hadn't left her bed since his sister's death, notwithstanding.

Rodderick kept his gaze focused on Nicholas, much as a hunter might a wild animal. Something stirred in the depths of his eyes, not entirely of the man himself. "You are nothing more than a deceiver. A liar."

Nicholas inclined his head in a subtle acknowledgment of the accusation and let his suspicions fall to the ground unvoiced. "And so I am what the world has made me."

Realization and pain morphed into fury, filling Rodderick's eyes. He fought an inner demon that shone in the dark depths. The gun went off.

Nicholas watched in horror as the shot struck him true. Crimson bloomed across the front of his white shirt, spreading like paint through a jar of mineral spirits. Odd how no pain registered.

The paintbrush dropped from fingers that no longer worked. Sound became a distant, hollow thing. A scream came from behind him, but even that had the quality of a train entering a tunnel, the whistle fading into the dark earth.

If he'd had the ability, Nicholas would have laughed. A mortal wound would not kill one such as him; it only released him into the hands of the fae master, Azgarth. And therein lay his real fear. Servitude on this plane was one of commerce, a way to provide for his family in the manner they'd become accustom. Being one of the chosen in the fae realm for eternity was not the thing of beauty Azgarth promised. The thing he'd seen welling in Rodderick's eyes.

The only one to derive any pleasure from such an association was Azgarth himself. However, it might give him a chance to see Juliana again. To see if she'd been taken into the fae realm on her death and protected.

Rodderick stood over him, his face white, lips pale. Tears streamed down his face. The darkness had faded from his eyes. "Look what you made me do."

He was unsure if Rodderick meant Nicholas, Clarissa, or Azgarth. He moved his arm to try to cover the wound and staunch the flow, but could do nothing more than watch as the blood began to soak into the carpet beneath.

Lady Clarissa finally rose from the bed. She stood over Nicholas, looking down on him. Her mouth was pinched with displeasure, no doubt for the stains that ruined the Aubusson. "I knew your jealousy would one day be your downfall."

Rodderick still held the pistol. Disbelief pulled his mouth down at the corners. "I've killed him."

Nicholas tried to inform Rodderick that he was very much mistaken—he still lived and heard every word they said. The one to kill him was much worse than Rodderick could ever imagine.

Lady Clarissa took Rodderick by the arm. "No. We will keep this between the two of us. Call Charles and have him dump the body in Whitechapel. No one will bat an eye for one more murder in that part of town."

Rodderick nodded mutely. He started out of the room, then turned back as Nicholas took one last shuddery breath.

Figures moved around him in a haze. A head blocked out the light, creating a unique halo around a face cast in shadow. Dr. Mikhail Stanslovich attempted to focus on the image, but his eyes refused to cooperate. The sweet scent of opium tried to pull him under in blissful oblivion.

Small hands and pointy ears made him question his sanity, but then nothing was sane in the midst of an opium-induced haze. The creature began to tug at his shirt, hair, and ears—anything little fingers might grab to get his attention. It failed to stir him. He might have swatted at it a time or two, as one might a particularly nasty bug. Finally, it got the hint and left him alone. Mikhail closed his eyes, taking more of the smoke-laden air into his lungs as he fell deeper into the haze.

A slap to his face and a quick biting reprimand brought him back to consciousness, though he had no idea how long he'd been out. Another reprimand, this one coarser, angrier than the first. He knew that voice and hated the fact he'd been found by the one person who had the ability to make him feel small.

"Leave me alone." He might have struck out at his attacker, or simply thought he did. With the amount of mind-numbing drugs in his system, it was hard to tell.

"Valentine, grab him under the other arm." A voice very close to his ear breathed hot breath on him. "We will carry you out by force, make no mistake, Mikhail."

The sensation of being lifted, floating along a surface of jagged rocks propelled him through the dark room and into the harsh bite of the chill night. He tried to turn away from the effects of fresh air—or not so fresh, as the alley smelled of human waste and vomit. Why were they doing this to him? The indignity of being carried from a drug den against his will was too much to endure. Did they not realize opium was the only refuge from truth? That his entire existence had been called into question? Meeting Azgarth—knowing he was real—had implications on Mikhail's work and success he'd never anticipated. How was one to react knowing their life was directed by a being with an agenda as fanciful as it was vile?

A few short months ago, he'd believed himself to be the forerunner of scientific breakthrough in the reanimation sciences. He'd given new life to celebrated violinist, Andres Valentine. Literally brought Valentine back from the dead, only to discover that no matter how triumphant Mikhail's accomplishments, they were not his at all. No, all the most glorious of his achievements he now knew were solely the actions of the fae master, Azgarth.

Mikhail tried to fight against the arms that held him. For his efforts, he was tossed unceremoniously into a carriage. Someone fought with his sleeve. A tiny pinprick of pain came as warm calm filled his veins, chasing away the effects of the opium from his system. He closed his eyes, wishing to hold on to the sensation of oblivion as long as possible.

"You are a disgrace to your profession." The voice was angry, hot.

"I'm a visionary. No, wait. I tell a lie. Azgarth is the visionary; I'm merely a puppet."

"For God's sake. Pull yourself together, man." The voice held more than a measure of disgust. "You don't see Henri and me falling apart. Lord knows someone has to keep your practice going as you bask in your self-indulgent breakdown."

Mikhail cracked an eye open and regarded Dante with a frown. "I never asked either of you to interfere with my grief."

"Grief." Dante made the word into an epithet. "The only grief you feel is in the fact you were wrong. Well, you know something, my pickled friend? It was bound to happen sometime."

"I really hate you when you're self-righteous." Mikhail turned away. "You're pompous too."

"I'm also the man who is saving you from yourself, though why I'm bothering I have no idea." Dante turned away and looked out the carriage window. Some best friend he'd turned out to be. Traitor.

The carriage cut through the London streets. Mikhail tried not to sit too close to Dante, nor pay attention to Valentine. They were against him—all of them.

Even Henri had been distant and moody.

"Tell him," Valentine whispered.

Mikhail gazed over at Dante. "Tell me what?"

"There's been a murder. A painter of some recent fame."

Mikhail sat up as much as his weakened, drugged state would allow. Dante's antidote had given him a somewhat clear head, but his body remained weak. "What have I to do with a painter?"

"Only the fact it was a fresh kill, the body dumped. I thought perhaps you might return to the land of the living by performing a resurrection."

"If the bugger was careless enough to get himself killed, it is of no consequence to me."

Dante glared. "You're pathetic and not the man I thought I knew."

"And the world isn't what we thought either."

"Is that reason enough to let a great talent die? One who paints portraits of the fae realm?"

Mikhail turned in his seat to fully face Dante. "What did you say?"

"Nicholas Alexandre's favorite subject is the fae realm. The court of Azgarth."

Air eased out of Mikhail's lungs. Nothing he'd heard so far had captured his interest as much as that fact. "You should have mentioned that first."

"I'm not sure it would have penetrated the veil of opium."

That stung. Dante was a just and moral man. A good man. He'd hate seeing anyone he cared about lose themselves to the oblivion of drugs. The set of his shoulders alone was enough to prove he was irritated at Mikhail.

Shame burned right below Mikhail's heart. He rubbed a hand over the spot. "How was our subject killed?"

"Shot. Dueling pistol. Lead ball to the gut."

Mikhail let out a moan. The newer revolvers didn't do near the damage the old dueling pistols did. "Bad?"

"Devastating."

The carriage stopped. Mikhail's head was a bit clearer, but he was certain they'd not traveled all the way to his estate. "Why have we stopped?"

"We're here."

He looked out the window to the gates of Dante's house. "Why are we here?"

"You'll see."

Dante climbed out of the carriage, and then he and Valentine helped Mikhail down. His legs remained unsteady. Whatever Dante had used to counteract the opium, hadn't quite made it through to Mikhail's limbs. His head started to pound. Light hurt his eyes.

They walked through the rooms to the surgery where a man lay on a table, covered by a sheet. Blood hung in glass bottles, going into a large vein in his arm. Henri sat next to the table, monitoring the subject. On the subject's chest was the compressonator, pumping out a steady beat, doing the work of the heart.

Mikhail motioned for Dante and Valentine to bring him closer to inspect the subject. He had no doubt Dante had already fixed the wound and stitched up the abdomen.

He pulled down the sheet and studied the straight stitches transversing the torso. "Did you have to remove much of the small intestines?"

"No. A few repairs, but the worst part was that the ball ripped through the abdominal aorta. I suspect he bled out before the body was dumped."

Mikhail narrowed his eyes. Doubts of the feasibility of saving this particular subject rose. "We're going to lose the window. There isn't time for a full transfusion before the serum is administered."

Dante gave him a wicked smile. "I may have found a way around that small problem. I added the serum to the blood. It's being infused along with the transfusion. Premixed before going into the body."

Mikhail gave a bark. Weariness rode him and he sagged down into a nearby chair. "If you thought of all this, you hardly needed to drag me from my activities."

Dante cut a haughty glance his way. "*That* was not active. It's an excuse, and a poor one at that."

"Did you bring me here to abuse me?"

"If that's what it takes to get you sober and clearheaded." Dante closed the space between them and held out his hand. "Come. Let me see you to a room where you can sleep."

That was the first sensible thing Dante had said all evening. Pride had him shooing the offered hand away. He might be shaky as a new foal, but he'd make it to the room under his own steam or not at all. Not after Dante had the audacity to speak to him so in front of Henri and Valentine.

Mikhail pushed off from the chair and held his hand on the back until he felt stable enough to walk. He shot a glance to Henri. Both he and

Valentine had turned away. Shame gouged a pit under his heart. Some mentor he'd turned out to be.

He cleared his throat. "Lead the way."

Dante gave him a dubious look, then turned and walked slowly from the room.

"You can move faster, Dante."

"I don't want you to fall, and since you refused my assistance, prudence must prevail."

His life had become such a shambles. For that, he had no one to blame but himself. Oh, it was easy to place the responsibility squarely on Azgarth's shoulders, but there had to be better avenues to defeating the fae master than falling into a cloud of mind-numbing smoke.

Weren't there?

They climbed the stairs. Mikhail had to stop every few steps and steady himself. A wave of dizziness washed over him, causing cold sweat to break out on his brow and coat his back. A reaction to the opium mixed with whatever antidote Dante had injected into him.

Dante stopped a few stairs up from him. "Are you unwell?"

Mikhail swallowed down the rising nausea. "Give me a moment."

Dante came back to him, placing a firm hand on his back. "No one is here to see if I help you or not."

"I'll know."

"And you are the most stubborn, stupid man I have ever met."

The charge stung in more ways than Mikhail was willing to admit. If he acted as if the words had no impact, perhaps Dante might not use them as frequently.

Mikhail closed his eyes and waited for the wave of sickness to ebb. With any luck, he'd not make himself a further fool by vomiting all over Dante's marble staircase. Not that he'd eaten anything that day in order to come up.

Dante studied him closely. "Now what's wrong?"

Mikhail lifted his hand to say it didn't matter. He wasn't going to admit that he didn't remember the last time he'd eaten or what kind of meal it had been. The idea of food put him off in a bad way. His stomach roiled and pitched.

He took Dante's hand and squeezed it. "I think I need to lie down."

"Let me get you to a room."

"No. Here."

He started to lower himself to the hard stairs, but Dante scooped him under the arms and picked him up.

By Sir Issac's balls! This was the final humiliation.

He closed his eyes and allowed Dante to drag him down the hall like an oversized rag doll.

They stopped. A door banged open. Mikhail was helped to the bed, and then dim light started to build behind his closed lids.

Slowly, he opened them. Concern filled Dante's face as he stood staring down at Mikhail. "You have some tough decisions to make, my friend."

Mikhail rested his arm on his forehead. He knew. He just didn't like others pointing out the obvious. "If you are going to lecture me on my drug consumption, you can save your breath."

Dante let out an aggrieved sigh. "Then perhaps you'd like to discuss your funeral arrangements."

A cold fist grabbed his heart and squeezed. Death was a sure way to give Azgarth triumph. If he died before finding the book with his and Dante's names, neither of them would ever be free.

"I'm not going to die."

"Says the man hell-bent on killing himself."

"It won't come to that." Mikhail put no conviction behind the words. He hadn't any to spare. Kicking the lust for a potent drug wasn't so easily done, not even by a man of his experience and knowledge.

"You might believe that, but as one who has to sit by and watch as you fall further into your despair, I see nothing but a bad end to you and it's killing me." The last of Dante's words were choked off in emotion. He turned away, heading for the door. "If you need anything, just ring the bell."

Ring the bell? Mikhail glanced around and could not locate the bell pull anywhere in his vicinity.

He closed his eyes. Immediate and horrific dreams rose. This wasn't the restful sleep of a man under the influence of drugs, but a nightmare born of his mistakes. So many to account for over the past few months.

Visions of potential failures in reanimation poked and prodded him. Faces with sloughing skin gazed at him accusingly. One lifted a clawlike hand to point a skeletal finger. The mouth opened, but the words that issued forth were garbled, unintelligible. He'd never seen any of those people—had never used so many human subjects. So what was this, some preview of his bleak future?

A voice whispered in his ear, counter to the ones who threw doubts like rocks at his confidence.

He might have had his share of failures when he first began to experiment in the new science of reanimation, but his human subjects had lived. Valentine was a triumph. But could he be counted? Did Azgarth have more a hand in keeping him alive than any of Mikhail's ingenuity?

Another blow to his pride? Would they never end?

"Leave me alone."

The visions dissipated on command, so much smoke on the air.

He rolled onto his side, tucking a hand under his chin. If he took nice deep breaths and let relaxation come, perhaps he'd fall into an untroubled sleep and wake in the morning to a new world.

Or perhaps the world would be as always—out of his control.

Chapter Two

Roman Cetanni trudged through the dirty, crowded streets of London. The stink of unwashed bodies, horse refuse, and urine filled his nose and made him want to gag. He preferred not to spend time in such places if he didn't have to and yet Nicholas Alexandre enjoyed the seedy parts of the city. Why on earth he'd want to do so was beyond Roman's ability to guess. Too many sad stories and blatant indiscretions rode on the wave of scents carried through the streets. Surely, there were as many amusements to be found in the drawing rooms and salons of the wealthier citizens of London as were in this forsaken corner of the world. They usually smelled better too. The wealthy had ways of covering up their olfactory tells that most of the lesser beings of society hadn't the means.

Nicholas had failed to meet him at the designated pub at the time they'd agreed. Punctuality was one trait Nicholas had in spades. He also kept his word, so the fact he'd not shown for their appointment was cause for some concern.

Roman took out his pocket watch and opened the cover. Many years had passed since time held meaning for him. However, most people kept their lives regimented by the segments on a clock face. Every hour of their day taken up with duties or responsibilities that only served to gain them more of the same. Senseless.

Time had dwindled down to the wee hours of the morning. Soon the sun would rise and a new day begin.

Where had Nicholas gone? Surely, he hadn't found a paramour to spend the evening. Lady Clarissa might be a handsome woman, but Roman doubted she'd turn Nicholas's head. He preferred to find his lovers in the gentleman's clubs.

Roman walked to the edges of the bad section, where more hope and better housing prevailed, hailed a hired carriage, and gave the direction. The confines smelled worse than the street. Questionable substances were smeared across the seats. He lifted a handkerchief to his nose and gazed out the window.

What mischief had Nicholas found this time?

The carriage pulled up in front of the home of Lady Clarissa. Roman jumped out of the carriage and flipped a coin up to the driver, who promptly caught it and bit into it. He took out the gold and inspected it.

"Are you for real, gov?"

Roman tipped his hat and melded into the scenery. The clop of the horses' hooves faded into the distance. All was still. He'd been in crypts that had been livelier than this neighborhood. Yet a pervasive evil clung to the houses, the cobbles, the very grass. He took a deep breath and assessed the situation. Just there, under the reek of humanity came the unmistakable tang of blood. Lots of it.

The stench came from directly in front of him—Lady Clarissa's address.

"Oh, Nicholas." Roman stepped up to the black iron fence and looked through the gates. If anything untoward had happened there, no visible signs showed on the outside.

All the lights were off with the exception of those that illuminated the exterior. If Nicholas was in there, he wasn't coming out anytime soon.

Roman turned back around and sniffed the wind. But that blood. That tinny, metallic scent imbued with life force and enough energy to light the entirety of London.

A sick feeling crept up from his belly. He followed the scent trail, hoping he was wrong and his nose had failed him. Instincts told him he was on the right track. A slight breeze bathed his face. Wind changed direction. The scent disappeared.

Damn, he'd lost it.

The sun cleared the buildings, painting the city in a soft pink-gold patina. Not knowing where else to look, he returned to his lodgings, defeated.

He stopped at the desk. "Are there any messages for me?"

The young man shook his head. "Sorry. No, Mr. Cetanni."

So Nicholas hadn't come to the hotel or left any kind of message saying he'd been delayed or changed his plans. He hadn't been at home either. His mother was not receiving visitors, and Roman doubted she knew her son's whereabouts anyhow.

Roman crossed the lobby and went to his room. The morning edition of the paper sat in front of his door. A headline screamed up at him from the black-and-white newsprint.

Body of Slain Man Disappears from Crowded Street.

He scanned the article but saw no description of the victim. Even without it, he knew. Felt it burning deep in his gut. He'd failed Nicholas in the most basic of ways.

Damn the man.

The article might not have described the deceased, but it did give the section of the city where the body had been found. Blood scent was unique to the individual. If he went to the scene of the crime and compared the ambient blood scent to that of what he'd caught in front of Lady Clarissa's, then perhaps it might give him an idea of what happened—or at least if Nicholas was involved.

If he only knew the scent of Nicholas's blood. He'd had no occasion to become that intimate with the man. But if he could extrapolate the scent of Nicholas's blood from the other scents such as hair and skin, he might be about to make a positive identification. Sweat also had a unique scent. Each person carried a particular flavor on the wind. Creative people smelled sweeter for some reason—at least to Roman's refined nose.

After glancing over a few more details—gleaning what he could from the sensationalism of the article—Roman headed back out into the early morning light. With any luck, the crime scene would be devoid of gawkers, onlookers, and investigators. The last thing he needed was Scotland Yard creeping around the area, trying to find clues and impinging on his mission.

Even if he verified Nicholas's identity as the slain man, how would he locate the body? Who had stolen it?

He was almost certain who *hadn't* taken it—if indeed the deceased turned out to be Nicholas. In that case, none of Roman's problems would be as crucial, though recompense must be made.

A warning chill swam down his spine. He moved faster into the streets and cut across town. How many times in twenty-four hours was he going to have to make this trip? Nicholas had always been trouble, but in death, he was more so. And therein lay an even bigger question: if Nicholas was dead, wouldn't Roman feel it through their connection? If so, why hadn't he?

As he traveled, Roman tried not to see, hear, taste, and feel all the emotions swarming in a nest of angry bees around him. He blocked out the voices swirling around him, buzzing his ears. Distractions were problematic for him. Always had been. Being an effective agent meant he needed to keep focused. Most of the time, he heard too many voices, too many thoughts bleeding out of the huddled masses of Londoners to do his job properly. For that, he'd been punished hard and often.

He took a deep breath. No sense in dwelling on that now, it only led to panic and grief.

It took some time and a few misdirections before he found the street in question. The scent of blood was faint. It had washed away with the morning dew, gutter run-off, and general rubbish smell.

A few constables milled about, and a few men in plain suits—those from the Yard. Roman stood behind a barricade and tried to push the scents of the unwashed bodies and rancid clothing of the onlookers away from him. He stirred the air, shifting through all the different flavors floating about, until he plucked one out, a thread separate from the rest. This he recognized. Knew it well.

Nicholas had been there.

Roman took a deeper breath and let the strains of the bouquet that made up Nicholas bloom against his palate and tongue. Fear. Contempt. Arrogance. All the flavors that made Nicholas who he was had been present—save one essential ingredient: life.

He closed his eyes and followed the scent from the alley. The Yard was never going to find Nicholas's body with conventional methods, and for that, Roman was eternally grateful.

Mikhail rolled over and touched his forehead. Who had the audacity to drive railroad spikes through his frontal lobe? He moaned and pressed the heels of his hands into his eye sockets.

Shame that Dante had seen him in such a state was nearly as painful as the aftereffects of the opium. He slid deeper into the covers and pulled them over his head. Maybe if he fell far enough into the down and cotton, he'd leave the world completely. No telling where he'd end up and he didn't want to go back to the fae realm anytime soon. Once in his life was enough for him. The fun-house horror of the walk he'd taken with Dante had left a lasting impression on him. No mortal had control of their person or circumstances in that world beyond the veil and it was pointless to believe otherwise. The only things they'd managed to find there were more questions.

A knock on the door interrupted his quiet, fabric prison. The door opened. "Are you still alive, or should I put you into your own concoction?"

"Could you speak a bit quieter, lest my head explode and I ruin your linens?"

Dante's footsteps neared the bed. The curtains were pushed back, letting in more light than Mikhail ever wanted to see so early in the morning. "Get up. I'll not allow you to wallow in pity and self-indulgence."

"How about pain?"

"It's your own fault you feel like hell. I'm not going to feel sorry for you when you could have prevented this by staying out of the opium dens."

"I hate you."

A weary sigh filled the air above Mikhail's head. "I know."

Pain of a different kind filled Mikhail's chest as he heard Dante's retreating steps. Left alone to pull himself from the abyss, Mikhail rolled onto his side and hugged the covers to his face. Maybe he'd suffocate and then he wouldn't have to worry about what a fool he'd made himself into. Not that Dante would care. He'd probably get annoyed that his best sheets were dirtied.

No. That was unfair.

Dante had never been anything but honorable and just. He was a good man, even when Mikhail didn't deserve kindness in any fashion.

He must have fallen back to sleep, for the next he knew, the sun was overhead and the room warmer. Sweat drenched his body in a sickly, sweet stench.

Surely he hadn't fallen into withdrawal so quickly. Oh, by all the heavens, he felt a right wretched thing.

Coffee, he needed lots of it. Hot and strong and brewed thick as tar. Tea, no matter how strong, wouldn't do in this case.

He poked his head out of the covers and glanced around. On the bedside table sat a silver pot and cup with saucer. So Dante had thought to provide him with some form of liquid relief.

Mikhail swung his legs over and sat on the edge of the bed. His head still pounded and his hands shook. He reached for the silver pot, touching the body of it. Cold. It had sat so long the contents had grown cold.

Oh, well. He poured a cup and shot it back as if drinking the smoothest whiskey. It went down the wrong way, making him cough and choke.

Henri walked in as Mikhail wiped the tears from his eyes. His expression was one of crude disappointment. He rested his hands on his hips. "Do you require assistance?"

Mikhail held up his hand. "No. I can manage to choke on my own."

A reluctant smile lifted the corner of Henri's mouth. "I can see that. I meant with your ablutions."

"What time is it?"

"Half one."

Mikhail moaned at the lost time and tried to stand. He was still in the same clothes he'd worn to the den. They stank of smoke and neglect. "I need a bath and some fresh clothes." He rubbed a hand across his bristled jaw. "And a shave."

"I'll get one ready for you."

Mikhail held up a hand. "Have a servant do it. I'm sure you have more important matters to attend than to care for me."

Henri's look of sympathy made Mikhail turn away. "We may not see eye to eye all the time, but I still owe you a debt for taking me in. Consider it a small repayment."

"You have more reason than anyone to think ill of me." Mikhail rubbed a hand over his head. His hair even felt grimy with smoke residue.

"Well, you haven't always been an easy employer, but you haven't exactly been a tyrant either."

Mikhail gave a rueful laugh. "That is something, I guess."

He allowed Henri to help him to his feet. Once standing, it took a moment for a wave of dizziness to pass before he was able to walk to the small bathing chamber set off from the room.

A quick look in the mirror and he wished he hadn't bothered. Better if he avoided looking into the eyes of his reflection. There were things in their depths he knew he'd not want to see. Too many truths he'd rather leave buried for now. He possessed only enough strength to fight one demon at a time—right then, that demon was opium.

He washed his face, shaved, and ran a wet rag through his hair in lieu of scrubbing it proper. Enough time had already been wasted while he slept off his bender. A man downstairs needed his expertise to cheat death, and he had every intention of making good the promise Dante made when he'd recovered the body.

Henri remained in the bedroom. He'd laid clean clothes across the bed, working as efficiently as any valet ever had. "Dr. Savoy held dinner for you."

Food sounded neither appetizing nor interesting at the moment.

"Coffee. Preferably hot. I'll take it the laboratory."

Henri raised a shoulder as if to say it didn't matter to him one way or the other. "I'll let Feltch know."

Feltch was Dante's butler. The man would have a stroke if he knew coffee or any beverage other than alcohol was to be consumed outside of the designated perimeters of the dining room or main salon.

Henri left Mikhail alone to dress. When the door closed, Mikhail trailed his hand down the familiar shirt and trousers. Dante must have gone by the estate and retrieved some of Mikhail's personal effects.

Thoughtful. Behavior he'd expect of Dante.

He dressed with care, stalling for time and trying to think of what to say once he entered the laboratory. Apologies seemed inadequate. Thank you, not quite enough.

He ran his hand through his hair and steeled himself against the recriminations. What had Dante said that wasn't true? Painful as it was to hear, he'd been right on every count.

Servants were scarce as he crossed the townhouse to the ballroom-turned-laboratory. Not that Dante employed many domestics, but he expected to see one or two in the midst of discharging their daily duties. Maybe he'd given them time off with the exception of the kitchen staff and Feltch. Not every domestic who worked within the confines of London were able to withstand employment in a household where reanimation took place.

He entered the laboratory to the scent of fresh-brewed coffee and the quiet burble of a tank motor.

Where Mikhail had always submerged the subject in a suspended horizontal position, this tank stood upright and was comprised of two compartments. The first was a drum that contained the resurrection fluid. A series of wide-bore tubing fed into a standing glass tank, with a water-tight door on the front.

Mikhail turned to Dante. "Did you build this?"

"I might have been the inspiration for it, but Henri built it." A twinkle of excitement filled Dante's eyes. He rubbed his hands together. "It really is quite genius and improves upon your designs."

"I take it the fluid is pumped from the drum to the tank?"

Dante nodded and moved to the contraption to point out various levers and spigots. "The flow of fluid can go either way. It's a safety feature in case what happened to Valentine happens again. It will be easier to get a subject out of a tank, or lower the fluid level by draining it."

Mikhail frowned as he inspected the improvements. "How do you get the subject submerged over the head without drowning him?"

"With one of these." Dante picked up a mask apparatus. "It fits over the nose and mouth like so." He demonstrated by fitting the bridge of the mask to the corresponding place on his nose. "Then it is tied into place." His voice sounded muffled and far away.

A hole was located halfway between nose and mouth. Mikhail glanced inside. "I assume a tube goes here."

Dante took off the mask. "Correct. It is used to supply the subject with fresh air and a bit of pressure to inflate the lungs."

Mikhail made a noise in the back of his throat, considering the applications of such a device. "If we added a timer function to that, we could inflate and deflate the lungs to mimic respirations."

Dante smiled. "I'll get Henri on it."

The subject remained on the table. Henri's compressonator bounced up and down in a rhythmic pace. Blood continued to drip into the large vein of the left arm from a glass bottle hanging above.

"How many more pints does he require before his total volume is restored?" Mikhail walked across the room to study the subject and the infusion. "Have you added more serum to each bottle?"

"Yes. It seems to work well that way, or at least it appears to. We'll know more when we wake him."

Mikhail turned to Dante. "It looks like you don't need me at all. You have a nice setup here. You should be proud."

Dante's enthusiasm dimmed. "I didn't do this to usurp you. I did it to show you how important your work is—how the world needs men like you to carry on and advance the sciences."

Mikhail considered the laboratory and the improvements Dante had commissioned on the tank. He'd put a lot of thought into creating an environment conducive to reanimation. Not for competition, but to support. To bring Mikhail back into the science he'd poured his heart and soul into.

He squeezed Dante's shoulder. "I appreciate all you've done."

"You're welcome."

Mikhail gave a reluctant smile. "Thank you."

Why was it so hard to admit he needed his friends? That their support was important to him? He'd spent his entire life not needing anyone, being a man who success came easy to, and yet he would have nothing if it wasn't for Dante and Henri. They had made all the difference in his life and it was about time he repaid their loyalty.

"You never said how much more blood the subject needs before his volume is restored." Mikhail bent over to assess the subject's pallor.

"Two more after this one and he will be at an acceptable level." Dante checked the bottle much as Mikhail had done earlier. "It's going to take the rest of the night and into morning. I expect he'll be ready for the tank tomorrow."

With the artificial compressions, the color had slowly come back into the subject's body. What a difference a small invention made. Mikhail glanced over at the air machine and mask, considering the impact breathing for the subject throughout the course of the procedure might have on the outcome.

Dante raised a brow. "You've got that look on your face."

"What look is that?"

"The one where you are about to come up with something inspired."

Mikhail brushed off the compliment. "Nothing that clever, only an extension of your and Henri's brilliance."

Interest lit Dante's eyes. "Which is?"

"If the compressonator keeps the blood circulating to further our cause, then using your air pressure machine to give breaths will keep the ventilatory system functioning." Mikhail moved his hands in and out over his chest to mimic deep breathing. "If we had a way to vary the pressures in the lungs."

Dante narrowed his eyes. "Time and pressure." He took off for the laboratory door. "Henri! Henri, get in here!"

The sound of running feet moved across the floor above them, hurrying across to the main staircase. "Has the subject woken already?" came the returned shout.

Dante didn't bother to answer. He crossed the laboratory to the air pressure machine and switched it on. A loud hiss of air and vibration of motor filled the room.

Henri entered. He glanced at the subject and then to the air machine. "Are you ready for that?"

Dante switched it off again. "Not quite. Mikhail would like a few modifications made if it's possible."

"It's always possible." Henri slid his hands down into his pockets. "What would you like it to do?"

"Timed breaths with variable pressures to mimic the respiratory cycle." Mikhail watched Henri's face to see if the idea intrigued.

Henri pursed his lips. Already his face showed proof his brain worked on the problem and any solutions. "Let me think on this, and I'll get back to you."

For the time being, it was the best Mikhail could expect. A tall order needed time to be filled, even when the one assigned to the project did so under the auspices of a dark fae master.

Mikhail frowned and watched Henri as he went to the small desk in the corner and made himself at home with paper and pencil to draw out a schematic. No one who had known Henri before his *wolfsine* attack would ever detect anything different in the man. From the very first day he'd come to Mikhail's notice, Henri had proved his creativity, ingenuity, and intelligence. If he could dive headfirst into his work knowing the terrible connection he had with Azgarth, why did Mikhail have such a hard time getting past it all? Even Dante—fanciful and dramatic Dante—seemed to enter into his duties with enthusiasm.

Did it even matter what mechanism the power to create used to initiate ideas? If lives were saved because of what each of them had become, was it of any consequence? The only thing that should matter was the preservation of life.

Mikhail let out a deep breath and looked once again to the subject.

Nicholas, Dante had called him. Nicholas Alexandre. He had a name and a family. Hopes and dreams, fears and foibles. He was human, and he was worth saving.

Chapter Three

Roman stood outside the townhouse of one Dr. Dante Savoy. Glancing up at the edifice evoked no feelings of mystery or suspicion. The neighborhood was quiet and lined with decorative trees along the street. Across the way was a small park where people rode horses and walked along a promenade filled with flowers. The scene was idyllic, peaceful, and almost too congenial to be plunked down in the middle of London. Not and be the epicenter of the gruesome work that went on behind the closed doors and shuttered windows. A subtle pale hovered about the place as if at any minute the quiet surroundings would be filled with the screams of the damned.

Still if Nicholas had been brought there, he wasn't beyond hope and that was good enough for Roman.

The problem was how to go about getting access to the house if they turned him away? He had no power to travel through walls and bend dimensions. His only real talent was to see artistry hidden inside the soul and smell the various forms of life on a person. Odd talents, but they had served him well so far and he wasn't one to call a blessing a curse. And vice versa.

Laughter and screeching from the park startled him. Almost, but not quite on cue. He turned to see a young boy about twelve pull the hat from a girl about the same age. He took off at a dash, daring her to chase him.

Rude little bugger.

While others in the park had their attention turned to the antics of young misplaced love, Roman rang the doorbell and stepped back, folding his hands in front of him to wait.

A butler opened the door and looked down with one imperious brow raised, then briefly turned his attention to the commotion in the park. "May I help you, sir?"

"I am here to see Dr. Dante Savoy on a matter most urgent." Roman reached into his inner pocket and retrieved one of his calling cards. "It is in regards to Mr. Nicholas Alexandre."

The butler's dour expression changed only enough to let Roman know the name had some recognition. "Wait here, sir."

Roman did as told as the door shut in his face. The outrage across the street escalated. He turned around and caught sight of the young boy being jerked by the arm by a man twice his size.

Really, injustice of that kind chafed at his soul. Truthfully, it wasn't right that the boy snatched a girl's hat from her head, but it didn't justify being brutalized by a behemoth. Suddenly the boy cried out. His arm and shoulder stuck in an awkward angle.

Roman leapt off the steps and went charging for the park. He hit the brute full speed, knocking him to the ground. "How would you like me to break your arm?"

The man looked up, dazed, as if he'd never considered someone would dare take offense to the injustice of his crime. "Mind your own business."

"And if I had, would you have broken his neck?" Roman gazed down at the man, putting all the rage of hell into his eyes. Recognition lit the man's expression and he hunkered back in fear.

In the background, the boy held his arm and cried. The girl started to sob and pat the boy in comfort.

The brute started to get up, but Roman pointed down at him. "I wouldn't if I were you."

By this time, a circle had formed around the melee.

"Were you all going to just let him kill the boy?" A woman started to open her mouth, but Roman held up his hand to stop her. "I saw the entire thing from across the street. A reprimand and lecture of not snatching hats in future would have sufficed. Breaking a child's arm and dislocating his shoulder is really beyond the pale."

Some of the adults had the good sense to look chagrined at their behavior, others angry for his interference. He didn't care.

Two more men showed up at the park. "What in the name of all that's holy is going on here?"

Both men had the aura of being touched by the fae. Roman pointed at the boy. "If you are Dr. Savoy, I believe the boy could use your assistance."

Surprise lifted the good doctor's brow before he went to care for the badly injured arm. The other man stared at Roman, and he got the sense more moved underneath the surface than mere speculation.

The man approached and indicated Roman step to the side with him so they might speak in private. "You are Dr. Savoy's visitor?"

"I am." Roman glanced over his shoulder. "I'm sorry, but I felt I needed to intercede on the child's behalf before Goliath there tore him asunder."

The man gave a grunt in the back of his throat and held out his hand. "Dr. Mikhail Stanslovich, Dr. Savoy's associate."

Roman took Dr. Stanslovich's hand and shook it. "Roman Cetanni. I'm a friend and manager of Nicholas Alexandre."

"Manager? Do artists need a manager?"

"They do when they have a problem managing themselves."

Dr. Stanslovich cocked his head. "And why would you assume that Dr. Savoy knows anything about Mr. Alexandre?"

"The job of a good manager is to know the whereabouts of their clients, particularly if said client has run afoul of trouble."

Dr. Savoy started back out of the park with the boy in tow. "I'm going to set his arm and send Feltch to find the boy's parents. Call the constables to have that brute locked up."

The brute in question had gotten up and dusted off his pants. His brow was set low in a frown. "I'm allowed to defend a little girl."

Roman turned. Savage hate roared to life in him. He never did have patience for those who took out their aggression on smaller, lesser beings. "Perhaps! But you are not allowed to ravage those weaker than you. What would happen if a blood infection should set in when the bone heals improperly? Or if his shoulder will no longer support weight? How will he maintain a position of employment? Care for himself? Did you think about that while defending her? Did you once consider the consequences of *your* actions?"

The man grew angrier. Accusations of inequality in crime and punishment did not sit right with him. His expression said it all.

The little girl continued to cry. "I don't want Albie to die."

The big man held his hat in his hand, his expression softened. "He won't die, Little Miss. This here gent is just trying to scare you."

"He's going to get infected," she countered. "I heard him say so."

Roman closed his eyes. This was getting him nowhere. He centered his attention on the girl's mother. "I'd take her home to collect herself if I were you."

She merely nodded and patted her daughter, steering her away from the scene of the crime. Other bystanders remained where they were, waiting to see the final outcome. He pretended they were far away.

"As for you, I should do as Dr. Savoy suggested and call the constables. However noble your motives, they went too far. It is never right to prey on those smaller than you."

"It's not like I went looking for trouble." The protest did not move Roman in the least. He'd known too many like this man over the years. Some human, others not. The cycle had to end.

It started with one man.

"No, but it found you. Now it will never leave you alone."

With that, Roman turned and started for Dr. Savoy's residence. He'd already spent enough time involved in a situation not of his making. Sometimes, though, one had to get involved if only to balance the scales a bit.

Truly, the girl looked more aggrieved that Albie might be maimed for life than she did about her hat. If memory served, Albie's actions were more a way of misguided flirting than malicious intent.

Dr. Stanslovich caught up with Roman as he crossed the street. "What exactly happened back there?"

"The injured boy—Albie—snatched the little girl's hat from her head. The man took exception and hurt the boy."

"And you intervened?"

"I couldn't very well let a man more than twice the boy's size keep at him. No telling if he'd have stopped at a broken arm and dislocated shoulder or if he'd rip the appendage clean off." Roman shivered at the thought.

"And you let it go with a cryptic remark."

Roman gave Dr. Stanslovich a knowing smile. "Not cryptic."

They said no more as Dr. Stanslovich opened the front door of Dr. Savoy's residence and let them inside.

The home was comfortably appointed. Dark paneling gave the interior a warm feel. He followed Dr. Stanslovich down a long hallway and into an office of sorts. Medical journals, textbooks, and models of various mammals, human and otherwise, crowded the room. A large desk sat facing a bay window. Through another door, Dr. Savoy had the boy up on an examination table. With his back to the door and standing in front, it was hard to see if the boy's shoulder had been put back in place yet.

Such a painful procedure.

Dr. Stanslovich knocked on the door.

"Enter."

Roman followed the doctor into the examination room. An overwhelming scent of vomit and chemicals hit him as he crossed the threshold. Albie sat on the table, holding his arm up while Dr. Savoy placed a splint on it.

"How is the young patient doing?"

A glance to Albie's face showed it tearstained with red puffy eyes. "I got sick."

Roman crossed the room, searching for another door. "Pain will sometimes do that."

Dr. Savoy glanced over his shoulder. "I take it you aren't the boy's father."

"No. A concerned observer." Roman came closer. There was something eerily familiar about the boy's eyes. Otherworldly.

"Thanks for saving me." A light came and went in the depths of those eyes—a flash of acknowledgment. Was this a being from beyond the divide come to live among humans? It happened more often than one might expect, and in greater numbers of late.

They were called Watchers. Those who traveled between worlds, living in this realm but reporting back to their fae masters beyond the veil. Children made particularly good Watchers, since they tended to be overlooked by adults, thus their observations went unnoticed.

Roman doubted the butler would ever find this *child's* parents.

"You're most welcome. Perhaps you might try to curb your desire to snatch hats."

Albie laughed. "I only did it because she took my slingshot yesterday and hid it on me."

Roman raised a brow. "Did she? And why do you suppose she did that?"

"She called me a menace." Albie glanced up at Dr. Savoy. "Girls don't understand the hunting instinct."

Dr. Savoy gave a laugh. "I've known some in my time who would put any man's hunting skills to shame. They just don't tend to hunt in the same environment as men."

Nor as Watchers. The more Roman saw and heard of this Albie, the more he was convinced he wasn't what he seemed on the surface.

"What did you wish to see me about, sir?" Dr. Savoy tied off the end of the wraps that held the splint together.

"It can wait until you finish with Master Albie."

Those eyes twinkled in mischief again. "Master?"

Dr. Savoy finished and told Albie he could get down, then gave him instructions to care for the arm. Number one on the list was not to take off the splint or he'd have to put a locking mechanism in place.

"Have your parents come round to see me."

"I will. Thanks, Dr. Savoy."

"You're welcome." The arm was supported by a heavy sling, most likely to help immobilize the shoulder while it healed as much as to keep the splint from moving.

Albie gave Roman a knowing smile as he skirted around him and left the room. Dr. Stanslovich escorted the boy to the front. Sounds carried down the hall. When Roman was certain they were out of earshot, he turned to Dr. Savoy, all pretense of congeniality gone.

"Where is Nicholas? I know he's here."

Dr. Savoy gave nothing away in his expression. "What the devil do you mean?"

Roman stepped forward, sniffing Dr. Savoy, letting the scents of the man coat his palate and run over his tongue. "Hmm. He's there, lingering on your clothing. It will take me only moments to find him."

Dr. Savoy stepped back, his eyes wide and wild. "How—"

Roman shook his head. "Some things are better left unknown."

"He's very sick."

"You mean very *dead*, don't you?" Roman gave a brittle laugh at the degree at which the good doctor paled. "Come now, Dr. Savoy. We are men of the world. I am not ignorant as to the scope of your and Dr. Stanslovich's practices."

Dr. Savoy rubbed his hands together. "Very well. Come this way."

Nicholas walked among the scarlet veils of the fae realm. No matter how hard he tried, he hadn't the strength to penetrate that most subtle of barriers that would allow him full entrance. An unseen tether bound him to the material world. He'd tried unsuccessfully to break the bond, but it was stronger than he'd ever imagined.

What kept him bound to his physical body? Why hadn't he been allowed to move forward from one plane of existence to the next? Had all his manifest sins finally found consequence? He couldn't very well search for Juliana if his body held fast to the world of the living.

Even movement in this place was dulled, hard to negotiate. He could see his limbs move but had no sensation of the action.

Figures glided around him. Silent, fascinating. Their seamless locomotion resembled skaters moving over a frozen lake. Dressed as characters from the Enlightenment, Nicholas expected Marie Antoinette to appear at any moment in all her splendor with white makeup and high wig. Over a hundred years had passed since that time, fashions had changed, but the minds and hearts of courtiers had not. Nicholas would not be surprised if he discovered the fae populated every royal court.

All courts were basically the same. No matter if they appeared in the fae or the human realm. It was so in the court of his cousin the czar.

Pain shimmered through his physical body—if he'd had one at the moment. What was that strange sensation that felt as if someone sat on his chest, forcing his heart to beat? Didn't they know he'd died and was beyond the hope of mortal men? His only recourse was to allow his fae master, Azgarth, to claim him, though Azgarth had yet to make an appearance.

Oh, his courtiers stared and commented behind hands and painted fans, whispering condemnation for some perceived slight or outrage. Royal courts lived and died by gossip and intrigue. This one was no different and even more so in some instances.

Voices came and went, blowing by his ears in intimate whispers. They called to him, urging him to join them, yet he had no idea where they led. Always that scarlet veil kept him separated from the world before him.

He reached out and tried to move it aside, only for his hand to become tangled in the length. When he tried to pull it down, it wouldn't give. Instead, he was hoisted upward, falling skyward. A balcony looked down on the ballroom. Courtiers lined the gilded walkway, gazing down on the festivities below. From this vantage point, Nicholas saw what captured their attention and he gasped.

What he'd thought was a party was instead some kind of gruesome experiment. A man lay strapped to a table; his abdomen stitched together, the result of some horrific operation. On his chest sat a metal device that moved up and down, imitating the beat of a heart.

How horrible to be kept alive against the will of God or the heavens. To be unable to move forward due to the intervention of mere mortals. Didn't those with authority in the afterlife have something to say in the matter? Didn't they make the final decision about who lived or died?

Nicholas turned away, glad he had no such worries. The red veil caught on his face, making it hard to breathe. Why was it so hard to draw air? He tried to take a deep breath and noticed his chest wasn't moving.

Panic raced through his body, lighting tiny fires along all his nerve endings. All sensations were out of keeping with his prior experiences in the fae realm. Pain, fear, hunger, and neglect were all emotions unknown to this place where only beauty in all its facets was celebrated.

One man's beauty is another man's horror.

He started down the stairs, trying to make it to the ballroom floor to get a closer look at the night's entertainment. All in all, it was a most unusual form—perhaps it was a dramatic rendering put on by stage actors for the amusement of the court. Yes, that had to be the answer. Nothing else quite fit.

He struggled against the scarlet fabric. No matter which way he turned, it was there covering his head and obscuring his view. It moved through the ballroom with him, a constant uncomfortable companion. How was he to be rid of this curtain that kept him from interacting with the others in a place of opulence and style?

Hours passed—or at least he thought that it had—before his foot hit the bottom step then the floor. Dancers twirled in and out of formation, moving in the patterns of a waltz though no music played. He wended his way in and out of the dancers, trying to make his way to where he'd seen the man strapped to the table.

Why the importance of seeing the scene up close, he wasn't quite sure. Only that he felt compelled to verify they were only actors playing out a scene. Azgarth's idea of entertainment did not necessarily fall in line with human sensibilities. He found beauty in things that humans often saw only horror. Nicholas understood that sentiment to an extent, but oftentimes failed to grasp the aesthetics in a decomposing body.

Luckily, this specimen looked to be whole, which only reinforced his assumption that things weren't as they appeared.

Couples shifted on the floor before him, cutting off his path to the center. When they moved again, the scene had vanished.

No!

Where had the table gone? The odd glass storage container? The beakers and burners? All of the props had vanished.

Nothing remained on the spot but the floor patterned in the manner of the constellations.

He turned, trying to find where the body could have possibly gone, but he was alone. None of the courtiers remained in the ballroom.

For the first time in many years, he was glad to be alone.

Chapter Four

Mikhail rubbed his arms. A cold breeze stirred the hair on the back of his neck. A quick check showed there were no open windows in the laboratory. Not even the shutters were pulled back.

He looked around, not quite comfortable with the essence of the breeze. A ghostly presence invaded the room, searching over the body strapped to the table. A few months ago, he'd never believe such a thing possible. So much had changed in so short a time. Now he questioned everything about the material world. Even breezes were suspect.

His jacket sat on the back of a chair. For the work he planned to do, he didn't need the encumbrance of proper dress. Shirtsleeves would suffice. Still the feeling of not being alone—with the exception of Nicholas—continued to plague him.

The laboratory door opened and Dante entered with the man from the park in tow.

"Dante?"

Dante held up his hand as if to say he knew the arguments, but there were extenuating circumstances. "We can save him, Mr. Cetanni. We've saved others."

"Andres Valentine, perhaps?" Mr. Cetanni lifted a brow and neared the table where Nicholas lay. He touched a long finger to the sutures on Nicholas's abdomen. "What was the initial cause of death?"

"Gunshot." Dante came to stand next to Mr. Cetanni. He looked down at the fatally injured man, appearing for all the world as if sleeping. "I suspect he bled out before his body was dumped in an alley."

Mr. Cetanni closed his eyes. Pain reflected in every angle of his face. "How did you possibly get him out without the constables seeing?"

Dante gave a knowing smile. "Trade secret."

Mikhail prepped the next unit of blood as Dante walked Mr. Cetanni through the events that brought Nicholas Alexandre to the care of such unusual physicians. Let Dante play the diplomat while Mikhail continued to care for their...patient.

"Will he remember anything?"

"We have to wait until he wakes to determine the extent, if any, damage is done to his brain." Dante directed Mr. Cetanni to a chair. "You may have a seat if you so wish, or you can return in a few days when Mr. Alexandre is ready to waken. Until then, there isn't much to see and nothing for you to do."

"No. I believe I'll stay here if I'm not importuning you."

Dante exchanged glances with Mikhail. "You'll have to appeal to Dr. Stanslovich in this matter. It might be my home, but he's the doctor of note in this discipline."

Mikhail started to answer, but at that moment, a distinct scent of burnt paper captured his attention. A subtle movement of Mr. Cetanni's hand to his jacket pocket was a telling sign.

Manager? The man was a bleeding agent of Azgarth! The chance of Mikhail ever consenting to let the man leave had diminished significantly.

Mikhail painted a benevolent smile on his face and straightened from his task. "Surely, you have extra rooms, Dante? Perhaps Mr. Cetanni would like to be your guest until his *client* is well enough to leave?"

Dante glared, but Mikhail met his gaze, not backing down from the challenge in his eyes. After a moment, Dante turned back to Mr. Cetanni. "If that is acceptable to you? We can have some of your belongings sent for? What is your address?"

"I'm currently staying at the Imperial."

Dante's gaze shot back to connect with Mikhail's. Understanding dawned. "Very well. If you will draw up a list, I'll have my butler and valet attend to the matter."

Mr. Cetanni gave a slight incline of his head. "You are all things gentlemanly, Dr. Savoy. I thank you for the invitation but will leave tonight and return with a small case in the morning."

"Fair enough." Dante rubbed his hands together. "If you don't mind, we will be working. If you have any questions or concerns, feel free to voice them."

Mr. Cetanni raised a hand and snuggled back into the chair. "I will let you know, but I believe I'll simply watch the masters at work."

Concentration and focus were never hard concepts for Mikhail to grasp. He'd always been driven when it came to his work. The fact he performed his duties in a room not far from a man who posed as one of Azgarth's agents had the impact of a train crashing into all his good intentions and smashing them to smithereens. All he wanted to do was charge the man and rip the book from his pocket and tear the pages out, pitching them into a fire. Or at least look for his name.

He curled his hands into fists and then let the tension out slowly, uncurling them from thumb to pinky. Now was a good time to let his emotions go and bide his time. If Mr. Cetanni planned to stay with Dante to watch over his client, then there would be ample opportunity to gain control of the book.

A slight tremor started in his fingers, then moved up his hand. Need, raw and pure, spiraled up from the well of addiction rooted in the pit of his soul. Craving for a hit of opium blocked out all else. And for a blinding, mindless moment, he didn't even care about agents, Azgarth, or the state of his being. All he knew was he needed a hit and needed it then.

"Mikhail?" Dante whispered. Concern pulled his brow down. He placed a warm hand at Mikhail's back.

Mikhail locked his jaw and fought back the need. Cold sweat began to bead up on his forehead. It rolled down his back and into the waist of his pants. Oh, by Hippocrates, he couldn't work this way.

"Come with me." Dante nudged him to move in the direction of the door.

Mr. Cetanni glanced up. "Where are you going?"

"We'll be back in a moment. You can sit there, or go and speak with...your client." Dante had Mikhail by the sleeve now, dragging him along.

Mikhail let himself be pulled, if only to keep from showing their visitor a struggle. That might arouse more suspicion than the two of them leaving the room together. When they were safely ensconced in the treatment room, Dante opened a small cabinet and pulled out a large vial and a syringe.

"Sit down and roll up your sleeve."

Mikhail recognized the bottle. "Morphine?"

"A small dose to take the edge off. We reduce the amount each day until your symptoms are gone." Dante competently pulled up a dose and flicked the bubbles out of the fluid, then squirted the air out of the tip of the needle until a few drops bubbled up.

Uncertainty ran like a river in Mikhail's gut. He knew the properties of morphine. Knew how it worked and what it did to the body. He wasn't a novice when it came to pharmacology; however, fighting a drug addiction by introducing another into the bloodstream seemed an intense measure. Wasn't he then in danger of becoming addicted to that drug as well? Most addicts either succumbed to their drug of choice or the rigors of withdrawal. Very few of those treated enjoyed much of a life once the drug was taken away. The weeks or months of torment. Physical and mental pain. Symptoms that caused life-threatening ailments. Even if a patient was successfully removed from their drug of choice, there was no guarantee against relapse.

How had he ever allowed himself to travel down this road? Why, when he'd lived his life so committed to his science, did he let himself fall into the wasteland of drugs? Deep down, he knew his constitution was stronger than his addiction. It had to be. He'd overcome so much in his life to prove the art of reanimation was a viable option in medicine. So many sacrifices lay close to forfeit at his feet, scattered debris of a life torn to ruins by the introduction of a concept his mind failed to handle.

Dante tied a tourniquet around Mikhail's arm. "Hold your arm out."

"I know the procedure." Mikhail braced himself as the needle slid under the skin in the smallest of pinpricks. Morphine entered his vein, sending relief to the aching pit of want.

He sagged down into a chair, sitting there as the drug moved through his system smoothing over the rough edges, allowing him to think clearly again.

Embarrassment came quickly on the heels of relief. Mikhail kept his concentration on his arm as he carefully rolled down his sleeve, anything not to have to meet Dante's eyes.

Dante moved around the treatment room, cleaning the equipment and placing the needle and syringe into the sterilization cabinet. He kept his back to Mikhail, working quietly. Then, "I will give you another small dose tonight, to help you sleep. We'll see how it goes for a few days and then begin to taper it off."

"I appreciate it."

"I would hope, if the roles were reversed, you'd do the same for me."

A tight, uncomfortable feeling squeezed Mikhail's chest. "I think you know I'd walk through fire for you."

Dante didn't turn, but his hands stalled over the instruments. He made no reply.

After a few more moments in silence, Mikhail stood and returned to the laboratory. Henri was there, fastening a new attachment to the air machine.

"Is that it?" The entire apparatus was only about the size of a bread box. Not very large at all. It fit in the back of the bellows, attached to the paddles that opened and closed the diaphragm where the air entered the system.

"Yes. And I hope it works to your satisfaction."

Mr. Cetanni watched from his seat across the room, brow furrowed but mouth closed. Odd how he'd not asked Henri to explain his presence or his invention. As an agent for Azgarth, did he already know Henri's role in saving the lives of those unfortunate enough to die before their time?

Damn! Instead of worrying about his addictions and Dante's feeling on the matter, they should have taken the opportunity to discuss what they were going to do with the agent while they had him in the house. Plans needed to be made and discussions voiced. He'd have to make it a point of capturing Dante alone later. Perhaps when he gave the second dosage.

Henri straightened from his task and turned a crankshaft on the front of the box. "I decided instead of using a power source, I'd make this a self-sustaining mechanism."

Brilliant. "You never cease to amaze me, Henri. If the power is cut off, the machine continues to operate."

"The only downside is the tension and size of the spring. In order to not have to use one the size of a city block, once the unit is primed, it must be wound again once every four hours."

"What did you use for gears?"

"I purchased an old grandfather clock and gutted it for parts. Those are the most efficient mechanisms and will keep accurate and precise measurements and time throughout the breathing cycle."

Henri stepped back and the bellows opened and closed, sending air down the tube and out to the mask. He pointed to a small lever on the side of the box. "This is how you set pressures. I wouldn't suggest going too high at first. Watch for the chest rise. When it looks adequate for normal breathing, you've got it."

"The only problem I can see is that with the compressonator in place, we won't have a clear view of how the chest is rising." Mikhail took the mask and stepped up to the table.

"Your other subjects didn't have the compressonator running the entire time they were receiving the serum. I doubt taking it off for a few minutes in order to adjust your pressures on the air machine will make much difference."

"True." Mikhail gave a nod to the heart-pumping device. "Go ahead and turn it off."

Mr. Cetanni rose from his chair and stepped forward as Dante entered the room.

"I see I've arrived just in time." Dante hurried over. His eyes sparkled with interest and awe. "I feel like a child about to eat his first flavored ice."

Such a simple, innocent comparison for a work that most considered dark and immoral. Heat stirred in Mikhail's belly as he glanced across the table at Dante. For all they had worked on different ends of the reanimation process, this was the first time Mikhail knew Dante really understood the passion for the work.

Henri reached over and turned the compressonator off. The machine stilled. Behind them, bellows creaked and wheezed. Mikhail placed the mask over Nicholas's face and strapped it on tightly, so no air leaked around the edges.

With a slow twist of the calibrator nob, Nicholas's chest began to rise. It fell again when the desired pressure was reached, the air forced into the bellows escaped, closing them off and priming the unit for the next breath.

"What do you think? Should we turn it up a little more?" Dante squatted down to be level with Nicholas's chest, his concentration fixed on the area as another breath went in.

"We'll observe any changes at this level and adjust accordingly." Considering they had no foreknowledge of how this latest device might affect the outcome, Mikhail didn't want to push their luck or jeopardize the patient in any way. At best, this addition to the procedure was experimental. At worst, it might cause a detrimental impact to the lungs.

As the air moved through the lungs and became absorbed by the capillary bed, Nicholas's color changed from the pale gray of death to something resembling a living body.

Mikhail glanced around the room, searching for the notebook that held their observations thus far. When he didn't see one readily available, he turned to Dante. "Tell me you are making notations on this case."

Dante gave a small knowing smile that did odd things to Mikhail's insides. "Of course, I am. You don't think I'd try to remember all the parameters. I might have a good memory, but that kind of recall is even beyond my abilities."

Dante walked to a hutch and pulled out a leather-bound ledger. "Excuse the lines on the paper. I only had a journal that I use for my bookkeeping for the practice."

Mikhail took the ledger and opened it. Penmanship, neat and straight, with the precision of a scalpel lined the pages with numbers, letters, and Mikhail's own particular nomenclature.

He blinked a few times. "This is much easier to read than the manner I keep a journal. I should have had you dictating the notes all along."

"Don't push it." The easy smile on Dante's face belied the gentle rebuke.

Mikhail found a pen and began to write down his observations. He almost hated to start in the middle of a procedure. Being the one to find the subject, first to administer the serum, that was his calling. Not taking over after others had done most of the work. However, there was brief satisfaction in knowing that he had trained Henri so well as to assist Dante in the fine art of the all-important initial steps.

The only thing left to do was wait.

Roman left Dr. Savoy's to retrieve his belongings at the Imperial. He'd not missed the looks exchanged when he gave his direction. The good doctors had obviously had some experience in that establishment. If they had only known a good portion of the staff were fae, they'd have never gone inside in the first place.

Azgarth liked to keep his agents all in the same place when in London. It made watching over them much easier. Not that they weren't allowed to come and go as required to attend their charges, but corralling the agents meant they were observed closer. Things had changed drastically since Herr Wilhelm Kering was sentenced to death. If one of the most infamous and successful of Azgarth's agents should run afoul of the master, no one was safe.

Roman suppressed a shiver and kept moving through the London streets. Several people turned to him as he passed by. Their eyes cold and knowing. Watchers.

Sweat beaded on his upper lip. A trickle ran down the small of his back to pool in the tops of his trousers. His heart beat triple time, pounding with every footfall that landed hard against the paving stones. They were following him. He'd caught the notice of the court and they were watching him, making sure he did not step out of line or make a run for it.

How did they know what was in his heart?

He'd never done anything contrary to Azgarth's wishes, no matter his own desires. Working for a fae master was not all beauty and joy—the ugly side of it reared its head soon after all contracts were signed in blood and fire.

Pay no attention to them.

Easier said than accomplished. Lately, he felt the walls were closing in on his world. The noose of his existence growing ever tighter. He had only to stay out of Azgarth's notice. Act and pretend all was in control and normal. If that was even possible. Azgarth always knew when things went sideways.

Did the fae master cause the problems? A little mischief to keep himself amused?

Roman wouldn't put it past the dark fae.

Legends dating back to the founding of civilizations spoke of the fae and their penchant for affecting human lives. Not always for the better. Most of the time for their own gain. A wager to be won against those who refused to believe in their powers.

Roman believed.

His introduction into the world of the fae happened on a dark night when he was sixteen.

Rain had pounded heavy and hard most of that day. As night fell, it subsided to a dreary mist—all save the reflections of the lamplights on the paving stones. Water made them shimmer like diamonds waiting to be unearthed in the street. Roman, on the way to meet his friends, had turned down a side street only to catch the glowing reflection of jewels at the bottom of a puddle. His first thought was some lady had lost a necklace in the street. As he neared, the puddle expanded to a pool, widening and deepening until he was submerged to his neck and fighting to reach the distant shore. Someone threw a lifeline to him. He caught it and let it pull him along, his mind in shock from the sheer magnitude of the event.

Close enough to touch his rescuer, he reached out a hand and let himself be pulled to safety. What he saw defied logic. For a long time after the incident, Roman had decided his mind had played tricks—that panic had filled in the blank places in his memory with visions from a dream or nightmare he'd once had. Even though he'd never gotten a good look at the face of the man who'd saved him, he'd always remember the searing pain of the brand on his skin and the stench of burnt flesh in his nostrils.

He'd screamed and begged for mercy, but the blurred image of his rescuer had assured Roman no one could hear him now. He was beyond the scope of human ears, beyond the veil of the mortal realm. Roman's life now belonged to Azgarth.

From that, it had taken him years to understand the implication of his actions and his service. His odd abilities had brought him into the notice of the fae, but pleadings for someone to save him from the raging torrent of the puddle-turned-ocean had sealed his fate. Azgarth gave no help that didn't come with a price.

And sometimes that price was too high.

Visions of his early years within Azgarth's circle haunted him all the way back to the hotel. The association had cost him much more than he'd ever gained. His family had stopped speaking to him—as a matter of record, they had him declared dead—and so he'd taken the name of a little-known painter who had died during the Renaissance. Only those well schooled in art history of the period would have even heard of him or how he'd given life to such works that would make angels weep.

Years had passed since his immediate family had all died off. No one was left to mourn him.

He entered the lobby and didn't stop at the desk or say hello to the staff. Head down and moving forward, he hurried to the elevator.

The operator opened the cage. "Where to, sir?"

Caught off guard, Roman glanced up. He didn't know this particular operator—had never seen him before.

"Fourth floor, please."

"Very good, sir."

The cage door glided closed without a telltale rattle or squeak of brass hinges.

Fear lodged in Roman's heart. He took a gulp of air and bit his lips to keep from telling the operator to let him out, he'd take the stairs.

No! He had to appear as if all was normal. As if he had complete control over the situation, when in fact he wondered if this was how Kering had unraveled.

Granted, Roman had not pushed Nicholas from a window as Kering had Valentine. Had not been the instrument of Nicholas's death. But he had a good idea who was. If he could bring those responsible to justice—fae justice—perhaps he might bargain his release.

Chances of success in that endeavor were slim. He'd never known Azgarth, in the entire history of their association, to actually grant someone their release. Not an agent. The only way out was through death or dismemberment. Generally, the dismembering was delivered personally by Azgarth. He left none of that to his lesser minions. One look into the watercolor depths of Azgarth's eyes as he punished one of his agents and it became clear he enjoyed playing the part of torturer. He had once told Roman while suffering upon him one of the worst punishments ever, that there was great beauty to be found in pain. Nothing was quite as exquisite as a soul teetering on the precipice between agony and ecstasy. Roman had not agreed with that assessment, though he'd been well schooled in Azgarth's moods to keep his mouth shut on the matter and opinions unvoiced. To Roman, pain was merely pain. Another dark cloud in an endless storm-laden sky.

He held his handkerchief to his face, covering his nose. A light citrus-floral fragrance filled his head. For some reason, the scent always helped him relax, brought him back to center, and reminded him of a time before his life had been forfeit to the fae.

Some days, he wished to go back to his life of idle gentility. Where the most crucial decision he had to make every day was what to wear. Still, living the life of an agent of Azgarth wasn't all bad. It did allow him certain privileges he might have otherwise not known. His every need was cared for with material possessions, food, and shelter. None of the agents ever wanted for anything that made life comfortable or even bearable. However, fundamental rights like freedom to travel, personal decisions, and pursuit of happiness were not allowed. Azgarth would be the first being to ask why anyone should want more than what he gave, since he gave the world. An easy question coming from a being that had the ability to move through worlds.

Roman arrived at his room. He knew before he tried the key that he would not enter the suite with any expectation of privacy. Already the air shimmered with the essence of the fae. Court who had come to the Imperial.

He'd probably not be allowed to return to Dr. Savoy's until morning.

Taking a deep breath, he turned the handle and entered, half expecting to receive a physical reprimand for his carelessness in losing Nicholas.

Nothing came by way of abusive correction. That did not mean the fae weren't in residence.

Music came from a distant place, far beyond the expensive furnishings and solid structure of the hotel. Out past the physical world and into another much more intangible arena where only one lord and master ruled over his subjects with an iron control.

He removed his coat and placed it in the wardrobe, then loosened his necktie. Did he antagonize to get a response or wait it out in silence? Better yet, he'd pack his bag to take to Dr. Savoy's and see if that brought the wolf to the gate.

After locating his luggage, he placed it on the bench at the foot of the bed. Several shirts, trousers, socks, and ties later, Azgarth arrived, lounging against the pillows as if he'd been lying there all the time observing.

"You are being remiss," the dark fae master pointed out.

Roman glanced up as he stuffed a coat into the case. "How so? I'm going to stay with Drs. Savoy and Stanslovich as they fight to bring Nicholas Alexandre back to the world of the living."

Azgarth waved his hand in the air as if it was of no consequence what happened to Nicholas. A well of anger rose in Roman. He stuffed it down and continued packing. Azgarth really needed to learn the fine art of coming to a point, but it most likely undermined his sense of drama.

Azgarth pointed vaguely toward the wardrobe. "Your jacket pocket."

"What about my—" Roman cut off and went back to the jacket he'd worn that evening. He'd forgotten all about the fact the name of a new prospective talent had been seared into the book used to capture the essence of a chosen. "Forgive me, but there has been a lot going on in the last twenty-four hours."

With a subtle, yet deadly grace, Azgarth leaned forward. "The name in that book has become your priority. I want to cultivate new talent in case the doctors cannot save Nicholas."

Curious. If the doctor's couldn't save Nicholas, he'd come to the fae realm and live among the court for all of eternity. That was the letter of the contract one signed when the name went into the book and the *wolfsine* left its mark.

"Are there doubts?"

Azgarth gave what might have passed for a smile if Roman had been able to make out any features. "I'm making it...interesting for them. They need to reaffirm their commitment to their calling."

Roman had a sinking suspicion Azgarth withheld a great deal of information.

Whether they wanted to or not, he supposed. Nothing like letting a man choose his own path in the world, then following it. No, Azgarth had to exploit and control a person regardless if their true talent was their passion. One way to get a man to hate everything about his life was to force him to do the things he loved until it became a chore. That way led to resentment, then hatred for the activity—no matter what it might be.

He'd never been allowed to follow his true calling. Whatever that might have been. The fact he'd been conscripted against his will proved that not all contracts were based in one's passions. Roman had long suspected his reason for being entrapped in the pool were his weird abilities to track by scent and see into a person's heart to know their talent. He'd had the skill since he had been very young. His mother had called it a parlor trick, though it had always been much more than that.

Roman found the book in his pocket and opened to the last page. "Aristotle King—a name born for success if ever I saw one."

Azgarth tapped the name with a long slender finger. "He represents the future."

The future? The fae moved in and out of time. No set parameters marked out their existences. So why was Azgarth worried about the future? Was that of the human race, or of the fae?

He gave a nod as if in understanding. Better not to ask the questions or risk tipping his hand too soon. There had to be a way to defeat the fae and release all of mankind. Perhaps he needed to enlist his own army to do so.

Chapter Five

Nicholas walked through a gallery. Whether this was real or a product of his imagination he had no way to verify. The pain that had followed him earlier—numbness and paralysis—continued to haunt him. The red veil fluttered over his eyes, turning all the paintings to a crimson monochrome. Some of the paintings he recognized as those created by the old masters. Others were at the Royal Academy, painted by his contemporaries. Still some of them were unfamiliar to him, yet stole his breath with their simplicity and lightness.

He grew closer to read the signature and was startled to see the familiar gold A in the corner of the canvas. Odd sensations poured through his being. He'd never created anything even remotely like that particular painting in the whole of his career. However, a feeling not unlike recognition filled him as he gazed at the portrait of a man, backlit as if standing in a blazing sunset. As he gazed at the face, he noticed it had that same quality of being underwater as Azgarth did. Not that he thought the painting was of the fae master—the setting was humble, the clothing normal and modern. Nothing like how Azgarth might dress.

So who was this subject who enjoyed an entire set of paintings similar of mood and tone? And why as he watched were the details slowly fading?

The gallery was deserted. Large curtains covered floor to ceiling windows. A breeze billowed deep red fabric, sending it outward to the middle of the floor.

He didn't know this place—not in the fae or mortal realm. How had he come to be there? If there was some deep and meaningful lesson to learn in this exercise, he had no idea what it might be.

Resigned to look for clues in the artwork, he moved on, studying the other paintings until he came to the end of the row. The opposite side of the gallery opened up into a balcony, overlooking an indoor courtyard. A fountain sprayed water into the air, creating a gentle burble of sound.

No stairway gave egress from the mezzanine. Not from this vantage point, it seemed. He moved by one of the windows and glanced out. No panes broke the portal. An archway led outside to a rooftop garden with what appeared a maze in the center.

Standing across from him, staring up at the maze in some confusion was Roman Cetanni.

"Roman!" His voice echoed back to him, stalling in his ears. Roman never turned or acknowledged Nicholas's presence. The red veil tightened, closing off his air, making it impossible to call out a second time.

He fought his way across the garden. Foliage tried to block him. Limbs of decorative trees became muscular arms that held him back from reaching his goal.

He filled his lungs, ready to yell for Roman, but at that moment, an eviscerating pain shot through his abdomen, stealing his breath and doubling him over onto the ground.

Memory of his injury returned brutal and hard. He had been shot and bled to death. He was dead. No, not dead maybe, but a half-life, lingering in the ether somewhere.

He put a hand to his midsection. Warm blood trickled over his fingers. Why was he reliving that moment and so out of context? He'd been shot in Lady Clarissa's bedroom, not in a garden.

What was the purpose of depositing him here to see a gallery of paintings he'd never create? To see into a world he might never know again. If Azgarth was to make good on his promise, why didn't he snatch Nicholas from the hungry maw of death?

He closed his eyes and hoped for darkness.

"Henri! I need help in here!"

Mikhail held his hand over the sutures in Nicholas's gut. They still held, but blood leaked out around them and ran down the sides of his belly, pooling on the table below. With the amount of blood leaking through, the internal sutures had to have ruptured.

The only way to tell for sure was to go back inside and have a look.

Henri slid to a stop beside the table. "What..." The question died on the air as he ran to get the instrument tray.

"Where is Dr. Savoy?"

"He went to lie down for a while."

"Damn poor time to take a nap." Mikhail grabbed a cloth off the tray and held it to the incision. "I'm going to start; you run and get Dr. Savoy."

Henri handed Mikhail a scalpel. "Or you can let him rest and I can assist."

Perhaps it was time to allow Henri a bit more latitude. He'd assisted in every other way possible in the lab, why not in the surgical phase? "All right. I don't have time to offer any protests."

Mikhail ran the scalpel through the sutures opening them in one efficient cut. The wound remained pinched together and blood rolled out in a steady stream, faster now. "Turn off the compressonator. I don't need blood pumping through while I'm trying to work. It's going to be hard enough as it is to keep him from losing what we've put in him already without adding to the amount."

Henri disengaged the device, then moved off to the far side of the small surgery. Mikhail took the instrument tray and placed it on Nicholas's thighs, so it would be close at hand. Without an actual assistant to hand him instruments, they needed to at least be a touch away.

Henri returned with a few large syringes filled with clear liquid. "Lavage for the wound."

Pride moved through Mikhail. "Good. We'll need that to see where the bleeding is coming from." Once inside, it might be anyone's guess and they didn't have that kind of time.

Mikhail pulled the flaps of skin back and studied the peritoneum. Henri squirted the water into the site and then dabbed with a dry cloth. Blood leaked from the abdominal aorta.

"Clamp that off."

Even though no blood pumped through the system, it still wanted to ooze. The hole was large enough to see, but it was delicate work when dealing with vessels. He didn't want and couldn't afford to make a mistake.

"I need some magnifiers."

Henri hurried to the cabinet and pulled out a wooden case. He placed the calibrated magnifiers on Mikhail's head, resting the bridge piece on his nose with gentle care.

"Turn the adjustment a quarter turn to the left," Mikhail commanded. "There. Perfect."

Henri donned his own pair and hurried to take his place across from Mikhail.

Looking through the magnification lenses, Mikhail noted the vessel bled not from the suture line, but higher. The injury not straight, but marked with the jagged lines of tiny teeth.

A feeling of ice ran down his spine and pooled in his lower back. Sweat broke out on his forehead. Tremors shook his hands, making it hard to hold the instruments of his profession.

The weight of Henri's stare penetrated the top of Mikhail's head.

"Dr. Stanslovich?"

Mikhail waited for a moment to see if the tremors would pass. He hadn't time to take a dose of morphine for his relief.

"Dr. Stanslovich?"

Mikhail glanced up to capture Henri's worried gaze. "Yes."

"I can perform the surgery if you'll direct me."

Mikhail let out a well of pride with his heavy sigh. Embarrassment bloomed, but it was nothing compared to the life he—they—might renew in Nicholas. "Very well."

Henri used the foot pedal under the table to raise it up to a comfortable level.

"If you look closely at the vessel, you will see it is jagged and torn. You will need to cut very delicately to even the edges before stitching it together." Mikhail picked up a slim scalpel from the instrument tray. It gleamed in the bright light. He turned it handle out and placed it in Henri's palm. "You may begin."

Mikhail watched as Henri showed the utmost competence and confidence as he cut through the vessel, leaving the surrounding structures intact. He was as fine a surgeon as the city of London had ever turned out. Despite his request for instructions, Henri needed none and proceeded with the surgery as if he were seasoned over years of practice.

The sutures Henri placed were delicate and fine. Mikhail tried to push the image of those ragged bite marks from his mind, but they refused to leave. How was it possible to chew away at the insides of a man with no readily available access? Such a situation was only possible by Azgarth's wretched hand. But how?

Could he move through a man's physical body as he could through the veils of worlds? Surely madness had overcome him to even contemplate a thing was possible. But how else would an injury be explained? Dante would never have made a mistake as to leave a hole that size in so important a vessel. As a matter of fact, Dante never made mistakes when treating patients—a very annoying quality.

"Finished."

At the sound of Henri's voice, Mikhail shook his head to clear his thoughts. His hands continued to shake and sweat ran down his face and dripped onto the lenses of the magnifiers.

He lifted them to rest higher on his head and wiped at his eyes. "Release the clamp and start the compressonator, then lavage the area to see if it continues to leak."

"Yes, Dr. Stanslovich."

Henri did as instructed. The lavage showed no further bleeding, even when blood pumped through the vessel.

"Very good. You may close."

Certain that Henri could finish without interference, Mikhail slipped off the magnifiers and crossed the surgery to the opposite side of the room to sit. Nicholas hadn't lost so much blood that he needed another transfusion. Once normal function was restored, he would begin to produce his own. They needed to develop a new plan. An accelerated one or they were going to lose him to Azgarth's pleasure, and Mikhail was damned if he'd allow that to happen.

A terrible itching started under his skin. It began in his arms and shoulders, then radiated out to his lower limbs. Merciful heavens! Was he to get no relief from this madness? He didn't dare administer the morphine to himself for fear of taking too much. Yet the symptoms of his withdrawal were severe enough to incapacitate.

Perhaps a spot of whiskey might dull the senses enough for him to at least get some temporary relief until Dante awoke. Anything to make the itching and shakes stop.

Unworthiness of body and soul, Mikhail stood and found the liquor cabinet, ensconced in the privacy of Dante's study. He took off the top of the decanter and poured a generous amount of the warm amber liquid into a glass. He kicked it back, letting the relief wash down his throat in a smooth river. A slight woodsmoke flavor bit at his tongue. It didn't have the same effect as the opium, but it did dull some of the symptoms. Not the itching—it remained a constant nagging harpy. Azgarth need not punish him, for he'd damned himself to all the rigors of hell with his fall from grace. No other punishment would hold quite the torment of breaking his addiction.

His eyelids grew heavy. Shapes formed in the dark corners of the room, imposing themselves on the material world. They danced, wiggled, and teased, mocking him with their every move.

He brushed his hand at them in dismissal. "Do what you will. It will be no worse than what I've done to myself. You see before you a broken man. I give you leave to rejoice in your triumph."

The figures halted their merriment as if jerked by an invisible string by a startled puppeteer.

"What? No fun if I don't play the part of the haunted and cower from you?"

One by one, the silhouettes vanished, leaving Mikhail alone with his drink.

He woke later to someone shaking his shoulder.

"Mikhail? Mikhail?"

Mikhail opened crusty eyes to gaze into Dante's dark ones.

Dante took the glass from Mikhail's hand and set it on the sideboard. "What are you doing? Did you self-medicate and fall asleep?"

"The tremors came on me again while I tried to mend a chewed aorta."

"A chewed aorta?" Dante raised a brow and considered the mostly empty decanter sitting beside Mikhail. "Exactly how much did you drink?"

"More than I should have but not enough to get drunk." Mikhail pushed up from the chair. "I'm more worried about the implications of what I found in a broader sense than the acute."

Dante made a face. "The agent."

"He's a complication and a direct line to Azgarth. We need to discuss how we are to proceed with him." Mikhail glanced longingly at the decanter he'd nearly emptied the night before, then turned away. "I'm confident you did not leave a sizable hole in the aorta when you put Mr. Alexandre back together."

Dante ran a hand through his hair. "Could the pressure from the compressonator and the breather cause it to rupture? Is it a complication we hadn't foreseen?"

"There's a bitter irony to this moment, Dante. You as the voice of reason and me the one to chase rainbows." Truly Mikhail thought this day would never come to this pass. Not in his lifetime. "To answer your question, I don't see how that is possible. There were no pressure marks on the skin. No free air in the abdominal cavity. There were no secondary ruptures and your sutures were placed much lower."

Dante went to the bookcase and pulled a large volume from the shelf. Gold leaf that had once embossed the title across the dark leather cover was now worn away from years of constant use. He turned to the table of contents, running his index finger down the entries. Halfway down the page, he stopped, then flipped to the middle of the book.

"Ah. I thought I'd read something along the lines of what you're speaking of in this arcane medicia." Dante glanced up, his gaze locking with Mikhail's. "Indulge me for a moment, if you will."

"Certainly."

"It is often found that men who serve beings not of this realm have occasion to show such allegiance by the spontaneous drawing of blood." Dante looked up, holding his place with a finger. "This is a book I found on esoteric and occult medicine. It subscribes that some of the illnesses we perceive as biological or viral really have their roots in infections we have no way to fight."

"And a few months ago, I would have sent you to Bedlam for even owning such a book." Mikhail gave a nod. "What else does it say?"

"Certain beings travel through the humors to attack and control the hosts as entailed by the master. To sever the connection to one who might intercede in their liberty."

"I'm not even sure I know the meaning of that line." Mikhail looked over Dante's desk and found a candy dish. He plucked a sweet from the top and stuck it in his mouth. The morning after a night of alcohol always met with dry mouth and thick throat, and here he'd not even been offered a morning cup of tea in which to wash down the observations of some long dead occultist.

"True, it is written in a rather fanciful manner." Dante gave a heavy sigh. "I purchased this during our first foray into the world and workings of Azgarth. I thought it might give us some insight."

"And how do you find it?"

"Hard to discern at times."

Mikhail smiled. "We already know Azgarth capable of walking through worlds, what's to stop him from reaching inside a man and causing injury, even death? And I doubt liberty of any kind was his goal."

"No matter what we do, we do so at Azgarth's mercy?"

"I sincerely hope not." Mikhail ran his hand over his jaw. Stubble from the overnight growth of beard scratched against his palm. "I am going to go wash and shave. I'll meet you in the surgery to assess our patient."

Dante rubbed his chin. "I've already been this morning. You—or rather Henri did a fine job. The infusion is finished. When you come down, we can place him in the tank."

A fine tremor moved through his hand, radiating out to his fingers. "Before we do that, I may need a dose of morphine."

Dante reached across and grabbed one of Mikhail's hands. "You do. Wait here and I'll get it."

Mikhail took a deep breath and rolled up his sleeve. If they stayed ahead of the symptoms, then maybe he'd be able to practice his vocation without asking others to act as his hands.

Dante returned with the medication and made quick work of administering the dosage. For his part, Mikhail closed his eyes and rode the edge of a perfect calm. He hated being dependent of another drug to get him off the one he'd abused, but if it was the only way to heal while allowing him to continue to enjoy some semblance of normalcy, then so be it.

With the morphine still flowing warm through his veins, Mikhail hurried through his morning ablutions and returned with a fresh shirt and waistcoat. He decided to forgo the jacket. Moving a man into a resurrection tank required free range of motion. Perhaps Dante's redesign would be easier to submerge a man.

It couldn't be harder than with a horizontal tank.

Mikhail made it to the surgery as Henri, Dante, and Valentine rolled Nicholas first one way, then the other in order to get him situated on the harness that would attach to the inside of the tank and hold him upright.

"Do you need help?"

Dante fastened the first strap across Nicholas's upper chest. The apparatus reminded Mikhail of something that was used in the madhouse to subdue violent patients. Another strap fit across the lower abdomen and hips, another came up between the legs.

"That looks very uncomfortable," he observed.

"At least he won't have to wear it for long once he wakes." Henri stood at the head of the table, his arms bent to push against it.

They rolled the table to the tank. Henri reached inside the chamber and pulled down the hooks for the harness. Each brass hook was fed through a jump ring in the straps. Once the hooks were secure, Henri moved to the outer back of the chamber and began to pump a lever that rolled the lead line to wind around a spool that sat above the chamber. With every pump, Nicholas was hoisted higher off the table. Mikhail stepped up to help guide the inert body into the chamber without doing more damage. Mikhail did one final check on the breathing mask to ensure there were no leaks in that quarter. He'd hate to lose a patient due to drowning him in the tank. Not after all Nicholas Alexandre had endured to get to this phase of the experiment.

The door was closed and the seals engaged, by pushing a lever, much like the lid on a canning jar, to make certain the tank didn't leak and the resurrection fluid run all over the floor.

Mikhail marveled at the time and care that had been put into the design. Not only did the vertical tank use less room in the surgery, but it also used less fluid. How that would affect the outcome he had no idea. Did it matter as long as the mixing ratios were equivalent to those used in the larger tank? He'd have to ruminate on that possibility. Either way, it was a bit late to worry about that aspect at the time, but it was important to take into consideration. Careful records had to be kept and adjustments made if it looked as if things were going afoul.

"You may fill the tank now, Henri." Mikhail nodded in the direction of the fluid drum.

Henri turned a large flywheel. Fluid spilled out of brass jets located around the tank bottom.

Even the amount of time it took to fill the tank had been dramatically reduced. Where it once took the better part of an hour, Henri and Dante had shaved it down to less than fifteen minutes.

Mikhail folded his arms and admired the process with wonder.

Dante came to stand beside him. "You have a peculiar look on your face, old friend."

"It's not every day a man sees his brilliance overtaken and surpassed by his own colleagues. It's rather humbling."

Dante frowned. "You aren't put out by the changes, are you? We weren't trying to surpass you or even step on your toes. We only wanted to work in the space we have. As you see, we had very little choice."

Without a workable laboratory in his own home, they really did have few options left in order to continue their work. He should shut up and be thankful that the opportunity presented to save another life.

Mikhail glanced up at Valentine who had moved out of the way in order to let Henri work. Now there was a work of resurrection art. The perfect melding of science and ingenuity. How much of that triumph could be placed at Azgarth's feet, Mikhail didn't even want to know. To do so undermined all his accomplishments.

Phosphorescent properties of the fluid filled the room in an otherworldly glow. Nicholas Alexandre floated, a sea creature captured for the observation of humans. An odd image to come to mind, but Mikhail found the fanciful thought stuck. The way the suspension in conjunction with the lights from the gas lamp played across the skin made odd patterns emerge, which were not there before.

Mikhail rubbed his eyes. The only thing left to do was to wait and let the resurrection fluid do its job.

Chapter Six

Roman found the direction for Aristotle King with very little effort or fanfare. As with his dealings with most men of talent, Mr. King proved to be an eccentric, who lived above his photography studio in the middle of a busy business district on the outskirts of London proper.

None of Roman's clients had delved into the newer mediums. A first foray into a different art form held a bit of excitement and fear as he had no idea what to do with pictures taken on film and plate instead of paint on canvas. He supposed even artistic expression had to change with the times. Not by only the difference of one school or movement to the next, but by as fundamental ways as the tools used to create the scene, mood, or composition.

He entered the shop to the sound of a drum roll. The unexpected herald of his arrival made him look up to the marvel of ingenuity. Instead of the drum and sticks he'd expected to see, the door was connected to what looked like a gramophone that played a cylinder whenever the door opened and a switch engaged. A man with that level of creativity had to possess incredible talent.

Framed photographs were displayed around the shop, interspersed with equipment for sale. Roman perused the evidence of Mr. King's craft. Each photograph illuminated an otherworldly quality, spoke of the fae realm. If he didn't know better, he'd swear Mr. King might have been there a time or two already. In almost all of the pictures, save one, the ghostly images of dancers were visible in the background. Most who viewed the photographs and knew something of technique would know that the photographer had used a double-exposed plate to create the illusion. However, Roman had been forced into the fae realm too many times to not know a courtly scene when he witnessed one. Aristotle King had tapped into the veil as no man had before.

No other customers were in the shop, nor had any come in while Roman enjoyed the displays. A young man, no older than his mid-twenties, came out from the back of the shop. A foul chemical smell rolled out with him, clinging to his clothes. He considered Roman with the gaze of a man who didn't know if he should try to sell Roman equipment or run for his life. Either way, Mr. King gave a nod and removed his spectacles to clean them on his shirtfront.

"Can I help you with something? Are you in the market for a camera, plates?"

In the past, Roman might have tried to sway him with the guise of becoming Mr. King's agent, he instead dangled a bit of a carrot of another kind in front of him.

He reached into his pocket and pulled out one of his cards. "My name is Roman Cetanni. I wondered if you might hire out your services for special projects."

Mr. King's dark eyes narrowed. Apparently, he was not a man who trusted easily or allowed his passions to be swayed by a few words. "What kind of project?"

A good question. A fair question.

Roman pointed to the clusters of photographs on the walls. "Was this a labor of love or commerce?"

Mr. King wiped his hands on a towel—a subtle way to show a tell. "Does it matter?"

Roman lifted his shoulder as if to say it didn't matter. "Has art for the sake of creation ever put food on the table?"

"I have no trouble providing for my family."

How, in both worlds, was he going to secure Mr. King's cooperation for what he had planned, if the thought of working on commission held no sway? Roman's attention was dragged back to the pictures hanging on the wall. Not all motivation had to be monetary in nature. Sometimes, what a man wanted most out of life was to be believed. To tell his story and have another act with wonder, awe, or compassion.

"Your technique for double exposure is very unique. Do you teach it to others?"

Anger filled Mr. King's eyes. "That is akin to asking Rembrandt his secrets."

Roman laughed. "Are you the Rembrandt of the camera?"

Mr. King offered no reply, nor did he seem disposed to helping Roman.

He turned back to the photographs. "A bit of free advice, Mr. King. Try pointing your camera at a mirror when the lights are low. The effect will capture those who dance beyond the veil much more reliably than catching them when they wish you to."

Roman started out of the shop and paused. "If you change your mind and are willing to assist me, you will find me staying a few days with Dr. Dante Savoy."

"You still never mentioned what type of project," Mr. King yelled after Roman.

Roman waited a beat, acting as if he wasn't going to answer, then turned. "No, I didn't, but I guarantee the beings will be much more interesting than the ones you've managed to capture on your own."

Back out on the street, foot traffic had gotten a bit heavier while Roman had been inside. People walked along the narrow pathway, their gazes trained downward, considering their steps.

Contact had been made. Azgarth had never once dictated the mechanism an agent used to hook their charges. The only importance was that they were consigned to the ranks of the chosen. The freedom gave him some room to maneuver. For Azgarth's benefit, Roman would appear to court Mr. King when in reality Roman planned to use him to find a way into the fae realm that wasn't by invitation only. It might be the only way to break Azgarth's hold over humanity.

At the corner, he turned and kept walking for several blocks until he found a hired carriage. Once inside and heading toward Dr. Savoy's address, Roman considered his surroundings. Clouds had rolled in overnight, casting the entire city into shades of gray. Soot turned this particular area even darker, more depressing than it deserved. Hope had come to this section and died, not with a triumphant explosion, but a choking whimper. He held his handkerchief to his nose and mouth, gazing out the window. An occasional knowing gaze would glance his way as the carriage passed. Watchers. How unfair they should come here and mock the poor. Though perhaps some of them might be scouting for new and varied talents to pass on to the master.

Neighborhoods changed, became cleaner, brighter as the carriage grew closer to Dr. Savoy's. The air wasn't as close, or stifling. His lungs finally felt as if he could take a full breath that reached all the areas of his lungs.

The carriage rolled to a stop. Roman got out and threw a coin up to the driver. Unlike the day before, there were no outraged sounds coming from the park. People were out strolling, enjoying a morning walk to invigorate them for the day ahead. Sunlight tried to peek from behind the clouds but did not give any great fight.

He climbed the steps, feeling a preternatural unease. No matter what condition he found Nicholas, it could not be worse than death. He rang the doorbell. A few minutes later, the butler answered the door and bowed.

"Dr. Savoy awaits you in the surgery. May I take your bag, sir?"

Roman handed the case over to the charge of the butler, who in turn handed it to a footman. He followed the butler through the house into the surgery.

An odd glow filled the room from the tank in the corner. Fluid bubbled and circulated. Nicholas hung suspended, upright, in some strange halter that looked more of a medieval torture device than that of modern medicine.

Did Nicholas know discomfort? Pain? Even though he was dead, did his mind still work? Artificial life was still life, wasn't it? No wonder Azgarth hadn't been confident that Drs. Stanslovich and Savoy could pull Nicholas back to the land of the living. Appearances could indeed be deceiving, but from what he saw before him, anything might happen to derail the procedure.

Dr. Savoy approached Roman, who hadn't advanced past the doorway.

"It's an impressive sight, I know. Quite a lot to take in, but necessary if we are to save your client."

Roman gave a numb nod to show he understood, when in reality his mind raced with possibilities too dark for even him to imagine. He who had seen so much, working for one such as Azgarth.

Roman took a few wooden steps toward the tank. "How long does it take before he wakes?"

"We like for subjects to stay in the fluid for a few days before we wake them. All that will depend on several factors we monitor."

Roman stopped and raised a brow. "What factors?"

"Temperature. Fluid levels. Ph, or potential hydrogen. To name a few. I won't bore you with details."

"I'm not bored, I assure you. Overwhelmed, bewildered, and in awe."

Dr. Savoy gave an easy smile. "If you like, you can have a seat by the tank. Dr. Stanslovich's assistant, Mr. Vauss, will be monitoring Mr. Alexandre this morning."

"Dr. Stanslovich doesn't stay with his...patients?"

"Not the entire time they're in the tank. It's a lengthy and tiring process. We take turns."

Roman gave a nod. He'd run out of questions, speculations, and conversation. Miracles needed no words, only keen observance. A drop of divine—or in this case fae—inspiration helped.

Mr. Vauss seemed a sturdy, trustworthy man. He moved around the surgery with a quiet efficiency that proved he belonged in this element. He also possessed the scent of someone touched by the fae. A recent conquest by the *wolfsine,* no question about it. The scent of a *wolfsine* bite had particular markers. Strong and briny at first, over the weeks and months, the fragrance morphed to a subtle mossy, earthy flavor that tickled Roman's nose.

Though he had heard of Drs. Savoy and Stanslovich, he'd not heard much on the assistant. Possibly because he was new to the fae, but most likely because his discipline fell so far outside of Roman's purview. Science had a beauty all its own. Without it, there would be no painting, or music. Architecture, bridges, or some of the newer marvels—like photography.

What images might Aristotle King find in such a place as this? Even now the edges of the tank blurred with the essence of the fae realm. Nicholas wavered between two worlds. Hovering as if waiting to see which way he'd fall. Given the level of skill that went into saving him, Roman had few doubts left that the good doctors would triumph in this endeavor.

If Nicholas wanted to live, the matter seemed entirely up to him.

Nicholas shivered with cold, desolation. What manner of place had he been brought to now? The walls were made of liquid, yet had a solid substance. If he'd been pressed to explain the possibility that any known compound might exhibit both proprieties, he'd have failed. No artwork or other personal items lined the walls of his prison. What had he done wrong to go from a lush garden to this place? And cold—he'd never felt such cold. Like a thief, it stole his thoughts, emotions, even his will.

After he'd given freely of his soul over to Azgarth, he'd imagined that once dead, he'd be free to cross over into the fae realm. He'd never believed there might be trials or negotiations. And still, he had yet to even catch a glimpse of his beloved and deceased sister.

He stepped through the maze of glowing pink waterfalls. Each shimmery drop of water contained the reflection of a tiny world, infinite dimensions. Inside those worlds were people pressing up against the barrier, trying to force their way out. He turned his gaze away, guilty he didn't know how to help them.

Nicholas ran his fingertips along one of the falls. Icy pain infused his hands. He had the horrible idea that if he tapped his hand along the walls, the limb from the wrist down might shatter into a million crystalline shards. The attempt had no effect on those wretched souls trapped within the drops. On closer inspection, the souls of the damned held expressions from agony to elation. Some mocked him, while others showed the results of their extreme torture. Every turn he made brought him closer to examining those things in himself he wished he'd never exposed. All his faults were laid bare. Was this his final judgment?

But wait. No. Was that a heartbeat pulsing deep in his chest? Air moved through his lungs. A strange sensation skidded through him—odder than those trapped within the bubbles. Odd light filtered through the room, sun through closed lids. He rubbed at his eyes. That changed nothing.

Hallways changed. Narrowed. Water began to trickle and run, splashing him in a gentle wash as he walked by. Cleansing him, making him as new.

He fought to surface from the murk and mire of this constructed world. To find his way back to the surface. No matter which way he turned, he only succeeded in coming back to where he'd started. Circular in thinking and movement, he'd made no progress in his bid for freedom. As a matter of fact, if his calculations were correct, he'd lost ground. Intervals between waterfalls closed, soon to become one large curtain of water. He raised his hands, trying to pass through, certain he saw figures on the other side, watching him.

"Help me."

The words were garbled, bubbles moving to the surface of a pond. A few steps brought him to the edge. He lifted his hand. Glass met his fingertips. Impersonal. Solid. Panic rose, choking off what little air came into his lungs. Every breath felt forced, worked against him.

He beat against the window, frantic to escape. Water rushed all around him, slowing down each strike, creating less of an impact. The scene before him shifted. People no longer looked in at him. Now he stood in a room—a study. A man sat in a chair with a hand covering his eyes. His shoulders shook with grief. An empty bottle of scotch sat on the desk at his elbow. A gun hung from the limp fingers of his left hand. Nicholas knew only one man who had a dominant left hand in most things—Sir Rodderick.

Bloody bastard!

Who was he to cry when he'd been the instrument to end Nicholas's life, or at least stranded him in this world between worlds? At least whatever had been inside him, infecting him had tried to kill Nicholas. He doubted even jealousy would move Sir Rodderick to raise a hand to Nicholas. Their affair had been intense, but it was never meant to be permanent. And yes, he realized Sir Rodderick was angry at the assumed intimacy Nicholas shared with Lady Clarissa, but he'd never bedded the woman. Never wanted to.

As if sensing a presence, Sir Rodderick lowered his hand from his tearstained face. "Who's there?"

Though Nicholas could not hear the words, he read Sir Rodderick's lips. A need to confront his killer rose like a phoenix in his blood. Heat scorched him from the inside out. What had taken hold of him in order to make him shoot? Damn but he couldn't confront Sir Rodderick now. Not in this state where he was neither spectral nor corporeal. What damage could he do against a man solid with life?

"Show your face!" Sir Rodderick stood. He gripped the pistol tighter, raising it to the darkness.

The door behind Sir Rodderick opened. He spun. Lady Clarissa stood there, staring at her husband with an odd expression. "Who are you speaking to?"

Sir Rodderick stood frozen for a moment before he shook his head, then placed the pistol on the desk.

Lady Clarissa crossed the room and laid her hand gently against her husband's face. "Have you been in here all night?"

Sir Rodderick moved past her. He rubbed a hand over his face. If he answered her, Nicholas didn't see the words, nor did he feel them resonate through his body.

Before the scene ended, the water shifted again, this time bringing Nicholas to see Roman, sitting in a chair against a window. His fingers were pressed to the glass as if trying to instill energy into the very pane. If anyone were capable of such a feat, it would be Roman. Loyal, canny, and irrepressible Roman.

If he ever had another chance to walk the paths of the living, he'd let Roman know how much his friendship meant to him. Above being an agent of Azgarth, Roman was a stable, sturdy character. He kept his word and then some. There were not many like him around. Not that Nicholas had ever found.

What made some men good and others...not so good? Was there some flaw of character that predisposed them to bad behavior? Nicholas had always wanted action and excitement. Had craved intrigues and scandals to amuse him in the court of his cousin. He'd learned no better manners on these wet English shores. Much to his peril as it turned out. Still, he was not at fault for his own demise. That lay square at whatever entity had infected Sir Rodderick.

This odd journey seemed never ending. At the moment he thought he might break free of the bonds of death, he came up against a new opposition. Did God decree him too tarnished to walk through the pearly gates? Had Azgarth changed his mind and decided the contract null and void? No sadder day for a man than the one where he learned neither heaven nor the fae realm wished to keep his wretched soul.

Sunlight filtered through a second set of windows, casting Roman in a burnished gold. An aura of divinity surrounded him, so out of place with the nature of his calling. Nicholas lifted his hand to touch his fingers to the glass, hoping to absorb some residue of grace.

Roman glanced up. Shock rounded his eyes. He shouted garbled words to someone beyond Nicholas's field of vision. Three men whom were vaguely familiar came to stand on the opposite side of the tank.

One of the men pushed a lever and the fluid rushed out of the tank, taking his breath, leaving him cold and shaking. Reality replaced the dreamscape—cold and unforgiving. Devices were strapped to his face and chest. When he tried to lift his hand to bat them away, he found his reflexes slow to respond. They weren't like that before the fluid released.

Nicholas was pulled forward. Pain etched along his groin. The harness he was strapped into to keep him upright dug into his thighs. One of the men removed the devices from his chest and face, while the other two guided him to a table where the clips for the harness were freed.

He tried to talk, but his mouth and jaw were tight, making it hard to form the words. Maybe he needed to warm up a bit more before communication was even attempted. The most remarkable thing was that he was alive!

None of the sensations from the dreamscape were present. Pain, cold, fear, were all visceral responses to the material world. All of them magnified by the systems of his physical body.

Nicholas watched, complacent as they dried, examined, and dressed him. They spoke to each other, bandying about medical terms and writing down notes in a journal. All the while Roman stood back, face white and eyes glistening with unshed tears.

Nicholas lifted his hand from the table in a feeble attempt to ask for comfort from the only one in the room he knew for certain would never hurt him.

Roman glanced to the others, and when they paid him no attention, he came closer, linking his fingers through Nicholas's. "Allow Drs. Stanslovich and Savoy to help you."

He squeezed Roman's hand as tight as he could, which wasn't to any extent, to show he understood. The doctors continued their assessment.

Movement beyond the range of light captured his attention. A movement in the shadows.

The third man glanced up. "What is it, Andres?"

"I only came to see the latest creation." Andres walked deeper into the room, giving Nicholas a chance to see his face in whole. Andres Valentine, the once famed violin virtuoso who left the stage after being tossed from a window by his maestro.

Was that how his life had been saved? By this same odd procedure Nicholas had been subjected?

Plucked from death by extremely skilled hands. How long would it take until he felt as if he belonged on this plane and not some reject from the afterlife?

Andres walked to the table where Nicholas lay. He looked down and their gazes met and held. No one else in the room would ever understand the knowledge that moved between them. They were unique in the world. Not many people had been pulled from the brink—or once crossed over only to be resurrected like some reluctant Lazarus.

Feeling returned to his limbs. Pain began in his belly, radiating outward. He'd been shot. The pain grew more intense as he began to thaw. He gritted his teeth.

He cleared his throat. "Pain."

Only a croak of sound came out, but it was enough to move at least one of the men into action.

"Where does it hurt?"

Nicholas used his free hand to run over the area on his belly where the greatest pain centered. Rough skin met his fingers. Sutures binding his skin together.

"If it didn't hurt there, I'd wonder at your ability to feel anything." The man gave a smile. "I'll get a topical agent to put on it."

Dr. Stanslovich mumbled something to Dr. Savoy. "Henri, get a vial of the serum. I want to see if it will accelerate recovery."

If it meant he might be able to use his body as before, he wasn't going to complain.

Roman remained suspiciously silent.

Nicholas turned to study his agent's face. Concern pulled Roman's brows down, mouth pressed into a grim line. He seemed on the brink of saying something but held his tongue. Whatever it was, he wished someone would say something beside the whispers coming in a steady stream from the doctors. He had a hard time discerning anything from that quarter. None of it sounded particularly encouraging—even for a man brought back from the dead.

Golden light continued to shine in the windows. Beyond the glass, bright green leaves danced on the wind, slapping against the pane. A garden? Oh, how he longed to go out into the garden and sit under the sun, his skin and blood warming from the rays.

The man known as Henri returned to the room with a medical tray holding a vial, a jar, and a syringe.

Dr. Stanslovich picked up the vial and syringe and pulled up a small amount of fluid into the barrel. "Normally, I'd put this directly into your heart, but since that seems to be functioning within normal parameters, I'll settle for your vein."

Henri tied a tourniquet around Nicholas's upper arm.

"Make it tight. He won't have enough strength to make a fist."

Nicholas tried, but his fingers were so stiff he only managed a rather loose closing of his fingers. At this rate, he'd never hold another paintbrush. His rising career might find a sudden change of direction and fall.

As the serum entered his system, a warm feeling of comfort moved along his veins. Panic ceased. His eyes grew heavy and he fell asleep.

Chapter Seven

Mikhail scanned the book of lore Dante had read from earlier in the day. Two subjects. Two outcomes eerily similar. Neither Valentine nor Nicholas Alexandre had lasted the entire prescribed time in the resurrection tank. More and more, he believed the reason for that was due to the bite of the *wolfsine.*

He'd not missed the telltale bite marks when they'd lifted him into the tank. The back of Mr. Alexandre's upper thigh was marked deeply with the scars of the fae creature. The mark had come dangerously close to the artery. How remarkable that his life had not been forfeit from the attack. But it hadn't. He'd lived and thrived and become an artist of some local renown.

What Mikhail really wanted was to interrogate the agent, Roman Cetanni. If anyone knew how and why the fae worked as they did, it was that man. For all the man appeared an agent for Azgarth, he surely didn't act like one might expect. That worried him.

The study door opened and Dante entered.

Night had fallen some time ago. Long shadows stretched across the dim expanse of the study, painting the corners in darkness.

"Mr. Alexandre is still sleeping. Peacefully, I might add." Dante crossed the room and poured himself a couple fingers of scotch. "How are you holding up?"

"More questions than answers." Mikhail rubbed his eyes and regarded the book as one would a puzzle missing several crucial pieces. Answers hid between those musty pages. He just knew it. "Has Cetanni said anything more about their relationship?"

"No. He's sitting by Mr. Alexandre's bedside, watching him like a mourner at a funeral."

Mikhail glanced up. "He almost was."

"That's true enough." Dante kicked back his drink, downing it in one swallow. He poured another. "I am surprised Alexandre woke on his own. My bet would have been another intervention by Azgarth before we were done."

"I'm glad there wasn't. We damn near lost him the first time. I don't know if we could have saved him again. No telling what mischief Azgarth might visit on him next." Mikhail turned a few pages of the book, hoping something might catch his eyes to explain why those who were bitten by the *wolfsine* seemed to wake before their time. Though in truth, the science as practiced by himself and Dante wasn't likely to be found in old books. "The harder we try, the more I'm convinced this is all orchestrated for our inconvenience."

Dante gave a grunt of a laugh. "Inconvenience indeed. What is your estimation of the initial assessment?"

"Sluggish, but better along than Valentine at that time mark."

"Agreed."

"Henri knows to summon me when Mr. Alexandre wakes, no matter the time?"

Dante paused with the drink halfway to his mouth. "I assume so. He knows we need to interview a subject post waking."

Mikhail raised a brow. "I don't want the same thing to happen this time that did before. Henri was the only one Valentine would speak with, the only one he trusted. It will do us very little good in practice if all the subjects feel Henri is their lifeline. We need to gain rapport with Alexandre. Gain his trust."

"I think that honor is already bestowed upon Mr. Cetanni. I doubt Alexandre will trust either of us the way he does his agent."

Truth rang in every word. The relationship between the two was of a different kind than that of Valentine and Kering. Cetanni seemed a different type of man. Kinder. Gentler. His behavior during the incident in the park was proof enough the agent had a decided sense of justice separate from any fae master he might serve.

Cold, clammy sweat broke out along Mikhail's brow and upper lip. One moment he was fine and the next the symptoms of his withdrawal were riding him with all the ferocity of the four horsemen.

Dante put his glass down with a decided click. "You're in a bad way."

"It comes and goes."

"I can see that." Dante left the room to retrieve the morphine, or at least Mikhail assumed.

He sat quietly, trying to force the feelings of need raging through his body to still. If he could bring men back from the dead, he should be able to overcome a drug addiction. Mind over matter.

"Not so much sometimes," came a lyrical voice from behind him.

Chills ran down his spine. He knew that voice. Had heard it when he and Dante traveled through the fae realm. Misdirected more like. Traveling intimated they had planned to go there when nothing was further from the truth.

Mikhail turned. "Have you taken to reading my thoughts?"

"I pick up a stray one here and there." Azgarth sat against the wall, hovering five feet above the ground. "Humans are very easy to read. Your minds are always filled with all matter of debris."

"Put there by beings who have no business in there in the first place." Mikhail stood in an attempt to get closer to his tormentor.

The air around Azgarth shimmered. He appeared to move farther away, out of reach. A reaction such as that only made Mikhail more determined to get close.

Mikhail took a few steps.

Azgarth moved back.

"Are you afraid of humans? Afraid we might contaminate your world if we should breach the veil when we are not under your complete control?"

Azgarth gave an uneasy laugh. "You are always under my complete control."

Mikhail shook his head. "No. I don't believe that for a minute. If we, who are your chosen, were always under your control, where is the amusement for you? The spontaneity?"

The laugh grew, followed by hollow applause that echoed through the study. "You are one of my brightest lights. Never forget that Mikhail Stanslovich."

The sound of Dante's shoes moving from hard floor to carpet heralded his return. As Dante grew nearer, Azgarth faded.

"Who are you talking to?"

Mikhail turned. Dante hadn't seen Azgarth. Now he wondered if he'd even been there at all. Was he hallucinating?

"Would you think me fit for Bedlam if I told you Azgarth was just here?"

Dante frowned and set the small tray he carried down on the desk. "Where?"

Mikhail pointed to the corner. "Over there. He appeared as soon as you'd gone to get the morphine."

Dante waved his hand in the area, testing the air for what Mikhail didn't know. "I don't feel even so much as a stir of a presence here."

Mikhail waved the exchange away. "It doesn't matter. He made his taunts and left."

"When I entered the room?"

"I understand the implication. Please do not labor under the illusion that I haven't thought of that myself."

Dante came back to the desk and prepared the morphine. "Do you see him often?"

"No, but if I do, I'll let you know."

Mikhail rolled up his sleeve and held out his arm. A pinch of pain and the morphine eased into his system. So small of a dosage in so short a time. "Are you cutting me down too fast?"

"Yes."

"No wonder you think I'm hallucinating."

"Assumptions." Dante laid the syringe back on the tray. "Your symptoms have diminished. There is no reason to prolong treatment if it's not needed."

Mikhail ran a hand through his hair. "I don't feel as if they are. Prison would have nothing on this feeling."

"We make our own prisons, Mikhail. Whether we choose to stay trapped is entirely up to the individual."

He scoffed at the notion of Dante ever being weak enough to build his own prison.

Dante walked around the desk to stare down at the book. His fingers skimmed the pages as he turned them. "Fear is never understanding what exactly it is we stumbled into that night in Paris."

"At least now we have a chance."

"Which seems slimmer all the time." Dante turned a few more pages. "There are things described in here that will turn hair white and make a man wish for death. If you thought the *wolfsine* were bad, they are nothing compared to the *neabré*."

Mikhail walked around the desk and leaned in to look over Dante's shoulder. "What is that?"

"According to the legends chronicled here, the *neabré* are a host of souls all mangled into one being no bigger than a child, but disfigured, as warped and corrupted as the souls within." Dante turned a few more pages, then spun the book so Mikhail might see it.

The picture was of a hideous figure of contorted flesh and piercing eyes. The attribution at the bottom of the page noted the artist as one A. Dominique, woodcarving on oak. 1437.

Mikhail closed his eyes and swallowed. He'd hoped it had been his imagination. That the smoke was thick and the opium pure.

He felt the world spin. Tip a bit off center. He nudged Dante out of the way and sat down.

Dante turned, a worried expression on his face. "You've seen one."

Mikhail nodded. Words were too hard to form, too solid. If he spoke of what he'd seen, it might be real. More so than the tales printed in an old book.

"Tell me," Dante urged.

"When you'd come for me in the opium den. One had been poking at me with a long, sharp object right before you arrived." Mikhail rubbed a hand down his face in hope of scrubbing out the memory. "I thought it only the drug."

"According to the book, a *neabré* is dispatched when one has strayed from the path placed by the inherent talents."

"A tool of punishment?"

"In a way." Dante turned a few more pages, then stopped at another picture. "Here is another interpretation."

This picture was even more disturbing than the last as it was rendered in pencil with fine details. More grotesque than anything Mikhail had ever seen, even in all his dealings with patients in various disease states. He ran a finger over the visage that resembled nothing of this world, nothing that might be compatible with life. The essence of the *neabré* was to torment and the form followed function in even the most basic ways.

Sparse dark hair hung in clumps around a bulbous head, disproportionate to the body. No discernible neck held the head. With such a configuration, lacking in cervical vertebrae, the being would have to turn the entire upper torso to move. Long arms hung down to the ground, dragging knuckles on three-fingered hands. One eye was hidden up high on the forehead, beneath the fall of hair. The other sat lower on the cheek. Nasal passages were open, like the holes in the skull. Large tusks protruded from the lower jaw.

Mikhail bent closer to the picture. He moved the gas lamp over to shine on the page. "Are those horns?"

"I believe so."

Having seen enough, Mikhail turned from book. "I wonder if Azgarth creates these creatures he unleashes on the unsuspecting, or if he's conscripted them into his court?"

"Who is to say. Probably does so for his amusement." Dante closed the book and leaned against the desk, a considering expression on his face. "Perhaps the opium worked as a conduit for seeing what was already there."

"Excuse me?"

"You've heard the stories of certain indigenous peoples throughout the world using hallucinogenic smoke to enter an altered state of consciousness. What if the opium worked for you the same way? It allowed you to freely see into the fae realm. You didn't have to wait for it to come to you."

Mikhail frowned. "This is treading down a very dangerous road, Dante."

"Yes. It is." Dante pushed away from the desk and paced around the study. "Suppose, for a moment, that we allowed ourselves to get pulled into the fae realm and have a look around. Only this time, we control the landscape."

"I can tell you I felt no control while under the influence of opium. I doubt going into the fae realm would change that. It might only make it worse."

Dante held up his hand. "I know. My plan is only in the forming stage. I'll work on it."

"If you really want to get lost in the other world, wait for Azgarth to appear and follow him in, or better yet, have your guest get you in." Mikhail went to the sideboard and poured himself a drink. After Dante's announcement, he needed a strong one. "I, for one, have seen enough of that world."

Dante turned pleading eyes to him. "Don't you want to know what it's all about? How it works?"

"I'd rather know how we were selected." A puzzle he'd had a hard time solving since they'd discovered their connection to the fae master. "Were we followed from infancy because we showed infinite potential or only since entering university?"

Dante looked so dejected, Mikhail felt compelled to make conciliation.

"If you want to go hunting around the fae realm, I'll go with you. What kind of a friend would I be to let you face that danger on your own? However, I won't succumb to using any kind of drug to do it. If we go, we find another way in."

Dante placed a hand on his heart. He seemed to sag a bit in relief. "Thank you."

Mikhail stood there watching his friend for a long time after, capturing the moment in time.

Roman sat in the corner of Nicholas's room. They'd moved him from the surgery to a guest room in the upper story of the townhouse. Morning was a few hours off yet, and the house had grown quiet and still. In the wee hours—that time between dark and dawn—was when Azgarth was the most active. He said he could walk freely among men as they slept, drinking in their dreams and reading their hearts. Desires were all nearer the surface. If the common man only knew that his dreams were forfeit to a fae master, they'd never wish to sleep again.

Nicholas rolled over. A moan came from deep in this throat.

Roman rose and crossed the room to sit on the bed. He ran a hand over Nicholas's brow. Fever had set in. He leaned over and grabbed the bell pull.

"Roman?"

"I'm here." He leaned in closer, touching Nicholas gently to let him know he wasn't alone. Often with fevers the ill had no notion of what went on around them. Just because Roman spoke, did not mean Nicholas heard.

"Roman? Close the window. Don't let him escape."

Roman tapped Nicholas's cheeks. "You're dreaming, Nicco. There's no one here but us." If Azgarth or any of his creatures had breached the room, Roman would have smelled their presence before they were ever seen.

"Close the window."

A tap sounded on the door seconds before Drs. Stanslovich and Savoy entered. Dr. Savoy rolled up his sleeves as he approached the bed. "What seems to be the problem?"

"He's burning with fever."

Dr. Stanslovich frowned and placed his hand on Nicholas's forehead. "Good God. He's on fire. When did this start?"

"I only noticed it. He's been quiet for hours. He just rolled over onto his side and called my name, so I rose to check on him."

"We have to bring his temperature down." Dr. Stanslovich stalked into the suite's private bath. "Do you stock isopropyl alcohol in your guest rooms?"

Dr. Savoy shook his head. "I don't know what they place in the rooms. Wet some towels with cold water while you're in there, and I'll go to the surgery for the alcohol."

Left alone, Roman began to strip Nicholas's nightshirt from him. Roman had few memories of childhood, but he did remember once having a terrible fever and his nanny stripping him down to cool his skin. She'd been afraid he'd have gone into seizures. He'd not thought of that in years.

Dr. Stanslovich returned with a couple of towels, wet but wrung out. "You've stripped him. Good."

"Only his shirt."

"It's enough." Dr. Stanslovich shoved one of the towels into Roman's hands. "Wrap his head in that one. I'll put these under his arms."

Roman merely stared down at the linen, not knowing quite what to do, half afraid of doing something wrong. What did it matter? Anything he did was better than nothing. He swirled the towel around Nicholas's head in a configuration resembling a white turban.

"Close the window."

Dr. Stanslovich glanced up from his work. "What is he saying?"

"He keeps asking me to close the window. But the window isn't open."

Nicholas thrashed on the bed. His legs working their way to the edge as if he meant to stand. "He's going to escape. Do not let him get away."

Desperate to reassure Nicholas, Roman took his hand and squeezed. "No. He won't get away. I promise."

Nicholas made what looked like a nod. He seemed to calm a bit and fall into a less troubled sleep. Meanwhile, the fever continued to rage.

Dr. Savoy returned with a bottle and some small hand-sized cloths.

"He's speaking out of his head, Dante." Dr. Stanslovich adjusted the towels under Nicholas's arms.

"What's he saying?"

"Nonsense things. Asking Mr. Cetanni to close the window."

Dr. Savoy gave a shrug. "There are worse things to say, I suppose."

Roman stepped back a few paces, allowing the doctors to see to their patient. Was there anything these two brilliant men couldn't do? Life and death lay suspended in their hands, theirs to dole out as they saw fit. Power of that kind was heady stuff. How easy it would be to abuse.

With their ministrations complete, the doctors left, giving Roman instructions in case the fever should spike again. Unfortunately, for all their skill as physicians, there was nothing they could do to prevent a fever. The body had to heal. Even if Nicholas hadn't initially succumbed to his injuries, he still would have had to contend with a fever.

Roman sat in the chair again, resolute on his intention to stay awake and watch over his charge.

The room grew quiet. Hours passed and the room lightened with the coming of dawn. Sleep came in fits and starts. Every move Nicholas made on the bed brought Roman back to full alertness.

Mr. Vauss came in near daybreak. He leaned over Nicholas and touched his forehead, then pulled the damp cloths off. Roman rose and shuffled to the bed, bone tired and soul weary.

"How is he doing?"

"Fever is gone. We'll have to watch him closely today to ensure it doesn't return."

"Do you think it will?"

Mr. Vauss gave a shrug. "It's hard to say in these cases. I fear we may not be out of the woods entirely."

"So it's a waiting game."

"I'm afraid so." Mr. Vauss straightened the bed linens where Nicholas had kicked them off in his sleep. He checked the wounds running down the center of Nicholas's belly, cleaning the sutures, then dressing it with gauze. "Go find your bed, Mr. Cetanni. You're about to drop where you stand."

"True spoken." He leaned over and touched Nicholas's hand. "I'll return after a good long nap. You need your sleep to heal, and I need mine to help you."

He started away from the bed but turned. "If anything changes or he wakes and asks for me, send someone to wake me. I'll not have him think I've abandon him."

"As you wish." Mr. Vauss went back to his duties.

Roman slid out the door and to his own suite. He'd not been there but for a few moments since his arrival. The appointments were comfortable enough, he supposed. As long as there was a place to lay his head, he didn't care if he was given lodging in the stables. In truth, he'd slept in worse places than a stable. Amusing how a man who had been born to privilege had learned quickly to take what circumstances were given as long as body and soul remained as one.

Once, after a horrible transgression to save a charge from certain folly, he'd been cast into a netherworld of sharp angles and prickly vegetation. Azgarth had made the bargain that if Roman survived the night, he'd be allowed to continue with his charges. If not...well, he'd be absorbed into the court as their permanent entertainment for the rest of eternity. To say he'd been motivated to survive was a gross understatement. As the night had worn on, he'd not been surprised to discover that the plants were carnivorous and had been promised human flesh for supper. Roman hated to disappoint them, but he'd fought like a demon from the bowels of Hell to get away from the hungry maws that chased him. Thorns as large as his arm had shot from the darkness, ejected from a towering tree seeking to protect its domain. It had taken every bit of his cunning to survive until morning.

To this day, he wore the scars of that night. If punishment had been the goal, it had not been met. That night, along with many others, had begun the kernel of resolve to find a way to free him and his charges from Azgarth's influence. Each day, each contact, hardened that resolve. The only thing he needed now was a way to make that vision reality.

Without thought to the fine clothes provided by Azgarth, Roman lay down on the bed, his eyes closed before his head rested on the pillow. All through his sleep, disquieted dreams haunted him. He tried to control the images, turn them from horrific memories and fears of retribution to those things he enjoyed in his youth—whenever that had been.

Years had moved into decades, into scores. Living in Azgarth's service prolonged life to an unnatural extent, with hardly any noticeable difference in appearance. Though he appeared a man in his mid-thirties, truth was he'd been born nearly two hundred years before.

Fashions came and went, but the existence of time did not show on his face. It marched across the inside of his eyelids in a panorama of his life. No rest for the wicked, indeed.

Roman rubbed his eyes and sat up. On the fireplace mantel sat a clock. It ticked in a precise rhythm, counting out the seconds. The face read half twelve. Judging from the ring of light coming from around the drapes, day was still upon the land, and he'd not slept it away.

His head pounded with all the authority of a kettle drum. Someone had poured sand in his eyes while he slept. No moisture coated his mouth. He needed to wash, dress, and head back to check on Nicholas.

A knock sounded on the door. His heart fell somewhere down on the carpet. Butterflies filled his belly. Bad news for certain. He'd told them only to disturb him if Nicholas had taken a turn for the worse.

"Enter."

The butler entered and bowed. "There is a Mr. King downstairs to see you, sir. Should I tell him you are indisposed?"

Roman hardly credited the words. "Mr. King? No. Please. Tell him I'll be down shortly."

"Very good, sir." The butler bowed again and left the room.

Roman hurried through his ablutions. The beard stubble would have to remain as there wasn't time to shave. No telling if Mr. King might grow cold feet and decide to slip out the door and into the park.

When Roman came to the bottom of the stairs, the butler waited. "I've put him in the consultation room, sir."

"Very good. Thank you."

Roman rubbed his hands together. Nerves shot through his body. This meeting might very well save him from showing his hand too early. No matter what, he must always maintain the appearance of compliance with Azgarth's wishes. To do less too early was to jeopardize his chance at freedom. Not to mention, the photographs were extraordinary.

He found the consultation room and entered. Mr. King stood gazing at paintings situated around the room. The subject matter was terrifyingly gruesome and showed bodies in various states of postmortem. In the shadows of the paintings were the silhouettes of people watching the physicians standing over the body of the deceased.

Mr. King turned at the sound of the door. His eyes were wide with surprise. He swallowed, causing his generous Adam's apple to bob up and down. "You said to come if I changed my mind." He raised his hand to forestall anything Roman might say before he'd finished. "Now, I'm not saying I've changed my mind, but I thought if I could have more information I might be able to decide what to do."

Roman narrowed his eyes and considered first Mr. King and then the paintings. "What is there to do? You either want to take on the project or not. I'll pay you for your time and expertise."

"I wouldn't expect otherwise." Mr. King rolled his hat in his hand a few times. It was a simple workman's cap. He wasn't a rich man by any stretch of the imagination, but he did make a living from his shop. "What is the scope of this project?"

"I need you to capture more of the beings you've so lovingly shown in your other portraits. Ones living in this world among us. I want to trace them back to their origin and find a way in without invitation." Roman put his hands up, indicating the room at large. "They can be anywhere around us. Point your camera in any direction and click."

Mr. King's eyes widened, and he shook his head. "You make fun of me."

Roman glanced up, leveling his gaze at Mr. King. "I assure you, that is far from my intent."

Mr. King frowned. "I know what people say behind my back. The whispers when they think I'm out of earshot."

"Might not be your neighbors."

"What's that?"

"What if I told you those scenes you stumble upon is truly another world bleeding into this one?"

Mr. King rubbed his face with a shaky hand. "I'd think we were both in need of the doctor's services."

"In need of dissection?" Roman gave a laugh. "A bit extreme."

"To give us something to calm our minds."

"There is nothing wrong with your mind." Roman neared one of the paintings and indicated the dark figures pressed into the corner. "They are all around us, and yet we fail to see them unless they wish to be seen."

"I've seen enough of them." Mr. King closed his eyes. His jaw set. "What will you prove by chasing them to their origins? They won't let you near them."

"Have you noticed more of them crossing over and invading our world? Something is coming and I mean to stop it, but I need your help."

Roman took a deep breath, allowing the scent of the man to fill his nose and filter down into his lungs. "You've paid dearly for the things you've seen. A lost love who thought you dead of an injury sustained by an animal from the very darkest corner of your mind. A nightmarish thing with scales and fangs—"

"No more!" Mr. King shuddered and cut his hand across the air. "Please. No more."

Agony of spirit twisted Mr. King's expression. Tears spilled from his eyes. His hands curled into tight fists, his knuckles blanched.

Roman turned and walked away, all the while nodding his understanding. "You have a decision to make, Mr. King."

Chapter Eight

Nicholas woke to a room he didn't recognize. Weakness kept his limbs firmly on the mattress when he tried to move. Something about the air felt familiar. He'd been there before, but not this room. Not this particular part of the house.

"Ah, you're awake."

A face came into his field of vision. It belonged to a young man, late twenties maybe. Dark hair and eyes. Like the air, he too was familiar, but not quite recognizable.

When Nicholas tried to speak, the man stalled him. "Don't even try until you've had some water. You're fluid-depleted and need to drink."

He poured a glass of water, then helped Nicholas to sit and held the glass while he took his fill. When he was finished, the man moved pillows behind Nicholas's back and propped him against them.

"Do you remember anything from your ordeal?"

Nicholas gave a nod. "Not you. Familiar."

"Name's Henri Vauss. I'm Dr. Mikhail Stanslovich's assistant. He and Dr. Dante Savoy saved your life."

Oh, yes. He remembered waking in the tank, covered in fluid, with some sort of electromagnetic appliances strapped to his chest and face. They'd made him into some sort of experiment.

"Where?"

"The home of Dr. Savoy. You have everything you need here for your care and comfort. There's no reason to be alarmed." Mr. Vauss held up a bowl with a silver spoon in it. "Would you like to try some broth? I'll admit it's probably gone cold, but it's nothing to have it warmed again if you like."

"No. Thank you." An appetite was the least of his concerns at the moment. Sir Rodderick had tried to kill him. The ignorant fool.

"Your agent, Mr. Cetanni is here. Would you like to see him?"

A spark lit in his belly. "Roman?"

"I believe that is his first name, yes."

Nicholas managed to move his hand enough to grab Mr. Vauss's. "Yes. Please."

"Very well. I'll go and fetch him for you. Will you be all right?"

Seriously, Nicholas had no notion of what he'd be if left alone for any length of time. "I'm not likely to meet with a mischief in this room, am I?"

An odd expression moved over Mr. Vauss's face. "One never knows."

Nicholas decided to wait and see. He wasn't afraid of the unexpected. Not having served Azgarth these few years. In the fae realm, he had witnessed events not even a Bedlamite could conceive. Horrible events had been known to occur in the fae realm. Even humans failed to be as uniquely cruel as what Azgarth could be if crossed. Thinking of his sweet sister alone in that realm without protection frightened him.

He had to get back there to find her. Make sure she was all right.

Tingles centered in his palms and moved outward. He pumped his hands, trying to get the feeling back into them. The desire to paint filled his body until it had nowhere else to go. He doubted in his condition he'd even be able to hold a brush, let alone apply paint to a canvas with any degree of skill.

A glimmer of an idea flashed in his mind. Inspiration pierced his soul, a Cupid's arrow hitting its target true. Colors, vibrant and bright, splashed across a canvas in thick smears, giving the painting not only life, but texture.

The door opened and Roman entered. "How are you feeling?"

"I need my paints and brushes."

"Nicco?"

"There are such scenes in my head I need to get out. I fear if I don't, I'll go mad."

"You need rest more than you need to paint." Roman pulled a chair over by the bed and sat. "Far be it from me to discourage you in exercising your craft, but you've been through a terrible ordeal."

"It's a compulsion. I won't be able to rest and heal until I get these ideas out into the world." He stared deeply into Roman's eyes. "Please, Roman."

Roman stood with a heavy sigh. "Very well. Do you have any materials at your studio, or did you take it all to Lady Clarissa's?"

Nicholas narrowed his eyes. He remembered painting her portrait as Tatiana, but there was something else about the session that was a bit off— above and beyond being shot by Sir Rodderick. "I remember being there. Painting Lady Clarissa." He waved his hand in a dismissive manner, not willing to go into the particulars of his attempted assassination. No, he'd catch up with Sir Rodderick and settle that score soon enough. "There's something else. It's a bit fuzzy at the moment."

"What is the last clear memory you have?"

"Waking in that chamber of fluid." Nicholas tried unsuccessfully to suppress a shiver.

Roman made a face. "You misunderstand me. What is the last memory you have from before you woke in the chamber?"

He decided on a little deception. Only a bit to bide his time. "We were supposed to meet for a drink. A little pub. The Stag and Boar."

"Correct."

"Sorry I was in no condition to meet you." Nicholas gestured toward his midsection. "As you see, I ran afoul of trouble."

"So it would seem." Roman leaned forward, placing his hand on Nicholas's. "Did you have any appointments between Lady Clarissa and when we were to meet? Did you write it in a ledger?"

"No. I am more fluid than to use such devices as a ledger." He frowned at Roman. "You should know that. You've encouraged me at every turn."

"Because I believe in you. I always have."

"That is your vocation."

"It's been a long time since you were nothing more than a vocation for me, Nicco."

Nicholas stared at Roman in wonder. Tightness pulled his chest. Afraid to ask for clarification, he remained silent. He didn't dare acknowledge that the feelings he'd had for Roman only grew the longer the association continued.

Roman knew all Nicholas's faults, foibles, and missteps. In all the time they'd known each other, Roman had never once acted as if he thought less of Nicholas for his wild, unchecked ways. Roman was the most sober, stable man he'd ever met. At times, he forgot Roman acted as an extension of Azgarth's influence in this world. They were so unalike in every way.

Guilt made an uncomfortable presence in his chest. Often were the times Roman took a punishment meant for Nicholas. Roman had never admitted as much, but Nicholas knew and it shamed him.

Nicholas rested deeper into the pillows and closed his eyes so he didn't have to look at Roman. "I don't know what I'd do without you."

"You will never have to find out."

Roman moved around the room, but sleep pressed down on Nicholas, making it hard to open his eyes again. Perhaps it was best if he slept a bit longer. Maybe then he'd feel as if some of his energy was restored.

Roman spoke to him, but the words were garbled, distant. Blessed quiet filled the room.

When he woke again, the sun had set and the lights were up, giving the room a soft glow.

Roman sat at the table, looking through a leather-bound book. Every once in a while, he'd jot something down before turning the page.

"Have you been here the entire time?"

Roman didn't glance up from his work. "No. I left for a while to collect some of your art supplies. Drs. Stanslovich and Savoy both thought it a very sound idea to aid in your healing."

"I don't know if I'll be able to even hold a brush for a while. I'm as weak as a half-dead kitten."

"The doctors were encouraged by the fact you even asked for your supplies."

Nicholas reached for the blankets in an attempt to throw them off his legs. "Help me up."

"Stay where you are. There's no need for you to get up and move around." Roman put his pen down and leveled a sharp glance Nicholas's way. "If you hadn't noticed yet, your abdomen is sutured together. You need to lie still until it begins to heal."

At the reminder, Nicholas placed a hand over his belly. Bandages cut across his body like a soft bastard corset. He didn't know if the tightness of the wrap was to keep his insides from spilling out or to encourage him to keep good posture. Possibly both.

"The way I'm trussed up, no one will ever know if I'm healed or not."

"Believe me, they check on you regularly. You've not been alone for any length of time while under their care."

"And how long have I been under their care?" Not that time mattered. He'd only felt as if he'd been gone for years.

"A few days. Long enough for Azgarth to notice your absence."

Nicholas never had any illusions where Azgarth was concerned. Considering it had been the fae realm and Azgarth's court he'd wandered through while between worlds, he doubted he was missed by the dark lord.

"Did you happen to bring my sketchbook and pencils?"

Roman tapped the top of a book Nicholas hadn't even noticed on the table. "Would you like me to bring them to you?"

"If you please."

Roman stood, picking up the sketchbook and pencil case on his way by. "Do not tax yourself. Only do what you can and don't push."

Advice came cheap when the person giving it had no notion of the creative process or how it worked. As far as Nicholas knew, Roman only had a good eye for art and did as his master bade him. No real talent was required.

Nicholas narrowed his eyes as he studied Roman. Other, different, talents were at work in the agent. Things Nicholas didn't even want to explore for fear it might change his feelings.

"What?"

Nicholas realized he stared and turned his face away as heat crept up his neck. He took the drawing implements with quiet thanks before he opened the book. Fingers that once knew how to hold a pencil for best effect were stiff and sore. The joints had a hard time moving and his grip on the pencil shaft was too loose to have proper control.

Instead of holding it the way he normally would, he slid his fingers up higher and let his wrist move back and forth, adding only a light line here and there with a feathery stroke. For what he had in mind, he didn't need to draw with any degree of accuracy, only to place items on the page where they might go when he transferred the idea to canvas.

Images flashed before his eyes like the pictures on a deck of cards when they were cut and shuffled. Each thought vied to be placed on the paper. Creative inspiration often came to him in sudden bursts, but this was an altogether different manner. He allowed his hand free rein, channeling all his talent into the end of the pencil. The favorite of his paintings had been completed in this manner—allowing his talent to take control. More stories were told in the depths of his subconscious than floated around in the known part of his brain.

Roman had taken a seat across the room again, content to sit quietly and jot notes in his book while Nicholas drew. No words were exchanged. They had been together for long enough there was no need to entertain or amuse one another. At least not that night. Now was the time for quiet reflection. Time to get his hands and mind working as one.

Time passed with the soft scratch of the pencil over paper. It sounded of comfort, industry, and a whole list of other words that brought satisfaction to his soul. To be doing that which made him happy helped to chase away the darkness.

And that commodity seemed to be everywhere lately.

Nicholas used his thumb to smudge the gray and soften the shading. He leaned back to inspect the overall effect and drew in a deep breath. What manner of being was this that stared at him from the page? Unlike Azgarth, this being's features were vivid. Long pale hair framed a thin face made of sharp angles. Tall pointy ears rose from the side of his head. An air of elegance and grace shone from a pair of light, piercing eyes.

Roman glanced up. "Are you in pain?"

"No."

"Then what's wrong?"

"Nothing." What was he supposed to say to Roman? Admit he'd drawn a being he'd never met, yet looked alive enough to touch?

"I heard you make a sound."

A twinge of defensiveness stung him. "I've been making lots of sounds."

"Forget I mentioned it or showed concern." Roman stood. "I need to see Dr. Savoy on a matter. If you need me, ring for the servants."

Nicholas held up his hand in entreaty. "Romo. Wait."

Roman stalled at the door, his hand on the knob. "Yes?"

"Please, don't feel you have to leave. I'm only tired and frustrated."

"Thank you for that, but I really must find Dr. Savoy."

The door opened and closed with a quiet click. Nicholas lay his head against the pillow and closed his eyes. He'd not meant to hurt Roman. No one had ever been as supportive and caring as Roman. Not even his mother.

A tremor moved through his body at the reminder of the shrew. Constantina Alexandre had never found anything but fault with her son. After his father died, he'd been old enough to inherit, but too young to really understand what that meant. It fell on older, wiser men in their family to assist with the running of their estate. In the end, those same men had undermined the family and used Nicholas's licentiousness against him to gain control of their fortune. Things only grew worse once they'd fled to England—until Roman had approached him to show his art to the masses. Recognition came as a sweet surprise. He'd never known how much he needed it, how much it meant. A lump formed in Nicholas's throat and made it hard to swallow.

Shadows pooled in the corner of the room, growing outward, though the light never changed. Silhouettes took form, shifting and moving in an intricate dance as they advanced into the room proper.

Nicholas set the sketchbook aside. "What do you want?"

Whispers filled the air, circling his head in a low taunt. An angry growl splintered through the murmurs, and Azgarth appeared, chasing his minions back to the other side of the veil. He did not seem pleased with his creations. Had they used initiative and worked without his express permission? A rift of such magnitude was a very interesting thing to encounter.

The shimmery outline Nicholas had come to know as Azgarth turned and glided across the room, taking up residence by the wardrobe. He stood with arms crossed and legs spread as if in an angry challenge. Nicholas simply stared.

When Azgarth did not speak or reveal the reason he'd come, Nicholas picked up the sketchbook and began to draw. He felt, rather than saw, Azgarth move closer to the bed. He stood gazing down at the portrait. Nicholas used his thumb once again to smudge the lines, but this time, he blurred the entire image, creating the effect as it appeared when looking at Azgarth straight on. No clean lines of demarcation between Azgarth and atmosphere. He seemed to blend into his surroundings as if he moved too fast for the naked eye to see.

"You've drawn me?" Surprise rang in the question.

"A close facsimile. I would have to know your face exactly in order to do any portrait of you proper justice."

Azgarth ran a long finger over the blurry lines of his image. "Human eyes cannot see the fae. You haven't the ability to view us properly. Not in the world of man."

"We have even less understanding of your world than the ability to see it."

Azgarth drew back. "You are angry with me?"

"And if I am?"

Azgarth cocked his head as if not knowing how he felt about such an admission. He straightened. "It's of no consequence to me."

Of course not. Why would Nicholas ever think Azgarth had any care for those he culled for his own amusement?

Without another word, Azgarth walked to the corner and folded back into the fabric of his own world.

Anger spiked red hot. He threw the sketchbook to the corner, following in the path of Azgarth's departure. "Take your bloody sketch!"

Damn! Was he to always be at the mercy of others? He thought when he agreed to this life that he'd still be his own man, not live under the thumb of his dark master's control.

No more.

When he finally made it out of this bed, he'd find a way into the fae realm and see his sister.

Roman entered the dining room. The others were already present, save for Mr. Vauss. His absence was no surprise as he seemed rather dedicated to his work and the care of the patient—in this case, Nicholas. Andres Valentine sat on the right side of the table with the doctors on either end. Roman took the left.

The dining room wasn't large but was well furnished. A chandelier hung from the ceiling, fixed with gaslights instead of candles. More lights were set at even intervals around the room but were turned low to create an intimate ambiance. An uneasy tension filled the room and conversation came in fits and starts. Roman hated to think he was the cause but knew in his heart the truth.

He placed his fork on his plate and dabbed at his mouth with the napkin. "My apologies, Dr. Savoy, if I've imposed myself too much on your good nature. Your kindness and hospitality is greatly appreciated, but I must beg your indulgence for a small matter."

The three gentlemen exchanged surreptitious glances.

Dr. Savoy leaned back in his chair and turned his hand, giving Roman leave to speak freely. "And pray tell, what is this indulgence you seek?"

"Your butler may have told you I had a visitor earlier."

"Yes, he did mention something along those lines."

"His name is Aristotle King, and he's one of Azgarth's chosen." Roman waited for the reaction, which was not long in coming. He raised a hand to stop any interruptions before they came. "His talent is photography and the fae are not shy around him."

Valentine frowned. "I've seen his work. He owns a little shop on the outskirts of the city."

Roman nodded. "The very one."

Dr. Savoy made a face. "I'm not sure what this has to do with me or my home."

"He captures things that leak over into our world. Things that Azgarth sends to watch his chosen and those who wrangle the chosen." Roman glanced down at his hands before looking up to meet Dr. Savoy's gaze. "I didn't ask to become an agent, just as most of the chosen don't ask to become one. This duty was thrust upon me for an odd talent or two I possess."

Dr. Stanslovich leaned forward. "Am I correct to assume you want to turn in your notice?"

Roman gave him a wry smile. "That's a diplomatic way of putting it."

"But accurate?" Dr. Stanslovich pressed.

Roman gave a curt nod. He dared not say it out loud. Even now, he felt the press of the fae world leaking over into the dining room uninvited. "To break a pact as an agent is not an easy thing. The manner in which you broke the covenant for Mr. Valentine placed him and all those in Kering's book in jeopardy. A few died as a result of the backlash of power unleashed when the book was burned."

The interest in the eyes of his audience turned to horror.

"We didn't know. We acted on instinct," Dr. Savoy defended.

Roman shook his head. "I need no justification or explanation for your actions. I'm here as neither judge nor jury. What I am asking is that you allow Mr. King to photograph areas of your workspace and home."

"Why?" Dr. Savoy did not appear disposed to give permission.

"I have reason to believe there are problems brewing in the fae realm."

Dr. Stanslovich leaned forward. "What kind of problems?"

"I'm not quite sure, but I fear for all of humanity should it spill over into this world more than it has already."

"And you believe my home is a nexus for this activity?" Dr. Savoy lifted a glass of wine and took a sip as if unperturbed by the charge.

Roman wasn't fooled; he smelled the fear on the physician. "Azgarth is drawn to your work. Your very vocation makes you almost as powerful as he. To control life and death the way you do is not a talent held by many humans. It also makes you vulnerable."

"So he targets us?" Dr. Savoy appeared unsurprised by the knowledge.

"Taunts is a better word. Challenges." Roman considered the physicians carefully. "But not to any degree of altruism. Not to teach, but for amusement. He's attracted to your work. It fascinates him and that can be a dangerous thing."

"Can't you simply ask Azgarth why he's sending more beings into our world?" Dr. Savoy gave the impression of a man who always chose the most expedient way to go about getting what he wanted. While an admirable trait, it did nothing in this instance but agitate.

Roman raised a brow and addressed Dr. Savoy directly. "Have you ever tried to ask Azgarth a question? He's not given to answering in anything short of a riddle, especially if he's of a mind not to answer."

Dr. Stanslovich and Dr. Savoy exchanged glances.

"You've had experience with this."

"A time or two," Dr. Stanslovich confirmed.

"Then let me do this. I promise to share any information with you to our mutual satisfaction." Roman reached into his pocket and pulled out his notebook. "Burned onto these pages are the names of every man and woman whom I've agented over my tenure with Azgarth. Each burning represents a person whose life has been my pleasure and honor to protect. Please, if you will not do so for me, do so for the lives represented herein— I beg you not to harm or foul this book in any way."

Their collective expressions said they wanted to chuck it into a forge, or emulsify it in acid.

Valentine was the first to nod. "I know how much pain it causes when a book such as that is destroyed. Knowing I gained my freedom at the cost of lives is a hallow victory."

"Given what I've already said, I'd be remiss in my duties if I didn't offer you full disclosure of the events which followed Valentine's freedom." The memory of the gruesome experience had been branded on his brain in blood and fear.

"Not a pleasant experience if your expression is any indication." This observation came from Dr. Savoy.

Roman shook his head. "No. It wasn't, but then Azgarth enraged is not a pleasant thing."

Dr. Savoy gestured to one of the footman who poured a glass of wine for Roman.

Roman nodded and took a sip. When he'd wet his suddenly dry throat, he began. "Kering was the first to fall. He'd angered Azgarth greatly when he'd been the one to push Valentine from the window."

He glanced up in time to see Valentine visibly shudder.

"Forgive me for my indelicacy," Roman said. "When he failed to regain control of you, he was thrown into an acid pit to melt away until there was nothing left of him. For the rest of Azgarth's agents..." Here Roman faltered. "We were held in a chamber to watch the process as a deterrent from stepping out of line in future. Afterward, one by one, we were stripped down and beaten with a lash. Once our backs were bloody and flesh lay open, he had us immersed into a pool of a foul-smelling sulfurous wash. The pain was enough to make most of the agents lose consciousness. More the better for them."

Dr. Stanslovich shook his head. His eyes were wide with awe and disbelief. "How did you stand it?"

"I had to. I have my charges to consider. Without me, who knows to what agent they may be reassigned. It might be another Kering and that will not do." Nothing would have done, save enduring the torture. He'd been right smack in the middle of the line of agents. The screams of those who had gone before him continued to echo through the caverns of the under-palace. Heavy breathing and fear came from behind him. He had alternated between envy for the ones who were finished with their punishments and anger at those yet to go, who did nothing but increase his anxiety.

The scars remained on his back, still purple and vivid. He'd carry those for the rest of his unnatural life.

Roman glanced at first one doctor then the other. He cleared his throat. "What say you? Will you allow me to see if I can discover a way into the fae realm without invitation?"

"Agreed."

"Agreed."

He gave a decisive nod. "Good. I will contact Mr. King in the morning. Until then, I have some research to do. If you will excuse me."

Roman bid them good evening. He left the dining room and climbed the stairs. One more check on Nicholas. Then he'd wait for Azgarth's summons. After what he shared with the others, it wouldn't be long in coming. Azgarth at least had that much predictability about him.

Lately, he only wanted to walk the halls of freedom. Maybe, just maybe, with a little information and the help of the good doctors, perhaps they might all find that end.

Chapter Nine

Mikhail gazed out at the garden below. Midnight came, and with it, a flood of silvery moonlight washed the small plot of land below, changing its face from daytime friendliness, to sullen nighttime. Too many dark shadows abounded. Sinister angles and malevolent recesses hid all manner of strange, exotic entities. None, he felt, were as kindhearted and caring as Mr. Roman Cetanni.

He was not at all what Mikhail had expected when he'd first realized the man was an agent of Azgarth. Weren't they all supposed to be evil bastards like Kering? Didn't the devil show in the details? If so, they'd know soon enough if Mr. Cetanni made them all fools.

A tentative knock sounded on the door.

"Enter."

In the dark, it was hard to make out his visitor, but he knew and his heart raced.

Dante closed the door and came farther into the room. "Why are you standing here in the dark?"

"Watching the moonlight, trying to decide if we're being taken in or if Mr. Cetanni is in earnest."

"And have you found any answers?"

"Not a one." Mikhail turned from the window. "I've decided to let this play out as it will and use it to our advantage."

Dante crossed the room and turned the key on one of the gas lamps. Introduction of light only chased away a few of the shadows. So many more waited for them that they'd never be completely free.

"That's better. How do you mean to accomplish that great task?"

"I haven't decided yet, but I'll know when I see it."

Dante leaned against the desk. He crossed his arms and regarded Mikhail with a look of concentration. "How are we going to destroy the books if we can't burn them? If doing so causes injury? I never want to be the cause of someone's pain, injury, or death. The day I took my oath to heal, I promised if I ever abused that office, I would never practice again. How can I live with myself knowing what I do now?"

"You can because you're the most conscientious man I've ever met and you know there are people out there who need your help." Suddenly, it was hard to swallow. "*I* need you."

"Mikhail."

He'd never heard his name sound more sensual, as if it had been drawn from Dante with a heady mix of pleasure and pain. "By now, you should have no illusions you're the most important person in my world. Thinking you might give up because you've caused a few unintentional injuries—"

"Deaths. Mr. Cetanni specifically said there had been deaths."

Mikhail pushed away from the window and crossed the room. He took Dante's hand in his. "Yes. Deaths. Ones you were unaware you'd caused."

"That doesn't mean I'm not responsible."

"Balance that against the lives you've saved."

Dante gave a pained laugh. "One life has no more value than another. All life is precious."

"And that is what makes you a great physician. You don't believe that the life of the shopgirl is any less important than that of the Queen."

Dante gave a sigh. "Then what are we going to do? How are we going to free those from Azgarth's control who wish to be set free?"

"I don't know." There had to be some sort of connection that fed back to Azgarth. Something esoteric, unseen by the human eye. "Perhaps the photographs to be taken by Mr. King will show us a thing or two we've missed."

"I will not hold out hope."

"Nor I. At the moment, I'm more worried about the beings Mr. Cetanni mentioned crossing over into our world."

"Me too," Dante agreed.

A sound came from the garden below. A mournful wail of one in danger.

Dante stalked to the window. "What the bloody hell?"

Mikhail came up behind Dante and peered over his shoulder. The sounds continued, though there didn't appear to be a disturbance. "Might it be coming from the neighbors?"

"They've gone to the country. I don't even believe their servants are in house." Dante started from the room. "Come on."

They hurried out of the room and downstairs to the parlor. A set of french doors opened onto a small patio that led to the garden proper. The yard wasn't large by any standards, but was big enough to hold a table for a morning or afternoon meal, a private bench by a stand of rose bushes, and a central fountain.

Water burbled and bubbled up in the center of the works. The wail continued from the direction of the fountain, echoing in a long chain of agony.

A figure billowed out from the spray, composed of droplets made from the rushing water leaving the spout. It raised its arms and reached for Mikhail and Dante, as if imploring a way to safety. The head and torso were man-shaped. A long column of water made up the trunk, sticking out of the main fall as a branch growing from the side of a tree. No legs appeared. It hadn't made it that far out of the fae realm.

"Trapped souls?" Dante pulled off his jacket and kept moving toward the fountain.

"I have no idea."

Mikhail followed suit. How were they to assist a being that was not solid? Or at least didn't appear to be. He rolled up his sleeves and stood at the edge of the fountain. The being reached out again. A horrible maw opened, emitting a shout that sounded as a thousand angry seas crashing against the shore.

Mikhail grabbed at the water. His hand passed through, leaving nothing but moisture against his palm. "What can we do? I can't get hold of it."

Dante kicked off his shoes, socks, and rolled up his trouser legs. The being continued to fight its way out to the surface. Water spewed in an arc with each pained swipe of its arms. He climbed into the fountain, wading toward the tragic figure. "Turn off the switch. If the motor is off, it might get sucked back into its dimension."

"To what, though? It's escaping for a reason."

Mikhail leaned forward again, trying to contain the frantic movements of the water creature. To no avail. Each time he came in contact, he only managed to get wet.

Dante stuck his hand under the water and pushed a lever. The fountain began to drain. "Kill the switch."

"Where is it?"

"Right side under the lip of the rim."

Mikhail bent down and felt around. A small toggle protruded from the gearbox. He flipped it in the opposite position and the water stopped cycling. The fountain spray stopped. The creature disappeared.

Dante stood in the fountain, breath sawing in and out. His face pale in the moonlight. A sheen of sweat and fear covered his skin. "God forgive me if I've hurt something else."

"What else could we do? I couldn't grab it. Lacking substance and form, our only alternative would have been to save it in a bucket."

Dante's shoulders slumped. "Damn it to bloody hell."

"It wasn't your fault." Mikhail stood there with his hands in his trouser pockets, staring at Dante in the moonlight. Helpless to aid his friend's distress. "But I might have another idea."

"What's that?"

"Is there always fluid in the canister that feeds into the resurrection tank?"

"Yes. Why?"

"Follow me." Mikhail picked up Dante's jacket off the ground and strode into the house, not stopping until he came to the surgery.

As he moved deeper into the room, he turned up some lamps. He'd had enough of dark places for one night.

"Remember when the *wolfsine* came through the tank in my laboratory and attacked Henri?" Mikhail stood near the controls for the resurrection tank. "The fluid acted as a conduit into the fae realm. Let's open a gateway and see if that being can find its way here. It made its way to your fountain. Another doorway so close is bound to draw attention."

Dante gave a swift nod. "Do it."

Mikhail turned the valve wheel and fluid began to rush into the tank. Images moved and churned in the depths of the solution, but nothing tried to push its way out. Reflection from the room or window into another world, it was unclear as to which it might be. A few months ago, he'd not have questioned what his eyes showed him. Now he neither trusted nor relied on anything around him. Certainly, his dance with the opium dens had not helped matters. Though how much of what he'd seen during drug-hazed nights had been real? The more he thought on it, the more difficulty he had separating the two.

When the tank filled, they brought chairs over to the edge and prepared to wait.

Dante spared Mikhail a glance. "I wonder if any of our intrepid chroniclers wrote about water beings."

"It wouldn't hurt to look as we wait. Who knows how long it will take for the being to find its way here, if indeed it ever does." Mikhail levered himself up. "I'll go get it."

Moving, engaging in a productive endeavor offered greater attraction than sitting by the tank waiting. He'd never been good at sitting still when action was required. Not that he knew what form that action should take in this instance. How did one go about saving a being that lived in a liquid state? Freezing would hinder movement and make the being shatter like glass. Heating would cause steam to rise, releasing it into a vapor.

Vapor? Perhaps that was the answer.

The point was moot until the being decided to show itself again. He hurried to the study and picked up the book from where it still lay on the desk and returned to the surgery.

"Any change?"

"No. Not a bit."

The tank had filled. Fluid stayed still, calm.

Mikhail handed the book to Dante. "This is wrong."

"What is? You found something in the book?" Dante opened the book halfway through and started thumbing the pages.

"No. The fluid." Mikhail pointed to the tank. "Stagnant fluid isn't going to call a being forth. Turn on the motor. Let the fluid move and agitate. That's how the tank was before, and the fountain with the recycling water. Movement is the key."

Dante reached over and turned on the motor. The tank came to life, making the water bubble and oscillate.

Mikhail sat down next to Dante as the fluid churned within the tank.

"Have you found another body?"

Mikhail turned. Henri stood in the doorway, leaning against the jamb. "Not in the strictest sense of the definition."

Henri stepped into the surgery, hands in his pockets. "Sounds intriguing."

"Another creature from the fae realm." Mikhail watched the scenes moving through the water, but nothing came close to trying to break free. "Come closer and look at the fluid and tell me what you see."

Henri did as instructed, staring into the glass. "Fluid, bubbles, motion."

"Is that all?" Mikhail studied his face. "Look closer."

Henri leaned in. Narrowed his eyes.

Dante frowned. "What do you see, Mikhail?"

Surprised, Mikhail opened his mouth to answer, then closed it again. "I'd rather you tell me what you see first. Then I'll tell you if it's the same. If not, I might be going mad."

Henri made a face. "We're all slightly mad if we're in this business."

"Look closer," Mikhail encouraged a second time.

Both Henri and Dante leaned closer, watching the fluid roil and tumble. Every so often, a face would appear near the glass, their mouth open in a silent scream.

How could they not see what was clear and plain as the noses on their faces?

Hands pressed against the glass, trying to find a way out. The walls of the container shook.

Henri and Dante jumped back.

Mikhail smiled. "You saw that, I take it."

"It's people. Trapped." Henri placed his hand on the glass, touching palms to one of the victims inside. "How did they get inside there?"

Mikhail indicated the book in Dante's hands. "Have you found anything that might help us?"

"Oh." Dante tore his gaze away from the tank. He flipped a few pages. "Swamps. Bogs. Rivers. Estuaries. Ah, here. Fountains, tubs, and aquariums." He moved his finger down the pages, skimming the information.

Violent percussion began hitting the inside of the tank. The entire structure shook.

Mikhail shot to his feet. "How are they even able to do that when they have image but not form? It breaks all the laws of physics."

"If we've learned nothing else from our brush with the fae, we have learned that they do not respect nor operate under any of the known laws." Dante didn't look up from his reading, but continued to skim the book.

"We have to do something." Henri stepped to the edge of the tank. "How do we separate them from the fluid without doing more harm?"

"I thought maybe changing the state to vapor, but I'd be afraid to heat up the fluid and cause injury." Mikhail considered the problem. "How about if we run gas through the system and break the fluid up into particles?"

Dante raised his head. His eyes were large and filled with compassion. "Listen to this. *The perinine, not to be confused with water spirits or nymphs, are believed to be the souls of humans trapped between the world of man and the fae after death of the physical body.*"

Cold ran down Mikhail's spine, whispering along his neck like a call to the grave. "So even if we had a way to save them, they'd have no corporeal form to return to?"

"According to this book," Dante quickly corrected.

Mikhail rubbed a hand around his mouth. "I hate this. I never signed up to be ineffectual. Saving a soul is infinitely harder than saving a body."

Dante's jaw tightened. "Henri, go wake Mr. Cetanni and see if he knows of anything we can do to help."

Henri hurried away, not stopping to look back at the scene.

"Does the entry give any other insights?" Mikhail asked. The activity within the tank eased a bit, though the faces were still visible as they churned in the fluid.

"None that are helpful. It does mention that the phenomenon is more prevalent in areas of greater hydroelectric conductivity."

"Which hearkens back to what we've already discovered on our own."

A few minutes later, Henri returned with Mr. Cetanni in tow. The agent skidded to a halt in front of the tank.

"*Perinine.*" Awe filled Mr. Cetanni's face. "It's been years since I've seen the like."

Mikhail grew closer, standing next to Mr. Cetanni as he gazed at the rolling fluid. "Problem is, do you know how to send them on their way?"

Mr. Cetanni broke his gaze and turned to Mikhail. "You can't. They are between worlds. Souls who have been denied both the grace of God and the favor of the fae. Without either opening their arms and taking them into the bosom of the afterlife, this is their reality. Their final resting place."

Mikhail had never been a religious man, nor particularly spiritual for that matter, but he did know and understand the concepts taught in Sunday school quite well. "This is their purgatory?"

Mr. Cetanni ran his hand down the side of the tank. "In a manner of speaking, yes. They can go neither forward nor back."

"What can we do to help them?" Dante set the book aside and stood as well.

Seeing the faces of those stuck in limbo was hard to watch. Their pain and agony stretched across contorted features, either from the movement of the water or the expressions of the panic it wasn't clear.

Mikhail wiped a shaking hand down his face. Sweat beaded on his face again. It had been hours since his last dose of morphine, and he could feel the need snaking through his body. "I hate this feeling of helplessness."

Mr. Cetanni cupped Mikhail's shoulder in a gesture born of compassion and understanding. "One of the hardest lessons I had to learn as an agent of Azgarth was the inability to change an outcome. Azgarth's will is strong, and a mere human is no match for a being such as him. Balance comes by helping those I can."

Respect for Mr. Cetanni grew. He was not at all what Mikhail had expected. Integrity showed the measure of a man. Some men were born with that virtue, others had to learn, some never embraced the concept. Mr. Cetanni had impressed with his benevolence on more than one occasion, and from what Mikhail detected, the emotion was genuine.

"Turn off the tank and release the fluid." Dante gave the order. Sorrow filled his eyes. "It's cruel to let them believe they have found a way out of the darkness only to deny it."

Words bubbled and rose in Mikhail's throat. Fluids flushed from the system as Henri released the valve. Cruel didn't even begin to define the act of sending those poor souls back into the dark void. Yet how did the living go about opening a doorway for them to pass on to the afterlife. No man had that kind of power, not even the clergy. Their powers were limited to that of prayer.

And he had never been one to pray.

Roman finally arrived to his room exhausted and slightly shocked.

Perinine.

Who would have thought that odd phenomenon had reappeared? But why now? He'd been correct in assuming something was afoot. The problem lay in proving what exactly all the separate incidents meant. Mostly, *perinine* stayed to their dark world, existing in the chasm between worlds. A frozen wasteland without beginning or end. Where even thoughts were denied.

Watchers. *Perinine.* He'd seen a sprite or two bleeding into the fabric of the material world. Tricksters the lot of them, Not to be trusted, and rightly so. Shakespeare had represented them true when he'd written Puck into *A Midsummer Night's Dream.* Though sprites were far from the worst beings to live in the fae realm. So many of them stood at the doorway that separated one realm from the other, longing on their collective faces. Nothing was so attractive to the fae as imposing themselves on the human race.

Tired beyond the ability to feel, Roman crossed the room, loosening his tie as he did. He'd managed to convince Dr. Savoy and Stanslovich to allow Mr. King to photograph the house. What he'd not expected was the task to be so easily accomplished. Other than one or two sensible questions, they'd all been very accommodating with the request. Surely his good fortune in that quarter wouldn't last. Not when Dr. Savoy realized the scope of the bargain he'd made. The very walls were going to tremble with the onslaught.

He hung his tie over the chair. As he bent, he caught something from his periphery. A small section of shadow near the wardrobe began to grow and shift. None of the edges indicated beings were on the other side, pushing their way through the void. No, this appeared more as if the very fabric of the worlds had developed a small tear.

An invitation or true rip?

A breeze sent cool air through the room, making the edges of the shadow billow as laundry on a line. This really needed exploring at closer range.

He took a few steps, lifting his hand to feel the escaping air move through his fingers. The window wasn't open, so it couldn't have come from there. Not in so great a gust. If so, Dr. Savoy really needed to get the glaziers in to fit new windows. Besides, the direction was all wrong. The window was located on his right. The air blew from straight ahead.

As he grew nearer, a howl rose. Wind rattling through trees or, in this case, a tunnel. He kept his hand out, feeling around the edges of the tear. A drop in temperature of at least fifteen degrees gave the opening a frigid chill. Roman reached out and grabbed his jacket and shot his arms through the holes. If he was going to explore the rift, he wasn't about to freeze in the pursuit.

In all the years he'd been in Azgarth's service, not once had he entered the fae realm unless invited. The more he thought about it, the greater the possibility this was less of an invitation and more of an invasion. If one didn't intend to entertain uninvited guests, one shouldn't leave the back door open.

Roman stuck his hand in the rift and wiggled his fingers. The air felt different there. Heavy. Melancholy. A horrible stench filled the entranceway. He gagged. Gods and devils, he'd been there before, but not from this position.

He reached into the wardrobe and pulled out a handkerchief. With quick efficiency, he tied it around his face to cover his nose and mouth. It probably wouldn't keep out all the wretched smells, but it might filter enough he'd not lose his dinner.

Stiffening his spine, Roman stepped through the breach and into the darkness of the chasm between the two realms. Immediate and crippling dizziness brought him to his knees. He hit the ground, striking his knees on a hard surface before tipping backward and tumbling through space.

The fall went on for an eternity. Entire worlds were formed and died in the time it took him to reach the ground. He hit with such force he lost consciousness, and came to he knew not how long later. If he thought the ambient smells moving through the rift were bad, they were nothing compared to the rotting flesh that permeated the area. Even with the kerchief on, the foul taste covered his tongue; bathing his mouth in a horrid flavor he'd never be rid.

Slowly he came back into his mind. Pain shot through him from a hundred different scrapes, cuts, and bruises. He pushed to a sitting position, then shook his head to clear the ringing in his ears. Under the constant hum came the unmistakable pop of murky, thick bubbles. Hot lava breaking the surface of a liquid death. God in heaven, he knew where he was and he cared not for the knowledge. He'd seen this place from above as Wilhelm Kering was pulled under by the acid bath. Witnessed the bubbling, sloughing of skin as the liquid ate Kering's flesh.

This was the place where Azgarth chose to punish with extreme prejudice. Fear filled him from groin to gullet. Speaking out loud and out of turn had brought him to this pass. A punishment for discussing what he'd witnessed with mortals. Some of the chosen, but mortals nonetheless.

Gingerly, he reached out a hand and felt away from where he landed. Darkness surrounded him. Not even a tiny spark of light illuminated the pitch black. Without knowing where he sat in relation to the pits, he had no way of ascertaining which way to go to escape. One step in the wrong direction and he'd be thrust into the unforgiving pool that fed off human flesh as payment for transgressions.

Stretched out all the way to the right, he felt nothing but solid ground. He explored to the left and came up against a wall. Comfort rose. If he stayed close to the wall, he might be able to negotiate his way out of the pits and back to another section of the fae realm.

With his back against the wall, he used his legs and pushed to stand. Every muscle and bone in his body screamed in agony. He bit his lip to keep from crying out in pain. If no one yet knew of his presence in this awful and forsaken place, he'd not alert them.

Taking small steps, he used his toe to feel in front of him, making sure the wall didn't meet the edge of the pit. Who knew when or if the walls would sheer off to a sudden drop. Inch by painful inch, Roman made his way through the twisting, turning chamber.

He moved his hand along the wall, reassured by the feel of the hard surface beneath his fingers. As he dragged his hand out before him, he came up with air. Panic rose. Was the wall gone, or did it make a ninety-degree turn?

Frantic, he felt around, not finding anything to use as a guide for his progress.

Carefully, he lowered himself back to all fours. Dignity be damned. He'd rather lose a bit of pride in this dark place than his life. Besides only he knew of his presence, no one need ever know of his fear that ran in rivulets of sweat down his back. His hair stuck to his forehead. Palms grew damp. Each breath became a struggle as his throat closed. He was going to die down there and no one would ever know. He'd become one of the *perinine*. Neither being embraced by heaven nor welcomed by the fae.

Whatever happened, he would not go down without a fight. He had been through worse, though nothing in his experience quite equaled the acid pits.

Girding himself to continue forward, Roman took a deep breath and said a small prayer to whatever celestial body or fae diva bothered to listen. He crawled over the rough rocky surface, feeling out in front of him as he advanced. Ambient sounds bounced off the walls, echoing, disorienting him. The information gave him no clue as to which way to go. His breath was loud in his ears, further distracting him.

His shoulder brushed against something hard. He lifted his hand and felt around. A doorway or arch leading into another chamber. Darkness faded to a dull brown. Light somewhere up ahead.

The acrid scents of the pits remained but were not as pervasive—either that or his nasal passages had been burned to the extent he no longer possessed the ability to smell. But no, with every foot he gained, it grew lighter. Perhaps he'd succeeded in moving away from peril.

Voices murmured from down the passage. None of the words were clear or made sense. He kept moving. The ground sloped upward. A little at first, then became a greater incline. The texture of the surface changed, where it had been hard and rough, it now smoothed out, giving him little purchase. Determined to climb out, he stayed to his hands and knees, not willing to risk a fall should he stand.

A ledge rose up in front of him. He had no way to advance unless he climbed up onto the step. Investigation of either side of him proved he'd entered a narrower part of the passageway. There was no choice but to advance or go back the way he'd come. Since he had no intension of heading back to the acid pits, he stood and levered himself up onto the ledge and straight into a nest of centipedes.

Squiggling, crawling bodies moved under his hands. Hundreds of legs from a gross of segmented bodies flicked against his palms. Movement twitched against his trouser legs. He tried to reassure himself they were only bugs and were not harmful, but in all truth, he had no way to know if centipedes in the fae realm were venomous or benign. Knowing Azgarth, the centipedes might spin a jeweled chrysalis and emerge as a sprite or fairy, then rally against him for killing their brethren.

He felt around for another ledge and found it about three feet above his head. Stairs. He'd found a flight of stairs. More light fell into the hallway from somewhere above. Each step brought him closer, made it easier to see; however, he was far from out of danger. The higher he climbed, the thicker and more varied the bugs. Spiders with bodies the size of his hands crawled along the walls. Their multitude of eyes shone in the rising light coming from the top of the stairs. If anyone were to ask, he'd swear they watched him, noting his progress to report to their master.

Spiders, bugs, and other crawly things had never bothered him much until that moment. Then again, he'd never encountered them in such numbers. They moved over his back and dropped in his hair from the ceiling. He brushed them away only to have another take its place.

Hard pincers bit into his flesh.

"Ah!" He batted at the offending bug, sending it to smash against the wall. Venom poured into his bloodstream, heating his arm as if set to flame.

Clicking pincers from hundreds of the same species of insect rose in a terrifying crescendo. They would have their revenge. He moved faster, trying to make it to the opening before the offended creatures swarmed.

Several orbited his head, looking for a way to attack. He batted at them with a forearm. Sweat ran down into his eyes, blinding him with salt. One of the bugs managed to get to his face, sinking its pincers into his cheek. He screamed and grabbed it in his fingers, pulling it away as hunks of skin came with it. Blood ran down his face, mixing with his sweat.

The scent of hemoglobin on the air stirred the masses to a frenzy. They came at him from all directions. Too many of them to fend off with his arms. He pulled his jacket over his head and tried for another step, but misjudged the distance and slipped.

Weightless he fell into a void, hitting the solid edge of each step as his body tumbled ass over end down the stone stairs to the incline. He hit hard, jarring his shoulder and biting his tongue. Blood filled his mouth, washing over his tongue. He rolled over to spit it out. Bugs continued to crawl over him—the fall not enough to dislodge them.

Back in the utter dark, he had no choice but to try to crawl back up again. Pain, both from the injuries of the fall and the shock of venom to his system, crippled him. He wished only to curl up into a ball and die, but knew that way lacked courage—a commodity he could ill afford to lose at this juncture.

Another bite gouged him on the back, digging in between his shoulder blades. Already the amount of venom racing through his system made it hard to hold up his head. But he had to. Needed to get back to the top of the stairs. He'd never survive the acid pits. Serious doubt whether he could withstand the bug-laden stairs a second time entered his mind, but he batted it away.

Survival left no room for doubt. He had to try. To persevere. He rose to his hands and knees with the intent to crawl up the incline a second time. Even positioned so low to the ground, dizziness swept over him in the worst case of vertigo he'd ever known. Right side up and upside down reversed without mercy. In the dark with his eyes closed, the sensation of falling stayed with him. He gripped his fingers into the rough stone. Fingernails split and broke, knuckles skinned with abrasions.

No. He'd not die in defeat.

One hand, one leg, over and over, slowly he started up the incline. Every few feet, he had to stop to swat at the angry bugs that continued to feast on him. The bright side of having so much venom in his system, he no longer felt the pain of the new stings and bites. Only a casual acknowledgment that another had chosen to make him their meal.

At the point where the gradient increased and the angle sharpened, a wash of slimy, slippery goo slid down the hall. It bathed his hands and knees, burning his cuts and bites afresh. Purchase became more difficult.

He fell back, sliding down, losing any ground he'd gained.

Walls moved by him in a rush. Only the wind from his passing indicated how close he came to the narrow passage. The fall spit him out, not in the acid chamber, but into a wild dark void, free-falling through space.

His breath caught. Held.

Had he died?

No. Surely not. If dead, he'd not feel so much pain. His head wouldn't be swimming and his heart racing.

Cold wrapped a chill blanket around him as he passed through a rift.

He landed with a jerk, not on a hard surface but a soft one. It gave as his body came into contact and he bounced a little, but not painfully.

Voices rose in frantic orders around him.

"Get his clothes off him. We have to assess the damage."

"He looks like he's been put through a meat grinder."

"I fear he has multiple broken ribs."

"He's swelling. There must be venom in the bites."

"Let's move him to the surgery."

The voices ceased as he was lifted and carried on a floating cloud—to where, he didn't know. He fought to open his eyes, to gain his bearings, but they were too heavy, too puffy to afford him more than the suggestion of light beyond his lids.

Soon he was set back down on a cold, hard table. His clothes removed. Movement brushed all around him as words danced an intricate pattern above his head. He'd lost the ability to discern their meaning, and didn't even attempt to try.

Whatever place he'd come to, wherever he'd landed, they seemed bent on healing his broken and abused body. For that, he offered silent thanks, then drifted off into oblivion.

Chapter Ten

Never, in all his years of practice, had Mikhail ever seen anything like the injuries sustained by Mr. Cetanni. Once he'd seen to a young woman who had been out picking wild berries and stumbled across a beehive. The bees had swarmed her, stinging her over the entirety of her body. Though not allergic to their stings, the number of them had ravaged her system for days, making her gravely ill. That incident paled in comparison to this unprecedented attack.

So far, Mr. Cetanni had not been conscious enough to describe how he'd been bitten or where the battle had taken place. Dante had servants searching the house for a possible nest. Judging from the degree of injury and pattern of bite, these were not insects with stingers, but with claws or pincers.

Skin had been ripped away from places all over his body. The white dress shirt he'd worn earlier was a macabre example of Swiss dot. Mikhail dabbed cotton into the pot of salve and stuck it to one of the bites. They'd decided the best course of action, after an injection of adrenaline, was to draw the poison out of the wounds using an old hedge remedy. Once in a while, the old ways were still the best. Since they had no idea what species of insect they were dealing with, it seemed quite logical to try to get the poison out as quickly as possible.

Looking over Mr. Cetanni, it was a wonder he'd clung to life this long.

Once the salve-soaked cotton covered the bites, Henri and Dante carefully wrapped gauze around the areas to hold the cotton in place. By the time they were finished, Mr. Cetanni looked like pictures of mummies Mikhail had seen in the papers. The dressings might have appeared as if he were ready to be interred with the Pharaohs of old, but as a medical procedure, it was sound care.

Mikhail went to the pile of Mr. Cetanni's clothes they'd dropped to the floor. He shook out each piece, hoping to find one of the tiny culprits in which to study. None of them had remained. They'd attacked with aggression and purpose, then left.

"We should move him back to his room." Dante had stepped away from the table and begun to close jars and tidy up the supplies they'd used.

"Not until we know if that room hides a nest. I'd hate to check on him and find they'd returned." Mikhail placed the jacket on the back of a chair. Movement from one of the pockets drew his attention. "I think he may have unwittingly captured one."

Dante and Henri both moved closer.

"Grab me a something to put this in. A container of some sort." Mikhail pointed to a shelf filled with empty bottles, jars, and pots. "One with a lid."

Henri made a face as he crossed the room to collect the item.

Mikhail gently took the pocket and closed the top flap to trap the insect inside. Henri offered him a medium-sized jar. "Hold it so I can turn the jacket upside down and shake the little bastard loose."

Henri took the jar in one hand and stood poised with the lid in the other.

"Bring it closer. I want to upend the pocket into the mouth of it." Mikhail waited while Henri adjusted his hold, then stuffed the pocket inside so the opening pointed downward. He gave it a quick shake, hitting the material against the inside of the jar. The insect spilled out. Henri screwed the lid down. They both backed up at the sight that scrabbled on the side of the glass, trying to gain purchase for an escape.

There had never been anything like it in the whole of England, of that Mikhail was sure. Insect was a misnomer. This creature was a pure work of art. About four inches long, it had a long, hard body, resembling a beetle. The wings were iridescent white, with gold edges. The appearance reminded him more of a piece of jewelry than a living thing.

"Extraordinary," he breathed. He tapped the side of the jar with a finger. "Where did this come from?"

Dante turned his head to get a look at the specimen. "I have never seen one so colorful, so detailed. Not in this part of town. That's not saying there weren't some acting as stowaways on travel trunks. Mr. Remly two houses down recently returned from India. We should consult Fischers. He might know the particular species."

Emmet Fischers studied the science of entomology. His case studies on beetles—*Coleoptera*—had been widely celebrated. Mikhail shook the jar. "Good idea. In the meantime, we should move Mr. Cetanni to another room. Even a servant's room will suffice."

Dante made a face. "I do possess adequate guest rooms that allow me to reassign Mr. Cetanni without displacing one of the domestics."

"I meant no offense. My apologies." Mikhail gave a mock bow. Lately, it seemed Dante's feathers were ruffled with the slightest provocation.

Instead of acknowledging the apology, Dante's jaw tightened. "If you will excuse me, I'll go prepare the room."

"You can't send a servant?"

"They are in their beds. Where we should be. For God's sake, I perform the most delicate surgeries on the human body; I am perfectly capable of turning down a bedsheet without calling a servant." Dante turned on his heel and withdrew from the room, leaving Mikhail to wonder what had just happened.

He turned to Henri. "Did I say something wrong?"

Henri shook his head. "Not that I could tell."

He'd make a point later of finding out what he'd done to offend Dante. At the moment, he didn't have the time or the concentration to spare. Currently, there were two ill or injured men in the house. One the victim of attempted murder; the other, attacked by insects. Both scenarios indicative of violence. What he had a hard time putting together was the number of bites inflicted on Mr. Cetanni with the fact only one beetle had been uncovered, and that one by sheer dumb luck.

Mikhail moved to the study to pen a letter to Emmet Fischers, requesting his presence to identify the specimen.

Noises woke Nicholas more than once through the night. He'd slept in fits and starts, never really falling into a blissful slumber ensured to promote healing. At one time, he'd thought he heard the distant shouts of a man in pain. By the time he'd fought his way up from a dream, the house had grown quiet again.

Sunshine created the barest of golden halos around the drapes. A whirring noise captured his attention. Dark shapes moved away from the window, trying to hide from the light. He threw the covers off and tried to get up, only to realize his legs were still not answering his commands as he'd like. They moved, but were heavy as lead.

Skittering of tiny feet came from the far corner. Buzzing. Insects.

His heart sank. He'd never enjoyed insects. Not even as a child. It wasn't that they were particularly dirty but the suggestion that so many tiny legs spread disease.

The sounds grew louder. Closer.

His breath came short.

He reached out and pulled the bell. While he waited, he inched his legs over to the side of the bed. Using the nightstand for leverage, he pulled himself up, leaning heavily against the tabletop. His legs turned to treacle. Knees weak and out of practice for supporting his weight. Slow but determined, he held on to anything within his grasp as he made his way across the bedroom.

The brush of insect legs darted across the top of his foot. He jerked his leg at the disgusting feel. Too quick, his balance fled. He wobbled, tried to keep from falling, but failed. Hard.

He lay where he fell. From this perspective, he saw tiny shadows scrambling beneath the bed. Did Dr. Savoy know he'd been invaded by insects? Beetles, if the shape was any indication.

A knock came to the door.

Nicholas pushed to a sitting position. "Enter."

Mr. Vauss stepped inside. "Bloody hell. Are you all right?" He hurried over to Nicholas and helped him back up to the bed. "Did you fall out of bed?"

"No. I tried to walk and lost my balance." Nicholas sat down, holding on to Mr. Vauss as he lowered himself to the bed. "There are bugs in here. They're under the bed and flying by the window."

Interest kindled in Mr. Vauss's dark eyes. He dropped to his knees to peer underneath. "Did any get on you?"

"One ran across my foot. Why?"

"They were in Mr. Cetanni's room, as well."

Nicholas gave a laugh. Roman was even worse in his fastidiousness. "Is he threatening to return to the Imperial?"

An ominous silence came from under the bed, and then Mr. Vauss popped back up, his mouth compressed into a grim line. "We need to move you now."

"Where to?"

"For now, it will have to be the hallway." Mr. Vauss stood next to the bed and proceeded to help Nicholas to stand once more. "I'll help you. There is a chair at the end of the hall. You can sit there while I get Drs. Savoy and Stanslovich."

"Because of a few bugs?"

"Yes." Mr. Vauss placed his arm around Nicholas's waist. "Put your arm across my shoulder."

"Is all this necessary? Have a servant chase the little bastards out and squash them."

Mr. Vauss didn't respond to the suggestion. He hurried Nicholas out of the room, stopping to close the door behind them. Nicholas was without slippers or dressing gown. The hallway had a breeze flowing through it that chilled him instantly.

The chair sat at the other end of the hall, near the windows overlooking a small yard with a fountain. Mr. Vauss helped Nicholas lower down onto the seat, ensured he was comfortable, then left him there.

Nicholas looked out the window. The day promised to be sunny and fine—a feeling that never quite reached inside the house. At least not to the hallway or down to Nicholas's soul. Sinister atmosphere swirled through the house and it came from none of the residents. This was separate. Other. The dark side of the fae realm.

Scratching came from the direction of his room. Insect feet moving over the door. It wouldn't be long before they found a way underneath and were free to roam the house. Nicholas reached up and opened the curtains wider, allowing the sunshine to bathe the hallway. If beetles were going to have free run, he wanted to keep an eye on where they had gone.

Mr. Vauss returned with Dr. Savoy.

Dr. Savoy stopped at the door and placed his hand against the wood. "How many did you see in there? It sounds like an entire invasion."

"I counted seven, but they were moving around and it was dark under the bed."

Dr. Savoy ran a hand through his hair. He looked beyond exhausted. A night's growth of beard shadowed his cheeks and jaw. "I have no idea how to get them to move other than smoking them out."

That sounded fraught with danger. What if he burned his house down in the process?

Nicholas cleared his throat, gaining the attention of both men. "If I might make a slight suggestion."

"You may." Dr. Savoy cocked his hands on his hips.

"They sound determined to get out. So get a broom and open the doors all the way outside. Brush them in the direction you wish them to go. It might take very little encouragement to get them to leave."

"He has a point, Dr. Savoy."

"Indeed." Dr. Savoy motioned with his hand. "Go get a broom from the scullery. We'll give it a try."

Mr. Vauss left again. Silence grew, save for the determined click against the door. Dr. Savoy closed his eyes for a minute. Nicholas wondered if he should offer his chair. The man looked beyond his endurance.

"Are you quite well, Doctor?"

Dr. Savoy opened his eyes. "It's been a very long night. One of many. A good long sleep and I'll be right again." A frown grew between his brows. "I do apologize for your sleep being disrupted by this invasion. I've never had trouble with insects since taking up residence."

Nicholas brushed the apology away. Insects were an unfortunate part of life. No place was immune to at least some form of the multilegged pests.

"While we are both here and waiting, let me examine you." Dr. Savoy came down the hall to stand in the sunlight. This close, Nicholas noticed the dark circles under his eyes as well. "Henri said you had tried to walk."

"Yes. Until one of those things ran across my foot. I lost my balance."

"It will take time to regain full equilibrium." Dr. Savoy held his hands out, index fingers extended. "Grab on to my fingers and squeeze as hard as you can."

Nicholas performed the maneuver, feeling as if his hands only wanted to close partway. "I noticed yesterday I can hardly even grip a pencil to draw."

"How does it feel today as compared to yesterday?"

He thought about it, concentrating to squeeze harder. "A bit better."

"Improvement of any kind is encouraging."

Nicholas's expression must have been dubious, because Dr. Savoy was quick to add, "Yesterday, you couldn't even swing your legs to the side of the bed, and today, you walked with assistance. Not a great distance, but enough. Give it time."

How did he explain that a nagging feeling in the back of his brain kept counting down? Time was a luxury he didn't have.

Mr. Vauss returned with a broom and Dr. Stanslovich.

"Those bloody things are a menace." Dr. Stanslovich drew nearer. "Did they bite you?"

Confused, Nicholas looked at each man in turn. "No. Should they have?"

Dr. Stanslovich shook his head and patted Nicholas on the shoulder. "Are we ready? They sound anxious to be set free."

"Ready, Henri?"

"Ready."

"Open the door."

Dr. Stanslovich opened the door, and the beetles raced out. They scattered, moving in all different directions, seeking darkness. They faded into the shadows. Alarmed, Nicholas threw open the curtains wider, capturing one in a beam of brilliant sunlight. Smoke rose from the beetle's back. It screeched in an air-splitting pitch, then exploded into a puff of gold dust.

"Hurry! Henri. Cast them toward the sunlight," Dr. Savoy ordered.

Mr. Vauss began to bat at the little creatures as if playing crochet. He caught one of the beetles, sending it flying; it hit the light and burst into dust that showered down onto the floor in glittery residue.

Amazed, Nicholas could only stare. He'd never seen anything like it before in his life.

When the majority of the beetles had been dispatched, Dr. Stanslovich bent down and ran his finger through the remains. "What in all the living hell?"

"Photosensitive?" Dr. Savoy offered. "Though this is an extreme case."

Dr. Stanslovich rubbed his fingers together and held them up for the others to see. "It's gold. I bet if you put it through the spectrometer, you'd find it's pure."

"But how?"

Yes, Nicholas wanted to hear that explanation as well.

Dr. Stanslovich lifted a shoulder. "Chemical reaction when the body of the beetle hit sunlight. As you said, photosensitive."

"But instantaneous?" Dr. Savoy made a face.

"We've lost a few of them." Mr. Vauss leaned on his broom handle. "They're very fast."

"You did well. We'll just have to check all the rooms and make sure the curtains are open. The dark gave them plenty of places to hide." Dr. Savoy ran his hand through his hair again. "I'm not going to sleep until I know those things are gone."

Didn't Mr. Vauss say that Roman was sleeping? Why was he still in bed when the rest of the house was awake?

"Where is Roman?"

All three turned away with guilty faces.

Cold dread trickled down his back, wrapped around his body, then settled low in his gut. "Did he leave?" Even as he asked the question, he knew Roman was in the residence somewhere.

Dr. Savoy's expression of compassion was Nicholas's undoing.

He glanced away, unable to see the apology there. "Let me see him."

Dr. Savoy rested his hand on Nicholas's shoulder. "He's resting, so I don't want you to wake him. Will you promise you'll let him sleep?"

"Of course." How selfish of a reputation did he have in order for Dr. Savoy to ask for such a promise?

"Henri, will you retrieve some slippers and a dressing gown for Mr. Alexandre?"

Mr. Vauss excused himself, setting the broom to rest against the wall. Dr. Savoy watched him, then turned back around to face Nicholas.

"We've been unable to determine how the beetles breached the house, or how Mr. Cetanni became the object of their attack, but they are extremely dangerous."

Nicholas's throat threatened to close. "Attack?"

Dr. Stanslovich shot his colleague a quelling glance. "He'll have you believe Mr. Cetanni is one step from death. The truth is, he is ill, but we are encouraged he will improve. Not much time elapsed between when he was bitten and when we discovered him."

No wonder Mr. Vauss had asked Nicholas if he'd been bitten. "Are they venomous?"

"We believe so, though we have no knowledge of the potency of the venom. I've sent a message to an expert to give his opinion."

Mr. Vauss came back out into the hall and helped Nicholas on with a pair of slippers and a dressing gown. Once he was semidressed, Mr. Vauss helped him to stand. His legs were still heavy, but not as weak as they'd been earlier. Perhaps it was as with any long illness and each day, every movement brought him closer to being well. He placed his arm around Mr. Vauss's shoulder but tried not to lean on him only enough to remain steady.

They walked down the hallway and turned to another wing.

"Are you tired? Do you need to sit and rest?" Mr. Vauss offered.

Nicholas shook his head. Determination kept him moving. He wasn't about to stop when they were so close. The closer they came to the door, the more he dragged his right foot. Damage from his illness? Worry crept into his mind, hovering there like a demented hummingbird.

They arrived at the door. Nicholas leaned down to turn the knob for them, and they hobbled inside.

His first sight of Roman, lying in the bed wrapped in gauze from head to toe became permanently etched onto his mind.

"Good God" escaped on a harsh breath as Mr. Vauss directed him to a chair. "How many bites did he sustain?"

"Many. His shirt offered some protection, but not enough. The pincers went right through the fabric."

"Has he said anything?"

"Not yet. He's been sleeping. At this point, it is the best way for him to heal." Mr. Vauss leaned over and touched the pulse at Roman's throat then his forehead. "His heartbeat remains strong, but not fast. His breathing is normal, and he's not fevered. It's a good sign."

Nicholas would take Mr. Vauss's word for it. Despite the positive news of Roman's vital signs, the undercurrent of concern emanating from the physicians canceled out all their reassurances.

"How safe is it for any of us in this house if there are flesh-eating beetles here?"

"You've seen for yourself how easy they are to kill."

"Provided they are herded toward the sun." Nicholas pointed to the corners of Roman's room. "How do we know they aren't hiding in here? Open the drapes, for Christ's sake."

Mr. Vauss hurried to comply. At least with the addition of sunlight, the beetles were less likely to breach the room proper. The sudden introduction of sunlight caused Roman to stir. He mumbled something in his sleep, then quieted.

"If you need nothing further, I'll search for any stragglers that might have gone into hiding. Should you need anything, pull the bell cord."

"Yes. Thank you."

Mr. Vauss left. The door closed with a quiet click, securing Nicholas in the room with Roman. He turned back to the only person in the world who truly cared about him, and his heart cracked. It started as a small spot, glass under pressure, only the tiniest of pings with fissures webbing outward. Seeing Roman like this, dressed up in pain and gauze, cut Nicholas to the bone. Had he been asleep and woke to the attack? The mere thought of such a ghastly incident caused him to shiver in revulsion.

Guilt cut a river through his soul. If not for wanting to be closer to Nicholas as he healed, Roman would not have been in a position to become so grievously injured. The same thing might have happened to him had he not woke to the sound of skittering insect feet.

Roman's hand lay across his stomach. Wrappings went down to the knuckles but left the fingers free. Even from where he sat, the edges of deep scrapes were obvious along the backs. Whatever had happened in his room, he'd fought a battle.

Valiant. Caring. Compassionate.

He'd never found a man who more resembled the ideals of a gentleman than Roman Cetanni.

Nicholas reached out and took Roman's hand, cradling it gently in his. He studied the fingers, thick and blunt. The nails were broken and torn as if he'd tried to grab at a rough surface or break his fall. The tips of his fingers had not faired any better than the backs of them.

"Christ, Roman. What happened to you?"

"I fell through the fae realm." The words were little more than a dry whisper, but Nicholas's breath caught in his throat.

"How did you manage that?"

Roman's injured hand tightened a bit. "Please get Dr. Savoy. I need to speak with him. There is no time to delay."

"Yes. Of course." Nicholas leaned over and pulled the bell and kept pulling at it until running feet sounded in the hall.

Chapter Eleven

"Roman. Roman, wake up."

Nicholas's beloved voice roused Roman from a deep sleep. Confusion swirled around him. He'd been speaking with Nicholas only a moment before and been awake. He knew he had. He didn't remember falling asleep again.

Roman opened his eyes to find his bed surrounded.

Dr. Savoy stood on his left, looking down on him with a worried expression. "So you decided to come back."

Roman smacked his lips together. His tongue felt thick, mouth dry. "Water?"

"Henri, will you pour him a glass, please?"

Mr. Vauss was quick to comply. He threaded between Dr. Stanslovich and Nicholas, then helped Roman to sit up. That's when Roman glanced down and noticed he'd been wrapped in burial gauze.

"Did I die?" He asked the question, even knowing that to die meant he'd have been visited by Azgarth. To his knowledge, no such audience had occurred.

"No. You were ill, however." Dr. Savoy sat down on the bed, facing him. "Your eyes appear clear and your color is good. I can't say the same for when we found you."

"You must think me the worst of houseguests."

Dr. Savoy's expression illustrated a man sorely aggrieved. "Believe me when I say you have done nothing wrong. If I had known there was an infestation, I never would have placed you in that room."

Roman frowned, then remembered how he'd returned to the realm of man. "You have a bigger problem than a simple infestation."

"Explain," Dr. Stanslovich commanded from the foot of the bed.

"There is a doorway into the fae realm in my room. Curious as to why it opened and not under Azgarth's direction, I followed the path where it led." He rubbed a gauze-covered hand over his face. "Sometimes, I hate being right."

Nicholas leaned as close as his chair allowed. "What do you think it means?"

Roman started to shake his head, but the pain from the bites stopped him. "I never got far enough to figure it out. The entire way was fraught with traps and punishments." He held up an arm. "As you can see. I suspect Azgarth knew of the earlier conversation I had with the doctors."

Dr. Savoy made a startled movement. "Are you saying you received your injuries in the fae realm?"

"Unfortunately, that is exactly what I'm saying." He tried to sit up, but again, the bandages and sores pulled. "I fell and landed on a nest of beetles."

Dr. Stanslovich raised a brow. "That explains a lot."

Roman regarded him with caution. "Like what, for instance?"

"Why Mr. Alexandre was able to kill them with sunlight." Dr. Stanslovich crossed his arms in a mutinous stance. After a few moments of charged silence, the doctor seemed to come to a decision. "The longer I think on this, the more I believe Mr. Cetanni here. We need to mount an expedition to the fae realm. Not that I ever wanted or planned to return there. However, there have been too many odd happenings lately to put me at ease. I've been uncomfortable with the fact they cross worlds as it is. Knowing they are doing so more frequently makes me feel we need a few spies of our own."

Roman let out a weary laugh. "You see what comes of trying to breach their defenses when you are uninvited."

"Opening a door is invitation enough," Nicholas countered.

"Yes, but it all depends if it is the front door or servants' entrance." They might not see the distinction, but Roman did. Going in the front door to the fae realm meant Azgarth invited you to see what *he* wanted. His reasons might not align with human understanding, but they did have a distinct point of a fashion. However, Azgarth's penchant for cruelty to those who had offended or disappointed him far outweighed the benefits of living in his glorious presence.

Dr. Savoy touched Roman's arm. "What did you see?"

"Darkness. Complete and utter darkness. I might have taken a wrong step, but for the unimaginable stench." Roman swallowed down the revulsion. His belly quivered. It took a moment to gather his strength to continue. "There are many pitfalls in traveling through the outer reaches of the fae realm—or should I say the lower realms of Azgarth's palace. Not all areas are opulent and filled with light. Some are straight from the origins of hell. A nightmare landscape that tortures and terrifies. The acid pit for instance."

Nicholas's gaze swam with worry. "And this is where you entered?"

"Yes. First, I fell; then I crawled; then I fell some more." Roman let his gaze lock with Nicholas's. He moved back and forth in the fae realm with regularity. Time had come for him to realize all the dangers. "Azgarth has a room—it's a cavern, really. A pool filled with an acidic soup comprised of the decomposed flesh of those who have transgressed. He is a very dangerous enemy to have. His punishments are not half measures."

The worry in Nicholas's eyes turned to sorrow. Tears brimmed the blue, making them sparkle like diamonds. "You've been punished."

"With a frequency I'm embarrassed to admit." Roman held out his hand, which Nicholas took. "I have made it my mission to stand between Azgarth and my charges. It's often an uncomfortable place to be. However, I have never had a hard time getting you to play the role you've been assigned for Azgarth. Your paintings have been very well received in both realms. This has allowed you certain latitude to enjoy your intrigues and scandals. Azgarth might have coerced a few of your more outrageous ones himself in order to see what you might do."

Color rose in Nicholas's cheeks, whether from anger or embarrassment, Roman couldn't decide. His hand tightened on Roman's. "No more. I promise you. No more. I'd not have you take my punishment for either world."

Dr. Stanslovich watched the scene with quiet consideration in his expression. If Roman read it right, he was busy making plans while listening to the conversation. He shifted his stance a bit. "Whether you want to or not is immaterial to Azgarth."

Nicholas's expression changed to one of bitter determination.

"He's right, Nicholas. Azgarth doesn't care if you wish to fulfill your destiny. He will ensure compliance one way or another."

"That's not necessarily true." The voice came from the doorway.

Those assembled turned to watch as Andres Valentine entered the room as if he were taking the stage for a performance. Since coming to stay at the home of Dr. Savoy, Roman had not seen much of the violinist, his particular skills unneeded in a home devoted to science and discovery.

Valentine spread his hands out beside him. "You see before you a free man."

"A freedom bought with the price of other men's souls," Roman pointed out.

"But free."

"Yes," Roman agreed. "The only one of us in this room who can subscribe to that state."

Nicholas returned his attention to Roman. "So how do we gain our freedom without sacrificing others in Azgarth's thrall?"

Roman had no idea and told Nicholas, "If I would have been able to do so, I would have died long ago."

Nicholas frowned. "What do you mean?"

"Agents are not what we appear." Roman held his hand up for an example. "Oh, we are flesh and blood enough, but the process by which Azgarth makes us, changes us, extends our natural lives. It's a way of making good returns on his investments."

Dr. Savoy glanced back at his colleague, who raised a skeptical brow. Mr. Vauss appeared intrigued. Nicholas looked unconvinced, but Valentine was not surprised.

Dr. Stanslovich gave an incredulous look to the man he'd saved only a few months earlier. "You knew about this?"

"Having lived around Herr Maestro since I was a child, I had many occasions to learn his secrets. One of those being his surprising longevity. He loved to brag to me he had musicians performing at the court of Marie Antoinette."

Dr. Savoy gave an ironic smile. "Not for long."

Roman gave a huff of sound. The group turned back to him. "You may be surprised to know the uprising, the very turn of the tide in most political situations, was orchestrated by Azgarth. He grows bored so easily."

"Nothing like a revolution to inspire a new artistic movement." Dr. Stanslovich's dry tone underscored the entire turn of conversation.

This particular detour Roman had not thought to take but was now glad he had. The more information they had at their disposal, the better prepared they would be. But for now...

He lifted his hand in a shooing motion. "If you would excuse me, all this talk has made me quite weary."

"Yes, of course." Dr. Savoy rose and ushered the others toward the door—all except Nicholas who stubbornly stayed by Roman's side.

When the others had gone, Dr. Savoy approached Nicholas and laid a hand on his shoulder. "Do not stay too long. You need your rest as well."

"I won't and thank you."

When the door closed behind Dr. Savoy, Nicholas sat on the bed next to Roman. "What are you hiding you wished not to say in front of the others?"

Roman gave him a teasing smile. "How do you know I'm hiding anything?"

"Because I know you."

"I'm not exactly withholding information, but I do wish they would reconsider their own efforts to cross into the fae."

"Then why didn't you tell them so? If you feel they'll be in danger, then it makes sense to warn them."

Roman nodded. "True, but I also need their cooperation. Now I have it, I want nothing to upset that balance."

Nicholas let out a disgusted sigh. "You play as many games as Azgarth."

Roman raised a brow and shot Nicholas a look. "Not quite."

Contrite, Nicholas threaded his fingers through Roman's bandaged ones. "I hate seeing you like this. You, who is everything brave and strong. It makes me fear what we're walking into."

Roman squeezed Nicholas's hand as much as his injuries allowed. "You aren't walking into anything. I forbid you to get anywhere near where I'm going."

"And you mean to stop me? If so, you're in no condition to physically restrain me."

Roman doubted he was in good enough shape to restrain a feather. But he did need sleep and to plan his next move. If there was a rift in the other guest room, then it was imperative to get Mr. King in to photograph the space. Only through careful study would he know if that particular gateway opened only to the caverns or if it was a door to the multiverse of the fae realm.

Once he found a point of origin and how to properly navigate a back door into the fae dimension, he'd make solid plans for what to do inside. There had to be some mechanism other than the books and bindings that held the chosen to their contracts. What he needed was a bit of divine inspiration or assistance.

What he needed was another fae.

Mikhail searched Mr. Cetanni's previous room for any suspicious shades of darkness. Nothing overt struck him as out of place or untoward. No areas of heavy atmosphere or unexplained cold. Absence of ectoplasm on the walls or furnishings. He checked the wardrobe for any secret openings or rips in dimensional fabric. The only things inside were a couple of jackets, shirts, and trousers.

Had the rift opened to entice Mr. Cetanni to follow the path? From the way he'd spoken, punishment was a natural order of Azgarth's world. Quite a bad position to be in when one never asked to be selected for such a gravely singular honor. Man chose to live in society and adhere to the rules. Those who didn't were punished. However, the choices were known. Either conform or don't and pay the consequences. With Azgarth, there was no choice given. You were chosen and were expected to play by rules only he understood. No contract, written or implied, had been executed. No signatures were scrawled across the bottom of parchment. And yet, the names scrawled across the book and burned into the parchment pages were as binding as any legal document.

He moved to the bed and dropped to his knees, searching underneath for some proof of access. Nothing. Not even a beetle lying in wait. He stood and brushed at his trouser legs.

At least three rifts had centered on Dante's home the previous night: the one in the fountain, then in the tank, and the one in this room. Commonalities in the locations included what? He glanced around the room, trying to think of something to connect the areas of greatest activity.

Both the fountain and the tank used water and power to run them. Current flowed through the system, bringing the motors to life. The bedroom had no water, and gaslights. Not even the same form of power. As for location, the bedroom was neither located above the surgery, nor close to the fountain, but stood in the other end of the townhouse.

Since he couldn't recreate the rift in the bedroom, he had to try to do so in the surgery under controlled circumstances.

Mikhail hurried out of the room, closing the door behind him on the off chance the rift opened again. He went straight to the surgery and the tank. It sat empty, where Dante had given the order to flush it the night before. A turn of the valve and fluid splashed and filled the bottom.

Dante stalked into the room. Anger filled his face. "What are you doing? Inviting disaster?"

"Trying to determine what it is that opened the rift in multiple points in your house. To do so, we must recreate the event."

Dante hitched his hands on his hips. "I thought we agreed it cruel to let those trapped believe they'd found a way out?"

Annoyed with the accusation in Dante's voice, Mikhail continued to work. He shot an emotion-filled glance in Dante's direction. "Not all the beings trying to make their way out are trapped between life and death. Some are only trapped between realms. I want to know why you suddenly have not one but three different points of entry in your home. What is different today than yesterday? Are there conditions that exist now you've not had present before?"

Dante gave a frown and looked around his surgery as if seeing it truly for the first time. "Short of burning the place to the ground, I'm not sure how we might close them. We came damn close to razing your house when we tried that strategy the last time."

As if Mikhail could ever forget that night. The memory alone made his stomach cramp and cold sweat coat his back and palms. He turned the wheel again, opening the valve wider. His hands shook.

Damn! Could he do nothing without the specter of his addiction riding him as a nagging nursemaid? A hit of opium would be a wonderful thing at the moment. Only enough to take off the edge.

"Mikhail?" Dante had moved closer. He stood above Mikhail, gazing down with a worried expression. "Are you all right?"

He fought back the empty feeling—the screaming voice of need in his head. "Yes."

"I don't think you are."

Mikhail straightened. "Then why did you ask?"

"Because you're hurting again."

"How can you tell?"

Dante relaxed. He placed a hand on Mikhail's shoulder. "I know you better than you know yourself these days."

"I don't want to rely on morphine to get me through a day."

"And yet you're standing here grinding your teeth, wanting to hit the hookah and smoke opium until your eyes bleed."

Mikhail rubbed a shaky hand down his face. "No. I want to feel normal again."

Dante watched the fluid fill the tank. "What *is* normal?"

"Not what we once thought, apparently." Mikhail spotted the book sitting on one of the desks. Maybe it had some information on spontaneous rifts. Even a small hint might go a long way to understanding why the fabric between worlds had suddenly grown as thin as lace.

He thumbed through the pages, wondering if they had stumbled into areas where they would find no documentation to aid them. Surely, the devices available to them were not even a consideration when most of the entries were penned.

"What are you looking for?"

"If there is any mention of rifts opening that are uncontrolled by Azgarth."

"Even if there had been, do you think an observer would recognize it as such?" Dante leaned against the desk and folded his arms over his chest. "I have to admit, I'd have loved to have followed Mr. Cetanni into that opening."

"Agreed." Mikhail flipped a few more pages, coming to the same section where they'd found the information the night before. "Where is your ammeter?"

"In the cabinet. Why?"

"For the same reason the *wolfsine* was able to come through before. We need to check for current, voltage, and magnetic properties. I'm not convinced we'll find any in the bedroom, but the tank and fountain are possibilities."

"How do you think one opened in the bedroom if not through the same mechanism?"

Mikhail had no idea, but a guess was as close as he'd get to an answer. "Residue left from when Azgarth opened one."

"It's as good an explanation as any." Dante crossed the room and pulled an ammeter from a cabinet. "But how does it help?"

"Perhaps it won't help at all, but the more information we can gather on all aspects of these infringements, a more effective plan we can formulate to stop them."

Dante's weary expression showed the strain of the last few months. "What good will it do, if we close one and they find another one to open?"

Mikhail looked down at the ammeter in his hand. "I have an even better idea."

"And that would be?"

"Measuring the temperature and wavelengths of light in the areas we've seen rifts. If we can pinpoint fluctuations, perhaps we can predict where they will open next, or create a generator to force one open."

Dante narrowed his gaze as if drinking in a bitter brew. "What do you plan to do once you've found a way in? That is, assuming Azgarth doesn't find you first."

"Figure out why he's so interested in us. Why does he care about humans?"

"According to Mr. Cetanni, Azgarth bores easily. Mankind offers infinite variety. We are also an unpredictable lot. He is the zookeeper and we are the exhibits."

Mikhail didn't care for that observation, though it seemed accurate enough. "That is even less appealing than thinking ourselves an experiment."

Dante glanced around his surgery. "I have no instrument to meet your needs at this time."

The formality with which Dante spoke struck like a spike through the heart. Mikhail stood staring after Dante for a moment before excusing himself to find Henri.

He found his assistant hunched over some gadget that erupted with gears and wires.

"I'm returning to the manor for the thermal spectrometer. When I return, I want to do a scan of all the areas where we've seen rifts open into this plane."

Henri moved the goggles he wore to the top of his head. "Do you want me to get them?"

Mikhail shook his head and looked at the back of his hands. "No. Thank you."

Henri continued to stare at him for a beat or two. Mikhail turned away before any questions arose. He really didn't want to articulate what was only a vague feeling at the moment. The fact that worry stemmed from his friendship with Dante. Something had changed that night in the opium den and Mikhail didn't know how to fix it.

Perhaps there wasn't a way. He'd gone past the point of amendment and even Dante had recoiled. For the first time in longer than he cared to remember, he felt truly alone.

What would he do without Dante in his life? The truth was he never wanted to find out. Dante had always been the best part of him. The one who listened to his creative side as much as his intellectual.

Mikhail donned his hat and overcoat, then made his way across town to the manor. The laboratory remained boarded and unusable. A lingering stench of smoke still hung in the rooms—had wicked into the drapes. Depression became a steady occupant, filling the hallways with its unwanted presence.

So many hours had been spent in this house, this laboratory, experimenting, learning the secrets to bring the dead back to life. Triumph had once dwelt within the walls, but now even that had lost its shine. All his accomplishments were tainted, all because of Azgarth. All his problems could be placed directly at Azgarth's feet.

Or whatever he used for locomotion.

Mikhail went into the laboratory and rummaged through the remaining debris. He hadn't the heart to put the place to rights, not after the initial cleaning, not after Azgarth had seen to the room's destruction. Glancing around at the rubble and ruin, hatred for himself and the untenable situation rose like a phoenix.

For this continued insult, he had no one to blame but the man in the mirror. He'd not hired workmen to repair his house. Instead of doing anything constructive, he'd lost himself to pity. By allowing Azgarth to win, he'd lost.

After a lengthy search, he found the instrument he'd come for. He doubted the delicate device would work. Part of the panel was smashed, the dials stripped. He put it in a satchel. Henri might be able to manage a repair in short order.

On the way back to Dante's, he stopped at several places to engage the services of carpenters, masons, and glazers.

With the workers secured, he returned to Dante's and found Henri, still seated in the same place, working on a device only he understood. Mikhail pulled the thermal spectrometer out of the pouch and set it on the worktable.

Henri slid the goggles up again and rubbed a finger beside his nose, depositing dirt as he wiped. "Is it broken?"

"The case is rather crushed. Must have happened during Azgarth's temper tantrum."

Henri turned the instrument over and studied the back. "I'll take the cover off and look inside to see what's salvageable. This might take a while. I'll let you know when it's finished."

With nothing to do but wait, and not wanting to run into Dante, Mikhail went upstairs to check on the patients. The first room he came to, he found Mr. Cetanni sleeping comfortably. His breathing deep and even. Pleased with the progress, he stepped back out into the hallway and closed the door.

Mr. Alexandre had been moved to a room at the end of the hall. Mikhail gave a soft rap to the door, listening closely for any movement inside. No sound came in reply, not even an invitation to enter. Slowly he swung the door, cringing when the hinges creaked in the silence. Mr. Alexandre lay against a mound of pillows, sleeping. A drawing tablet rested on his lap. His fingers were loose, pencil fallen to land on the bed beside him.

Mikhail drew closer. He angled his head to see the drawing rendered across the page in pencil. The sketch depicted a desolate place. Caverns opened to a central room, with many passages going off in all directions. Eyes shone in the dark recesses, watching. In the background, a dark column rose from floor to ceiling. Mr. Alexandre had used the sharp edge of the pencil lead to color in the column opaque, suggesting the absence of light in the area.

The image intrigued. Was it a representation of a rift? Had Mr. Alexandre felt them or sensed them during his time serving as one of Azgarth's chosen?

Mr. Alexandre took in a deep breath. His eyes fluttered and he woke, gazing at Mikhail as if he had trouble placing his face. "Dr. Stanslovich?"

"Yes. I didn't mean to wake you. I came to check on you and your drawing captured my interest."

Mr. Alexandre frowned and lifted up the tablet to glance at the picture. His frown deepened as he studied it. If Mikhail didn't know better, he'd swear Mr. Alexandre had no idea what he'd drawn. His expression was one of a man seeing something for the first time and unsure of how it got there.

"I drew this?"

"Though I was not present for the composition, I am relatively certain you did. The pencil remains near your right hand." Mikhail tipped his hand to indicate the pencil where it had gotten caught in the linens.

Mr. Alexandre felt around for it. "I started drawing without really thinking about a subject. This, though—" He tapped his finger against the page. "This looks familiar."

"You've been to this place before?"

Mr. Alexandre shook his head. "No. I've seen a painting of it."

"Where?"

Another frown. Concentration pulled his brow in. "In the in-between. The place between life and death."

According to Valentine, the musician had seen and known nothing as he hovered in the chasm. The account given by Mr. Alexandre differed in fundamental ways. Then again, their injuries were not the same, nor were their recoveries. Valentine had woken with very little deficit to his motor skills beyond the first day or so. Alexandre still had a hard time standing and walking without assistance. When Mikhail had time, he very much wanted to sit down and analyze why those differences had occurred. Was it due to the variables in the extent of procedures provided or the way the treatments were delivered?

Was Mr. Alexandre's condition directly related to the fact he'd bled out and had to receive his total blood volume from transfusion? Mikhail considered the problem from a purely medical standpoint—which, given the recent climate in which he worked, was hard to do. Frustration at not knowing the exact line of distinction rode him like a harsh master. He wanted only to have control again.

Then he wondered if he'd ever had it in truth.

Mikhail cleared his throat. Embarrassment bloomed. He'd been staring at Mr. Alexandre in silent contemplation for longer than was comfortable for either of them. "It appears your memory might be returning. In fits and starts, but it is something."

Mr. Alexandre gave a skeptical look. "I remember quite a bit, but some of it, I'd willingly forget if I could."

At the moment, it occurred to Mikhail that he'd never fully remembered his own brush with death at the fangs of the *wolfsine*.

Chapter Twelve

Nicholas sat staring at the drawing long after Dr. Stanslovich's footsteps faded into the lower floors.

He pushed to sit upright. Lying about, flat on his back was not going to heal him any faster. He needed action. A plan to regain his strength. To prove to Roman he was well enough to aid in his quest.

Truthfully, he'd rather have had his money stolen than his health. Money he could earn—enough to fill his coffers and those of his friends— so long as he had his health to create his paintings.

Damn his body for betraying him.

In his mind, he felt well. Weakness of body was something he'd never had to face, and he didn't care for it in the least.

Determined to combat his fatigue, he placed his hand on the bed and swung his legs over. He pushed up. He'd will himself healthy if he had to. One foot then the other. Shuffle. Shuffle. At the pace he moved, he might make it across the room by midnight.

How could any man go from being the toast of society, able to dance and ride without giving the movements of his body another thought, to one who had to concentrate so hard to walk that beads of sweat broke out across his forehead? The fact he was even alive to tell the tale was a miracle. A power granted by the same being that had sent flesh-eating beetles to attack Roman.

His heart ached and breath caught.

No, he'd not think of the pain Roman endured. Doing so only intensified his own. Roman might be an agent for Azgarth, but he'd been a fair and just one. Many were the times that he'd tried with deep desperation to pull Nicholas in, but the pleas had fallen on deaf and stubborn ears.

Roman had even tried to warn him off from disastrous affairs. Nicholas had disregarded that advice as well. The consequences of that fatal mistake was evidenced in a line of sutures down his abdomen.

In essence, both their injuries were his fault. Roman had tried to instill sense and reason, and Nicholas had refused to pay attention. Now they were both scarred for life.

And the punishments. How many had Roman endured because of Nicholas's indiscretions? Guilt tore at his insides. He'd never be able to properly repay Roman.

He placed his hand on a table near the door to steady himself. Taking a few deep breaths, he attempted to place the anger at Azgarth in a compartment of his brain to use as fuel for his healing.

Still, he needed the benevolence of Azgarth in order to find what happened to Juliana. Loyalty to Roman and love for his sister warred inside his head. Could he find a way to satisfy both goals and betray neither?

He opened the bedroom door and proceeded out into the hallway. Delicate violin music rose up from the floor below. Valentine. Did he often give private concerts to those living with Dr. Savoy? Nicholas followed the sound, taking the stairs as a child who was just learning to walk might. The music changed several times during his descent. A warm-up to an actual song? Practicing scales? Nicholas had no idea, only that the sound coming from the violin was uniquely Valentine.

Nicholas came to a closed door at the end of another hallway. He gave a ginger knock.

A long pause filled the air as the last note died. "Enter."

Nicholas opened the door to a small salon littered with sheet music, both filled with drying ink and bare but for the lines. Valentine gave Nicholas a startled glance, then set his violin aside and rushed to intercept him.

"Should you be out of bed, Mr. Alexandre?" Without waiting for confirmation or invitation, Valentine helped Nicholas to a chair, lowering him down with all the care of a nursemaid.

"Perhaps I walked too far, but I have no intention of staying in that damn bed any longer. I will not let my murderer win."

Valentine released Nicholas's arm and stepped back. "I have some knowledge of what you speak."

Nicholas considered Valentine for a moment. He cocked his head. "You of all people in this odd little residence know what I'm going through. What it's like to be pulled from the arms of death."

Valentine shook his head slightly. "I know waking up to find I hadn't died from my injuries. Yet something about that blackness where I traveled felt familiar."

"Familiar how?"

Valentine picked up his violin and began to pluck the strings. "As if perhaps I'd been there before."

The look in the violinist's eyes put a shiver down Nicholas's spine. "If you traveled to the fae court, you have been there. After this, I'm convinced they are one and the same."

Valentine strummed his thumb across the strings. "What brings you to my improvised studio?"

"The music. I heard you playing."

Valentine gave a nod. "I've wanted to speak with you since you woke but have not found an opportune time." He glanced up. His gaze sharp enough to cut. "You and I are in a unique situation."

"That is stating it rather mildly."

"Perhaps, but think about it. How many people have crossed over to the realm of death and returned? There might be those who have come close, but none of those who have been."

"Your murderer received his punishment. Mine, I believe, might have been working under the auspices of another."

Valentine stared off into space for a moment, as if listening to something far away. He then turned and jotted notes down on one of the papers. Then he picked up his bow and began to play. The song only lasted for a few measures, but even from so small a sample, Nicholas's breath caught.

"Were you afraid severing your ties to Azgarth might squelch or relieve you of your talent?"

Valentine frowned. "To me, going from celebrated to mediocre was worth the price of freedom. Teaching others how to play would have made me happy if only to allow me to choose my own direction. To no longer be at the beck and call of a mercurial host."

"How did you free yourself, if I may ask?"

"Dr. Savoy burned the book of names Herr Maestro carried."

Nicholas sat in silence as Valentine returned to work, playing a few chords and then writing them down on the music sheets. For a long time after being chosen, Nicholas hadn't yearned for freedom. He'd enjoyed the benefits of his association. Lately, it seemed the connections were filled with more shadows and subtexts than he'd ever known or accepted.

And his sister—Christ, Juliana had been a casualty of that war.

Sickness grew inside him, bubbling up from a well of grief so profound he'd had a hard time keeping it buried with her. She'd barely been over the bites from the *wolfsine* when a backlash of power ripped through their house, centering on her heart. One triumphant concert and it had all been taken away.

Valentine stopped playing. His eyes widened. "Mr. Alexandre, are you unwell?"

Nicholas closed his eyes against the crippling pain. Juliana didn't deserve to be snuffed out as if her life had meant nothing. Guilt swamped him, threatened to drag him down as it always had when he thought of his part in Juliana's death. If he'd only discouraged his mother from accepting the tutelage of Herr Maestro, Juliana might still be alive.

"Let me at least help move you to the sofa. You'll be able to stretch out there."

Nicholas allowed Valentine to help him to his feet, arm slung around the musician's neck. "It should have been me, you know?"

Valentine sent him an uneasy glance. "I'm sure I have no idea what you mean, Mr. Alexandre."

"To die. My sweet sister cut down for my presumption and arrogance."

Valentine stiffened. His expression closed. "Here we are. Lie down. I'll find Henri or one of the doctors."

Tears blurred his vision. He grabbed for Valentine's sleeve. "No. Don't leave. You are the only one who truly understands what it's like living under this terrible and beautiful yoke. To taste death on your lips and wish for it to take you in truth, yet all the time cursing the darkness for the failure of its finality."

"I can listen, but I can't do much else to aid your present condition."

Nicholas stared into Valentine's eyes. "Play a song to soothe me."

Valentine squeezed Nicholas's shoulder. "If you like."

Valentine crossed the room and gathered up his violin and bow. He placed the instrument under his chin and moved the bow across the strings. Tones sweet and calm fell to the floor around Valentine's feet. If Nicholas squinted just right, he could see the notes moving like dust motes in sunshine.

An awesome power was at work there, and not through the benevolence of Azgarth. Valentine had been freed and along with his freedom came a superior talent that no other being could lay claim to. He was born blessed to play an instrument with such care and devotion the music made love to the listener.

No, freedom had not robbed Valentine of his talent—it had torn from the shackles and bloomed into something more awesome than ever before.

If only Juliana had known such power without the sacrifice.

In time, Nicholas drifted off into a troubled sleep.

Mikhail turned the fountain back on. Water sprayed up into the air, then settled down in soft burbles as it recycled through the system. He'd not asked Dante's permission to do so, and had not run into him since returning from the manor hours before. Both patients remained asleep, though Mr. Alexandre had left his room to seek out the company of Valentine. After playing for almost a half hour, Valentine had put down his violin and sought out Mikhail to tell him of Mr. Alexandre's wretched state.

The man grieved for his sister. It was not clear how or why she'd died, but Mikhail vaguely remembered seeing an article in the paper shortly after the events of the night they'd confronted Azgarth. Was it possible that Miss Juliana Alexandre had been one of the casualties when Dante burned the book? Knowing of the deaths was bad enough, being able to put a face or a name with one was horrific.

They simply had to solve this mystery or risk injuring others. No amount of freedom was worth the price of a few innocent souls. Never should innocence pay the price for arrogance. The duty of men in his station was to protect those who had no protection. He'd taken an oath to preserve and prolong life, not to cut it down while executing a desperate plan. There had to be a way to free one of the chosen at a time. To keep body and soul intact in the process.

Henri exited the house and entered the garden. He held the thermal spectrometer. "I was able to repair it and use a different filter. This should help you distinguish shapes in the water by measuring the distance from drops. Instead of a flat picture, you'll see everything in three dimensions."

Mikhail turned the box to face him, studying the cover. It didn't even look the same. Not only had Henri added an extra filter, but he'd gone through the trouble of placing a few more dials on the front.

"What are these for?"

"Fine tuning. You can adjust the picture for sharpness on either the horizontal or vertical plane. This one—" Henri tapped a knob at the bottom. "—allows you to control color contrast."

"You would think by now I'd fail to be amazed at the thought you put into your work, but still, you manage to exceed my expectations at every turn. Thank you."

Henri took a step back, braced his legs apart, and crossed his arms. An expectant look filled his eyes. "Well, fire it up. Let's see how it works."

Mikhail used the hand crank on the side of the box. Tension wound the coil. He let go and the small screen came to life. He held up the viewing box to the cascade of water in front of him, scanning the area for any variance and found nothing but a constant, predictable flow.

Henri leaned in, looking over Mikhail's shoulder. "Do you see anything?"

"Nothing to analyze. I wonder if it is something that happens only at night when the moon is at zenith."

"Might explain why the beetles were photosensitive, but not why the rifts open. Andres told me of encounters during the day."

"Yes, for Azgarth. I imagine a being able to walk between worlds can do so at will and is not encumbered by something as insignificant as time of day." He scanned from side to side, moving to the back of the fountain. "I want to know about the secret entrances, like the one that took Mr. Cetanni through the dark passage."

"For that, you may need to wait until one presents itself and then analyze."

"Or return at night." The crank wound down, and Mikhail plowed his hand through his hair. Evening was coming, but full night was still off by a few hours. Patience was never one of his virtues, and especially not when an enormous clock ticked in the back of his head. If they didn't figure out the mystery of the rifts, of what Azgarth wanted or hoped to gain from humanity, Mikhail had an awful feeling, as a species, humans might not be long for this world. Not in any sense they now knew.

"True. If you isolate the spectral signatures when a rift opens, they will be easier to see as they begin to appear." Henri reached over Mikhail's shoulder. "Excuse me." He turned the color dial and leached the scan to grays and whites.

Images began to appear, but he had no confidence that they were anything more than scenes found in clouds. Imagination and optical illusions could make it seem as if a thousand and one possibilities were found in the rolling water.

"I think we need the temperature array to locate any pockets of cooler air."

A wind blew from the southeast, bringing with it tiny eddies of crisp air. "I'm not sure isolating temperature gradients outdoors will give us much information at the moment. It will be too difficult to determine what is caused from natural weather and what is byproduct of the rift."

"Then we go indoors and try to bring something forth from the tank."

Mikhail rubbed his head again. For some reason, it helped him think, when thoughts became muddled. "All right. We'll keep this on for now, in case we need to come back later."

Henri canted his head. "If I could only rig an alarm to let us know when something of value occurred."

"How would such a thing work?"

"Attach the warning mechanism to sound when certain parameters on the box are breached." Henri gave a Gallic shrug. "It's really not so hard to figure out a way to get the results we want."

"Once again, I'll bow to your creative wisdom."

They left the garden and headed back into the surgery. Dante was there looking over the equipment. He glanced over when they entered the room. "Did you find what you were looking for?"

"If you mean a rift, no." Mikhail walked over to the tank and cranked up the thermal spectrometer. "The fountain gave away no secrets."

"Well, if you're expecting the tank to give you anything, you're going to be terribly disappointed." Dante fiddled with the controls. The oscillations inside the tank increased. "The higher the frequency, the more excited the energy around the tank."

Mikhail gave a tight smile. "Recreate the scenario from last night, down to the tank settings. We must be precise in this."

Dante raised a brow. "At the risk of sounding as if I've not studied the scientific method, I happen to disagree."

"I can't see how that's possible. We already know a rift occurred under the conditions as found last night. We aren't positive these will even elicit the response we are after," Mikhail argued.

Henri cast a nervous glance at first one then the other, then stepped between them. "We can set up one of each. I have enough materials to make another tank or two. One can be used as a control tank, the other two running at various speeds."

Mikhail frowned. "That will take days, weeks even."

"Not now that I've put one together, a second isn't going to be that complicated, and if it gives us more information, it's time well spent." Henri gave Mikhail a hopeful look. "At least think about it. Bickering is not going to get us the answers."

Mikhail tried to act shocked. "I wasn't aware we were bickering."

Henri didn't reply. He turned his back and walked to the other side of the surgery, waving as he did so.

In the quiet that followed, Mikhail turned to Dante. "Are we bickering?"

"I'm not pleased with you, but I'm not going to fight you over it."

Mikhail let out a breath. If he'd been kicked by a horse, he'd not have felt worse. "Is it the addiction or an unnamed offense I've committed?"

Dante's jaw grew tense. He turned his face away. "You are hell-bent to run into danger without the proper precautions or strategy. I want to find answers as badly as you, but I'm not willing to kill myself and others to do so. And not a day or so ago, you said you never wanted to enter the fae realm again."

"I'm doing this so others won't die."

Dante stilled. "You aren't the only one who feels guilt over those deaths. And now, knowing the death of Juliana Alexandre wasn't some sick coincidence, I am doubly distressed."

Dante was correct. Learning the truth about Juliana Alexandre had been a blow. How could morale get any lower once it was discovered they were directly responsible for ending a promising young woman's life.

"Then don't be angry with me, Dante. Join with me in the venture, wherever it takes us."

"I'd never consider doing anything else, but I want to exercise a bit of caution. The thought you may come to harm or end up wrapped in gauze like Mr. Cetanni pains me."

Mikhail's belly clenched, low and tight. His breath stalled. More often lately, he had the same reaction whenever Dante spoke tender words.

He steeled himself against the feelings roiling in his gut. "You and Henri are more than qualified to tend me if I become injured. However, for your peace of mind, I'll promise to be careful."

"Sometimes, circumstances are out of our hands. We cannot predict time and place, especially when it comes to confrontations with Azgarth."

"I'm not so much after another confrontation as I am information. You know this. I've been upfront from the start."

"But I know what you want to do with the information after you gather it and that is what I oppose. Not until we can predict the consequences."

Mikhail gave a snort of laughter. "Predict the consequences with Azgarth involved? You'd have an easier time predicting when a volcano might explode or a sun to grow dark."

"Doesn't mean we shouldn't try. We do, after all, know more people who've spent time in his company than previously."

"True." Mikhail rubbed his forehead. The ghost of a headache had started between his eyes. His skin prickled. He looked down at the thermal spectrometer and wound it a second time. Images came through the lens, in shocking clarity. "We've got something."

Dante and Henri moved in closer, looking over his shoulder.

Henri pointed out a line of what appeared to be marching soldiers moving through the water. None of them paid any attention to the rift. They passed by as uniformed dragoons on parade; however, they looked like no men Mikhail had ever seen. Long hair fell to the center of their backs. Long ears were pointed at the tips and curved toward their skulls. Only an impression of their features was captured in the heat signature, mostly in shades of blue. Cold. Extremely cold. They kept in step, perfect in their precision.

"Who are they?"

"Shades of warriors from a bygone era?" Dante leaned closer. Heat from his body suffused Mikhail through their clothes. "They look like no humans even Darwin could conceive."

Mikhail glanced over his shoulder. Dante's mouth was close enough to taste. Mikhail shivered and turned his attention back to the screen. "More of the elfish variety."

"Storybooks come to life."

Henri moved from beside Mikhail and closer to the tank. "If there is a fae master, why not elves? Who knows what else there is in the universe?"

"Golden flesh-eating beetles, for instance?" Mikhail adjusted one of the knobs to see if it would bring the marching figures in sharper. No matter what he adjusted, the figures grew less defined. "We're losing the image."

Dante traced the line of soldiers as they diminished. "They're moving away from the tank, going deeper into the fae dimension."

"So we caught them magnified in the water while they were on route to their battleground." The thought alone was enough to make Mikhail want to recoil. "A war. How do you think that will affect our world?"

"I fear to even contemplate the possibilities." Dante rested his hand against the tank glass. "Makes me question whether that was why the beetles fled, or if they went on the offensive for Mr. Cetanni breaching their environment."

Henri turned back from the tank. "He said it was a punishment. I think we have to believe him."

"I'd like Mr. Cetanni's expertise about now." Mikhail made a few more adjustments, but the pictures faded.

"We shouldn't dare wake him." Dante stepped back from the tank. "Is Valentine working? Perhaps we should bring him in. He might have seen these odd beings before."

"Good idea." Mikhail turned to Henri. "Was he working last you saw him?"

"He's not here. The incident with Mr. Alexandre disturbed him so much he went for a walk."

"Then you can talk to him when he returns." Mikhail adjusted the dials again. The soldiers might have been gone, but other interesting creatures followed in their wake. Large siege machines and wagons pulled by animals he'd never seen the like before crossed through the surface of the water.

"This looks more and more like war." Dante turned a worried gaze Mikhail's way. "Who can they possibly be fighting?"

"Other inhabitants of the fae realm," Mikhail guessed. "If they wanted to make war on the human realm, they would have already crossed over, don't you think?"

Dante shook his head. "I can't even think about it." He chafed at his arms. "Has it grown colder in here?"

Mikhail spread his fingers, moving his hand through the air to get a feel for the ambient temperature. "Not to me, but then I'm running a few degrees above normal these days." He turned from the tank, setting the thermal spectrometer on the room at large. "Most of the room is scanning in the colder ranges."

Dante crossed to the cavernous fireplace. It had been converted to gas a few years earlier. He flipped the switch and the flames grew in the grate. "That should warm it up in here."

"The chill is from the passing rift, even if it hasn't fully opened yet."

"It must be close." Dante picked up another meter—this one for measuring kinetic energy—and waved the wand on the outside of tank. The needle pegged to the far end of the spectrum. "If we only had a way to go through the glass without disturbing the water, we might be able to follow them."

Mikhail smiled. "Lines of moving troops have been known to go on for miles. Maybe they've appeared in the garden fountain. I suggest we go out there and discover it."

Chapter Thirteen

Roman woke with a start. All his bandages were gone and in their place full court dress. Instead of a bed, he lay on a fine sofa of red velvet. Fires roared in the grates, though no change in temperature ever infiltrated the fae realm. At least not this part of it. Not where Azgarth stayed most of the time. Now he had only to wonder why he was brought here at this time.

He sat up and took in his surroundings. Voices drifted in from the next room. Laughter. Music. Not only were his bandages gone, but now he'd moved, the bites no longer pulled and tugged.

The light changed slightly. Darkness leaked into the corners. Flashes of sparkles floated through the air as so much metallic confetti. A sweet scent of honeysuckle filled the air. Roman waited, not quite certain what manner of being meant to manifest. In this realm, it was anyone's guess.

As more light and color played, a figure drew clearer. More so than Azgarth ever allowed. Then the figure was in motion, moving toward Roman in an airy glide. The confetti effect shifted, stirred, then reconfigured into one of the most beautiful people Roman had ever beheld.

Long blond hair shone silver in the firelight. Eyes the color of a summer sky stared into Roman's, with odd vertical pupils. His cheekbones were high and sharp as blades. However, the most amazing things were the long pointed ears that curled delicately up the side of his skull. He bowed at the waist.

"Welcome to my home, Roman Cetanni. I am Oiredon."

"Why am I here? And why did you heal me?"

Oiredon pursed full lips. "I would think that obvious. I want you to be my ally."

"Your ally? Now that's not an offer I hear every day, especially not on this side of the veil."

A cagey smile lifted the corner of Oiredan's mouth. "Let this time be different."

A motto near and dear to Roman's heart popped into his head: *beware of smiling fae.*

"What will this change of status entail?"

"Status." Oiredon rolled the word over his tongue like an epithet. "You will have your freedom from Azgarth."

"Ah, there it is, the golden carrot, left to dangle in front of me so I'll do your bidding. I'll be trading one master for another. One who I don't know on either temperament or promises."

Oiredon gave a grave nod. "After all your years in service to Azgarth, I would expect such an answer."

Roman grew ever more skeptical. "You know about my service, and you've never approached me before?"

"I had no need until now."

Trying to get a straight answer out of a fae creature was akin to getting one out of a Parliamentarian. "And that need would be?"

"All in good time." Oiredon came around the side of the sofa, running long, elegant fingers along the back. "For now, we will leave it with this. Your wounds are healed and you have never to fear the pearl beetle again."

"In exchange for my service to you."

"Your assistance."

Roman glanced around the room. "With the ability to heal my injuries and afford me such fine clothes, I wonder at how I can assist you."

"I'll let you know when the time comes."

Another saying came to mind: *never trust a fae whom you owe a favor.* However, if freedom was promised, it might be worth it to at least see how it was to be achieved.

"In order to agree, I need more of the particulars." Roman attempted to rise, but a firm hand on his shoulder kept him in place.

"I understand how Azgarth recruits his agents. It is not my way of doing things."

He'd very much like to know Oiredon's way of doing things. Azgarth lived for passion. He consumed it as humans did food. That small detail was an aspect most of the chosen didn't understand. Azgarth was more parasite than protector. He lived off the creative energy that fueled the human soul. Simple enough concept if one looked at is as merely a transfer of energy. However, it went deeper than that. Azgarth rode the backs of his chosen, working them until they failed, drinking every last drop of their essence here on earth. When it came time to die, they lived a prisoner of his palace forever, their creations nothing more than the shades of what had been. The energy more an appetizer than a banquet.

Roman gave a reluctant smile and wondered at the mechanism Oiredon used for fuel. "Yes, yours is by healing wounds and promising freedom."

"Still you will consider my offer." It wasn't a question.

Roman looked down at the hand that remained on his shoulder. Strength and power radiated out of Oiredon's palm. "Is it an offer or a mandate? If I don't agree, do you return me to my injured state with a few new ones thrown in as punishment?"

"No." Oiredon raised his hand. "Consider it a gift."

Roman offered a quiet thank-you. The light shifted, and he became so sleepy he couldn't keep his eyes open a moment longer. He lay back down on the sofa or risked falling. The room bucked and turned, only righting itself when he sat upright once again, ensconced in Dr. Savoy's guest room.

The soft nap of fine clothes had given way to the rough weave of bandages. A dream? A very real one. The scent of honeysuckle remained on the air. He moved his arm and felt no pull, no pinch from his injuries.

He pulled the covers down and unwrapped the bandages from his left hand. Knuckles that were once ripped and bleeding now showed new, pink skin. The healing had not been complete, but was accelerated on a scale even the good doctors would appreciate.

Evidence of a visitation or a reaction of being a little less than immortal? He couldn't decide.

He got off the bed and slowly stood to unwind the gauze. Standing in the room naked and exposed, he studied his reflection in the mirror. Whichever mechanism had seen to his recovery, Dr. Savoy's miracle salve, fae magic, or altered flesh, the results were amazing. He dressed and left the room.

Healing skin on the backs of his knees moved stiffly when he walked. Each step a bit freer than the next, but remained uncomfortable. Walking down the staircase caused immeasurable pain. Not all of the injuries were healed, and he'd felt suspect if they had been. No, it was better this way. Believing there might be another fae creature who wished his service was too unsettling to contemplate. He never wanted to be the piece of meat fought over by two deadly predators.

Voices came from the direction of the garden. He followed the sound to find Dr. Stanslovich, Dr. Savoy, and Mr. Vauss standing by the fountain. Figures moved within the flowing water. Strange, sensual. Familiar. Bows, firearms, swords, hung from straps. Bandoleers crossed muscled chests. Sunlight filtered through the trees. Water sparkled, giving the warriors the appearance of being composed of crystal.

Roman hedged forward. "Who are they?"

The three turned as a unit. Dr. Stanslovich had an odd device in his hand. The wand pressed into the flowing water.

Surprise rounded his eyes, but Dr. Stanslovich shook it off and glanced down at the equipment he held. "We haven't determined yet."

Their manner of movement and the physical traits were so close to Oiredon they had to be of the same fae race. What in all the living fires of hell was going on? He didn't dare tell them of his strange dream, not yet, not until he'd sorted it out in his mind.

"Where do you think they're going?"

Dr. Savoy stuck his hand into the waterfall. The images fell through his fingers like quicksilver. "We haven't determined that either, but we've decided they are off to war."

"That seems obvious, but I wonder who they are going to war with and is there a way to protect ourselves if they invade this world?"

"An angle we've discussed. At this point, there's no way to know." Dr. Savoy withdrew his hand. Water dripped from his fingertips into the catch pool below.

"Should we follow them? See where they're going?"

"That didn't work out so well for you the last time," Dr. Stanslovich was quick to point out.

"It might answer some questions."

Dr. Savoy shook his head. "I tried to penetrate the veil, but all I come up with are wet hands."

Roman put his hand into the waterfall as well. The result was the same as for Dr. Savoy. "Then they don't want you to know just yet."

"Why show us if not to tempt us to follow?" Mr. Vauss adjusted the dials on a box in his hand. "Seems pointless to me."

"No telling with the fae." Roman might have left it there if not for the fact one of the warriors chose that moment to turn and look over his shoulder, piercing the veil with a glance. "Did you see that?"

Dr. Savoy started forward at the same moment Cant Roman stuck his hand back inside the spray. His fingers brushed up against hard leather and brass grommets. As he was about to go in after the warriors, the solidity slipped through his fingers, once again turning to water.

"The walls are coming down." Roman turned and looked back to the house, half expecting to see a parade of fae soldiers marching through the yard. "We have to find a way in."

Dr. Stanslovich nodded. "I agree, but we've not found a way yet to force a door open."

As if a messenger from God himself, Mr. King was shown into the garden by the butler.

"Ah, salvation comes."

A grand commotion was going on below stairs. Was Dr. Savoy holding a ball? If he was, it was a bloody odd time for one. And with the house in uproar over his illness and that of Roman.

Roman!

Nicholas pushed up from the bed and walked in a jerky gait to the door. He flung the door open, but no one was in the hallway. God, his head hurt from grief and his heart ached from guilt. Whatever he'd been given to calm him tasted rancid on his tongue. He'd never been one to fall into hysterics, or fall apart when things didn't go his way, but knowing why and how Juliana had died shook him at the foundations.

He should have brought her here, let Dr. Savoy save her. He'd not thought of it at the time. Had been unable to think of anything other than a bright light had been snuffed out too early.

What he needed were his paints and canvases. His next series of paintings would be dedicated to Juliana. He'd show her as famous women from myths and legends. Guinevere, Miranda, Ophelia, Juliet. Tragically beautiful characters. Yes, that was what he'd do. A tribute to the person who loved him best in all the world.

He tucked back inside and picked up his sketchbook along with some pencils and headed down to the library where Valentine had practiced earlier.

The musician was no longer there. The violin and empty sheet music gone. Nicholas made a place by the window where the light was good, set his sketchbook on the table, and plotted out the paintings the way he imagined them in his mind. Bit by bit, the scenes came together, weaving a tale of misery, one fable, and one real.

"You can set up in here."

At the sound of voices in the doorway, Nicholas looked up. Roman escorted a swarthy young man into the library, photography equipment in both hands.

The sight of Roman walking around as if unaffected by recent injury jarred Nicholas. Had he dreamed the illness? Was it another residual product of having died and slipped between worlds? Seemed bloody unlikely when it had felt so real. Unlike his experiences in the fae realm.

Roman stopped when he noticed Nicholas staring at him. "You're awake."

"It appears so." Nicholas sat in awe of Roman. No injuries healed that fast. "You are much better than you were the last time I saw you."

"Yes." The abrupt answer came as Roman showed the other man where to place his equipment.

Curious.

They turned their backs on Nicholas as if he wasn't even there. Jealousy spiraled up from an open maw in his chest, burning and biting as it sought release.

He pushed the feeling away and gathered his belongings.

"Where are you going?" Roman stood with his hands on his hips, brow furrowed when Nicholas started out the door.

"To find a new place to work." He lifted the sketchbook. "I'm a bit more portable than your friend there."

Roman held out his hand. "Please stay. I want to test a theory."

"You've been in the company of the doctors too long. You're starting to sound like them."

"That's not necessarily a bad comparison. Rather a compliment." Roman indicated the chair Nicholas had vacated. "If you would take your seat again, I want Mr. King to photograph you while you work."

Nicholas gave a snort of laughter. "Chronicling the artist at his craft?"

"In a way. Mr. King has the ability to capture the fae realm on photographic plates."

Nicholas carried his sketchbook back to the desk and laid it down rather harder than he intended. "I still don't understand what that has to do with me."

"You will."

Nicholas opened to the page he'd been working on and tried to pick up where he left off. Odd scribbles lined the edge of the page. He'd not consciously drawn those, nor did he see where they added anything to the overall composition. However, they did look familiar, though he didn't know why or how.

He held the book up closer to his eyes and realized they were words. Not English. Not any language he'd ever seen before. The script was elongated, slanted, filled with loops and curls. Written out it was as decorative as lace.

"What's the matter, Nicholas?"

"Nothing. Only trying to find my place." What was he going to say? He had started drawing and writing things he'd never intended? That he was no longer in control of his creative side?

More disturbing was the fact that if he no longer had control, who did? Azgarth? Though none of the images he'd taken to unconsciously drawing gave even a hint of Azgarth.

He used the side of his pencil to begin shading the areas where he'd place darker colors and quickly fell back into the rhythm of creation. As he worked, he was aware of the sound of the flash powder and smell as it burnt. He did not pay attention as Mr. King moved his tripod to another location in the room.

The sun changed position, faded farther down in the late afternoon. Long shadows fell across his page, hinting at another level of the picture before him. Darkness often revealed what the light faded from sight.

"Now we will move to other parts of the house."

Nicholas glanced over his shoulder. Mr. King gathered up his equipment with Roman's help, and the two left the room.

Feeling like yesterday's fish, Nicholas turned back to his drawing. He needed to get paints and brushes into the house. Could he send someone to fetch his from his home, or would it be best if he dressed and made the trip across town himself?

He glanced out the window. By the time he got dressed and made his way home, he might as well stay there for the night. His paints were there and he might be able to lay at least the bottom layer on the canvas.

Why did he even need to return to this mad house of walking corpses and fae invasions? If he started feeling poorly again, he'd send for Dr. Savoy or Stanslovich.

He stood. The world slid a bit to the right, but he caught himself before he managed to fall. Damn, he should not have moved so fast. If he was going to be independent and live his life, he needed to at least be able to stand without falling over.

Getting upstairs was a struggle. It had been much easier going down than up—that was no lie. By the time he reached his room, he was sweating and shaking like a drunk in a dry town.

He sat down on the bed and woke up later. Darkness folded from outside the windows, sneaking in the panes to slither around the room.

Nicholas lay on his back as tiny pockets here and there coalesced into grotesque faces staring down at him from the canopy of the bed. No matter how hard he tried to move, his muscles remained paralyzed.

"You don't scare me."

They didn't seem to care if he was frightened or not. All they seemed able to do was stare at him as if taking his measure.

"So I should go? Is that what you're telling me?"

Still no answer.

They were ugly little creatures with heads as round as melons, long tusks that came up from a horrendous underbite. Their eyes were big and black as buttons.

One held a grubby little hand out to him.

Did he dare let the thing lead him around? Where were they thinking to take him?

"You do realize I cannot go through the ceiling. I'm mortal and bound by the laws of gravity."

The creature that seemed to be the leader of the little group frowned and turned his head to the side. Obviously gravity meant nothing to these members of the fae world.

"Where are we going?"

No answer.

"At least let me get my robe."

He stood. The creature placed its hand on his head, and a great shift pulled him off his feet and upward. All right, so maybe gravity was not a concept the fae worried too much about. At least not in the sense humans understood it.

Scenery flew by them. Streams of colors and lights sped by his periphery. Too many to take them all in. A distinct echo of vertigo rang in his ears, bringing back the earlier dizziness.

He closed his eyes. It was the only way to keep his head and stomach friendly with each other.

Probably not the smartest thing he'd ever done. If he had to give it a classification, it would probably be tucked somewhere between encouraging Juliana to sing and his own brush with Azgarth. He doubted this excursion would kill him, but it was damned uncomfortable.

The sensation of movement slowed, then came to a stop. His feet hit solid ground. Tiny hands slipped into his and tugged.

Nicholas opened his eyes, looking down on the creatures who pulled him along to some unknown destination. All around him, light danced in tulip-shaped sconces. Soft music played on instruments from the woodwind family, though if pressed he'd not have been able to pick out which ones, they sounded so foreign.

They moved past the sound, away from where a party ensued. The little creatures waddled in front of him, looking from side to side, as if searching for a particular room. That's when he noticed there were doors all along the corridor.

"Are we going to go into one of these?"

Apparently not, as they continued to drag him farther into the fae world. They finally stopped in a front of a door that was wide, dark oak. A brass knocker invited a knock or two. When he would have waited for leave to enter, the little creatures pushed right in and landed them squarely in Sir Rodderick's library.

Sir Rodderick sat in a chair by an empty fireplace. A glass of whiskey hung from limp fingers. A vague sense of déjà vu filled him. He'd been witness to a scene like this before but had no idea when or where. The truth of the matter was he'd seen Sir Rodderick drinking on more than one occasion but not with such melancholy.

The creatures pushed against an invisible boundary that separated this world from the human. They weren't taunting him; rather they were trying to soothe him. Contrary to how these odd things looked, they were kindhearted.

"What do you want me to do?"

One of the creatures turned huge eyes to him and made a low whining sound.

"I cannot move through walls and worlds as you do."

It pointed a stubby finger at Sir Rodderick.

"I will promise to call around tomorrow. That's the best I can do."

That seemed to appease the creatures, and they brought Nicholas back to where he'd started.

Arrival back to his room wasn't as he'd imagined. Where he thought he'd fall through the ceiling, or come out of the wardrobe, he kind of materialized in the middle of the room.

His body remained on the bed, sleeping.

Shocked, he stood still and waited to see if his chest expanded as he took a breath.

Yes, right there. He was still alive, just separate. When he lifted his hand, he still had the look of a corporeal being. He'd not been turned into a ghost or shade. He had substance, mass. What in all the hell was going on?

Nicholas turned to his escorts. "Did we exit at a different point than we should have?"

The leader stuck a finger into his mouth and gave a frown. He made a grunting noise to the others. They returned the sentiment. A hard shove from behind, propelled him forward. He stumbled over the end of the rug, crashing onto the bed. Force from the blow knocked him against his body.

He sucked in a breath and bolted upright.

Alone and once again a singleton, Nicholas glanced around the room. No trace of his visitors remained. Sweat ran down his forehead. His hair stuck to his head.

A dream. An odd and crazy dream.

He put his hand to his incision, but noticed it was no longer there. Healed as if it had never been—or at least the pain was gone. He ripped at the tight corset-like binding that kept his sutures closed. The lacings peeled away as his fingers tugged at them. Finally, he got the garment free and felt around. He lifted the bandage and gave a timid peek. The sutures remained, but the skin had fused as if he'd not been cut asunder.

Now why had they gone and healed him? What purpose did it serve? Or was it payment for saying he'd see to Sir Rodderick?

Not for the first time, he wished the fae were straightforward in their wants and expectations.

Another day had dawned. Morning birdsong came from the trees directly in front of the window. He'd slept longer than he thought. Perhaps he'd needed it after moving up and down the stairs without assistance. If so, how was he ever going to manage to make it home to collect his paints?

Years might have passed in the time it took Nicholas to rise, wash, and dress. However, with most of the pain gone, he'd no doubt move faster.

He'd been in pajamas so long that when he searched for regular clothes, he had none in the wardrobe. No shoes, no jacket, no hat.

He laughed.

Eccentric, but he'd dare cross London in his nightclothes. He'd be inside a carriage. Once he was home, he'd have his choice of clothing and a valet to assist him in dressing. If anything, it might give the society pages more fodder for gossip. The headline would be outrageous and grab readers' attention.

Infamous Artist Seen Dashing Through London in Nightclothes.

He put on clean pajamas and donned his slippers and robe. If he was going to do this, he was going to do so with at least a bit of decorum about it. Now trying to hire a cab might be a bit difficult. Perhaps he could send a servant to the local livery stables and hire one. Yes, that might have to do, but he didn't want anyone inside the house to know he planned to leave. They might try to stop him, and he'd not spit in the face of their kindness by refusing to obey. This way, he simply never asked if he might leave.

Truly, he didn't believe they were keeping him prisoner. Not for one moment did either of the doctors intimate he would not eventually be allowed to leave. They were merely concerned for his welfare as he healed.

Nicholas sneaked down to where a few servants were sitting in a hall. To say they were shocked by his appearance understated the case. One shot to his feet, causing the chair he'd vacated to shoot into the wall. Another started choking on his tea. The third simply stared in silence, cup poised halfway to his mouth.

Nicholas took it all in stride. "I wonder if one of you might go around to the livery stable and hire me a coach?"

"Are you going someplace, then? Dressed like that?"

"Yes. Home. Please see to it, or you'll force me to walk."

The one who had sent his chair flying, bowed. "I'll go."

"What do we tell Feltch when he sees you've gone?"

The young footman looked back. "The truth."

Nicholas nodded to the servants and left the hall.

Now he had only to wait.

Chapter Fourteen

Mikhail stood in the surgery, going over notes from Valentine's case, comparing it to that of Mr. Alexandre. No two patients could ever be more different, though the mechanism for saving their lives had been basically the same.

Death due to blood loss was not an angle Mikhail had had a chance to study in so intimate a manner. Not the aftermath. Blood leaving the body meant less available hemoglobin to carry oxygen enriched blood to the brain. The effects were devastating for the patient, though at this point, he hadn't seen any deficit in the painter.

Dante came into the surgery, slamming and banging. Temper erupted in eddies around him. "Damn him!"

Mikhail turned and raised a brow in query. "Damn *who*?"

"Nicholas Alexandre." Dante brushed a hand through his hair. "The blasted idiot just hired a carriage to go home wearing his nightclothes."

"Why did he do that? Is he confused or combative?"

"He didn't relay to Robert why he needed the carriage, only that he did. I'm torn between going after him and waiting to see what he does with his clandestine freedom."

Worry pinched Mikhail under his ribs. His heart gave a pang. "Have you formed an attachment to him?"

Dante turned a surprised glance to Mikhail. "No. Not in the way you mean. I'm attached as a point of interest in our field of study. As a patient I helped to heal. Nothing more."

Mikhail considered the problem. Emotion eased from him. "It's a delicate situation. He's well enough to return to his home with supervision. His servants should be able to look after him and his physical needs in a reasonable manner. We cannot force him to stay. Unlike Valentine, he has some place to go and most likely wants to be in familiar surroundings."

"Of course he does." The fight left Dante. He sat down on a chair, defeated. "I don't want to see harm come to him because he didn't exercise caution."

"Tell you what. We give him a few hours and then we follow. Mr. Cetanni knows Mr. Alexandre's direction. It shouldn't be too hard to get from him. Or better yet, he knows him better. We send him to fetch Mr. Alexandre."

"And in the meantime? How am I supposed to work, worrying if our patient is suffering seizures or taken ill somewhere that we can't find him?"

"I don't know. How did you work when you worried over me?"

Dante locked gazes with Mikhail. "I concentrated on creating something to bring you back. That is what drove me and kept me going."

The pang turned to a heated rush. "And I thank you for that."

Dante brushed the gratitude away as if uncomfortable to have a close friend in his debt. "What are you working on?"

A change of subject, he should have anticipated that reaction. Whenever talk sailed close to their feelings, Dante changed the subject.

"Trying to find correlations between Valentine's course of convalesces and that of Mr. Alexandre. So far they are chalk and cheese."

Dante gave a lame smile. "Which is which?"

"I'll let them decide."

"All right. Fair enough." Dante twisted around in his chair to study the resurrection tank. "Have you noticed any inconsistencies this morning? Any figures moving through the fluid?"

"None. It's been silent." Mikhail looked up from the pages he'd returned to. The only figure he saw in the glass was that of his own reflection. "Sometimes, I believe we're in a collective hysteria caused by trauma or overwork. Too many inexplicable things have happened to us in a short span of time to properly process it all."

"And even bigger, weirder events on the horizon. I think we best prepare ourselves for the worst."

Mikhail turned to look at Dante. The gas lamps brought out the deep russet highlights in his hair, making him look like a dark pagan god. Emotions too large to contain threatened to overcome him. He looked away.

The chair where Dante sat creaked as he changed positions. "How are you feeling?"

"Odd. Still not myself. I'm trying to make it longer between doses." And still the need for the drug cut ribbons through his blood. He ignored them at most turns, grinding his teeth and making fists until the urge became too much and he feared madness if he didn't get a small hint of relief.

"I wish I could do more for you. Ease the burden."

If Dante only knew how dangerously close he skated to learning the truth of Mikhail's deepest feelings, he might think twice.

"You've done enough. This is a burden I must bear on my own. I did this; I have to carry it." Mikhail glanced back down at the pages. Ink wiggled and squiggled, coming alive on the ledger sheets.

He rubbed his eyes.

The words turned and twisted, reforming into something new and not of any language Mikhail had ever seen. "Come look at this."

Dante hurried to him, standing to look over Mikhail's shoulder. "What is that? What's it trying to say?"

"I have no idea. Do you recognize the language?"

"Maybe." Dante rushed from the room.

Mikhail continued to stare as the enchanted ink looped around, remaking itself into words both beautiful and foreign. He grabbed the thermal spectrometer and waved it over the ledger. Colors exploded across the grid. Cold bloomed in a frigged floral pattern as the new words emerged from the ones left behind.

A true phenomenon was in play. Of what kind exactly, Mikhail couldn't be sure. About the only thing he knew was it had to do with the fae, as most of the odd happenings did. He'd be surprised if it came from any other source.

Dante returned with his reference book and flipped through the pages. "I've seen that same script in here."

Mikhail made space for Dante to place the book on the desk between them. He took the ledger and set it so they could reference the altered passages. "Does the book mention a cipher?"

"Give me a moment to find the reference I'm looking for."

Near the end of the tome were two pages of examples of the text that had appeared in the ledger. The writing appeared the same, though the words were different. No key was given to explain the beautifully rendered characters.

"Another clue with no explanation or a way to understand the meaning." Frustrated, Mikhail crossed his arms and sat back in his chair, hoping the words might suddenly make sense.

"What do we do with this?" Dante turned another few pages. "This gives us nothing. Only the verification that it has happened before when dealing with the fae."

"Which is hardly helpful, though I suppose we should find some comfort in the fact we aren't sailing in uncharted territory as we once thought." Trying to take comfort in so flimsy a reason was akin to using lace to block a blizzard.

Light shifted. The letters shot out across the page in a ripple of ink, recoiled, then settled back in Henri's familiar script.

"Whatever caused it is gone now," Mikhail observed. "It didn't even last long enough to get a clear message."

Dante closed the book. "That's the type of subject we need Mr. King to point his photography equipment at."

"Each piece of evidence, or this puzzle we're set to solve, only drags us deeper and leaves us wanting for answers. I've yet to decide which way this will take us."

"Is it up to us? Because I'm under the impression Azgarth holds all the cards." Frustration punctuated Dante's words.

"Then it's up to us to stack the deck in our favor."

Nicholas let himself in through the back door. Servants were nowhere to be seen, and the kitchen had been ransacked.

His mother! Oh God, where had his mother gone?

He hurried to her room—or as fast as his infirmity allowed. She wasn't there. He went to the wardrobe and found most of her clothing missing as well. Had she been taken elsewhere? What about the nurse he'd hired to care for her? Where had she gone?

Nicholas walked around the room. His mind splintered and confusion clouded his thought processes. How on earth was he going to find his mother in a town the size of London when he had no idea where to even start looking?

He sat on the bed, stripped of linens and personal effects, and stared down at his hands, hopelessness swelling inside him. First Juliana and now his mother. He'd failed them both so spectacularly.

Though he'd never been close with Constantina Alexandre, she was still his mother and he did feel a sense of duty, and yes, love for her.

Paralyzed with loss, he had no idea how long he sat and wallowed in his failures. When he glanced up, he noticed a letter addressed to *Master Nikolas Alexandre* set up on the fireplace mantel. The handwriting was unfamiliar. He rose and retrieved it. No sooner had he opened it than he glanced down at the signature. It was from Mrs. Stanton, the nurse he'd hired to care for his mother. Starting back at the beginning, he read with much relief the fact the nurse, fearing the servants after they rifled the house, fled with Mrs. Alexandre to a rooming house owned by Mrs. Stanton's brother. She'd be well cared for there until he was on his feet and able to set the house to rights again. She assured him she did not believe the rumors of his death.

He'd collect his things and then go to check on his mother. Perhaps seeing him in the flesh would jog something resembling life from her. At the least, it would show Mrs. Stanton that her faith in him was not misplaced.

Weary, he didn't have the strength to inventory the rest of the house to see what his errant servants had taken in his absence. Did it really matter? The only things he treasured were those that had belonged to Juliana. If he lost her personal effects, he'd kill the ones who took them and feel no guilt.

He sat at his mother's writing table for a long while, trying to gather himself. Colored lights danced before his eyes. Not those of the fae realm, but to herald loss of consciousness. He curled his fingers into the table, in an attempt to hold on to the world. Staying upright required a solid strategy.

Nicholas opened his mouth and took a deep breath in, held it, then exhaled slowly. He repeated the process a few more times, trying to suck in enough air to drive back faintness. Sensation, not unlike tingles, raced up and down his arms. Hair stood up from wrist to elbow. Only an electrical field would have so much power on this side of the veil.

Why these frequent attacks? Being reanimated after death was not his idea or doing. Why should he be punished for daring to live when death had come to call? Short of ending his own life—which he'd not do—he was stuck in this world and planned to stay until his time came around again. That did not mean he wasn't going to fight back.

Azgarth had made a true enemy when he'd tied the ledgers to the chosen. Ironic how Nicholas should live, but Juliana died when her only crime had been allowing the mark of the *wolfsine*. No one, least of all he, had known the repercussions destroying the book would have on those whose names littered the pages in a catalog of human bondage. As a deterrent for destroying other books, it worked. They needed to discover a proper way to release people from their contracts without harming the innocent. Perhaps ripping out a page at a time, or obliterating only the name who wishes release?

More determined than ever, he pushed up from the table to tour the rest of the house.

Most of the furnishings remained. Taken were the items small enough to be concealed in pockets, purses, or satchels. No constable walking the streets of this neighborhood would stop to question a servant carrying what appeared to be a normal bag from their employer's house.

All the mantels were picked clean. The Faberge egg his mother coveted was missing. Even the stand gone. The only thing left behind was a coating of dust where the maids had not been in to clean for days.

His home, his very life, lay in wreckage. There had to be some recourse. A bit of revenge for all the wrong done him. Part of the blame did sit on his shoulders for allowing Azgarth into his life, but this latest insult was the work of those who he'd paid to care for him.

He left the main salon and headed to his studio. Surely the servants hadn't thought to take his paint supplies or works he'd left drying. Of course, if they had believed him dead, his paintings would automatically increase in value. While he found little fault with their ability to make a profit, he found great anger at doing so off an employer they believed dead.

The studio door remained locked. At least they hadn't found a way to breach the locks and raid his sanctuary. Unfortunately, he didn't have the key on him at the moment. He usually carried it with him in a small pocket on his waistcoat. Borrowed pajamas very rarely had those small details, which were conveniently added to clothes made special for the owner.

He'd had a second key made and hidden it in the house. But where? It had been some years since he'd had to use it. Not the library or study. The safes had been too obvious. Yes, he remembered now. A small false bottom of the piano bench. Most of the time, Juliana had been sitting on it and no one would have thought to rifle through her music storage.

He cut through the small ballroom to the music room.

Sheets of printed music were scattered over the floors, chairs, and sofa.

Anger curled like a wakening beast up from the depths of his troubled soul. How dare they invade Juliana's sacred space? Defile the place where she'd been happiest. Rage burned his blood and turned his vision.

They had no right!

His faith in the goodness of man wiped out in a single day. No that wasn't quite true. There were still those who were trustworthy. Who had tried to help him and had asked for nothing in return.

Nicholas crawled around the floor, picking up the music and stacking it in his arms, cradled as a fragile child at its mother's breast. Tears clouded his vision, ran down his face, and dripped off his nose. He curled up into a ball of sorrow and sobbed. She'd not deserved this. Had done nothing to insight the looting of her prized possessions.

Noise from the kitchen startled him.

He scrambled to stand, looking for anything he might use for a weapon. Metronomes made poor defenses, but the heavy wood might make a decent club if hit from behind.

"Nicholas? Are you here?" A beloved and trusted voice echoed through the house. "Nicholas?"

He set the metronome back on the piano top and went to the door. "In the music room, Roman."

Roman turned the corner and stepped over some portraits that had been stripped from the walls, but not taken. The culprit probably gave the heavy pieces a second thought before lugging them through the London streets.

"What happened here?"

"I've been ransacked by my own servants."

Roman glanced around, his dark gaze taking in the destruction. He shook his head. "You can't stay here. Not in this state."

"I'll have people in to clean." Nicholas walked back into the music room and fell into the sofa cushions. "The thought of tackling this alone is a bit overwhelming at the moment." He gestured to the room at large. "Look what they've done to Juliana's things. No respect or regard for her memory. The only thought was for their own greed and lining their pockets by selling off what little my family managed to take out of Russia."

Roman sat down beside him, placing a firm hand on Nicholas's shoulder. "They are but things. Your life was spared and you can rebuild."

Nicholas narrowed his eyes at Roman. "You aren't outraged they did this to me?"

"You mistake me, old friend. I am relieved you weren't here and ill when they turned on you. That you didn't come home in your weakened state to find them robbing you. This time, you might not have survived." Roman picked up Nicholas's hand and placed a tender kiss on the knuckles. "I don't know what I would have done."

Heat spiraled up and exploded. "Roman." The name was thick on his tongue. He bent his head forward, brushing his lips against Roman's. Beautiful, honorable Roman.

As soon as the kiss began, Nicholas pulled away to study Roman's face. The confusion in Roman's eyes mirrored Nicholas's.

"What's wrong?"

"The bites. I saw you in the bed, covered in bandages. Did I dream it?"

Roman gave a slight frown. "An odd experience that. I don't know what to make of it."

"Azgarth healed you? Or did the salve Dr. Savoy used heal so quickly?"

Roman rubbed his jaw and put space between them. The subtle shift was a kick to Nicholas's gut. "Neither. I had a visit from a fae lord very unlike Azgarth. I don't know what to make of him or his request."

"How do you know he was a fae lord?"

Roman merely looked at Nicholas as if the question had a predestined answer. "I'm fairly certain it could be no other race but the fae."

"What was he like?"

"Ethereal. Beautiful. Like no other being I've ever seen. Unlike Azgarth, he doesn't keep himself hidden in veils and shadows." Roman put his hands together. "I've the suspicion something massive is about to take place in the fae realm that might send ripples out into this world. Already we're seeing more and more evidence of beings crossing over."

"What did he say? What did he want with you?"

Roman shook his head. He mouthed words Nicholas couldn't quite make out.

"Wait. Stop. I don't understand. Can you write them?"

Another head shake. "I don't dare. The last time I did...well, you saw the evidence."

They sat in silence for a moment. For all appearances, Roman was at a crossroads and Nicholas had no way to help him. Not unless Roman decided to explain exactly what the being wanted.

"The oddest thing," Roman continued, "is the fact Drs. Savoy and Stanslovich were able to find similar beings—or the impressions of them—walking on the other side of a garden fountain. A line of them, marching to war."

Nicholas leaned forward on the cushion. "Say that again?"

"Water is a conductor. It is also a gateway for fae creatures. Cairns, waterfalls, hills, they all have properties that cause a thinning of the veil in those places. The fountain in Dr. Savoy's garden acts as a window into the fae realm. We were able to see a line of fae soldiers marching. Provisioned for battle." Roman rose to pace to the fireplace. He stood with his back to

Nicholas, staring into the empty grate. "I—the doctors as well—feel we are in great peril."

"What do they propose to do about it?"

"We have to find a way into the fae world. One that will allow us access to figure out what is going on and how we can stop them from encroaching more on our world."

Nicholas gave a bitter laugh. "And here I was worried about Juliana's soul trapped in the fae realm."

Roman stalked back to Nicholas and cradled his face with warm hands. "Juliana is well. Do not let that have power over you. Please. Leave it in the past. You are alive and healing. That is all that matters."

Nicholas pulled back in outrage. "Do my feelings mean so little to you that you'd allow her to live in a horrible limbo?"

"Never." Roman lunged forward, taking Nicholas's mouth in savage hunger. He rested his knee on the edge of the cushion, bending into Nicholas. The kiss tasted of love, desperation, and sorrow. When he pulled back, he rested his forehead against Nicholas's. "I love you too much to ever let you believe that."

God in heaven. He'd been such a fool. All this time, Roman had been right in front of him and he'd never seen it. Never thought to take the comfort or solace offered. Instead, he'd sought meaningless dalliances with others who wanted to control him in more ways than even Azgarth considered.

Nicholas tipped his face, bringing their mouths together. They kissed and touched in a slow, gentle exploration, but the interlude went no further. For that, Nicholas was grateful. He hadn't the stamina for more than a few healing kisses at the moment.

Roman sat back, his hand still on Nicholas's shoulder. "Why did you come here in the first place?"

"I needed some clothes and my paints."

"You could have asked me. I would have come and retrieved them for you."

Nicholas laid his hand on top of Roman's. "I need to do for myself."

"Ah, well. I can't fault you for wanting your independence, but I'd like you to slow it down a bit." Roman stood. "We should get your belongings and return to Dr. Savoy's. There's no sense in you staying here. Not when all around you are painful memories."

"What if I want to stay here? I can't very well have people in to clean when I'm not here. I won't be robbed again." Not when everything precious to him had already been picked through.

"No. Please. Leave it to me. I won't let a single item leave this house without your permission."

Nicholas relaxed. He'd trust Roman to hire people to set the house to rights.

Roman gave Nicholas a hand up. "Come. We'll get you dressed and pack a bag. Then we'll tackle getting your paints and canvases."

As they started for the door, Nicholas stopped. "Thank you."

"Thanking me is not required. It's what one does when they care."

They continued on, leaving Nicholas wondering what he might do in return.

Chapter Fifteen

Roman functioned as valet while Nicholas dressed.

The servants hadn't done much to raid their former employer's wardrobe, but his shaving kit and other grooming tools were nowhere to be found. Seeing how they were made of silver, Roman had no faith they would be recovered. He'd surprise Nicholas by purchasing a new set and presenting it to him.

Time and again, Nicholas had lost so much. Now perhaps it was time to receive. Together, they packed Nicholas's luggage and started for the door.

"I'll put these downstairs and then meet you in your studio."

Roman glanced over his shoulder, waiting to see if Nicholas followed. Instead of moving, Nicholas stood in the center of the room, looking around as if trying to catalog the space in his mind. Concern nagged at Roman to turn back, but he continued on, giving Nicholas a bit of privacy. Whatever went through Nicholas's mind had him appearing as if he believed he'd never return.

Roman carried the cases downstairs and then turned to go to the study but stopped. Standing in the middle of the foyer, faded as a negative on glass plate, was Oiredon. The fae lord raised his arm, holding it out, calling Roman forward.

Roman set the cases down and walked to where Oiredon stood. As he neared, the scenery around him changed along with a dip in temperature. A rent in the veil allowed Roman to stand on the precipice of both, straddled between that of the human realm and the fae.

"Have you made a decision?" Oiredon's voice came as if from the end of a long tunnel.

"No. I require more information."

"I need your word. If I secure you, others will follow."

"Other what?" Roman was almost afraid to know the answer but thought he knew it instinctively.

"Come now. You don't believe you're the only agent I've contacted. I want this to be a successful undertaking and will leave nothing to chance."

Roman made a huff. "Chance? I didn't think your species believed in chances. You make your own."

"There is much truth in that statement." Oiredon raised a hand and started to fade from sight. "As you humans say, I'll be in touch."

The sound of shoes across hardwood caused Roman to glance to the left. Nicholas stared at the place where Oiredon had stood, his eyes wide as if he'd seen a ghost. "Was that him?"

"Yes. But still not forthcoming on what he means to do." Roman studied Nicholas closely. "You've seen him before."

"In a manner of speaking. I drew him after I woke from reanimation."

"Drew him? And you'd never seen him before?"

"Never. It was as if my fingers worked independently from my mind."

Roman made a face. "I think it more a case of him using the medium as means of introduction to you."

Nicholas made no comment to that revelation but held up a brass key. "I've located my spare key. We can collect my supplies."

Thankful for the change of subject, Roman followed Nicholas to the studio. Nicholas unlocked the door and entered. The room stood preserved as if Nicholas had only left the day before.

"What would you like to take?"

Nicholas crossed the room and picked up a basket, then put tiny pots and jars inside. He picked up a few and shook the bottles, then set them down. A frown drew his brow together. "I'm missing some pigments."

Roman went cold. Would he go to retrieve them from Lady Clarissa? No telling what Sir Rodderick might do if he knew Nicholas lived. As far as the papers reported, the body dumped in the alley had never been seen again.

"Are you sure?"

"Positive. I had a new jar of cobalt. And some gold." The search turned frantic as Nicholas went through his brushes. "I'm missing all manner of things. My favorite brushes, a palette knife, my favorite palette. Fucking wretched servants. If I ever see any of them out on the street, I'm going to punch them straight in the head."

That wouldn't do either.

Roman came to stand behind Nicholas. "Make me a list of the items you require, and I'll get them for you."

"That isn't the point, Roman."

"I realize that, but you aren't going to get them back by making idle threats to the walls. We'll get your supplies for you. Please don't fret over it. Take what you need now, and we'll get you the rest." Roman placed a comforting hand in the center of Nicholas's back. "Getting upset while you're trying to heal feels counterproductive."

Nicholas let out a long, shuddery breath that vibrated through Roman's palm. "Intellectually, I know you're right. Emotionally, I have to fight or surrender. There are no other choices. All the other insults I've suffered since being shot by a former lover makes me lose faith in humanity."

So he did remember. Roman swallowed. "Perseverance is what got you this far from your homeland. It has seen you through your darkest hours. Don't let a few servants, who probably saw their employment coming to an end and meant to use the items in lieu of pay, bring you down." When Nicholas started to protest, Roman held up his hand to stop him. "No. Listen. I am not condoning or excusing their actions. They had no way to know if you were the man found in the alley or on an unscheduled trip to the continent. What they did was wrong, but my outrage on your behalf does not place me above understanding their actions. What it does make me want to do is plan for a solid, better future for you. So this won't happen to you again."

The fact remained that Azgarth should have been the one to ensure Nicholas's belongings were safe while he was incapacitated, unless the fae master was angered that Nicholas survived. But that wasn't the impression he'd left with Roman. Far from it. It seemed more a test for Drs. Savoy and Stanslovich.

"What do you propose? Because frankly, I'm out of answers." Nicholas placed a few more items in the basket. The brushes looked little used, evidence they were not his favorites.

"Whatever it is, I believe it may involve my visitor."

"That's the frying pan into the fire if ever I saw it." Nicholas hefted the basket. "If you'll grab that easel and a few of my stretched canvases, we can go. I don't want to return here until it's been cleaned and set to rights."

"Then that's what you shall have."

"I've seen this writing before." Henri stared at the pages in the tome, hand on chin in thought. "You say it formed before your eyes in the ledger sheets and then disappeared?"

Anyone else hearing the unlikely scenario might scoff at the possibility, but not Henri, he tended to take recent events in stride. Only the most outrageous of circumstances had shaken him. For that, Mikhail was eternally thankful.

"If it had been only me who witnessed the event, I'd put it down to long hours, eyestrain, and withdrawal. However, Dante saw it, as well, and as far as I know, he only suffers from two of those three factors." Mikhail had placed the ledger under a light that mimicked the ultraviolet portion of the spectrum, hoping that might either produce a reaction or expose some hidden property in the ink that caused it to shift.

Henri shook his head. "No. I believe you; otherwise, I'd not have been exposed to this script."

"How long ago?"

"Recently. Within the last day or so." A light lit behind Henri's eyes. He put his hand up, wagging his finger. "I got it. I know where I've seen that writing."

"Where?"

"Mr. Alexandre's sketchbook."

"What? When?" Mikhail stood and stalked to Henri.

"As I said, over the last few days. I can't say I was familiar with his work before he came here. When do I get the opportunity to attend an art exhibition?"

Mikhail frowned. "Maybe we should."

Henri canted his head. "Excuse me? Why would we? I don't see the point."

"Artists, musicians, tinkers, all facets of creativity have a connection to Azgarth. Why not see if we can find more examples of this. We've studied books, why not paintings?" Mikhail held onto the idea like a lifeline. The only way to understand a phenomenon was to gather more information. No matter the cause. In this case, the only way to discover more was to find other instances of it and research the origins.

"If this book"—Henri tapped the cover with his finger— "doesn't provide information, I'm not sure there are any other resources. The book Andres bought at the bookstore only talked about physical manifestations of creatures and sightings of oddities. I don't recall an entry about morphing text."

"Which is why we need to discover the reason this is happening, why the portals are coming so close together and why we are targeted for these visitations." Mikhail had studied the book under the light until his eyes only detected the negative of the light source. He turned away and rubbed at his lids. "I am afraid if we sit by and do nothing, we're all going to painfully regret our inaction."

"I know." Henri started away. "Let me find the sketchbook and show you the picture where I saw the writing. Compare it first and see if it's similar. It appeared so to me, but don't take my word for it."

Mikhail started. "I would trust you with my life, Henri. And have on more than one occasion since this business started."

"Yes, but I think going forward we all need to be in agreement on every step of the journey." Henri moved away with a mocking smile. "Safety in numbers."

Mikhail returned his attention to the ledger. Still nothing. It sat there under the purple lights and mocked him. "Come on, you bastard, dance for me."

Despite the name-calling, the ink did not change form. Nor did he expect it to. Not in truth. The fae had their own timetable and did not jump when mere humans called. To them, mortals were playthings to be moved around a board like chess pieces. Perhaps they had been singled out because they had dared to stand up to their fae oppressors. Were they the only ones to try such an outrageous plot? There was no way to tell. And surely the fae would tell no secrets where they did not hold the upper hand.

He sat at the desk and pulled out paper and pen. In all the chaos over the past few days, he'd not collected his thoughts enough to write them down. It helped to put things into perspective.

On a clean sheet of paper, he started with the number one and began to list all the anomalous occurrences to take place over the last few days. Though he'd been in a drug-hazed stupor at the time, he included the incident with the *neabré* that happened right before Dante came to rescue him from the drug den.

The more he sat, the longer the list grew. From the list, he took a second sheet and fleshed out the details of each occurrence. Words poured from him with as much force as rain from a thunderhead. He let them come as they would; afraid if he thought about them, it might censure an integral detail and strike it from the record.

Henri returned with sketchbook in hand. "It took longer than I thought to find it."

Mikhail didn't look up. "One moment."

He'd finished writing the account of the shifting script when his pen slipped. Ink blotted the line above, marring a portion of the account. A small, thin line feathered outward, reaching to the line above. As it touched the serif of a lowercase *g,* another line extended up to the line above. The process repeated over and over until it stretched all the way up the page, running through the paragraphs in an inky vein. It moved slowly, but with purpose.

"Something is happening," Mikhail alerted Henri.

Henri set the sketchbook on the corner of the desk and leaned over to watch. "Is this how it started before?"

"No. The first time, it morphed what was already on the page. This appears as if the very words are reaching out to one another. It all started here, when the pen slipped." Mikhail pointed to the blot.

"And you don't believe the ink just ran?" Henri gave the page a skeptical glance.

"Not in this manner." Mikhail held up the page. Across the surface now lay a detailed map of a place he didn't recognize, labeled in the same odd language. "What do you make of this?"

"All right. I take it back. That's no running ink." Henri took the map and held it up to the light. "Why a map?"

"To find our way around the fae realm." Did they have an unexpected ally on the other side? Or did it lead them into a trap? Either way, Mikhail was prepared to take his chances if the occasion presented.

The front door banged opened, echoing down the hall. "Hello! Help!"

Mikhail exchanged glances with Henri before they both ran for the front of the house. Dante met them in the hallway as a man trudged toward them carrying a boy, stretched out unconscious in his arms.

Dante lifted the boy out of the man's arms and started toward the examination room. "What happened?"

"Bastard ran him down with a carriage. Didn't even stop. The poor boy spun out like a top and landed in the park." The man took off his hat, squishing it between two beefy hands.

Horror untold filled Mikhail at the news. When Dante laid the boy down, they all looked to one another. It was the same lad whose arm Dante had set a few days before.

They stripped the boy, to assess for injury. The sling was no longer on the arm, nor the splint that had been so carefully placed.

Dante glanced up with fire in his eyes. "Are you the lad's father?"

"No, sir. I seen the boy around the neighborhood, but I couldn't rightly tell you who he belongs to." He wiped a trembling hand around his mouth. "I'll tell you something else. That carriage was pulled by horses I ain't never seen the likes of before."

Mikhail sensed a potential for information and possible disaster. "Let us take care of the boy. Then you can tell us what you saw."

As he pressed on the boy's abdomen, searching for the telltale signs of internal bleeding, he felt nothing. It was as if the lad's insides had been turned to gelatin. Even the ribs were gone. How hard did you have to hit a child this size in order to sustain so much damage?

The boy opened his eyes. He reached a bloody hand up to Mikhail's shirt, grabbing the front. Mikhail covered the boy's hand with his own, marveling he was still alive.

"Take...care. Take...care." All color drained from the boy's face. Little by little, he began to fade away, moving from solid to sheer in only seconds.

The man who had brought the lad in, fell like a tree under a woodsman's ax.

"Henri, revive him. He has information we need."

Dante remained by the examination table, staring down at the empty bed. "What in the hell is going on?"

"A very good question." Mikhail held out his hand. "Come. We need the picture of a *callif*, to see if that is what our Good Samaritan saw pulling the wagon. If so, we have bigger problems than injured children who dematerialize before our eyes."

Dante glanced up with resentment painted on every line of his face. His eyes dark pools of contempt. "Do not patronize me, Mikhail. I know that child was real, of flesh and blood. I treated him not a few days ago. Felt the bones and muscles under his skin. Felt his arm move back into place when I set it." He stabbed the table with his finger. "This should not have happened."

"Not by any sense we know," Mikhail agreed. "But it did."

The man who brought the child in stirred. He shook his head to clear and looked around.

Henri helped him up and to a chair. "The doctors need some information from you."

The man shook his head again. "I'm going mad."

Mikhail pulled up a chair to the man and leaned forward to promote confidence. "What is your name?"

"Gerald Higgins." Mr. Higgins wiped a hand over his face and mouth.

Seeing his distress, Mikhail nodded to Henri. "Can you get him a glass of water, please?"

Henri left to do as asked, leaving Mr. Higgins with Mikhail and Dante.

"Do you remember what happened and why you're here?"

"Lord bless me, but I wish I didn't. I've never seen anything like it." He rubbed a hand over his face again, repeating the action in a constant motion. "That boy, he was there and then not. I've never seen anything like it."

"You need to stay on point. I know this is distressing, but I need you to go back to the time right before the wagon hit the boy. Do you recall anything odd?"

Mr. Higgins thought for a moment. Henri returned with a glass of water and handed it to Higgins, who tipped up the glass and drank most of it before stopping. He lowered his arm, a distant look in his eyes.

"I remember thinking how quiet the day seemed. Not even the birds were singing. The entire world sort of held its breath for a moment. I thought it kind of eerie. Not right. This time a day should be filled with people taking a turn in the park, carriages going by, foot traffic on the sidewalks."

"No one was out?" Mikhail prompted.

"No, they was there. They just didn't make any sound. Not that I heard. I thought I'd gone deaf, until the clop of those awful hooves came down the street." Higgins shook his head, closing his eyes to the memory.

"When did the boy come into the scene?"

Higgins paled. "Oh God. Oh God."

Mikhail didn't speak, deciding to let Higgins work through what he'd seen.

Dante had left the room and came back carrying the tome. He stood across the room, careful not to encroach on the scene. Sometimes, more information could be gained by letting someone talk without impinging on their thoughts.

Higgins took a deep breath. "The bastards run that boy down. Chased him. I wondered why the boy didn't jump into the park, but the driver was so determined. I don't think he'd have stopped if he'd hit a wall."

"Did you see the driver?"

"I did, but I can't seem to recall his face. It's all blurry-like."

A familiar tingle slid down Mikhail's spine. This had all the hallmarks of a visit from Azgarth. What had the boy done to be executed in so public a manner? On the street, in front of human witnesses?

"And those horses—something sent from the very bowels of hell." Higgins turned to Mikhail. "I thought never to see the devil in daylight."

Dante came forward, his finger stuck in the pages of the book. He flipped it open and held it so Higgins could see. "Is this what you saw?"

Higgins glanced at the picture, then looked up sharply. Surprise widened his eyes. He shook a grubby finger at the page. "Them's the ones!"

The idea the creatures had been shown in a book seemed to cheer Higgins immensely. Mikhail didn't want to be the one to squash that bubble where uncertainty met reality. Where a man's fears were put to rest that something from his nightmares had been seen before and documented. Given Higgins's state of dress and hygiene, he was of limited means and education. Not that it made him a bad person, only one who had a small circle of educational experiences to draw from. Telling him that the horses were really *callifs* from the fae realm would probably be met with disdain. Then again, superstitions seemed to take root and prosper in the lower classes. Still, better to just pretend they were a breed of ugly horse and leave it at that.

"Anything else you need to tell us about the events? Other than losing the sound before the attack, was there a change in air quality or a particular smell you remember?"

"Not that I can think." Higgins looked to Mikhail, as if waiting for an answer or prompt. "What happened to the boy? Where did he go?"

Mikhail exchanged glances with Dante and Henri. Truth must prevail, but in certain circumstances, it was, indeed, better to lie.

Dante cleared his throat. "Go? I patched him up and sent him home with a servant."

Higgins frowned. "No. I saw him disappear."

Mikhail pushed to his feet. "What you saw was the beginnings of unconsciousness. It's possible, as your vision dimmed, you only believe you saw him disappear. You were already shaken from witnessing the boy being run down. Your brain told you he disappeared and registered the phenomenon as real."

Higgins scratched his head. "No. I'm sure I saw it."

Dante gave a shrug of apology. "I fear I agree with my colleague. It's possible that the crisis in the street caused a reverse reaction when a threat was no longer visible. Such a thing can make even the strongest man falter. There's no shame in it."

"So the boy is sent home? He's alive?"

"He was when he left here." And that was the truth.

Higgins shook his head. "I'll be damned. It felt so real."

Mikhail patted Higgins on the shoulder. "Would you like my assistant to see you home? You still seem a little shaky on your feet."

Higgins waved away the offer. He pushed to his feet and lumbered to the door. Henri went with him, to ensure he got out safely.

As the footsteps receded down the hall, Mikhail turned to Dante. "What do you make of all that?"

"I'm afraid to even contemplate it."

Chapter Sixteen

An odd stillness infected Dr. Savoy's home. Nicholas shrank back from the door, afraid to go inside. Violence had happened there in his absence.

He glanced to Roman, who had gone tense beside him. "What is it?"

Roman sniffed the air. "The stench of a fae death. It smells like no other kind. This one violent. Damning. Azgarth has taken revenge on one of his own."

Called into action, Nicholas threw off the shackles of fear and rushed into the foyer—or as much as his injuries allowed. "Dr. Stanslovich. Dr. Savoy. Mr. Vauss."

He shouted the names, letting them fill the hallway, projecting all the way back to the office and surgery.

The three men in question came rushing out of the surgery. Their eyes wide.

Immediate relief flooded Nicholas's veins, taking his knees out from under him.

"Nicholas!" Roman swooped in from behind and grabbed Nicholas under the arms before his bottom managed to hit the ground. The rest of the way to the floor was done in a controlled manner.

Dr. Stanslovich speared Roman with a blazing gaze. "What's happened?"

"Much. None of which matters at the moment as much as the violent death of a fae I smell surrounding this house." Roman bent over Nicholas, rubbing a steady, firm hand over his back in comfort.

Nicholas held up his hand to let Roman know he was well. "Not to worry. Just moved too fast too soon is all."

Dr. Savoy bent forward. "Come. We will help you to the surgery. I want to examine you. We can talk there."

Nicholas allowed himself to be helped to his feet. Still unsteady, he leaned heavily on Roman and Dr. Savoy as they brought him into the surgery.

Beside him, Roman sniffed the air again. "It was a Watcher who was taken."

Dr. Stanslovich gave a nod. "A young boy. The same one you rescued from the bully in the park."

Nicholas had no idea of the events they spoke of and concluded it must have happened while he was walking the realms between life and death. "Why was he killed?"

Dr. Savoy took Nicholas's wrist and felt the pulse. "We don't know. Only that he was run down by a carriage pulled by a team of *callifs*. From the description of the driver, we believe it was Azgarth himself who caused the injury."

Roman paced away from them, then turned back around and stared. Agitation vibrated through him, filling the room. "Azgarth inflicting punishment on one of his own constructs? What had the boy done to gain Azgarth's displeasure?"

"Or for him to risk killing a child in full view of human witnesses?" Dr. Stanslovich added, then turned and walked to a writing desk in the corner where he picked up a sheet of paper and returned. He thrust the offering at Roman. "What do you make of this?"

Roman took the sheet. His expression changed from one of anger to awe. "Where did you get this?"

"It materialized from a blot of running ink." Dr. Stanslovich stared at the top of Roman's head as he bent over the paper. "You might even say it grew."

"If you wished to make a journey into the fae realm, this is all you really need."

Nicholas longed to see the paper. He leaned forward as far as he could without falling off the examination table. "What do you mean?"

Roman held up the paper. Across the expanse was a detailed map of Azgarth's palace. Nicholas had been there enough times to know the layout. Familiar writing labeled the areas.

"You might have a map, but you don't want to go there."

"It's an invitation." Mr. Vauss had stepped away from them, working on a small brass disk. "The least we could do is show up."

"You say invitation. I say trap. He means to get you all there and not let you go." Nicholas shook his head, sure of his convictions. "It's not worth the risk."

Roman held up his hand for Nicholas to wait a moment before passing judgment. "Though it is most definitely a map to Azgarth's palace, it does not stand to reason he was the one who brought it here." Roman lifted the paper and sniffed. "If I had to place a bet, I would say our benefactor is Oiredon."

Hearing that name again brought chills to Nicholas's skin. He chafed at his arms. "He's just as dangerous, maybe even more so."

"Who is this you speak of?" Dr. Savoy stepped away from the exam table, helping Nicholas down.

"Another fae. One who doesn't hide behind shifting lines to conceal his appearance." Nicholas found no comfort in that fae's boldness or his persistence in trying to recruit Roman. Not to mention the way his presence underscored lies told by Azgarth.

"Would he be disposed in helping us free ourselves from Azgarth's hold?"

A sudden drop in temperature plunged the room into icy coldness. "I would be disposed to giving you anything you ask if you join with me."

A being composed of gold and light strolled across the surgery as if only waiting for an opportune time to make his grand entrance.

Neabré trailed after him, holding onto his coattails as if afraid of being left behind.

A sly smile belied any sincerity he tried to portray. "I will grant you your freedom, if you agree to help me."

Nicholas pulled his coat closer. The cold penetrated his skin, causing a dull, deep ache to open where the doctors had put him back together. "Why should a being of unlimited power and grace need the help of mere mortals? Surely our gifts are not up to any tasks you might set out for us."

"You are very much mistaken." Oiredon lifted his arm and a panorama of Nicholas's works superimposed themselves over the walls. There, but not quite. Tangible, but illusion. "Have you not painted with precision and detail the very realm I inhabit? Have you not introduced the masses to beauty beyond their wildest imaginings?" Oiredon waved his hand again and the subjects in the paintings began to move, as if captured like animals in a zoo. "Have you not given life?"

"Only to the visions in my head."

"Life is life, Nicholas Alexandre."

Oiredon turned in a slow circle, taking in the others assembled in the surgery. "Every one of you have the gift of giving life. The doctors through their process of healing the sick and, to a larger degree, reanimating the dead." He took a few steps forward and slid his arm around Henri's shoulder. "Mr. Vauss is perhaps the most creative of you all, medicine and engineering. My brother chose very well when he had you bitten by the *wolfsine*."

Nicolas hung his head. A laugh built up from a crack in his soul—a place where hopelessness and irony collided. He'd seen this scenario play out one too many times to feel anything but contempt for the participants.

The others looked to him as if he'd lost the remainder of his mind, but he had no more control over his response than if he'd had a seizure.

He flung his hand out to indicate Oiredon. "Don't you see? We've been pulled into the middle of a family dispute. Two beings from across a gateway want us to choose sides in a conflict not of our making. Oh, they'll dangle our freedom before us as incentive, but in the end, we're nothing more than target practice and cannon fodder."

Oiredon cocked his head. "You couldn't be more wrong, Nicholas Alexandre. Humanity is the prize, not the sacrifice."

The cold intensified, either through Oiredon's displeasure or another rift. Nicholas stood huddled in his coat. Puffs of air were visible as he breathed.

When Oiredon looked as if he was going to leave, Dr. Savoy stalled him. "What about the ledgers? Will our names be erased?"

Oiredon gave a rather human shrug. "That depends."

"On what?" Dr. Stanslovich called out as Oiredon and the *neabré* began to fade.

"On whether or not *your* agent defects from my brother's side."

With the terrible words lingering on the air, Oiredon was gone. Dr. Stanslovich sat hard and wiped at his face.

"I guess that answers our question on whether or not he can free us if we follow him." Dr. Stanslovich glanced around the room before shaking his head and looking off into the distance where Oiredon had departed.

"Not entirely," Roman offered.

That ray of hope captured everyone's attention.

"Care to explain what you mean by that?" Dr. Savoy leaned against the desk. "Because if you know a way we can make this work and gain our freedom, I'd be most eager to hear it."

Roman placed one hand behind his back and the other on his chin as he walked a circuit around the room. Intense concentration pulled his face into a frown. "When Oiredon first came to me, he asked for my cooperation, though not the extent or scope it might take. For that matter, he still hasn't, and it worries me."

Roman came to the end of the circle and started back the other way. "However, he's sweetened the pie by saying he will grant the freedom of those in my ledger should I defect. It's a sure way to gain my compliance, as I'm confident he's offered the same to other agents. However, as you've seen before, not all agents care for the well-being of their charges. Not all of us wish to see them grow and prosper with happiness and abundance."

Nicholas's love for Roman grew. He'd been so lucky to have been granted an agent who cared so much for him. It might have easily gone the other way.

Emotion clogged his throat. He cleared it. "No one is more appreciative of your caring heart than I."

Roman threw him a gentle smile, eyes lit with passion before turning to make another circuit. "You are most welcome, but be that as it may, it still leaves open the question of how we should free the good doctors here. We still have no knowledge of the identity of their agent. Nor Mr. Vauss's, for that matter. Being a man of multiple talents, does he have one or more?"

Mr. Vauss put a hand to his chest. "You don't know?"

"I assure you, I do not. If I possessed that information, I would gladly give it to you. Azgarth is nothing if not efficient in keeping his agents apart. He gives us certain tasks to perform, which many times keeps us out of each other's spheres. I knew of Wilhem Kering, of course, but then he had a way of making his presence known to all."

Dr. Savoy and Dr. Stanslovich exchanged glances.

"Is there a way for you to discover the identity? A ledger perhaps or place where the names of the agents are kept?" A desperate hope shone in Dr. Stanslovich's eyes.

Roman lifted both hands. "If there is, it would be in Azgarth's palace. However, there is no guarantee he doesn't keep such information in his head."

"Still we have a map, which is more than we had before." Dr. Savoy held it up.

"But no way to get inside," Nicholas reminded the group.

"What of the photographs Mr. King took. Do you suppose there might be something on those to show the way?" Mr. Vauss suggested.

Roman nodded. "That might be our quickest way of finding an area vulnerable enough to open a rift on our own."

"And then what?" Nicholas was afraid to know.

"And then we search the castle for clues."

Mikhail used a drawing box to trace over the lines of the map, making an exact copy. Mr. Cetanni sat across from him, waiting to translate the odd writing into something they all could read without having to learn the language.

Dante and Henri were across the room, working on a device to detect and pry open a rift once they were able to pinpoint a vulnerable area. The premise was to reverse the process they used for closing one—minus the fire.

If they were going to raid Azgarth's palace, they had to make the very best attempt possible. Chances were, they'd only get one shot. Even then, they took the real risk that Azgarth already knew their plans. It seemed that Azgarth's agents were very active in their charges' lives. Why then had he never met his?

Mikhail glanced across the table. Mr. Cetanni was nothing like Mikhail had imagined when first they'd learned his connection to Azgarth.

"Is there something you wish to say or share, Dr. Stanslovich?" Mr. Cetanni looked up from his translations.

"No." But the emotions kept at him, working their way to the surface. "Well, there is one thing I wish to know. You are very active in Mr. Alexandre's affairs, and though he was an evil man, Wilhelm Kering had direct contact with his charges. At least the charges of which we are aware. As far as I recall, I've never even had a passing acquaintance to an agent."

Mr. Cetanni held Mikhail's attention in an earnest stare. "I don't wish to alarm you, or cause you undo worry, but we are governed by rules. Imposed by Azgarth, but they are rules. The first mandate is that we have continual contact with our charges. If you are a chosen, you do have an agent. There is no compromise on that point."

"Even if Azgarth himself takes special interest in the chosen?"

Mr. Cetanni raised a brow as if to educate a simpleton. "He takes special interest in all those he's culled. Agents included. One of the functions of the agents is to keep the talent working, ensuring Azgarth has a steady supply of sustenance."

The information didn't help. If anything, it unsettled Mikhail even more than he had been. Someone who had been in his life—possibly for years—worked as his agent. His gaze strayed to Dante, speaking in whispers to Henri.

As if sensing Mikhail's attention, Dante turned. His expression quizzical. Dante patted Henri on the shoulder and left him to join Mikhail. "Is something the matter?"

"Yes, but I never meant for you to stop working to come over here. Go back to your task."

"Henri is creating. There's really nothing I can do at the moment but watch and marvel."

Working. Creating. Giving life blood to Azgarth. Their creations kept him going. Was it possible to starve him? He asked Mr. Cetanni as much.

"An undertaking of such magnitude would be near impossible. Even if we could contact every human on the planet to get them to stop creating, stop thinking, it wouldn't work. Humans are driven to create. It's what makes you human. From the lowliest scullery maid telling stories in her head to pass the time to the top surgeon in the world. Every one of you create something whether it sees the light of day or not. One does not simply turn off their minds. Thoughts are always there under the surface, churning."

Dante pulled a chair over and sat down. His gaze moved over the finished copies of the map stacked at the end of the table. "What are you discussing?"

Mikhail gave Dante a long, silent look. Then, "Alternate means to bring down Azgarth. I was merely speculating."

Dante turned a grave look to Mr. Cetanni. "That sounded rather final."

"I don't mean to give that impression, but if you are to defeat Azgarth, or at least gain your freedom, you need something more."

Dante nodded in the direction Oiredon had vanished. "Or someone."

Mr. Cetanni's features tightened. "I think he did all he can for now. His poaching might be the reason the Watcher was killed. You saw how the *neabré* held to him. He's a protector, though I'm not sure I quite trust him."

Mikhail didn't either, but then again... "We're running out of options. Oiredon himself said he wants to stop his brother. I think we should help him or at least sign a truce."

Mr. Cetanni gave him a considering look. "What you do affects only you. What I decide affects all my charges. I must be responsible and answerable to them. I haven't the luxury of making a mistake with their welfare."

Dante rescued the conversation from the silence that followed. He glanced down at the maps they worked on. "You managed a great deal in so short a time."

Mikhail raised a hand to indicate Mr. Cetanni. "It helps working with someone who has been there and knows the layout."

"Only parts of it," Mr. Cetanni interjected. "I won't admit to knowing all. I'm positive there are parts of the palace Oiredon doesn't even know exist."

Dante turned to Mr. Cetanni. "You believe this came from Oiredon then?"

"I have my suspicions. What better way to draw us into a war of his making than to give us not only incentive but also a way to find what we're looking for." Mr. Cetanni raised the map he worked on and blew across the ink.

Dante picked up the map at the top of the stack. "Makes more sense in English, though the names are a bit pretentious."

Mikhail found a smile. "Only you would find fault with the nomenclature of a fae race."

Dante gave a small shrug. "Pretension of any kind bores me."

"I know." Mikhail traced another line around the edge of what was possibly the central ballroom. He'd as yet looked to the translations to discover the exact areas the map entailed. The sweep of ink turned from black to a deep red to blood.

The scent of it hit is nose, thick and metallic.

He set the pen aside and pushed the paper away. "I believe we have been made."

Mr. Cetanni continued to work. "It appears so."

"You don't seem worried." Dante pulled the paper closer to him to get a look and winced.

"It's a warning shot across our bow." Though the words were said with casual ease, a tightening appeared around Mr. Cetanni's eyes and mouth. "You did the right thing. Set it aside."

Flames erupted from the stack of finished maps. Dante scooted his chair back so fast he nearly fell over. Mikhail reached for a pitcher of water on the table and tossed the contents on the burning stack.

"Well, that's a day wasted." Mikhail went to the linen cabinet and grabbed a few towels to sop up the mess.

"Not entirely." Mr. Cetanni gave a cunning smile. "What is the single most effective means of teaching?"

Repetition popped into Mikhail's head, but he dared not say it aloud for fear Azgarth might strip the memory of repeatedly tracing the maps from his mind.

"All is never truly lost." Mr. Cetanni watched as the map he worked on suffered a similar fate as the others. The burned paper curled inward at the corners, turning to black ash, crisp and brittle.

"Is something burning?" Henri called from the other side of the room.

"Not any longer. Keep working," Dante answered. "Where does this leave us?"

"Moving to plan B." Mr. Cetanni rose from the chair. "If you will excuse me, I have a man to see across town."

As he walked out, Dante said, "We have a plan B?"

"Apparently so."

"Should someone go with him?" Dante rubbed at his chin. "My gut tells me none of us should be alone for long—even while using the privy."

The words struck Mikhail. Dante was not one given to fear. He embraced the strangeness and tackled it head-on.

"What are you thinking?"

"That it takes very little to snatch one of us into the fae realm. It happened to Mr. Cetanni and we know what condition he was returned to us."

"In all fairness, he admitted to walking into that rift of his own free will."

Dante gave a rusty laugh. "Free will." Mockery dripped from the word like burned candle wax. "I seriously question the last time any of us were able to direct our destinies. We've been manipulated longer than we've ever suspected."

Truth rang in the accusation. How long had they been herded toward this confrontation? Since they had chosen medicine or become interested in reanimating the dead? Had Azgarth watched them, waiting until they showed particular potential, or had it been a single incident that drew his attention? The questions shouldn't bother Mikhail, but they did. Gnawed away at his gut, tiny parasites of thought that feasted on his confidence and sense of self. And he'd fed off their inventions and art more hungrily than even Bram Stoker's monster.

They had entered a house of trap doors and dark passages. No maps to guide them or directions out. Mikhail had never enjoyed not having the answers. He'd pursued medicine and reanimation because he wished to unlock and conquer the greatest mystery of them all.

Dante stood. "I'm going after him. After the way that boy was killed, I don't want to run the risk of Mr. Cetanni suffering the same fate."

"Do you think there is anything you can do to stop it if Azgarth's set his mind to it?"

"I don't know. I'll have to wait and see when and if it happens." With that, Dante was heading out of the room.

Mikhail's heart dropped into his stomach and a knot formed in his throat. His breath came harsh and mind spun as any number of horrible scenarios played through his imagination.

If Mr. Cetanni found trouble, Dante would too, without the benefit of an agent's longevity.

A scene flashed through Mikhail's mind out of time and place. *Dante lying on the ground, facedown, blood pooling around him in the moonlight. A thunder of hooves galloped away from the scene. Mikhail bent over him, unable to catch his breath for the fear and grief.*

A hand touched his shoulder, startling him. "Dr. Stanslovich, are you unwell?"

Mikhail glanced around. The vision faded around him, leaving him sitting where he'd been only moments before. Hallucination? But it had seemed so real. He had smelled the grass and dirt. Tasted rain on the air. Felt the warmth of Dante's skin as well as the absence of breath.

Mikhail stood. "Come. Follow me."

Henri fell into line behind Mikhail as he stalked to Dante's office and the medicine cabinet. He opened the door only to find the morphine gone. Sweat broke out on his back. His hands shook in panic.

"What are you looking for?"

"The morphine! I need it." He pulled out a number of little brown bottles and clear vials, searching the labels, hoping Dante had only hidden it in another container.

"All right. Sit down. I'll bring it to you."

Mikhail stopped his frantic pursuit and took a deep, shaky breath. Anger and betrayal boiled to the surface. "He told you?"

"Yes. But not to shame you. Only to make me aware should you need my help." Henri gave a self-deprecating smile. "And because one day the treatment may be something I'll need to administer in my practice."

To his logical mind, the explanation made sense. To the side shamed by his addiction, the anger continued to simmer.

He sat down and rolled up his sleeve. "He's been reducing the dosage."

"Yes. I know. He's kept me abreast of the changes."

"Damn him," Mikhail huffed under his breath.

"Begging your pardon, but do not think so harshly of Dr. Savoy. He only has your health in mind." Henri went to the bookcase and pulled out a vial hidden behind a copy of an anatomy text.

"He didn't trust me with the medication."

"And by you asking me to administer it to you, tells me you don't trust yourself either."

Truth stung with the lash of a whip. No. He didn't trust himself to administer only the prescribed dose.

Henri competently gave the drug. Mikhail slowly calmed, but he couldn't quite shake the vision in his hallucination. And why now? He'd been off the opium and on the morphine for a few days. Other than sweating and shaking, he'd had no other symptoms. Had the morphine dosage been decreased too quickly?

Henri stood over him with a frown. "You still look pale. Maybe you should lie down for a bit. I can work on the devices alone."

With Dante and Mr. Cetanni gone, there wasn't much else for Mikhail to do—not until he knew what Mr. Cetanni planned. However, the thought of closing his eyes and possibly seeing the vision of Dante lying on the ground dead was enough to keep him stubbornly upright.

"There has to be something I can do while I wait for them to return."

"It's almost time to gather the temperature readings around the fountain and tank."

"I'll do that. Let me sit here for a minute and collect myself." Weakness only added another layer to his shame. He hated for anyone to see him like this, but especially someone in his employ.

No, that was extremely unfair. Henri had progressed to be far more than an employee or assistant. He was a respected and talented member of a very tight circle Mikhail trusted.

As Henri started away, Mikhail grabbed his hand. "I hope you realize how much I appreciate you, though I may not always show it."

Henri grew uncomfortable under the praise. He gently removed his hand from Mikhail's grasp. "I know, or I wouldn't still attend you."

"No, this goes beyond that. You've proved yourself time and again. I don't know what Dante or I would have done these last few months without you."

"I shudder to even contemplate it, Doctor." With that and a nod, Henri went back into the surgery, leaving Mikhail alone with the visions imprinted behind his closed lids.

He glanced out the window. Full daylight continued to paint the city. Sunset was still a few hours away. The vision had taken place in full dark, with a moon large and bright. The full moon was still a few days off. Whatever the portent of the vision, it would not happen that night. Time remained to warn Dante and have him take care.

Disturbed but a little more settled than before, Mikhail rose and went to gather the materials to take temperature readings of the fountain and tank. Tedious, yes, but a very important part of data collection. The more information gathered on the ambient conditions, the better chance they stood of finding a way into the fae realm.

Since the air in the surgery was better controlled than at the fountain, it took no time to take readings and record them in a ledger they'd started for the express purpose. Finished with the surgery, Mikhail stepped out into the garden.

Strange lights twinkled from the hedgerow, thousands of grounded stars in a vast sea of green. Odd that he should see them in full daylight, as if tiny mirrors were positioned throughout the garden. As he moved closer to investigate, the lights winked out.

He rubbed his eyes. Perhaps he'd not given the morphine enough time to work. He shook his head to clear it and moved to the fountain.

Changes in temperature were more easily explained outdoors, but Mikhail had accounted for that by adding a column for variances to explain wind speed and direction at the time of the reading. Those must be taken into account, though a breeze might not drop the temperature by much. A sudden, drastic drop in temperature was more what they'd come to expect from the opening of a rift.

He wrote down the information, careful to record conditions in the garden. The temperature plummeted. Water splashed across the ledger page. Mikhail glanced up, only to find an arm composed entirely of water molecules reaching out to him. It grabbed him with icy fingers and pulled him toward the fountain.

He dug his heels into the ground, pulling backward from the being. How could something comprised of water have such a tenacious hold? It defied every law of physics.

The ledger slipped from his fingers, sucked into the fountain, disappearing into the gurgling water. Mikhail dove into the spray to retrieve it, but it had disappeared, along with the entries they'd made thus far.

One by one, all their attempts to breach the other side of the veil were being eliminated. How long until they were too?

Chapter Seventeen

Roman glanced surreptitiously at Dr. Savoy as they alighted from a hackney. The good doctor had moved with considerable speed to catch Roman. Almost too quickly. The action more what he might expect from a fae than a human.

He sniffed the air. An involuntary response to the scent hidden beneath layers of human decay—a condition associated with being born on this side of the veil. At present, Roman had no time to address the odd phenomena as they stood outside the shop of Aristotle King.

The shop remained closed up tight, though the hour was late for the opening of business. Roman sniffed the air again but caught no scent of fae intervention that might explain the odd circumstance.

"Perhaps there's a back way in," Dr. Savoy suggested.

"Most likely."

They hurried to the alley and came up the back side of the building. A door to a small foyer stood open. Inside were two other doors; one, straight ahead, the other to the left. Roman knocked on the forward-facing door.

"Mr. King. It's Mr. Cetanni and Dr. Savoy. Are you well?"

Dr. Savoy stepped back outside and looked up to the second-story windows. "I ran out of the house so fast I didn't think to bring my medical kit."

"If he's been bit by the *wolfsine,* you may not need it. Azgarth isn't about to let him die."

Dr. Savoy cast a sharp glance to Roman. "He hadn't been bitten yet?"

"If he had, his name would have appeared in my ledger before a few days ago. Generally, the name appears for agents to make contact before the *wolfsine* attacks. It's a way for us to vet those tagged before they're culled. However, I have reason to believe he has prior knowledge of them."

"And what happens if you find they are not up to standard? Are they simply let go?"

Roman turned his head slightly. He had no stomach for the truth Dr. Savoy deserved. The entire affair made him sick. "No. They most assuredly are not."

Silence filled the space between them. The import of the words and those not said grew heavy with significance. The less talented the subject, the more vicious the *wolfsine* attack. Azgarth didn't want what he couldn't use or turn to his satisfaction. His philosophy was the world was better off without mediocrity.

"Have you ever agented such an unfortunate soul?" Dr. Savoy inquired with a harsh whisper. The answer meant a lot to him, and by God and the dark fae he served, Roman hadn't the heart to lie.

"Once or twice, but I stayed with them every moment until the infection had passed." He swallowed down the gorge that rose at the memory of flesh decaying and sloughing off in the bed. He lifted his hand again and pounded on the door—harder this time, expending his hatred and hopelessness on the hapless wood. "Mr. King! Please, we need to speak with you!"

A sound, low and mournful, carried through the door.

"He's been injured." Dr. Savoy took a step back. "Move. I'm going to kick in the door."

Roman gave a nod and took a few steps back with him. "On three."

They counted it down. On three, they charged and led with the legs, kicking at the door and breaking the wood away from the locking mechanism. The door flew open, banging against the wall.

A rush of chemical stench and *wolfsine* filled the hallway.

"God!" Dr. Savoy covered his face with his neckcloth. "Remind me never to take up photography."

Roman led with his nose in the air. "This way. I fear he's badly hurt."

A faint metallic scent of blood gave a counternote to the developing solutions. They found him in his darkroom, lying on the floor, his shoulder and neck rent by fang and claw. Undeveloped plates were shattered around him, lost proof of the fae dimension.

Dr. Savoy bent over the prostrate man. "Mr. King, can you hear me?"

A gurgling sound was the only response.

"Jesus Christ. We have to get him to where I can treat him." Dr. Savoy removed his jacket and began the process of assessing Mr. King's injuries. Roman stood at the ready in case anything was required, but the way he saw it, neither of them knew where supplies were kept or if there were even any in the shop.

"Find me some towels or sheets. Any kind of cloth I can use to bind this wound enough for me to get him to my surgery."

Roman hunted through cabinets and drawers. He found a hamper with dirty rags, but nothing clean.

"From what I can tell, it looks as if the major vessels in the neck have been spared. All this blood seems to have come from smaller ones, and those in the shoulder. Not a happy proposition, but not as dire as could be." Dr. Savoy glanced up. "How is that search coming?"

"Nothing but dirty ones."

"Keep searching. Our jackets won't make for decent bandages."

No. Roman doubted they would. They'd not come prepared for this, and for such an oversight, Roman was heartily sorry. He should have known after all this time; something in his brain should have alerted him to pay closer attention to Mr. King. Not that the *wolfsine* attack could have been avoided, but so he'd not have been alone.

Roman pulled open another cabinet and found a stack of cloths, folded neatly, and placed on the shelf with great care. He grabbed the entire stack and hurried back to Dr. Savoy and Mr. King. "Here. These were all I could find."

"Thank you. Those will do nicely."

Dr. Savoy picked up the top one and snapped it open. He wound it around the shoulder injury, over, under, and around the arm. Blood soaked through the fabric. The crimson stain spread like water on a wet sidewalk, pooling, puddling. Was it just him or had the injury begun to bleed faster after their arrival?

"Damn it! Go hail us a carriage. Immediately. I have to keep holding pressure on the wound. I think my manipulations have burst open a vessel that might have only been partially torn."

That explained the fresh rush of blood.

Roman hurried into the street. No carriages were available in the immediate area. The livery stables were some distance from the lowly street. He had no choice but to return to Dr. Savoy's and collect both the carriage and the medical bag.

He ran down the lane, taking as little time as possible, wishing for once the veil might open and he could take a shortcut through the fae realm. Unfortunately, that service seemed to be reserved for only those who ruled in the land of the fae.

Sounds faded into the background as he traveled—save for the soft clop of hooves that grew closer. Roman dared not turn around and see who followed. Already cold air whispered along the back of his neck. The sensation of frigid air expanded, grew to encompass his entire being. Momentum slowed, until it was hard to go forward.

Wishes were dangerous things.

A gleaming white carriage pulled up alongside him. Roman kept walking, ignoring the conveyance.

"Do you care for a ride?"

Roman lifted a hand. "No. Thank you."

"Now don't be that way, Roman Cetanni." Oiredon's voice lilted down from the driver's box.

The sun beat down brighter than usual. Two albino *callifs* stamped in place, eager to run. Their pink eyes studied Roman with haughty disdain.

"It seems a shame for Mr. King to bleed to death because you are too stubborn to accept a ride." The taunt hit close to the mark.

Roman stopped. "What price for his life? If you help me, am I then beholden to you to help overthrow your brother?"

Oiredon raised a brow. "You have objections when your very soul is on the line?"

"Is it?" Roman knew very well, if the fae brothers stood on the precipice of war, then any communication between himself and Oiredon was fraught with danger. "If Azgarth wants my soul, he's in a fair way to taking it."

"Come now. You know you'd rather be free than live under your master's control." The carriage door opened in invitation. "I have everything you and Dr. Savoy need to save the life of Mr. King."

"If he dies, Dr. Savoy is more than capable of bringing him back to life."

A terrible laugh came from all around Roman. Feline-like eyes watched him from dark recesses.

Oiredon seemed to grow larger on the driver's box. He leaned down into Roman's face. "Why should he *have* to?"

The truth of that statement brought Roman up short. What he hadn't told Dr. Savoy, what his fears were of the degree of attack, was the bite was more retribution than turning. The turning he'd taunted Mr. King with hadn't been the man's own but that of a lover killed years before in front of him. He'd been unable to save the woman, but he'd never forgotten or forgiven himself for his failure.

He'd not let Mr. King share a similar fate.

For better or worse, he gave a nod and threw his lot in with Oiredon.

The carriage door opened of its own accord. Roman peeked inside. White velvet seats, matching curtains, gold flourishes, the inside was as opulent as the outside. On the seat was a white leather doctor's bag. Dr. Savoy would definitely notice the difference, but did it really matter?

He climbed up and took a seat. The door closed behind him. The motion of a fae carriage was not the same as a human one. This conveyance seemed to glide above the cobbles—wheels unnecessary. When Roman glanced out the window, he noticed the scenery went by in a blur, faster than a normal carriage traveled. Oh, he'd entered the fae realm all right. It only remained to be seen if Oiredon allowed him to exit in time to be of use to Dr. Savoy and Mr. King.

Dizziness swirled. Roman closed his eyes. Waves of nausea rose. He'd been driven into a vortex where up and down had lost meaning. The carriage rolled to a stop. He cracked one eye open. The view swam in streams that refused to settle.

He hung his head in his hands. *"What did you do to me?"*

Breath stirred on the back of his neck. Cold. Indifferent. "I untied the bindings placed on you by Azgarth. It can be a bit unsettling."

Roman tried to draw in a lungful of air but failed. The more he panicked, the harder the task. He needed to calm down. To think. Had Oiredon placed his own bindings? Most likely. It wasn't like a fae master to let his servants wander around freely. He'd only replaced one prison for another.

The carriage door opened. Cool air blew in from the street, reviving him. Slowly, his lungs filled. He let out the breath and slid from the seat onto the walk. He reached in for the medical bag.

Time ticked down. How long had he been gone already? Was Mr. King even still alive, or would they need to cart his inert body back to Dr. Savoy's to place in the resurrection tank?

Roman hurried to the back of the business and the door. He slipped inside.

Dr. Savoy glanced up sharply. His gaze strayed to the odd bag. "You've returned fast."

"I had assistance." Roman went down on his knees and opened the kit. "I didn't look inside to see what you've been given."

"Take over holding pressure and I'll look through the bag."

Roman placed his hand where Dr. Savoy's had been covering Mr. King's injury.

"What are these? I can't read the labels." Dr. Savoy made a frantic search of the bag, pulling out vial after vial of substances. He held one up. "Useless."

Roman scanned the handwritten label. Fae script spelled out *regeneration*. "I don't think that one is."

"You can read the label?"

"It says regeneration."

Dr. Savoy frowned. "That's too ambiguous."

"Let me see some of the others."

There were vials for hair growth, talon removal, wart restoration, runny nose, dyspepsia, wall-eyes, wattle neck, and halitosis. Given the current situation, only one seemed even remotely feasible. "Go with the regeneration. If it doesn't work, you aren't any worse off."

Dr. Savoy raised a brow. "You say that knowing this comes from the fae realm. It might grow an extra head for all we know."

"Use it!" Roman commanded with more force than he'd intended. "If you only knew what I compromised to get back here so quickly, you'd not scoff at the offerings."

Dr. Savoy went still, taking in the admission, and then his shoulders slumped. "What have you done?"

"What I did was make a tough choice. Know I did it in order to save Mr. King and any information he might possess."

"No matter how noble your motives, did you even weigh the consequences? How will this impact those who count on your protection?" Fury put lines around Dr. Savoy's mouth and narrowed his eyes.

"I've done much worse than save a life in my time. I'll find a way to make it right if it all goes sideways. What choice did I have? Imposing on you and Dr. Stanslovich to resurrect yet another dead body didn't seem fair when I had the means within me to keep him alive." Even now, blood soaked through the towel, baptizing Roman's hands in proof that life was a tenuous concept.

Roman nodded to the puddle growing between his fingers. "You better decide now if you wish to use it or not."

Dr. Savoy removed the lid, releasing a repulsive stench into the air. The doctor made a face. "Lift your hands so I can pour it into the wound."

"Get closer and we'll do it at the same time."

Dr. Savoy scooted in a bit. "Now."

Roman lifted his hands, taking the blood-soaked towel with him. A gaping wound stared up at him. Bone and muscle visible in the rent flesh.

Dr. Savoy tilted the bottle and poured the contents into the injury. "I have no idea how much to use."

"I don't think it matters. Either it works or it doesn't."

They stared in silent fascination as the open skin knitted back together, first blood vessels reattached themselves, lacing under the sinew and muscle. Next, the shredded pieces of muscle fused and mended. Last the layers of flesh. The only thing left behind was the blood, covering the skin where they had held pressure.

"Impressive." Dr. Savoy prodded the area. "He's still lost a lot of blood. We need to get him back to my house so I can monitor him."

Roman rose. "You get him to the carriage out front. Let me look for the photographs we came for."

"Please hurry."

Roman waved him away. "If you have to leave me, then do. Trust the driver to get you where you need to be."

Dr. Savoy gave him a questioning look as he leaned over and picked up Mr. King and hoisted him over a shoulder. "I'll wait for a few minutes, but no more than that."

"Fair enough."

Roman went to work, once again opening cabinets and drawers, this time in search of photographic plates. They were stacked according to location, or so it appeared. None of the plates taken at Dr. Savoy's were present. Had Mr. King not developed them yet? The possibility did exist that Mr. King didn't place the same importance on the project as did Roman.

Undeterred, he continued to search.

The light dimmed. Either from a cloud blocking the sun, or the passage of time, he wasn't sure. What he did know was the knock that sent him sailing across the room, broke a few ribs on impact. He slid down the wall, gasping for breath as Azgarth stood over him with the taint of revenge shimmering in the air.

Nicholas sat up in a panic.

Roman! Something is wrong with Roman.

After returning from the disaster he found at his home, he had decided to nap. He'd been exhausted after the day's ordeals. The usual disquieted dreams didn't plague him and he had slept soundly, until a vision of Roman falling through a dark eternity came to him. Roman's mouth hung open on a scream Nicholas could not hear.

Fear became a fine tremor in his hands. He slid off the bed and hurried through the house, shouting Roman's name. Dr. Stanslovich met him on the landing.

"Mr. Cetanni isn't here."

"We have to find him." Panic threatened to close his throat.

"He'll be along shortly. Dr. Savoy has returned with an injured Mr. King. Mr. Cetanni remained behind to search for the photographic plates. There's no need for alarm."

"Yes, there is. He's fallen. I know it as surely as I know I died. Please. He's in grave danger."

Dr. Stanslovich leaned over the banister. "Dante. Come here. Quickly."

Dr. Savoy appeared at the bottom of the stairs. "What is it?"

"Mr. Alexandre is worried for Mr. Cetanni. He is convinced Cetanni has run afoul of something."

Dr. Savoy closed his eyes. His color drained, and he started for the door. "I'll go back for him. Please see to Mr. King."

Dr. Stanslovich turned grave eyes Nicholas's way. "What exactly did you see? Not that I place any credence in portentous dreams."

No, of course he didn't. "Just as I've already explained. A black hole and Roman falling into it." He brushed his hair back with a shaking hand, resting his palm on top. "He might have been screaming, but I couldn't hear him."

"All right. Try to stay calm. Dante... Dr. Savoy has gone back for him." Dr. Stanslovich helped Nicholas back to the suite. "Try to rest a bit more before they return. It might be they pass one another on the street and it will all be resolved in minutes."

No matter how much Nicholas wanted to take that advice, it failed to ring true.

Alone with his thoughts, he had no intention of sleeping. He might not have stamina at the moment, but he had plenty of determination. How was he to save Roman when he didn't even know his location? Only Roman had known Mr. King's direction. He'd not revealed that information to anyone else.

"Why, Azgarth?" Nicholas challenged the fae master. There was no one else to blame. One did not fall into a dark pit of nothingness for no reason. Azgarth was always behind such misfortunes.

No answer came.

Not surprising. Azgarth also didn't deign to answer lowly humans when he didn't feel the need. Still, there was an odd emptiness right in the very center of Nicholas's soul. It wasn't there when he'd lain down for his nap. He'd only felt it, plunging into his body like a knife when the image of Roman being swallowed by darkness had come to him.

A vulnerability he'd not remembered feeling since before they'd fled Russia filled him. That sense of being without protection or anchor continued to grow, seeping into the very morrow of his bones.

A knock sounded on the door.

"Who is it?"

"Mr. Vauss...Henri."

"Enter."

The door opened to reveal Dr. Stanslovich's assistant. He wore a curious expression that did nothing to relieve Nicholas's fear. "What is it?"

Flags of red stained Henri's cheeks. "I took the liberty of setting up your canvases and paints."

"Thank you. I appreciate the gesture."

Henri held up a hand. "No. You don't understand. Please, follow me and I'll show you."

Intrigued, Nicholas followed Henri down the stairs to the second level and a small parlor of sorts. Inside were three canvases that had been bare that morning, but now showed the most amazing scenes of the fae court. In every one of them, Roman stood before those gathered as if on trial.

"No. Tell me this isn't true." He touched his hand to the canvas. Paint covered his fingers. Fresh. Sticky.

"It might only be meant to goad you. Try to look at the paintings objectively, maybe we can find a clue as to what they mean." Even though it sounded like an attempt at being helpful, Henri had no idea what he asked.

"All I can see is Roman in trouble. Nothing else matters at the moment."

"I understand how you feel, but please try. These occurrences aren't random. They are structured to provide us with information."

Nicholas ran a hand through his hair. "I know. It's just hard to figure what some fae being's reason is for using my canvas and paints. Why not write us a letter? Or show us a vision?"

He studied the paintings but didn't find one single stroke of the brush that told any story but that Roman was at Azgarth's mercy.

Chapter Eighteen

Darkness gave way to light. Blinding, brain-stabbing light. Roman rubbed his eyes, then tried to stand. Shackles clanked as he moved. The iron weighed him down, made it hard to keep his feet. It wanted to drag him back down to the marble floor.

When he finally managed to open his eyes, he wished the light had struck him blind. He stood in the middle of Azgarth's grand ballroom. Courtiers pressed in from all sides. Their painted faces hidden behind decorative fans and ringed fingers. Whispers grew as he stood in the center of the room, the object of their full attention and scorn.

He lifted his head. He might be damned for his decisions, but he'd take the punishment with dignity and pride.

Pain radiated from his broken ribs. He'd not be allowed to escape this place without feeling immeasurable pain. It was his penance. He lifted his head and looked to the throne.

Azgarth sat draped across the seat, languid in repose. Though he looked relaxed, Roman knew he was filled with anticipation for the punishment to come.

He blinked and Azgarth shifted, sitting up straight.

"My beautiful courtiers, you see before you a horrible wretch of a human. I've given him everything, and in return, he sides with my brother." Azgarth slapped the armrests of his golden throne and stood. *"My brother!"*

Roman swallowed.

"What say you, my loyal subjects? What is his punishment to be?"

Courtiers called out varied and heinous acts Azgarth was known to visit on those who fell out of favor.

Azgarth held his hand behind one ear as if having trouble hearing the choices put before him. "Nothing that will kill him too quickly for there is much amusement to be had in watching him suffer."

"The pit!" The suggestion came from over near one of the windows overlooking the gallery.

Not the pit. There were so many awful and terrible things down in the pit. Too many crevices each with their own horror to choose from.

Azgarth clapped. "The pit. Shall we just chuck him in and see where he lands?"

The courtiers yelled a resounding yes.

Roman fell through the floor and into darkness. The rank scent of decayed flesh filled his nostrils, causing him to gag. The action of retching put pressure on his sore ribs. He held a hand to them, splinting as best he could.

Unlike the room near the acid bowl, the air was cold, bitingly so. If he'd been able to see in front of his face, he might have appreciated the curl of his warm breath as it wafted into the air on little puffs.

A steady drip of water kept a constant beat. Its echo filled the chamber. Judging from the resonance of the sound, he could make out a rough estimate of the room's size.

But that stench. He'd smelled plenty of dead things in his long life, but this had a decided flavor of still being half alive. An underlying quality of tissue not yet tainted by the hand of disease.

A feeling of not being alone prickled up his spine.

He turned around but saw nothing save unrelieved black. A few shuffling steps and he ran into a protrusion in the floor. He reached out and rubbed his hand across the prickly surface. The slim column ended in a point about waist high. A spike. His heart dropped and stomach turned sour.

He'd fallen into Azgarth's oubliette.

Not as final a punishment as falling into the acid pit, but it ranked up there on Azgarth's list of favorites. How to escape such an impenetrable place, Roman had no idea. Add to his problems a couple of bad ribs and it didn't make for an easy climb out. If that might even be managed. How he'd fallen in without impaling himself on any of the spikes amazed and confounded him.

Azgarth had seemed rather furious on learning Roman had changed allegiances. But then he had said he'd wanted to draw out Roman's death. What if it had been Oiredon's influence?

If Oiredon had intervened when Azgarth cast Roman into the oubliette, then perhaps he'd made other plans of escape as well. A search might very well be worth the effort in this case. He'd have to search by touch and scent. He had no other resources at the moment. The darkness was so complete, his eyes never adjusted. In order to do so, there had to be some source of light. Here in the lower bowels of Azgarth's prison, light was forbidden.

Roman leaned against one of the spikes, crossing his legs at the ankles. He needed to contemplate his problem. Where to start? Feeling around the edges of the structure seemed a waste of time. Though he was not a short man, he still had no way to reach the top of the oubliette. He doubted there were any secret passages or doorways out. An escape by that means was even too bold for Oiredon to orchestrate.

The spike Roman leaned against moved. "What?"

Had it broken? He'd felt or heard no crack as the material gave way. Roman got down on his knees, holding his ribs as he moved. The spike sat on a track. Down near the base, he felt a lever. When the lever was pushed in, it allowed the spike to move along the track. Now, if he could push all the spikes into one area, he might be able to use them to stand upon, reach the edge of the oubliette, and pull himself out. Provided he didn't fall and do more damage to himself than a couple of bruised or broken ribs.

One by one, he began to move all the spikes to one side of the chamber. With that task completed, he climbed up on the structures, balancing as carefully as he could along two or three spikes per foot. He felt like an unsure performer in a demented circus act. Walking across the tops of the spikes required a steadier foot than he possessed at the moment, but he hadn't a choice. Either he did so, or he died. Simple as that.

Since he had no intention of dying and leaving all his clients to fend for themselves against an angry Azgarth, he had to get climbing. Gingerly, he moved to the wall and felt in front of him. The surface was smooth with very little hand or footholds. None of the crevices were wide enough to place his foot—at least not while in a shoe. He dared not take his shoes off for fear of sending the spikes through the bottom of his feet. All the while, his side ached with a fierceness that nearly blotted out rational thought. If he moved the wrong way, he winced and guarded in pain. He simply had to forge on and pretend the pain wasn't there. Take as deep a breath as he was able and thrust the ache away.

Easier said than done. He wanted to scream in agony.

Slowly, he rose, stretching his arms over his head to feel along the wall face, trying to find a ledge. Pain shot down his side as his injured ribs slid and popped. His loud cry sounded harsh in the enclosed space. Each subsequent breath came hard and fast.

"Do not lose consciousness, man. You only have this one chance to make it out."

He doubted he had the strength or wherewithal to do this more than once should he fail in this attempt. He stretched a bit more, finally feeling where the lip of the oubliette began. Not much room to grab onto, but he'd have to make do. He gripped the edge as tightly as he could, then kicked off first one then the other shoe and walked up the face of the wall.

Sweat ran down into his eyes—not that he could see a damn thing. The salt burned, and he almost lost his grip. His side screamed in agonizing pain. White hot and enough to make him forget to breathe.

Finally, he located the edge of the wall with his toes and pulled himself up with his arms. By the time he landed on the ledge, he was exhausted and soaked through with perspiration.

Darkness continued to surround him. He had no idea if there were more chambers such as the one he'd escaped. Perhaps there were others dotting the pitch-black landscape, waiting to capture him again. He'd not put it past Azgarth to devise a place devoid of light but riddled with death traps.

The pit tortured by the nature of its ever-changing construction. One never knew what might be done there or what to expect.

Roman used his sense of smell to guide him through. A distinct scent of death filled the air whenever he came close to another hole. Some of them smelled fresher than others, meaning the corpses therein were not long since dead. Must have been a very busy time for Azgarth. He was punishing transgressors with frightening regularity.

He kept moving forward, trying not to pay attention to whatever it was that squished under his feet. Some of the little buggers crawled over his feet. He shook them off and kept going.

Each time he believed he'd made it to the end of the larger, upper chamber, the wall seemed to move back a ways. This was the real danger of falling into the fae realm—walking forever and never quite getting to the end.

He kept his hand along the left wall as a means to help guide him through the passage. Moving forward in complete darkness with only sound and scent to show the way stretched his abilities. It also wore him down.

The passage ended without warning.

Roman moved both hands along the surface of the dead end before him. Had he made a wrong turn when he came up from the oubliette? A hint of air moved against his hands. There had to be an opening somewhere in the vicinity.

He lifted his hand, following the flow of air. His fingers met rough stone. A crack between two large slabs allowed air to move down a passage of some sort. Whether the crack was merely a fissure or a hint of a larger cavity behind the wall, he knew not. Above the split was another stone that fit awkwardly with the others. Judging from the feel, it was a different kind of stone, this one smooth as glass. Some of the other agents he knew had the ability to feel the vibrations in stone. He was not one such man, though the talent would be handy at the moment.

He pushed on it. A decided click echoed through the room. Roman straightened away from the structure as movement began all around him. Light bled in on the sides, giving a hint to his surroundings. Wedges of the wall shifted this way and that, spinning and turning. He glanced around, unable to believe his eyes. The part of Azgarth's dungeon where the oubliettes were housed was so much more than Roman had ever imagined. It appeared as if he were trapped inside a giant puzzle box. As the parts moved into a new configuration, giving him a break from total darkness, he tried to glean something of the new set.

Too soon, the darkness returned.

Mikhail heard the carriage pull up in front and Dante shouting. He'd not heard the words, only the intent. Whatever he'd found when he went back to Mr. King's shop was bad indeed.

Mr. Alexandre appeared at the top of the stairs. Mikhail used a hand signal to stall him there. Now was not the time for the painter to take a tumble down the stairs because he didn't wait for help.

Mikhail threw open the door and rushed outside. Dante carried Mr. Cetanni over his shoulder like a sack of laundry. "Let me help."

"I've got him for now. Open the doors for me and help me when I put him on the exam table. He's broken a few ribs and I don't know what all else. There's a cut on his head, near to where one of those damn beetles got him."

"The poor man has no luck but bad." Mikhail opened the door to the surgery. One table was already taken up with the sleeping form of Mr. King. "You're going to need to open your own hospital in order to care for all those being tormented and injured by the fae."

Dante stood near the exam table. He tilted forward as Mikhail eased Mr. Cetanni into a supine position. The injuries didn't appear too bad from the outside, and he was alive. Respirations were normal and his heartbeat was strong, steady. The veins in his neck were soft, supple, no distention. His stomach soft.

"He might only be knocked out, Dante. I'm finding no external evidence that he's been injured more severely than the broken ribs. If he has a head injury, it's all internal." Even the cut along Mr. Cetanni's temple had no bruising or lumps under the skin. "I suggest we monitor him and interview him when he wakes."

"Normally, I'd agree. However, he may have done something—nay; he *did* do something to anger Azgarth." Dante lifted Mr. Cetanni's lids and flashed a light into them. There was little to no reaction. "He's thrown his lot in with Oiredon."

"And these are the consequences." Mikhail made a survey of the man from head to foot. He placed his hands on his hips and stepped back from the exam table. "Then there is nothing we can do until whatever spell he's fallen under wears off or he's released."

"You have to do something," Mr. Alexandre said from the doorway. He was pale as a sheet. His cheeks appeared sunken. Dark circles ringed his eyes. "You can't leave him like this."

Mikhail placed a restraining hand on Mr. Alexandre's arm. "We haven't the means to bring him from whatever stupor he's fallen into. Even if the problem is physical, he'll wake when he is able."

Mr. Alexandre tore his arm away and took a seat next to Mr. Cetanni. "Do not die on me. I will not allow us to be separated by worlds or the fae."

The passionate words tugged at Mikhail's heart. To be loved like that—he'd never want for anything more. When was the last time he'd been the focus of such devotion? To his surprise, he failed to remember one person in his life to ever fall on a sword for him. Not that he wanted a lover to risk all for him, but it might be nice to know someone cared as much.

Feeling the weight of regard upon him, Mikhail glanced up to catch Dante's eye. He was also moved by the uninhibited show of affection.

Into the quiet tension, Henri carried a canvas. Images on it were odd to say the least. A man stood in the middle of a dark room with jagged edges of a wall in front of him. Light came in around the stones in a zigzag pattern.

"What is that?" Mikhail pointed to the painting. "Is that a new work, Mr. Alexandre?"

Mr. Alexandre glanced up and then stood. "Roman."

"What do you mean?" Dante came forward, putting his hand out to steady Mr. Alexandre should the excitement prove too much after his illness.

"That's Roman. He's trapped. We have to get to him."

"How? So far, all of our plans to travel to the fae realm have met with disaster." Mikhail had no intentions of mounting another expedition until they knew their plans were solid. They had to take into consideration how to get there, but also how to get back.

Mikhail came around the table, shifting the canvas to better see the impression. He studied the painting closer. An idea formed. "Of course. Why didn't I see it before?"

"See what?" Dante glanced up, then back down at the image. His gaze skated over the surface.

"This is simple communication from the fae realm. When the telegraphs were invented, people marveled at the ability for two-way communication between points A and B. Since there are no telegraph poles between London and the fae realm, the beings on the other side had to find another way. What we've been seeing as clues—and they might be that as well—is them trying to get a telegram to us." Mikhail looked to Henri. He was the only one with enough wit and intelligence in that area to manage what Mikhail was about to propose. "We need to find a way to send messages back to them."

Dante narrowed his eyes. "Don't you think they already know? Everything we've done has been under the scrutiny of Azgarth and I'm not sure how frequently we're seen by this Oiredon character."

"It might not matter." Mikhail turned both ways, looking over his shoulder at the desktops. "Where is the map to Azgarth's palace?"

"It should be on the table. Perhaps slipped between the pages of the book." Dante went to the desk and rifled through the papers. When he found it, he held it up. "It's here."

Mikhail gave them all a smile. "This is the information we'll feed to the other side. Transmit it to Mr. Cetanni. If he *is* trapped in there, he needs to find his way out."

"And how do you propose we get the information to him?" Dante raised a brow. "Provided he doesn't already know the way."

"The light box theory." Mikhail turned on the light and held it up. "The same way one might use light to trace silhouettes on paper."

Henri caught onto the scheme. A myriad of ideas shone in his eyes. "We will need to make the map larger. Instead of putting it on paper, use a large sheet of glass. I can set up a lens above the light source and we can project the image of the map wherever you wish."

"The tank," Dante suggested. "We already know it conducts images from the fae realm. We make it work for us."

From the corner of his eye, Mikhail watched as Mr. Alexandre lifted Mr. Cetanni's hand and kissed his knuckles, then pressed the limp hand to his cheek. "We'll get you out of there. I

promise."

Mikhail brushed his hair back with a shaky hand. If he had a way to go back in time and tell his younger self to leave his heart and mind open to possibilities no matter how fantastic, he'd gladly take the chance and go.

His thinking had changed so much since his first brush with Azgarth. So many things had been seen and experienced. Too many to account for by his former set of beliefs. Oh, he still believed and trusted in science—and who was to say that the magic of the fae realm wasn't some form of higher science the human world had yet to discover? Future generations might very well develop ways to transport themselves through the veils of multidimensions.

"All right." Mikhail clapped his hands together. "Henri, you get started on the projection equipment. I'll secure a piece of glass large enough for our purposes. And Mr. Alexandre, I'll have need of your skills to paint the map in question."

Mr. Alexandre stared at Mikhail as if he'd lost what little mind had not been transformed through heavy drug use. In truth, Mikhail had traced that map enough that if he closed his eyes he could recall every black line and detail. However, his point was to not only include the artist in their efforts, but to give him something to do except worry.

"I know you want to be of comfort to Mr. Cetanni, but you'll feel much better if you keep your hands and mind busy."

Mr. Alexandre gave a stiff nod of agreement. He went back to giving Mr. Cetanni encouragement in low, intimate tones.

Dante came up behind Mikhail and placed a hand on his shoulder. "Leave him be for now. There's plenty of time for him to begin work. Come. I know where we can obtain a glass plate for our purposes."

Mikhail followed Dante through the house and out to a storage area on the other side of the garden wall, situated between Dante's residence and the neighbor's. He took out a key and unlocked the door. The wooden door opened on squeaky hinges.

Dust and cobwebs abounded. The air smelled stale and heavy. "I haven't come out here in a long time. There's not much call to. The gardener uses another shed on the other side of the property for his tools."

The little building sat abandon by time. Ravaged by the elements, it lived in a state somewhere between neglect and decay.

Mikhail raised a skeptical brow. "If you have any glass in here, I'm sure it's broken by now."

"Nonsense." Dante brushed the suggestion away. "No one ever comes out here to break it."

"Things can happen whether they are witnessed or not. All it takes is one old piece of wood to rot and give way to gravity, fall and hit the glass to break it." Mikhail surveyed the interior of the shed. His eyes adjust slowly to the dim light. Remnants of a former life lay scattered and forgotten amid layers of dust and grime. Water had seeped into the structure, encouraging mold and lichen to grow on various objects. Old picture frames, furniture, travel trunks, carriage wheels, an odd assortment of junk were included in the piles of debris.

"Did this all come with the house?"

"Most of it, yes. There are a few items brought over from my previous residence, though why I kept them I can't rightly remember." Dante moved what appeared to have once been a chair frame out of his way. He stepped around that and came up against a large wardrobe. "Help me shift this. The glass plate is in the back near the loom."

"For God and country, why don't you sell some of this?" Mikhail stooped to grab hold of the lower half of the wardrobe.

Dante peeked around the other side, squatted down in a similar fashion. "Because some of it belonged to family members and I dare not part with it."

"I never figured you for the sentimental type."

The comment annoyed Dante if the look on his face was any indication. "Lift on three."

They counted together. On three, they lifted. The wardrobe was heavier than it looked. They only needed to shift it a few feet in order to make their way back to where an old abandon loom sat near the far wall. Dark shapes moved in the darkness. Not bleed-over from the fae realm. No, these occupants were very much of the human world. Their little feet made scratching noises as they ran for cover.

Mikhail followed behind Dante as they wended their way through generations of lost items. He picked up a vase here, teakettle there. No rhyme or reason had been used on what objects were stored, or even a basic order. It appeared they were all tossed in and the contents shaken, then sprinkled with dust.

As they grew closer, a faint reflection of light on glass sparkled from between the loom and the wall.

"I set it there to keep it somewhat secure," Dante explained as he grabbed the end of it and slid it out from its hiding place.

"But why is it here at all?"

"At one time, I thought to renovate the office and place a large window there, looking out into the garden. It's too dark in there most of the time. As I got further into my research, I decided I liked the privacy a closed environment afforded me."

The glass came free, and Mikhail hurried to hold one end while they carried it from the shed.

Grime covered the plate. Seasons full of rodent droppings, spores, and God knew what else, covered the surface. Cleaning the damn thing was going to be a major project.

They finally got the glass into the house. Dante set it on the long table in the kitchen.

"I better clean this quick before Mrs. Stooks lays an egg."

If Mikhail knew Dante's cook, she was going to cause her employer bodily harm for putting that dirty piece of filth on her clean table.

Dante returned to the room a few moments later, carrying a container of vinegar and some rags. "Mrs. Stooks is also not going to be pleased I pinched her vinegar for a cleaning agent."

"I think in this instance she might forgive you." Mikhail took one of the rags and doused it in the pungent liquid.

They worked for a while in silence. Grime came off onto the rags in long streaks. More than one pass was going to be needed before the glass would be ready to use.

Feeling the quiet regard of Dante on him, Mikhail looked up. "What?"

"Just remembering a certain class at university and a long night of dissection."

Mikhail smiled at the memory. They had been students at the time. Eager to make their mark and earn a place among the best and brightest. They had formed a lasting bond over a corpse, ironic how their paths should lead them where it did.

"We're a long way from the eagerness of youth. I feel we've more than proved ourselves capable healers."

Dante pursed his lips and looked down at the glass as he cleaned.

"You don't believe that?"

Dante took some of the vinegar and poured it on the glass. "I think we are in way over our heads. When the most skeptical of the lot of us proposed to communicate with the fae realm by sending over projections of maps, the world has indeed gone mad."

Mikhail could not hide his sour expression fast enough.

Dante pounced. "You don't believe this is going to work?"

"In a word, no. I have my doubts, but I would as soon try to give the appearance of an attempt to Mr. Alexandre. This is as much about his peace of mind as it is an experiment in our abilities to breach the fae realm on our own."

Dante made big, sweeping streaks with the rag. Dirt and green mold ran and smeared. "When I think what Roman sacrificed to try to save Mr. King...I am humbled."

Roman?

Mikhail knew a pinch of jealousy. When had those two become intimates? Instead of calling attention to the breach of propriety, Mikhail continued to clean and contemplate their next move. If this didn't work, what were they going to do? What could they do? Mr. Cetanni might have sacrificed himself to the other fae master, Oiredon, but the link hadn't provided them any protection as yet. Nor a way in.

Chapter Nineteen

Nicholas studied the map. Underneath the schematic depicting Azgarth's castle were lines written in a bold, masculine script. Not many of the words were visible. Only a few here and there, but enough that he recognized it for someone's attempt to make sense of the events of the past few days.

So much had happened he scarcely believed he remained awake and not plunged into the midst of an odd dream, though he'd lived a few years under Azgarth's watchful eyes and he knew very well the fae were real.

The glass plate he'd use for his canvas to transfer the map was the size of a large window. The surface imperfect, but it made the work more of a challenge. As did the fact his hands were still stiff, a residual from his ordeal. It hadn't been but only a few days since he'd woken from the resurrection tank to a new life.

Henri wandered over, wiping his grimy hands on a towel. He stared down at the glass. "Do you plan to use the entire surface for the map?"

"I believe that was the point. To use as much of the surface as possible so it will project and be seen farther."

Henri held up a hand in surrender. "That wasn't an attack on your artistry, I only wanted to know so I can get a rough estimate of the size bed I need for the projector."

Nicholas frowned. He'd not meant to snap at Henri. "My apologies."

Henri patted him on the back in an absent manner. His attention riveted to the glass.

"I believe I know how Dr. Stanslovich feels when he realizes you have an idea forming."

The corner of Henri's mouth curled into a knowing smile. "Sometimes, I do that just so he remembers how valuable I really am."

"Oh, I know. Trust me." Dr. Stanslovich entered the surgery. His shirtsleeves were rolled up to the elbows and hair mused as if he'd run his hands through it a thousand times. "But Mr. Alexandre is right. You have that look."

"Yes. And you are going to love my idea. Not as much as Mr. Alexandre, but you'll love it." With that, Henri started away.

"Where are you going?" Dr. Stanslovich called out.

"To find a place to sell me some telescope lenses." Henri stopped and turned back to look at Nicholas. "Do not start working on that glass yet. If anything, use one maybe an eighth that size."

"An eighth?" Dr. Stanslovich stared at the glass plate with concern. "Where are we going to get that?"

Dr. Savoy rose from where he'd been working at a desk. "I saw some in Mr. King's shop."

"If you're suggesting we take one from his shop, I have some very strong feelings against that sort of pilfering." Nicholas raised a brow. After the way his servants cleaned him out, he'd never steal from another. Not even if the reason was for the common good.

"I am not." Dr. Savoy's gaze narrowed. "I am suggesting we get what we need and pay him for them. He can purchase more to refill his supply."

That more than pacified Nicholas's sense of justice. Paying for the plates was an acceptable compromise. "All right. I will agree to that."

"Glad to hear it." Dr. Savoy started for the door. "I'll procure the plates while Henri is gone."

Nicholas sat down. He picked up the map and traced the lines with his finger. In all the times he'd been to the palace, he'd never seen some of the rooms. At least not that he remembered. But then Azgarth only let his chosen see what he wanted them to. There was no such thing as wandering around or taking an unguided tour.

Flashes of dreamscapes filled his head. A long gallery of paintings. A rooftop garden. An operation in the middle of the grand ballroom. All around him a red veil that kept him from seeing too much, or too clearly.

"Are you unwell, Mr. Alexandre?" Dr. Stanslovich placed a warm hand on Nicholas's shoulder.

"Only contemplating my memories of my time in the fae realm. The time between life, death, and new life."

"What about it?"

Nicholas kept his own counsel on what he'd seen. He didn't want to pry the lid off those memories. Something dark and hateful lurked there. Something Azgarth had not wanted him to see.

But was he still under Azgarth's rule? If what Dr. Savoy said was true, Oiredon had liberated Roman from Azgarth's service and thus all those he commanded. Nicholas was now free of the dark fae master. It felt different and yet not. The sensation had shifted, but not completely gone away. Pressure from his association with Azgarth still lived in a tight ball under his sternum.

Perhaps with a trip to the fae realm, he might be able to find what Azgarth hid.

Mikhail separated himself from the group. He needed time alone to think. Things were moving in an odd direction—one he'd helped along. Perhaps he shouldn't have encouraged the thought they might communicate with those living on the other side of the veil, but he'd be damned if he would sit idly by and appear as if he did nothing.

Really, he didn't know which was worse.

Dealing in the impossible or obscure had been his stock and trade since medical school. Bringing the dead back to life wasn't exactly an occupation most men aspired to. It put him several rungs above a shopkeeper, but many more below the upper classes. Not that he worried where he came on the social ladder. It was more in how he might be perceived.

Horrible to think a man of his status and education might worry of how others saw him—especially when that same man had spent months in a drug den.

He picked up the list he'd been making earlier and studied it carefully.

Guideposts. Lanterns in the darkness. He'd been brought to this point through constant contact with otherworldly beings. Had they set a path for him? If so, had he followed it to their specifications?

Did he even want to?

The struggle of free will versus fulfilling the wants of a fae being took its toll. If they all agreed to pay no attention to the fae, would they be left alone? Was it because of the fact Valentine had entered their sphere in a violent way, they were dragged into the middle of the maelstrom? Not that he regretted saving Valentine, but the act of saving him had drawn attention to them as they hadn't been in years.

Too bad he hadn't taken as much care to record the dates, times, and other ambient conditions of his experiences as he had with the subjects in the resurrection tank. Information might have been lost, a way to connect the occurrences beyond that of random one-way communication.

Movement from the corner of his eye captured his attention. Oiredon stood there in all his golden glory, a frown firmly on his elven features.

"You worry over unimportant matters when the fate of the worlds hangs in the balance."

Mikhail hadn't the power to keep his gaze on Oiredon for long. The light shone too bright. "Trying to figure out a way to send messages back through the veil is not an unimportant matter."

"It will take more than that to assist in my endeavor."

"If you're after my soul, you'll have to queue up."

"I cannot claim that until I have the allegiance of your agent." Oiredon lifted an elegant hand to inspect his fingernails.

For that, Mikhail set the list aside. "You know the name of my agent?"

"Of course. What kind of master would I be if I didn't keep a running tally of all those who my brother has conscripted into his ranks?"

"I'll have a name."

Oiredon gave a cagey smile. He wagged his finger at Mikhail. "Not until I have your solemn promise to side with me in the coming conflict."

"I give my oath and Azgarth arranges my premature death. I've done my research into these matters."

Oiredon waved his hand as if his brother's threats meant nothing.

"We know about the boy—the Watcher—who was killed. If he's picking on those of your own kind, he shouldn't have any compunction about killing one human doctor."

"True, but he can't afford to. You are too valuable to him. You see you and your Dr. Savoy keep him very entertained by bringing back the dead. The first of your kind to do so successfully, though there have been those throughout the world who have tried. You're a banquet for him." Oiredon raised a brow.

"The art of reanimation is being discussed in medical schools and symposiums. It might be a relatively new discipline, but it is gaining some notice." Not all of it good, but Mikhail did not share that information. Besides, Oiredon probably already knew. "What did you come here for, if not to taunt?"

Oiredon's expression grew serious. "Roman is being held in the heart of Azgarth's dungeon. A place known as the box. It shifts and changes configurations with regularity."

"He's in the surgery. I've examined him myself." Mikhail frowned. Guilt that he'd not truly believed Mr. Alexandre's fear sat like a stone in his gut.

"His body may be, but his mind is indeed trapped."

Mikhail took a deep breath in an attempt to calm himself. "How did he get there?"

"A miscalculation on my part, I am afraid. However, I am unable to assist him to guide him out of the box."

"So much for your influence and protection."

"You misunderstand me. My power is null in the depths of the dungeons. I know where he is, but I cannot send him a message or render aid. It's damn frustrating to be powerless." Oiredon made a face to show his distaste. "Now I know how humans feel. I don't believe I care for it."

Mikhail leaned back in the chair and crossed his arms. "You also know how we feel when we realize we're under the control of a race that can bend time and space."

The frown deepened. "I suppose so."

Mikhail leapt to his feet, all angry energy and smoldering resentment. "You suppose so! You suppose so! Well, isn't that just a grand concession on your part? You and your brother decide who is worthy of your regard and you have them bitten by an animal out of a damn nightmare, then seize control of their lives so completely they—we—don't know if any of our achievements or ideas are really our own or a construct you've controlled. You might need us for sustenance, but I assure you, humans don't need you."

Oiredon gave a haughty look but offered no other outward proof of offense. "Do you still know so little of how the bite from the *wolfsine* works?"

"Honestly, at this particular moment, I don't fucking care."

"You are a very passionate man, Mikhail Stanslovich."

"Which is what I thought drove me all along. Then I discover I'm beholden to your brother for all my scientific discoveries. Quite a blow to the old pride." Mikhail paced away from Oiredon before he put his hands around his pale, slender throat and choked the living hell out of him.

He stopped to turn around and pace the other way, only to look up and find Oiredon had moved in front of him.

"You labor under a misconception, my friend." Oiredon lifted his hand and rested it on Mikhail's shoulder. Stray energy from the fae realm sparkled around them, tingling through Mikhail's flesh as current runs through copper wire.

"Really? How so?"

"The thoughts, ideas, innovations, and inventions you conceive are all a part of you. None of it comes from the fae realm. What need do we have of your devices or medical advances when we have magic? We don't. This is your world. You shape it as you see fit and by seeing what it needs to run better. We are not of this world. Your achievements might amuse us, but we do not benefit from them."

"And the arts? We have a musician and an artist here who do not create to advance mankind, but to embellish it. Do you get anything from them?"

Here Oiredon graced Mikhail with a benevolent smile. "Oh, yes. We get to see into the human heart."

"And that is important to the fae?"

"Perhaps not all of them. My brother…" Oiredon paused either for dramatic effect or to find the words, Mikhail wasn't positive which. "He lost his heart a long time ago. Taken. Stolen by a mortal."

"He has no heart?" The thought rather shocked Mikhail. Being a physician, he found it hard to believe anything that looked so human could live without a heart. Then again, he knew nothing about fae physiology.

"In the way we think of them." The mysterious answer hung on the air.

Curiosity almost made Mikhail ask for him to elaborate, but he didn't wish to feel any sympathy for Azgarth, not even to solve a biological quandary. "So why have you come? Are you here to offer assistance in breaching the veil?"

"Yes."

To say Mikhail was surprised by the quick and decisive answer was an acute understatement. "In that case, we thank you."

Oiredon held up a finger in caution. "Since my powers are null in the dungeon, I can hold the gateway open for you a level above. It will be up to you or whomever you choose to go into my world to deliver your message."

Mikhail thought about the problem for a moment. "I won't send anyone inside. Not alone. Not again. However, what if you merely open a passageway enough that Henri might use one of his devices to keep the rift open? Could you open the fabric only on this side of the veil?"

Oiredon thought about a moment. "I don't see why not. I could open it until right before the breach into the dungeons if that helps. Then your Henri can use whatever clever device he's designed, and I will not be null, and he will not have to worry about generating enough power to pierce both veils."

"All right. That's settled. Only if we can't get through, will I resort to going through to the dungeon myself."

"You? You'd go?"

"Of course, I would. I'd not ask anyone to do something I'm unwilling to do. Also, I am a trained physician. If Mr. Cetanni needs assistance, I'll know it."

Oiredon smiled. "Now I know why my brother covets you so much."

Chapter Twenty

Nicholas had never painted on glass before. The texture was so different, the paint tended to smear and run on glass, unlike on canvas where the fabric nap grabbed and held. Learning the differences while making a map was a challenge; however, the experience gave him ideas for future works. Perhaps he might even develop his own pigments that allowed light to pass through them. The results would look like stained glass, but with more and greater detail.

"How are you coming along with that, Mr. Alexandre?"

Nicholas dipped his brush into the black paint, not bothering to glance up at Dr. Stanslovich. "Slowly. This requires a different technique. I had to practice for a few moments before I hit on a process that would work."

"Excellent. Keep working."

He planned to. Working was the only thing that kept him from jumping out of his skin. Roman remained asleep and that worried him in no small measure. It took every bit of his restraint not to take Roman by the shoulders and shake him until he woke. But that way meant the possibility of greater injury.

Henri entered the surgery carrying a large clear plate with a light source attached underneath. On one side, a metal arm rose up, extending over the plate. On the end of the arm was a wooden box with lenses on either side.

Nicholas marveled at the contraption. "Is that what you're going to use to send the map into the fae realm?"

"I hope to. I didn't have anything to test it on." Henri positioned the device on the ground and left the room again.

Dr. Stanslovich knelt near the object. "I hope this works."

A knot tightened in Nicholas's gut. He stalled in his painting, brush poised midair. "You have doubts?"

The doctor avoided looking up or even acknowledging Nicholas had spoken.

"Please tell me."

Dr. Stanslovich pushed to a standing position. "We have no idea what we're doing. The only thing we have going for us is assistance from Oiredon, who I suspect is the reason Mr. Cetanni is in this state in the first place."

Nicholas compressed his mouth into a line to keep from yelling accusations or making threats. A riot of emotions swirled inside him, and he hadn't the energy to exorcise them. Nor would he.

What good would it do but show the world—or these few people in it—that he was not in control? He finished the map in silence. If Dr. Stanslovich did not wish to share his concerns, then Nicholas was in no position to try to draw them out. The only part that concerned him was the risk this scheme might have on Roman's health. That detail had to be the bottom line.

He stood from the table where he worked and started from the room.

"Mr. Alexandre, are you unwell?" Dr. Stanslovich called after him.

Nicholas turned at the door. "No. Only tired."

The lie fell easily from his lips. Mentally and emotionally, he was quite exhausted. Physically, he felt like a dreamer who only walked through various scenarios that made no sense when placed together. No moment in time seemed to fit with the next. If that was what living in the fae realm was like, he wanted no part of it. Neither as Azgarth's chosen nor Oiredon's guest.

Not all inhabitants of Dr. Savoy's home seemed disturbed by the events. There was one who had remained conspicuous in his absence.

Valentine had kept clear of the distractions in the house. Nicholas envied him the ability to lose himself in his work. Music often filled the house, quiet and soothing, as the master musician composed.

Knowing the circumstances surrounding Valentine's freedom from Azgarth made speaking to the man more difficult than it should be. But each time he caught a glimpse of Valentine, Nicholas choked on rage. Why did Juliana have to die in order for Valentine to live? Why did one soul weigh more than another? Juliana had been an innocent. Her only sin was the desire to sing on stage. Not a heavy crime for any god or deity to find fault. Yet, she'd died for that want when others had lived.

Nicholas followed the music to find Valentine in the small study he used for a music room. When he saw Nicholas, he set his violin aside.

Guilt mixed with compassion filled Valentine's expression. "How are you feeling?"

"I've had much better days than these last few." Nicholas took a seat in one of the wing-back chairs. "I have managed to fall as far as any one man might and still decide life is a better choice than the alternative."

"Life is always a better choice."

The spark of anger grew. "Some aren't given a choice, though. My sister, for example."

Valentine looked down at his hands. "We had no idea what we did would harm the others under Kering's direction. I would have never sought to destroy the book if I'd known. Please believe me."

Nicholas raised his hand. "Your sincerity moves me, but it doesn't bring my sister back."

"No. It doesn't."

"If I might make a request of you."

"Of course, anything."

Nicholas looked to the violin and empty sheet music. "Write something in her honor. Tell her story. Tell of her death. Make the world know her and miss her as I do."

Valentine gave a nod. "I'd be honored."

Nicholas looked across the room, staring at the spines of books on the shelf. There were none he recognized, or many he could even read from the distance. "I think Sir Rodderick might have fallen under the influence of the fae while I had my back turned. He'd never shown that side of his personality before, nor had his eyes ever turned to that deep pool of nothing before. I fear he might be a Watcher for Azgarth. If so, what can we do about him?"

Valentine shifted uncomfortably in his seat.

Nicholas waved his statement away like a stink on the air. "I didn't mean to burden you with my thoughts. You, who have probably never known a moment's ill thought or bad feeling in your life."

"You labor under illusion, if that's what you believe of me. I have plenty of ill thoughts for those who have wronged me. Luckily, my list is much shorter than yours. Most of them were lain to rest when Kering was killed." Valentine leaned forward. "Don't let the bitterness win, my friend. You've been given a second chance. Make the most of it. Grab it with both hands and do not let it go over some petty emotion like revenge. It's not worth it."

Nicholas ran his fingers along the spine of the books. "You mistake me. I feel no ill will toward Sir Rodderick. He had no more control of his hand when he shot me than I did in dying. I blame Azgarth. Oh yes, I feel the need for revenge for what he's put Roman through. And believe me; it's worth the price of dying again."

"So you seek revenge not for yourself, but for Mr. Cetanni?"

Nicholas gave a hollow crack of laughter. "For that and being the catalyst that allowed for my servants to rob me blind and steal all Juliana's belongings. For once again having to start over."

"Those are heavy sins." Valentine rose and went back to his music. "And what will you do if you get the chance?"

A sense of being between worlds and times stole over him. His hands turned cold. He pumped his fists to help restore heat and feeling to his fingers.

"I have no idea. I hope that when the time comes, I'm ready to face what's in front of me. Making plans in regards to the fae doesn't always come off as planned."

Nicholas rose and walked to the pianoforte where Valentine stood. He used the top as a table to rest the sheet music as he composed. "I feel blessed to have been found and returned to the land of the living, but I do lament the residual effects."

Valentine nodded. "Each day for me is a blessing. To think I may have missed these experiences, the chance to gain my freedom if Drs. Stanslovich and Savoy had not been at the concert that night. Azgarth may have chosen me, but the Lord protected me."

Nicholas gave Valentine a sad smile. "You believe that?"

"Every day."

To have such faith after all he'd seen was quite remarkable. Nicholas only wished he had half of that optimism.

Henri appeared in the doorway. He spared a glance and loving smile to Valentine before turning his attention to Nicholas. "We're ready to start the experiment if you care to attend."

If he cared to? Of course, he did. If nothing else, he wanted to be there if and when Roman awakened.

The pit of despair lodged in his belly opened again. Misery leaked out, sending numbness out along his limbs. He pushed the horrible feelings away, determined not to show his emotions to others. If he was to get out of this situation and rise above it, he needed to show the world his strength, not his weakness. It served nothing but his self-pity to wallow in his fears.

He pushed away from where he leaned on the pianoforte for support. "I'll be there momentarily."

Henri exchanged another look with Valentine before he left.

Nicholas knew an intimate undercurrent between the two men and smiled. Would others feel the same when he and Roman were together? He didn't rightly care. All he wanted was for Roman to be well and whole again. Another great loss in his life would put him completely under.

He tightened a fist at his side.

No matter the outcome of this experiment, he had to be grateful that they at least tried to bring Roman back. Nicholas wasn't even certain of the mechanism or how it all worked and he'd been to the fae realm on several occasions. This, though, this was an entirely different operation. Roman's consciousness had been forced outside his body and hidden in Azgarth's dungeons. No good ever came of a situation where Azgarth held one prisoner. The fact Oiredon confirmed Roman's whereabouts and was willing to help break him out was enough proof for Nicholas.

The surgery had been altered as much as any room could in the short time Nicholas had left to speak with Valentine. Liquid filled the resurrection tank. Lights cast an odd glow through the room. Henri's projection device sat on the floor. Next to it sat another device Nicholas had never seen before. It consisted of a box with gears, a fan, two metal plates and a spring with a crank handle.

None of the items appeared at all promising for what they meant to accomplish. Doubt filled Nicholas and dragged what little hope he had like a sinking ship to the bottom of the ocean.

The exam table where Roman lay was pushed near the resurrection tank. His skin had paled considerably over the last few hours, as if the prolonged exposure to the fae realm had drained away his life force.

Fear that the scheme might do more harm than good whispered through his mind. He'd never forgive himself if Roman came to harm and he'd not raised even a minor objection. Yet, he knew it was probably their only chance to save him. Azgarth would not let Roman go. Not until his sentence had been served—and no telling how long that might be in mortal time.

Nicholas glanced around. "Are you sure this will not harm Roman?"

Dr. Savoy glanced at his colleague before raising one shoulder. "We have no idea. We've only been able to use this method to close a rift, not keep one open."

Dr. Stanslovich was more circumspect. He capped a hand of comfort on Nicholas's shoulder. "If he is harmed, we can help him."

It was poor compensation, but the best he'd get.

Oiredon entered the room as a king making a grand entrance at his coronation. "My men have infiltrated Azgarth's palace and now only await my command."

Dr. Stanslovich narrowed his gaze. "I thought you said your magic isn't good in your brother's house."

Oiredon raised a slender finger in the air. "Ah. Yes. Mine is not. My men have not been sanctioned. They can use theirs, but they'll not need it. They have…more interesting ways of subduing those in Azgarth's thrall."

That sounded neither good nor promising.

"And you can guarantee Roman will not be hurt in the crossfire?"

Oiredon made a face. "I would never go so far as to give my word on something so nebulous as injury."

Nicholas wished he didn't understand that statement, but coming from one of the fae, it made perfect sense.

Dr. Savoy stepped behind the large piece of glass they had tipped up to make a shield. "Are we ready?"

Dr. Stanslovich glanced around the room. "Places everyone."

Nicholas stood aside as the others took their position in a demented play with a dreamer for a director. And yet, there was no other way he knew to save Roman.

Oiredon lifted his hands. His gestures were subtle, elegant. Cold air rushed at them from the rent in the veil. He struck through the heart of the resurrection tank, bending glass and channeling the liquid into columns. Not one drop splashed onto the floor, but remained orderly under the hands of a fae master.

Oiredon didn't take his attention from his work, but motioned to Henri. "Focus your generator in the core of the power stream."

Henri turned on the box and then adjusted a few dials. Electricity fed through the wires, then hummed out of the side. Pistons oscillated at a frequency too high for the eye to see. The beam hit the water and lit up the surgery like the eye of an electrical storm.

Shockwaves rolled down the wires. Explosions from inside the fae realm spilled over into the surgery.

Nicholas stepped up to Roman's exam table, meaning to push him out of the way, but came too close to the edge. A terrible vacuum tried to suck him into the void.

He grabbed hold of the table to hang on. His feet lost purchase on the wooden floor.

Dr. Savoy held onto his arm, keeping him secured and anchored in place.

Warriors ran down a corridor toward a large black box. Their bows shot arrows the likes of which the civilized world had never seen. Each of the tips were laced with an explosive that, when it struck stone, blew it away with very little regard to anyone who might be stuck inside.

"Wait! You can't blow the puzzle box!"

"How else do you expect us to get inside?" Oiredon threw the query out there as if speaking to an ignorant child.

"Use the combination."

Oiredon raised a brow. "Do you possess such knowledge? I assure you, I do not." He glanced around the room. "And I doubt any of your compatriots do either."

Nicholas's breath came short. Hard.

He couldn't watch the destruction of one he loved so dearly. One he'd never be able to tell.

Under his hand, Roman's finger's twitched.

By all the fae...it was working.

Roman stood in silence, listening intently for the unmistakable sound of stone on stone. Clues as to the movement of the puzzle box might be found in so small a way. He held still, waiting to feel the vibration in his feet. Nothing. He had to try to force the box to change shape. Perhaps if he timed it right, he might be able to slip through the openings and gain freedom that way. In order to do so, two criteria must be present: one, the opening had to be big enough for a grown man to push through without being crushed; two, he had to be standing close enough to the opening.

Without knowing exactly where the cracks would occur or the configuration the puzzle moved to, it was hard to anticipate where he needed to be within the core.

So he listened and waited.

Unfortunately, he'd never been a very patient man. Not when his life and limb were on the line. If he didn't survive, his charges didn't either. They were vulnerable without him. If Azgarth chose to retaliate against him, he had no compunction of taking out his aggression on those weaker.

Which included the entire human race.

No telling how far apart the changes in the puzzle came. It might be entirely whimsical. Given the nature of the fae realm, and Azgarth's palace in particular, that was an entirely possible supposition.

He placed his hand on the wall. Even a small protrusion might indicate a lever or mechanism to force the puzzle to change. As far as he could tell, the surface of the walls was smooth where he stood. That didn't mean they all were.

A rumble shook the foundation under his feet. Not the same as when the configuration changed. This was on the scale of an earthquake—but in the fae realm? Unheard of.

He flattened his back against the wall, hands spread, trying to hold on. Feelings of intense anger roared through the core of the puzzle. Not from him but from Azgarth. He was near and very angry.

Explosions roared on the other side of the stone, muffled but still noticeable. What in the hell was happening out there? Had the war they feared come?

The floor beneath his feet cracked. Light shone from below, sending golden fingers skyward. Afraid to fall into an even worse place, Roman moved to the side, trying to see into the fissure to the lower level. Figures moved back and forth, though he hadn't a notion of whom or what they were, friend or foe. In Azgarth's dominion, it had to be foe.

However, it appeared the only way out at the moment.

Movement beneath him grew more violent. The fissure expanded. He tested the edges. Still not wide enough for him to fit through. The entire room pitched to the left, knocking it off center. Though made of stone, it appeared it had been placed on a pedestal and did not intend to stay there under the onslaught.

But the light. That light was different. Resplendent. Magical. The palace heart.

If he could get in there and destroy the heart, he'd have Azgarth by the balls.

He braced his hands against the wall. No spot in the puzzle was good if it fell. Either side, up or down, he was sure to be crushed by the stones. His heart raced and breath came short. A second fissure opened under his feet, joining the other crack.

Another explosion hit, ripping the front of the box off. Light and air rushed in through the opening. Roman pushed off from the wall, running toward the corridor, holding his sore ribs.

Each footfall against the hard ground shot pain up his side to radiate along all his nerve endings like a rush of Greek fire.

Arrows whizzed by his head. He sank back into the safety of the box entrance, afraid of trading one peril for another. A map of the palace lit up one wall like a marquee in the theater district. He recognized the brush strokes as if they were his own.

"Nicholas." The name eased from his mouth, dripping off his lips. In that moment, he knew he only wished to return to the man he'd loved so well.

An arm reached around his waist and pulled him back into the darkness. He tried to shake it off, but the hold was too tight, too secure. Air squeezed out of his lungs and refused to fill.

He looked down, trying to force the arm away from him. The very edges of it moved and shifted. Azgarth had him in a hold, dragging him to an even deeper region of the palace.

"Oiredon has invaded my palace in an attempt to rescue you. I will never let him have you."

Try as he might, Roman hadn't the strength to respond. So many words and accusations vied to pour forth, but they were stuck in a throat that no longer worked.

The scene shifted and changed. He found himself in a small, dim chamber strapped to a rack. Hot breath bathed his naked back as Azgarth bent over him.

"Not even the broken pieces that are left when I finish with you."

Roman tried not to shiver at the promise in those words. If he'd ever wondered what happened to those who'd crossed the line with Azgarth, he was about to find out. Toying with him was only a means to draw out more emotion. Fear and passion were often neighbors. Feeding off either one would sustain Azgarth for the coming battle. Strengthen him. Make him impossible to defeat.

Roman wouldn't give Azgarth that satisfaction. He tried to close off his mind to the torture. To make his mind a blank slate so not even those things that gave Roman comfort would fuel Azgarth's strength.

The sharp edge of a fingernail caressed Roman the length of his spine. Flesh rent and opened, stinging as the cool air of the torture chamber hit it. Blood trickled down his sides, dripping onto the slab where he lay.

A moment of respite as Azgarth moved away. A high-pitched whistle sang, then a crack of leather against skin as the whip found its mark. Roman gritted his teeth and refused to give into the pain.

"I will have your loyalty back. Your soul is mine."

Another lash lay across the open line on his spine, making a cross. Roman bit back his cry. He wound his hands in the straps tying him to the slab, gaining strength from the connection.

Each strike of the whip tore more of his back apart. Roman closed his eyes and held on, hoping when Azgarth didn't get the response he was after, he'd let up.

It wasn't to be.

Instead of lessening the severity of the punishment, Roman's silence only infuriated Azgarth more. The lashes became stronger, ripping down to the muscle and bone.

"One strike for each offense against me, plus another for each year you've been in my service. I will have my payment one way or another."

Christ in heaven, he'd lost count of how many times he'd been hit—of how many years he'd served.

Heat poured into the room. Azgarth's minion stoked an unholy fire below, turning the room into an oven. Sweat built on the skin that remained intact and ran down to douse the injuries in salt. Acid wouldn't have burned more if Azgarth had upended a bottle over Roman. Tears ran down his face and still he refused to give in.

Azgarth might be battling for his home, but Roman fought for his soul.

"I will break you." With the wave of a hand, Azgarth turned Roman over onto his ruined back. Stars exploded behind his lids and a grunt of sound escaped his throat.

He tried to close his eyes as the whip descended, but couldn't. Azgarth had made it impossible. Now he not only had to feel each strike, but had to watch as the lash arced and connected.

Harder to ignore, harder to fight.

The torture continued.

He was dying.

Chapter Twenty-One

Mikhail monitored Mr. Cetanni for any changes in appearance or vital signs. All were elevated and his hands began to show signs of tremors. From a purely medical standpoint, it didn't appear promising. From a metaphysical standpoint, he had no idea what to expect inside the puzzle box or if the structure might afford Mr. Cetanni even a bit of protection against the war that raged outside its stone walls.

A bright light and the rumble of an explosion lit the corridor inside the fae realm. The percussion from the blast knocked those in the surgery back. Mikhail fell to the floor.

"Mikhail!" Dante was to him in a blink, helping him to his feet.

"I think Mr. Alexandre was correct to worry over the state of Mr. Cetanni's being. We can't control what's going on over there, any more than we could control the oceans."

Dante raised a dark brow of agreement. "I think we've bedded down with the devil," he whispered.

"No!" Mr. Alexandre took off at a run for the veil.

"Come back here!" Mikhail dove to the ground, tackling Mr. Alexandre around the legs. They slipped through the void, crashing into a null space where up and down were the same concept.

Mikhail held his breath. Hitting bottom was going to hurt. He braced for impact.

And landed with a splash in a lake.

Another splash landed next to him, soon followed by frantic movement and a burbling request for aid.

Mikhail swam a few feet to where Mr. Alexandre panicked his way to near drowning. "Calm down. I've got you. You're safe." An odd thing to say given the circumstances of where they'd landed.

None of the scenery looked even vaguely familiar from the last time he'd fallen through worlds to land in the fae realm. The lake was not the same, the countryside appeared a bit more realistic and in focus. The colors appeared more Pre-Ralphealite than Impressionist.

With one arm secured around Nicholas Alexandre's chest, Mikhail swam for shore. It didn't take long to find his footing. "It isn't too deep here. You'll be able to touch bottom and walk the rest of the way out."

"What happened?"

"My guess? We got too close to the veil and became trapped in the vortex." He glanced around again as they trudged out of the water and onto the bank. "I can't speak for where we landed, though."

Mr. Alexandre gazed at their surroundings. "We're about a quarter mile—in human distance—from Azgarth's palace. Now, if he decided to add onto the journey, we might be trying to find our way all night."

"I've played that game before." Mikhail pulled his shirt tails from inside his trousers and wrung them out. Water in the fae realm had all the wet properties it did in the human world. "Which direction?"

Mr. Alexandre made a vague motion with his arm that put them on a western course. "That way."

"Well, let's go."

Hope was a fragile thing. Even when one held it secure and used tender care, it shattered like a robin's egg on cobbles. Until they had fallen through another damned rabbit hole, Mikhail had begun to believe they might pull Mr. Cetanni from Azgarth's hold with success. With each passing footstep, his belief waned and hope grew a little dimmer.

They walked in silence. The only sounds that of their passage through high grasses and their labored breathing. They climbed a hill, forded a stream, then came to a forest where the trees took on that odd charcoal look Mikhail had come to expect from the fae realm.

"We're getting closer." Mr. Alexandre held onto the trunk of a thin tree, using it to pull him up the incline that steepened with every step.

"Believe it or not, I have already reached that conclusion." A quick glance to his unwilling companion and Mikhail halted their progress. "You look unwell."

Mr. Alexandre compressed his lips into a tight line. "I'm fine. Let us make haste."

Mikhail kept an eye on him as they continued to climb. Not once—other than the near drowning—had Mr. Alexandre uttered one word of complaint or offered any resistance. His determination to reach Mr. Cetanni was admirable in the extreme.

A brief thought caressed Mikhail's mind. What had Dante thought when he'd seen Mikhail and Mr. Alexandre fall through the veil? The roar had been so great in his ears, he'd heard nothing from the human side. Not one call of his name. Not one shout of rage.

What if they'd hit the electric field and suffered electrocution only to be separated from their bodies as Mr. Cetanni had been? How were they going to help him?

Mikhail touched his face and ran frantic hands over his shirt. The fabric remained damp from their fall in the lake. No. All that felt real. He took a deep breath in and smelled the rich scent of disturbed earth, recent rain, and rotting vegetation. Scents such as those were not products of his mind or remembrances from walks in the woods in his youth. They were here and alive and surrounding him.

Finally, they breached the crest of the hill. Down below lay a lush verdant valley. Too green and too perfect. High walls secured the main building from outside invaders. At the moment, lines of fae creatures, large and small, poured through a breach in the structure.

Mikhail put up his hand to stop Mr. Alexandre from going down the hill. "We need to think this through before we go storming in with the invading hordes."

"What is there to think about? I'm going to find Roman. Period."

"Do you even remember the map?"

"Yes. And I bet you do, too." Mr. Alexandre shrugged his arm from Mikhail's hold. "I've come this far. I don't intend to stop until we find him."

"Just so you know, I'm not certain we aren't outside our bodies now too."

Mr. Alexandre frowned. "What do you mean?"

"We could have fallen through the veil intact, or been separated when the electric charge hit our bodies." Mikhail shook his head. "I have no way of knowing which it is at this juncture."

"I don't believe it matters here. Azgarth will take of you what he can get. If that's only your mind, well, your body is of little consequence to him."

"So I'm beginning to learn."

Noise rose on the hill behind them. Mikhail turned as one of the fae warriors arrived behind him. Slanted, amethyst eyes stared at Mikhail as if seeing not only the physical but down to the seat of his soul.

"Follow me to the palace. Azgarth has taken Roman Cetanni."

"Where to?" Mr. Alexandre started down the hill, never questioning the validity of the statement or even if the being was in Oiredon's employ.

"To the Garden of Souls."

Mikhail made a face. He didn't like the way that sounded. "Is that what it sounds like?"

The being's expression never changed. "Worse."

Mr. Alexandre was not as good at hiding his emotions. He stumbled and nearly went down, if the fae warrior hadn't grabbed his arm and stood him on his feet.

Mikhail raised a brow. "You've been to this Garden of Souls."

"Once." Mr. Alexandre rubbed a hand down his face, then placed his arms out to the sides for balance as they scaled down the hill. "I didn't know what it was at the time."

"When were you there?"

Mr. Alexandre spared a glance at Mikhail. Suspicion and guilt mixed in the depth of his eyes. "In the between, before I awoke in the resurrection tank."

Mikhail left it at that. No more words were needed.

The fae turned around and stabbed a flinty purple stare their way. "Do you humans always talk so much?"

"Excessively," Mikhail said just to be annoying, though why he thought to poke at a fae creature who was obviously there to help, he had no idea. Perhaps it was the tension of the situation or the panic slowly rising the closer they got to the palace. The not knowing what they'd find once they arrived.

Somewhere in the distance the low, long note of a horn blew. Barks, growls, and snarls erupted onto the air, stirred by the horn's call.

"Aladair!" came a voice from the valley. "Hurry!"

The fae warrior beckoned them to move faster. "Azgarth's called in reinforcements. We do not want to be caught in open ground when they arrive."

Mikhail picked up his pace. He reached out a hand to Mr. Alexandre, helping to keep him steady as they went down the last third of the hill. Once on level land, they ran. Mr. Alexandre moved faster than Mikhail credited him, but he still lagged behind. He held his side and his face twisted in pain, but he still never uttered a word of complaint or asked them to wait.

Admiration for the man grew.

Over the top of the hills to the south came a black horde of snarling teeth and vicious jaws. Mikhail had never seen anything like these animals. They were not *wolfsine,* but bigger, more aggressive. Red glowing eyes trapped their prey, freezing Mikhail in place. Aladair continued to run. Mr. Alexandre called for him, but Mikhail was rooted to the spot.

What were these creatures that slobbered and spat and scared human hearts until they were unable to beat properly? They ran on all fours, lumbering like a bear but with a speed unmatched by any mammal Mikhail had ever studied. Now these moved with an agility and grace only seen in the fae realm, only created to overcome and subdue those who had gone against Azgarth's wishes.

"Dr. Stanslovich! You must hurry!" Mr. Alexandre shouted. "You'll be eaten."

Mikhail frowned, the words failed to penetrate any area of his mind that induced him to move. Instead, his body did the most unnatural thing—he turned and held his arms out from his sides, waiting in hypnotic anticipation for the horde to arrive.

A voice deep in his soul told him Azgarth would not harm him.

He remained one of the chosen. As long as that tie was intact, he'd not suffer a horrible fate on this side of the veil. His connection to Azgarth protected him. Perhaps not the others, but it would shield him—at least long enough for the others to get to safety.

He hoped.

He prayed.

The gap closed.

The stampede rumbled under his feet. Their stench like rotted meat and fetid breath filled his head. He clamped his teeth together to keep from vomiting. He continued to stand his ground. Arms out. Stoic.

Between one heartbeat and the next, they were on him. He closed his eyes and gave himself over to the moment as the creatures moved around and through him. Vile thoughts, chaotic and foreign, filled his head. Not words, but pictures. These...things...were bred purely for punishment. To tear at tender flesh and expose the gore inside. He also sensed a slight flair of ozone and got the impression they not only ate flesh but consumed magic.

These creatures were dangerous to both human and fae alike. God forefend if they should ever breach the veil.

The last of the things passed through him, leaving a rancid taste in his mouth. He turned as they continued on their journey to the palace, and spit on the ground.

A dark man rode behind him, seated atop a large *callif*. He turned his head as he passed Mikhail, but the features were too distorted to tell if it was Azgarth or another of his minions.

Mikhail started for the palace, chasing after the horde. His body felt heavier, as if his bones had been replaced by lead pipes. Each step came slower, harder to maneuver. Then he stepped on a soft bit of ground and fell through.

The hole sent him down a spiraling tunnel. Falling and falling until he reached the bottom and landed in a dungeon.

Nicholas hid behind the barricade. He'd lost sight of Dr. Stanslovich. All he'd seen before he leapt was a black wall of fur, fury, and fangs. He sat now with his back to the barricade wall. Breath sawed in and out, and every one of his limbs screamed in burning pain. He'd never been a physical man, save what he did during vigorous bouts of sexual congress, and he hated like hell he had to start now—especially after his illness.

The fae warrior known as Aladair sat beside him. He'd nocked an arrow and waited until the creatures breached the barricade. It was only a matter of time. Nicholas remained still. Afraid if he moved even an inch, the creatures might find him.

He closed his eyes. Images of Dr. Stanslovich standing there in the open, frozen in place rushed behind his closed lids. Oh God. What was he going to tell Dr. Savoy? How did one make up for so great a loss? Nicholas knew there was no way to make it right or offer condolences to those who had been close to him. And seeing the viciousness of the creatures, there was no way he'd survived.

"Do you know how to shoot?" Aladair nodded to another archer down the line.

A bow and quiver full of arrows was thrust in Nicholas's hands. "A little and mostly for amusement."

"Did you ever hit the target?"

"Yes. Many times."

"Good. These arrows do not require a great deal of accuracy, only that you can strike the *fasails* somewhere on their body."

"All right." Good to know, but these targets were moving and had murder on their minds. He'd never tried to hit anything that was moving before and had never been on a hunt. Not even with his cousin the czar.

The *fasails* reached the barricade. Their bodies hit the walls in a crash of thunder. Up and over the top, coming down with bellies exposed to those hiding on the other side.

Arrows flew, trailing golden tails behind them. As the projectile found its mark, the *fasails* exploded into nothing more than black soot.

Nicholas nocked an arrow and let the magic fly. It found a target in a large beast that had turned and started for the line of warriors. Dust rained down on them from above. A stink of death floated on the air—either promise or lament, Nicholas wasn't certain.

"Come on." Aladair rose from his hiding place and gathered the arrows that now lay on the grass.

Nicholas did the same, looking back out to the field and hoping to see Dr. Stanslovich.

Disappointment tasted bitter on his tongue. Had Dr. Stanslovich sacrificed himself for him and Aladair? Why? There wasn't a need. They all could have made it to the barricade in time.

"Behind you!" Aladair yelled, but the warning came too late.

Nicholas was seized from behind. His body lifted off the ground as if he had no more substance than a small child. He jackknifed his body back and forth, trying to lose his captor's hold. The arm tightened on him.

"Getting rid of me is not so easily done, Nicholas Alexandre. Not by half." Azgarth's words filled his head in silky threat.

"I am no longer yours to command." He tried to pry Azgarth's hold away, but he might as well have tried moving a mountain with a teaspoon.

They rode toward the palace proper. Nicholas only hoped he might end up in the same place as Roman.

However, given the identity of his captor, that seemed unlikely. They'd be seen as conspirators in cahoots to overthrow Azgarth in his own palace.

Aladair aimed an arrow at the *callif*.

Blackness bled in from the edges of Nicholas's vision. Frigid air froze his nasal hair. His breath crystallized, falling like tiny snowflakes onto his shirt. They came out in an area not at all like the faded scenes from his memory of death. Decorative fruit trees and interesting topiary had been reduced to dry, brittle branches. Cobwebs fluttered on a distant breeze.

"Where have you brought me?"

Azgarth pushed Nicholas from the *callif*. He landed on the cracked, dirty paving stones. Pain shot up his leg. His knee hit hard.

"Don't you recognize it?" With that, he faded away.

The problem was he did recognize it. Only it didn't look like this when he'd last been there.

The Garden of Souls.

He'd not known, at the time, the name or the significance. The only clue had been the unusual shapes of the bushes. Yes, he'd known they were people—well, people shaped, but he'd never thought the garden was real. Is that what happened to those souls who had ceased? Had Azgarth brought his chosen there to cultivate them? Grow them? Then what happened when he tired of them?

Nicholas rose and touched the roots of one of the trees. The limbs were dry as old bones. He closed his eyes and turned away. If these were the remains of those who had displeased Azgarth in some way, Roman didn't stand a chance.

He pulled himself to a standing position. His knee throbbed with pain. The garden appeared empty save for the remains of what had once been beautiful shrubbery.

Broken statues littered the walkways, fallen soldiers of a lost campaign.

If this was all that Azgarth's chosen meant to him, then Nicholas was glad Roman had freed them. But where was Roman? Aladair had mentioned he was being held there? If so, there had to be some sort of prison or containment facility.

Frantic, he hurried over to one of the statues and looked at the face. Not Roman. But that didn't mean he hadn't been turned into one and smashed along with all the others. He moved onto the next one, then the next one. Each face he searched, he felt a stab of relief that Roman's likeness wasn't reflected back to him in the form of fractured marble.

Nor had he seen Dr. Stanslovich.

One statue stood off from the others. Alone. Forgotten. A woman.

As if propelled forward by one of Mr. Vauss's machines, Nicholas walked to the statue and stood, gazing up into the stone face he'd known so well in life.

Rage heated him. Fire lit his belly. How dare Azgarth? How dare he?

"I swear to you, before I leave here, I will set you free." He touched the delicate curl of Juliana's fingers as they rested against her heart. Her features were frozen forever in an expression of horror and disbelief. What had she witnessed before she'd fallen to Azgarth's spell caging her soul in stone?

His knees buckled in pain and sorrow. He rested his head against her pale stone feet and sobbed. Of all the people who deserved such a fate, Juliana had not been one of them.

This had been his fault. He'd not discouraged her from taking the assistance offered by Kering. Failed to warn his mother of the dangers of such an association.

Nicholas lifted his face, gazing through a veil of tears. In the end, did it matter at all? Azgarth would have taken his pound of flesh regardless if Juliana was a willing participant or a reluctant hero.

A cold wind blew. Bits of debris, fallen leaves, and dirt swirled in eddies. If he didn't know better, he'd think a storm brewed. Yet the garden was enclosed on all sides, and when he looked up, a roof kept the attraction away from the elements.

He pushed himself up and moved to the center of the garden, looking at the walls. An odd shimmery substance coated some of the surfaces. From where he stood, he had a hard time seeing what was behind the coating.

A crawling sensation moved along his neck and shoulders as he inched closer to one of the walls. As he grew nearer, he realized what he'd thought was a shiny coating was tempered glass. Figures, captured in time, were held in frozen horror. Faces contorted in agony told the story of certain torture at Azgarth's hands.

Nicholas hurried from one exhibit to the next, searching for Roman.

A few of the faces looked familiar; perhaps he'd seen them at Azgarth's court. No names filtered through his memory to connect with those lost to Azgarth's whims. What offense they might have given the fae master, he had no idea.

As he gazed into each soul cage, the thought he might not find Roman trapped behind glass urged him to move faster. Urgency spurred him on. The displays went from showing the subjects in states of pain to staged scenes of torture.

Feeling sick in body and soul, he came to the end of the row. Roman was stretched out on a rack, his torso laid open by lashes of a hundred whips.

"Roman!" He beat his fist against the glass. "Roman!"

Roman lay still as death. Blood ran down his sides and fell into puddles beside the contraption. Footprints were visible around the rack, where his torturer had stood.

"Roman. Wake up!"

No telling if Azgarth planned to show his face again and perhaps finish what he'd started on Roman. Nicholas had not the luxury of time to contemplate it either. He grabbed the remains of a tree. The window shattered under the impact with the planter. He threw the remains of the tree aside and stepped inside. Glass crunched under his feet.

"Roman. Roman." He tapped Roman's face a few times. "Wake up."

No response. Not even a flicker.

He had no choice but to release him and carry him out.

The rope used to hold Roman's wrists was so taut Nicholas couldn't pull the knot free. He grabbed a piece of broken glass and sawed it back and forth across the ropes. Fiber by fiber, the rope began to fray. Three more to go after this one. Each as thick as his wrist. Pressure, from his hand along the jagged glass as he cut, laid open a gash along his palm. Blood ran down onto his fingers. His hold slipped. Slashes opened on his fingertips, adding more blood to the already coated glass.

Despite the chill air, sweat dripped down his forehead. He brushed it away and smeared blood over his face. His eyes stung and closed involuntarily.

Only a few strands remained connected. He chopped at them and they broke free. Immediately, he moved to the next one. Oh, this was taking too long. Too great a fear of discovery.

Hysterical laughter rang in the confines of the cell. His. What was he thinking? Azgarth already knew where he was—he'd been the one to drop him there. For what purpose? Torment? Oh God. The images that rolled through his mind were too horrible to dwell on.

No time for his mind to splinter. He had to keep it together.

He worked vigorously, cutting through the ropes. At one point, he had to switch hands because his right was cut to shreds. It might be a long time before he'd be able to hold a paintbrush again, but the loss of a creative outlet was worth it to save Roman. He'd give his life to save Roman.

A light tinkling not much different than the sound of small silver bells came from the area of the shattered window. He glanced over his shoulder and stopped. Glass once again covered the opening.

The shard he held fell from his fingers to shatter on the floor. It had all been a trap. He'd let his guard down, and now they were both contained behind a window that showed only an abandon garden. And each one of the cells contained men like him who had been caught off guard and captured.

Do not panic!

Nicholas took a breath and tried to gain some composure. He'd never feared Azgarth more than he did at the moment. At every turn, he—they—could be interred forever. No one would ever find them. Nicholas would disappear, body and soul, and Roman merely a body, devoid of all that made him Roman.

He simply needed to keep moving forward. Get them out of this space first and worry about what came next after.

He found another piece of glass and went back to work on Roman's restraints. Finally, they fell away. Nicholas leaned over and lifted Roman from the rack, then sat him to lean against a wall. So far, Roman hadn't shown the least sign of waking. He also seemed lighter than a grown man. A spirit without connection to its body had to weigh less than the whole of the parts. It made sense but was more than a bit disconcerting. A less than subtle reminder that Roman had been torn in half, the material and esoteric.

Now to find something to break the window. He wasn't strong enough to lift the rack by himself. The damn contraption might be made of wood, but it was heavy as hell. However, the wooden lever that ratcheted the ropes and applied the tension might be freed from the device. If he managed to get that loose, he could use it as a pike to break out the window a second time.

He needed to work quickly. If he let this opportunity pass, no telling what Azgarth might choose next to cover the window. Lead. Stone. Brick. Glass was no real deterrent. Barring the ability to free the shaft, he always had the choice of breaking it with his arm.

He'd reserve that option as a last resort.

In order to remove the lever, he had to pull it from the metal casing that kept it in place. He glanced over his shoulder to check on Roman. He remained still, his breathing shallow and fast. Had they stretched him or merely beat him? Nicholas had no medical knowledge in order to tell by looking at him.

Instead of pulling the lever out of the casing, perhaps he would fare better breaking it off. He came around to the side, so he stood perpendicular to the lever. In his many nights of drunken shenanigans, he'd kicked in a door or two. It was always more effective for him if he kicked out to the side and counterbalanced with his body. He only hoped after his illness, he had enough strength to manage the act. Not to mention the lever was a hell of a lot slimmer surface than any door he'd taken down.

He centered his entire being into his foot. Concentration absolute. He kicked out. His foot went wide of the mark. Laughter echoed in from somewhere outside the cell. The sound rolling down a canyon wall into a cave.

Azgarth watched his every move. Ready to counter any attempt at escape with some new means of holding them hostage. Well, Nicholas, for one, would never stop trying to save them. Even when his energy was spent and spirit broken.

This time, he came in lower, closer to the base. The kick connected, but he hadn't enough strength on the first pass to do more than cause the lever to vibrate.

Frustration lit a fuse. A keg of emotions exploded within him, sending Nicholas into a frenzy of kicking, over and over. A crack sounded loud in the chamber. The lever listed drunkenly in the casing. Triumphant laughter poured from him. He kicked it twice more and it fell to the ground with a clatter.

Without missing a step, he swiped up the lever from the ground and used it like a cricket bat to smash the window. Glass cracked and fell down in crystalline rain. He beat it until none remained.

Roman stirred. Unintelligible mumblings fell from his cracked lips. Nicholas shushed him, then leaned over and hoisted him up on a shoulder.

Time to leave this awful place.

Pain lit low in his belly. Strain from lifting Roman's weight pulled at the newly healed skin. He rubbed his hand over the area, afraid the pink scar might rupture despite Oiredon's healing.

Tile cracked under Nicholas's feet. The garden swayed as if the supports beneath it were no longer secure. In the distance, the percussion of explosions punctuated the quiet. The battle grew closer.

God, he wished there was time to rescue all those frozen behind the glass and to free his sister, but he was only one man and he had only enough strength to carry Roman.

He'd send others back to search. If he came across others.

Another blast rocked the garden. It listed dangerously to the left. Nicholas almost lost his footing. He picked up his pace, dodging falling trees and gazebos that caved in under the rain of stone and marble.

The gates came into sight.

He sent a brief prayer to anyone listening that they were not locked.

Burdened under Roman's weight, Nicholas's strength began to fade. No. He had to make it through the gates. Once outside, he'd figure out the next step—but just get them through the gates.

Vibrations shook the ground. Nicholas lurched, his feet skidding over the moving ground. His knees started to buckle. He kept running.

Stumbling. They both went down hard. Roman's eyes flickered open but then shut again.

"I'm sorry. So sorry." Nicholas scooped Roman up. Blood from all the various lash marks had soaked through Nicholas's shirt, making it damp and sticky. He'd been cleansed—baptized in the blood of his lover. Washed clean of all the mistakes and pain he'd caused while under Azgarth's control. No more. From now on, he'd be his own man.

He shouldered the gates. They slid open with little resistance. The garden led straight to the gallery. As he moved by the paintings, details stuck in his periphery. He stopped.

He knew these paintings. Had crafted each of them, breathing life into canvases and oils. Hours of his time spent setting a scene and building a world from the visions in his head. Images of the fae realm.

To leave pieces of his work behind was foolhardy. No ties need remain for Azgarth to pull him back into this realm.

"Forgive me a moment." He gently lowered Roman to the ground and leaned him against the wall.

He glanced around, searching for something to use as a tool—sharp and pointed would work well. Better not to risk going back into the Garden of Souls. The way events were unfolding, he'd end up trapped there for good.

A ways down the balcony, pieces of the banister had fallen away, leaving the wooden pegs free. Nicholas hurried to the gap and worked one of the balusters from the structure. The top had been sheared away, leaving a point not unlike a stake. He lifted it and speared it through the first painting.

Pain tore through him. Eviscerating. He kept at it. Ruining that which he'd created with his own hands, leaving nothing behind but the destruction of his rage. Azgarth had taken everything from him and given nothing but hollow promises in return. Saving Roman wasn't assured. Not seeing him in this state.

Nicholas moved to the next painting, savaging it until there was nothing but the frame and a few smears of transfer paint left on the wall.

Roman stirred again. Nicholas finished destroying the last painting. He still had to find a way out of the palace and get them to safety.

He leaned down and lifted Roman. On wobbly legs, he headed to find an exit.

Chapter Twenty-Two

Mikhail searched for a way out. He'd landed in deep shit this time. From one peril to the next, this particular one having a rather more difficult extrication. No magic doors appeared. No holes in the floor to send him to another level. He'd tried all of that already, to no avail.

At least he was alone and not facing some fae creature doing its damnedest to skewer him through with a tusk. Thoughts like that might get him into trouble if he dwelled on them too long. No telling where Azgarth got his ideas for his creations. Wherever they came from, they were the stuff of nightmares. And he didn't think much of the prison he'd fallen into either.

He studied the ceiling. He'd fallen through at an angle where ceiling met wall. Not through a tunnel or hole as he'd first believed, but a space between spaces. It had been as if his body had compacted down to the size of a mouse and slid through an underground warren, falling in both distance and size until he'd been spit out there in the cage of a dungeon. Immediately, his body returned to normal and he'd been trapped.

A feeling of being watched by hundreds of little eyes crawled over his skin. Whether Azgarth or his minions, Mikhail hadn't a clue, but he didn't care for the feeling at all. Not in this place where strange insects could rend a man's flesh, or physical concepts like mass and weight had no common relation.

An explosion rocked the dungeon. Bits of rock and mortar rained from above. He'd run out of time and ideas.

But he'd be damned if he'd die in this place. Not now. Not here. He might give his life for his friends, but he'd not give Azgarth the satisfaction of killing him in such a stupid way.

Another blast—this one closer—buckled the wall across from his cell. Too close.

The bars rattled. Wait. Were they loose?

He gripped them with both hands and tugged. The metal moved freely, having separated from the mortar that sealed them in place. Odd how that detail captured his imagination in such a moment. Held by human materials, not magic. Not illusion or wishes, but science. He found comfort in that knowledge and pulled harder.

A third blast came from the opposite side of the dungeons. Too far away to do much damage where Mikhail was held, but enough to place more stress on the cracked stones above him. More of the ceiling gave way. Rocks fell, filling up the passageway to the left of his cell. Dust rolled down the corridor, obscuring what little view he had in that direction.

He pulled on the bars again. They came free, sending him to stumble back a few feet before he threw them to the ground and crawled from his cell.

He hurried up the corridor. Lost. Without direction or any knowledge of where he was going. The map he'd traced time and again did not show this area of the palace. This was uncharted territory. So he ran, keeping an ear out for any telltale signs he moved in the correct direction. Going the other way was not an option. Not with the passage caved in.

The hallway made a ninety-degree turn. An incline rose to a second-story level. Light shone above him, guiding the way. Either he ran to peril or freedom. No other choices remained. Not when the entire palace threatened to come down around his ears.

It only mattered where he stood when the final shot was fired.

Oiredon should have warned them the palace was going to be under siege. Sending in his army to clear the place was not the same thing as having a few forces there to aid in Mr. Cetanni's recovery.

Never trust a fae bearing gifts.

He moved to the light. The incline grew steeper the farther he went. At points, Mikhail had to sink to his knees and crawl up or risk sliding all the way down to the beginning. As he climbed, the floor became rougher. Obsidian glass cut at his hands until they bled. He didn't let it bother him but kept moving forward. Cuts and abrasions were only surface wounds and healed relatively quickly, all things considered. Nothing but a trifle when compared to all he'd been through, all he'd seen. It did make holding onto the slick surface somewhat more difficult. He stopped for a moment, resting his foot against the wall to steady himself. He grabbed the pockets on his pants and pulled. The seam let loose, ripping open his trousers, but the pocket remained intact.

Excellent.

He went to work on the other one. So what if he ruined his trousers. That's what a good tailor was for. When the second one came loose—with even more damage to his clothing than the first—he slid his hands in and used them as mitts.

A workable solution. Not a perfect one, but enough to get him up the incline of death and to the next level.

Shocks continued to rock the palace. He lost his grip, the fabric of his makeshift mittens made it harder to hold on the places where the stone was smooth as glass.

A figure appeared at the top of the incline, silhouetted against the light. Mikhail stared at the person. His heart in his throat.

"What are you doing here?"

"Looking for you." Dante threw a rope down to Mikhail. "Grab hold of it and I'll pull you up."

Afraid he was being fooled, Mikhail, nonetheless, shook off the hastily fashioned mitts and grabbed for the rope. He tied it around his waist. "All right."

Dante moved back, pulling on the rope. Mikhail progressed up the incline much faster than he had been going alone.

When he made it to the top, he threw his arms around Dante. "Thank you. Now we have to find Mr. Alexandre."

"He's not with you?" Dante's look of concern poked holes in Mikhail's slim belief that Mr. Alexandre had made it back to the human world before him.

"No. We became separated." Mikhail unwound the rope from his waist.

"I shouldn't do that if I were you."

Mikhail gazed at Dante. "That bad?"

"Henri is waiting to pull us back through the void. It's the only way to get out of here. Oiredon left us to our own devices. I believe things have gone sideways in his attempted coup." Dante took the rope and secured it to the one around his waist, essentially linking them together. "We need to get our people out and back to our own world. No telling what the fallout from this action will be."

"Believe me. I already know or at least have sampled a taste. I don't care for it." Mikhail nodded to the distance. "Give the signal."

Dante pulled the rope behind him. It grew taut and began to pull him back. He reached out for Mikhail, who grabbed at Dante's forearms. The line drew them to a portal that seemed held open by only wishes and a bit of aggressive science. Though the air in the void was bitter cold, a scent of burned circuitry and wood filled the in between. Energy crackled all around them. Lightning in a bottle.

A terrible noise of stones hitting each other with force came crashing through the void. The pressure sent a wave of air to them, pushing them through the artificial portal. It closed around them, snapping shut to leave Mr. Alexandre and Mr. Cetanni trapped on the other side.

Mikhail hurried to the inert body of Roman Cetanni. He was pale and waxy as death. They were losing him. He felt for a pulse. A faint beat remained, but for how long, he had no guess.

"He needs fluids. We have to keep his body alive long enough to get them back."

Dante left to get the supplies.

"Henri, try to get that portal open again. They won't be able to make it through on their own. Not with a war raging on the other side." Mikhail tried to concentrate on the struggle before him, but he had serious doubts that what they did on this side made a difference. If the fae realm fell, how would that affect those who had been touched by the fae? The two worlds were inextricably linked and had been for longer than Mikhail had been alive. The evidence was there in the histories of the arts and sciences.

Henri shook his head. "The parts are blown. I can't use these again."

When Henri held them up for Mikhail to see, sure enough, the pieces had turned to black dust.

"We have to get that portal open for them. We can't leave them there." A violent shudder moved through him at the thought of the creatures he'd seen. How many were even more terrible than those he'd faced?

"I'll see what I can do, but you aren't giving me much time."

"Time isn't mine to give," Mikhail said.

Henri left the room. To get his tools, Mikhail supposed.

Dante returned and they set up to give Mr. Cetanni fluids. The composition in question was of Dante's own making. It mixed dextrose with a base that mimicked the body's natural liquids. The idea was inspired and had helped them time and again while treating patients.

They worked in quiet as Mikhail stole surreptitious glances at Dante. He couldn't help but think about the horrible vision he'd had of Dante falling. So far, he'd been the stronger of them, the one who championed their cause and did not think twice about putting his life on the line for others.

"What?" Dante used a large-bore needle to puncture Mr. Cetanni's skin. He fit tubing onto the needle and began the drip.

"Protect yourself at all cost. Do not be a hero for me or anyone."

Dante gave an uncomfortable laugh. "A bit late to ask for that reassurance now, isn't it?"

"You didn't have to come to the fae realm for me. I would have made it out eventually."

"But you didn't have to. Did you?" Dante moved away from the treatment table and stood in front of the resurrection tank. "We need to move our operations out to the garden. Harness the power in the fountain. Figures have tried to come through it before. It's time we let them and use it to hold the doorway open."

A groan came from behind them. Mr. King stirred on his treatment table. Mikhail hurried to his side. Dante took up a place on the opposite side of the table.

He touched Mr. King's arm. "Mr. King? It's all right. You're at the home of Dr. Dante Savoy. You're being cared for."

Mr. King moved his mouth back and forth. "Terrible."

Mikhail exchanged glances with Dante. "We know. You'll feel bad for a while, but we hope it is of short duration. No one feels well after suffering a bite from a *wolfsine*."

"Punished," Mr. King corrected.

"Try not to talk or upset yourself." Mikhail patted Mr. King's hand and moved to the desk to retrieve the pitcher of water. He poured a glass and returned with it. "Help me sit him up, Dante."

Dante placed his arm around Mr. King's shoulder and lifted him. Mikhail held the cup and let him drink his fill. When he finished, he indicated Dante could lie him back down.

Mr. King rubbed his face with a shaky hand. "I thought I'd imagined it."

"No. The *wolfsine* are sent to hunt those with particular talents."

Mr. King gazed at them with haunted eyes. "You misunderstand. I saw them come out of my photographs."

Dante straightened. "Are you sure?"

"Positive. I was in the process of developing the plates I'd taken here when the images..." Mr. King covered his face with his hands. "The images grew larger, coming at me. I stepped back, but breaking contact did no good. One of the plates shattered, but it only released the images into the darkroom. I tried to fight them off."

A shudder moved through Mr. King's entire body. Gooseflesh broke out on his arms and back. "I'm never going back there. Never picking up a camera. If that's what this...this talent does, I want no part of it."

Mikhail gripped Mr. King's shoulder. "I can understand your reluctance to work. Believe me. We've seen things in the resurrection tank my scientific mind refused to comprehend. For the longest time, I thought it a puzzle to be solved or mystery to explore."

Mr. King raised his head, looking at Mikhail over the tops of his finger. "And now?"

"Now I know it simply *is*."

Dante sent Mikhail a troubled gaze. His jaw tightened, but he kept his thoughts to himself. For once, Mikhail didn't care to bait him into sharing his thoughts.

Mr. King made a long study of his hands and arms. He touched his neck where the skin had been regrown. "How did you find me?"

"Mr. Cetanni and I went to see if you'd had a chance to develop the plates. We found you in your darkroom." Dante moved away as he talked, going to the far side of the surgery to pick up a white medical bag. "Inside this are cures given to Mr. Cetanni from the fae world. One of those cures healed you. I don't know if I could have saved you without them. Your injury was too extensive. The damage certainly fatal."

Mr. King paled. He glanced over to the inert body of Mr. Cetanni. "Was he injured trying to care for me?"

"No. He stayed behind to search your studio for the plates. He...we...were afraid we might have lost valuable information on the fae realm. As it turned out, we didn't need the plates to find the entrance." Dante pulled out one of the vials and showed Mr. King the label. "I took a leap of faith that the contents were as advertised. I had little choice in the matter."

Mr. King took the bottle and studied it. "I'm rather glad you did. But what now?"

Mikhail lifted his hands to say he didn't know. "You were beholden to Mr. Cetanni. He changed allegiances to procure the cures that saved your life. That betrayal of his fae master is what locked him away in the fae realm."

Mr. King looked confused and pointed at Mr. Cetanni's inert body. "He's there. On the table."

"Physically, biologically, yes." Mikhail didn't know quite how to explain the difference. He had no knowledge of Mr. King's belief system, nor did he wish to disillusion or change it.

"His soul has been ripped away?"

"For lack of a better way to put it, essentially yes." Mikhail looked at Mr. Cetanni lying still as the grave. "But we're hoping to change that. First, we have to rescue him and Mr. Alexandre."

"I don't know what I can do to help. Is there anything?"

Mikhail thought about it for a moment.

He stared at Mr. King. Both he and Mr. Alexandre dealt in images, it didn't matter the medium. They brought to life things conjured from their imaginations. Both painted or captured scenes from the fae realm. "You're like a lightning rod."

"Excuse me?"

"You attract the fae to you." Mikhail warmed to the idea. "They allowed you to see and photograph them as they allowed Mr. Alexandre to paint them. However, even before you were bitten, you were marked. They knew you."

Mr. King looked away. He shifted on the exam table. "I've done nothing to gain their notice. Not on purpose."

"It didn't have to be intentional."

Dante had moved away to gather more supplies to take to the garden. However, Mikhail knew he listened intently to their conversation. "What do you think, Dante?"

"I think anything is worth a try. If he's working like magnetic north to the fae, then we owe it to ourselves and those caught in the fae realm to see if he can help us open a portal." Dante indicated Mr. King. "With your permission, of course."

Mr. King made a face. "You saved my life; I can barely begrudge you the chance to save your friends. Even if I don't know what to do."

"You might not need to do anything. Your presence alone might help." Mikhail lifted the projector, the slide of the map, and indicated the generator behind him. "I'll come back for that."

Mr. King slid off the exam table. "Where are you going?"

"To the garden. Interesting things move in the waters of the fountain. We'll have better luck there." He looked down at the holes he'd rent in his pants from removing the pockets. "But first a change of trousers."

Nicholas tried for the ballroom. Everywhere he turned, the ceiling caved in or horrible creatures roamed the halls in search of enemies. At the moment, he didn't quite know which side they fell on—though Azgarth no doubt saw them as guilty as Oiredon.

So much destruction.

All the beauty of the palace came crashing down with each terrible blast, exposing the ugliness under the opulence. Cracks appeared in the floor. Foul-smelling liquid oozed up, bubbling forth from the pits below. Nicholas was careful not to step in it. No telling if it was from the acid bowl or some other toxic place.

Once he reached the outside, then what? He had no idea which direction to go to find the human world or even if Oiredon's agents had the ability to open a portal for him. What if he ended up in some faraway place, much removed from London. How would he make it back to Dr. Savoy's home? He had no money. No resources.

Stop. You're finding problems before they arise.

He continued on. Roman's weight bore down on him, but he tried to push the pain and discomfort away. Roman would do the same for him.

What had happened to cause the war? It had to be more than previously stated. No one fought like this over a slight. This had the stamp of doctrinal or dogmatic differences to it. Well, he, for one, wasn't going to be a party to the arguments of the fae.

Warriors dressed in the black tattered clothing and shifting features of Azgarth's guard streamed down the passageway, swords raised. Caught with nowhere to hide, Nicholas did the only thing he could—stood his ground.

The warriors reached him. He gripped Roman tighter. If they were to die, at least it would be together. Without regrets, and with dignity. He didn't cower or turn away from the onslaught.

They moved through him. An edge of icy wind in a blizzard.

He lost his breath.

White vapor filled the air around his head, seeping from the rents where the swords had gone through. No blood leaked from his body. Only that essence of heat into the cooler air around it. Oddly, his brain registered no new pain. Metallic clicks came from behind him. He didn't dare turn to see the source of the sounds. He feared he already knew. He'd heard the clash of sword on sword before—though it had been many years ago.

He kept moving forward. When that proved impossible, he moved to the side, taking connecting hallways and corridors with the hope of eventually finding the way outside.

Sounds of battle rolled down the current passage they traveled. He needed to find a way to bypass the trouble. Nicholas stopped and hiked Roman up on his shoulder, getting a better grip on him.

It seemed they had walked forever. How long had they been on this endless journey? Hell must be an infinite series of corridors, never reaching any particular destination.

Loud keening came from behind them. The sound lifted the hair on his neck and caused a cold sweat to rise through his flesh. Primal fear blossomed in his gut, spreading outward to encompass his chest. He picked up speed. Halfway down the hall, his knees buckled. Nicholas pitched to the floor. Roman landed on top of him—dead weight pushing him into the ground.

He struggled to turn over. With throbbing legs, he rose to his feet. All the while, the keening grew louder, closer. Time ran down. They wouldn't have a chance to run.

The rents in his chest from the fae swords continued to seep. His life force ebbed out even as his heart and mind told him he had to keep moving. Had to keep *them* moving. For now, he grabbed Roman and brought him close, then sat in front of him.

Cracks appeared in the wall across from them, spreading a blinding light over the corridor.

Roman's mouth moved against his cheek. Air wheezed out.

Nicholas pulled back to see Roman's face. "Did you say something?"

"Destroy...you must..."

"Destroy what? I don't know what you're talking about."

"Palace...heart. Finish it."

The palace had a heart? Of course, it had to. Azgarth didn't have one, so he had to manufacture one inside the palace. Take out the palace heart and gain absolute freedom from the fae.

Light from down the corridor became eclipsed by a large object that took up almost the entire width and height of the structure. A whirring roar drowned out the keening. All the while the unmistakable *snip snip* of a dozen pairs of shears added an even more sinister crescendo to the already horrible experience.

Mechanical arms swirled while blades opened and closed, attempting to clip, snip, or amputate any appendage unlucky enough to be caught in the way. Nicholas rolled them away, tucking up as flush to the wall as possible. He leaned closer, trying to make them become one with the stone. His arms were clamped around Roman. His back exposed to the evil contraption.

Movement from the stone brought Nicholas's head up. He pushed harder and felt it give.

Tears of relief filled his eyes.

"Here." He tucked Roman into the space. "Stay here while I go take care of the heart."

He hated leaving Roman, but couldn't drag him along. Not when he didn't know how dangerous attacking the palace heart might prove. As it happened, the palace stood on very shaky ground. It might take very little in order for the entire structure to collapse.

He gripped the pointed stick he'd used to destroy the paintings and shimmied through the crack in the wall that led to the palace heart.

Pressure changed and swirled around him, making it harder to draw breath. Each step harder, as if he moved through sucking mud. The heart pulsed, sending shafts of colored lights outward, blinding in its brilliance. He tried to shield his eyes, but it penetrated through him, finding its way into his soul. It burned his throat like salt acid. He coughed to try to clear the pain.

No more dallying. He raised his arm and prepared to strike the heart when a blast blew him backward. He slid across the floor, landing near the entrance. When he looked up, Azgarth stood over him.

Fear filled his belly. He'd failed. Azgarth wouldn't let him go without punishment now. Nicholas would be lucky if death was the least of possible outcomes.

"You think to send me to a fae prison by striking out at the heart? It will never work. No mortal may kill a fae. You haven't the strength. It takes magic to fight magic."

Azgarth stalked Nicholas where he lay. The fae master bent down and pulled Nicholas up by his hair and dragged him back to the heart. "Look into the depths of the light and see what fate awaited your precious sister when she begged for your mercy."

Nicholas's eyes went wide. He didn't believe it. Juliana hadn't begged mercy for her life. She'd simply ceased to breathe, her heart to beat. But that was in the human realm—who knows what happened once she'd crossed to the fae. Had she bartered or begged to return? Had her stubbornness meant punishment?

"Such a beautiful creature." Azgarth gripped the back of Nicholas's head, shoving his face closer to the palace heart. So close Nicholas saw the faults in the structure. Instead of it being of sound construction, the heart was of no more strength than blown glass—fae glass. Cracks appeared in the outer shell. Brittle and delicate, the heart was every bit as mercurial as Azgarth.

Images in the depth of the lights, shimmered and shifted, showing Nicholas Juliana's fate.

"You see her?" Azgarth pushed Nicholas closer. "How beautiful she was before her grief led me to encase her in stone."

Horror filled Nicholas as the same blue veins spread through Juliana's skin as did his own. Christ, but he had to end this. Leave the fae realm for more reasons than to save Roman's life.

Anger struck. "You were supposed to protect her! That was the bargain. Not to punish her for being struck down before her time. She had no part in the events that caused her death."

"Someone had to pay." Azgarth waved his hand and the image changed to Azgarth's guards having their way with her even as she struggled to save herself from both them and her impending stone prison.

Nicholas struck out, sending the wooden stake through the palace heart. It shattered on impact, sending glass fragments outward. One struck his cheek, slashing it open, but he didn't care. Let him bleed as Juliana had. He deserved nothing less.

Azgarth screamed in agony. He held his chest as if his heart were ripped in truth. He fell back against the fractured shards, his face a study in pain and disbelief.

Nicholas scrambled to his feet as the palace quaked in earnest. What Oiredon's warriors hadn't managed to destroy, Nicholas had—a final nail in the coffin.

He hurried from the chamber and back to Roman as the walls around them shook with violence. He pushed at the loose stone. A few more shoves and it gave way. He dragged Roman through the tiny chamber just as the mechanical snipper whirled by again, unable to gain purchase on the horribly listing floor.

He leaned Roman against the wall, then went to work to pry the stone all the way free. If he got it out where they could shimmy through, then he could take stock of a possible escape route in that direction. Once he saw the other passage, he could decide which one to take.

White tendrils of smoke rose from his chest. With each expenditure of energy, more of his life force leaked out. He tried not to let the effects of waning strength matter, to give it credence. Truthfully, how was a mortal man to measure the damage done to a body by a fae blade? He'd probably expended too much of his life force by taking out the palace heart.

He'd used all his strength—the last of it to push the stone through the opening. The scene outside took his breath. A bridge, suspended high above a fertile gorge that led to the side of a mountain.

Birds called to others from tall pines. Ancient runes were etched into the side of the rock face.

"Nicholas Alexandre!" a voice called from the far side of the gorge.

A light shone from the ledge. He couldn't see a person or much else save rock and vegetation. And that light...it blinded. If someone stood behind it, Nicholas would never see them.

"Come on, Roman. We might as well go this way. I'd as soon get as far away from this falling palace as possible." Either that or they'd be crushed under stones and broken dreams.

The thought of putting Roman on his shoulder again was enough to make him stumble in weariness. He tried to pick him up but hadn't the energy to do more than stand in place and shake as his muscles spasm.

"No. Don't do this to me. We're almost free."

He sat back down on the bridge and pulled Roman along. Thus they progressed for the length of the expanse. Each foot they gained was a struggle. The distance seemed to grow longer rather than shorter. Illusion or fact? Hard to tell in the fae realm.

As he reached for Roman, Nicholas caught sight of his arms. Fingers of blue snaked down from underneath his shirtsleeves. He stopped and pulled up the fabric. Thick ribbons of icy stone had replaced and infiltrated his skin. Panicked, he opened his shirt. The gashes from the fae blade acted as points of origin for the strange phenomenon.

The planks of the bridge bounced with each precision step of booted feet. The movement caused vibrations under his buttocks. He looked toward the distant ridge. Warriors had moved out onto the bridge, coming closer, but wearing the colors of Oiredon.

Fog rolled into the gorge, closing off his view of the warriors. Sounds echoed around him in an eerie concert.

After trying so hard, and coming so close, he wasn't about to give up and let fae warriors overtake them. What if Azgarth's followers had worn Oiredon's colors to confuse? They'd not find Nicholas and Roman such easily plucked targets.

From behind the blanket of fog came the distinct *clink* and *clack* of large cogs in a wheel, turning. The bridge was suddenly in motion, falling down to the gorge below. Shouts called from behind him. He grabbed Roman once again, holding him tight to buffet him for when they hit the bottom.

This way was certain death.

They fell through the misty canopy. The ground came closer. A river flowed like a serpentine through the countryside. With a jolt, the bridge hit the water.

Chapter Twenty-Three

No sooner had Mr. King gotten near the fountain than the spray parted as a curtain on a stage. To say they were not prepared for the invitation was an understatement.

"Henri!" Mikhail shouted toward the house. So far, his assistant had not shown his face again once he'd started working on repairing the oscillating generator.

Mikhail realized some things could not be rushed, but the fae realm apparently waited for no man. Dante squatted down and went to work getting the projector working. Not that they were going to use it to project much at this time, but they needed the light to find their way to this particular entrance.

Even though his last experience in the fae realm was less than satisfactory, Mikhail tied a tether around his waist and prepared to enter the breach one more time.

"Wait for Henri to come with the generator. I don't want the rift to close prematurely on you." Dante got the light working. The beam cut through the rent in the water but did not reflect on the hedgerow at the back of the property, proving the light went into the portal rather than through it.

"I fear the longer we leave them in there, the harder it will be to extricate them." They'd already fought hard to bring Mr. Alexandre back from the dead once, no telling if they would be able to reanimate a man twice. He'd hate to lose him and find out later all their work was in vain.

Henri came out of the house, running to the fountain. The device in his hand was smaller, more compact that the earlier version.

Mikhail indicated the small box with a nod. "Is that going to work or have the output we need?"

"I've tuned it precisely to the output generated by the sound waves inherent in a rift. It should work more efficiently with less energy." Henri made it sound so matter-of-fact, who could ever dispute his theory?

"All right. Are we ready?" Mikhail glanced at his cohorts.

Mr. King looked as if he wanted to say something but held his tongue. No matter what objection he might pose, things had gone too far to change their minds. Mr. Alexandre and Mr. Cetanni needed rescued; Mikhail felt that all the way to the marrow of his bones.

Dante held the other end of the rope, using himself as an anchor. "If you get into trouble, yank the rope and I'll come after you."

Mikhail nodded and dove into the rift in the water.

Unlike his previous attempts to go through the fountain, this time, beads of water hit and bounced off him. He felt no wetness touch his cheeks or soak his clothing. Cold air shimmered around him, growing crystalline. He turned back to look over his shoulder. The beam of light was still visible from the opening. Good. They'd at least managed to mark their entrance, but how was he to find Mr. Alexandre and Mr. Cetanni in such a large and disorganized place during a time of war?

He didn't even understand the rules there, only that there didn't seem to be any. Time, space, physical principles all suspended as the fae realm closed in around him.

The channel opened into a small grotto behind a waterfall. Made sense in an odd sort of way. Once more, he turned back to see the light shining in the distance. The beam was barely a pinprick, but using the waterfall as a guide might help in his quest when he returned.

A small ledge separated the riverbank from the grotto. Mikhail crept around the edge, hugging the rock face to keep from slipping into the turbulent waters below.

He stepped out and looked up. Breath caught, suspended in the presence of such unimaginable beauty. The land was lush and green, rocks formed of glittering crystals made up the walls of the canyon. Majestic was the only word that came to mind. It was a shame that such beauty was hidden in a place where ugliness was concealed behind a very clever veneer.

Mikhail set out to walk along the river for a while. At one point, the rope pulled taut. He'd gone farther than he thought. It had been a risk doing it this way. They knew there was a possibility he'd have to travel deep into the fae realm to find the missing men. He stuck his hand down in his pocket and pulled out the copper slugs. If he had to leave the trail beside the river, he'd use the small disks to mark his way, but after those were gone, he'd have to rely on his memory and hope the scenery didn't change. One thing that stood out was this side of the landscape was crisp and real. No faded watercolors there either.

He hiked around a bend in the river, searching a hospitable way to scale the wall to the top of the gorge. From this vantage point, he saw nothing of what surrounded him. He needed higher ground so he might better pinpoint exactly where he stood.

Distance, like time, did not work the same way in the fae realm as it did in the human. One might walk for hours here and cover very little ground. It all depended on what Azgarth wanted, or how he tormented his visitors.

Birds called from high up in the trees that grew along the ridge. They were noisy. Stirred up. Something had upset the tranquility of the area, and it hadn't happened long before his arrival—at least not that Mikhail figured.

Another bend in the river, this one moving to the right. Mikhail followed the curve and stopped. A huge section of a bridge lay across the river, having fallen from the top of the canyon wall. Two figures lay washed up on the bank, rag dolls tossed about at sea. Mikhail hurried to them and turned the first figure over.

He tapped pale cheeks. "Mr. Alexandre. Wake up!"

Mr. Alexandre's eyelids fluttered. He mumbled incoherent words.

Above Mikhail, the unmistakable creak of wood about to give way echoed down into the gorge. He looked up only to find more pieces of the bridge about to come down. Not in a hurried broken and falling manner, but an eerily controlled one that suggested an unseen operator.

Mikhail tapped Mr. Alexandre's cheeks harder. "You have to wake now. I can't carry both of you out of here."

Mr. Alexandre took a gasp of air and sat up. His eyes popped open. His chest worked hard as he gulped each breath. The poor man acted as if he'd run with the hounds of hell nipping at his feet. His shirt lay open, revealing ribbons of blue lines spreading over his chest and up his neck.

"Roman."

"He's here, but I haven't checked him yet. I'll do that while you see if you can get yourself up and moving."

Normally, he wouldn't leave a man who had fallen from such a height to care for himself, but Mr. Alexandre's ability to sit straight up rather negated the need for him to sit still while Mikhail assessed for any internal damage. And those marks, what were they?

Mikhail stayed low to the ground and ever aware of the piece of the bridge coming closer. He did a quick assessment of Mr. Cetanni and decided he didn't like what he saw. Bloody slashes had ripped his chest and back open in savage stripes. How was that even possible? This was not Mr.

Cetanni's physical form. But then, what was the normal way for the subconscious to look when it takes on a slightly physical form? He had no standards by which to measure health and well-being.

Judging from the amount of blood leaking from the lash marks, this representation of Mr. Cetanni's mind and soul had as much substance as his corporeal. In that case, Mikhail had no choice but to treat it as such. He hurriedly checked a pulse and felt for broken bones. The only ones of note were the ribs.

He tried not to think of what happened when they walked through the veil. Would there be two Mr. Cetanni's? How were they going to integrate this aspect with the other? No matter what, he couldn't stay trapped here. That scenario was completely unacceptable.

Mikhail glanced over his shoulder at Mr. Alexandre. "Can you stand?"

"Not well. I hurt my leg. And...I took a wound from fae blades."

Mikhail tried not to contemplate the significance of that information. He looked around for something to use as a tool or a means of escape. Part of the bridge lay broken on the edge of the river. It looked seaworthy enough. Perhaps...

"Can you get over to the bridge? We can use it as a raft to float back down the river."

Mr. Alexandre did a broken-gaited shuffle over to the makeshift raft and sat down. Mikhail hefted Mr. Cetanni over his shoulder.

The bridge from above lowered ever closer. Snarls and teeth gnashing rained down like the promise of a bloody retribution. They had to move faster.

A rumble moved under his feet. Tremors of an earthquake. Or detonations.

Mikhail lay Mr. Cetanni on the wooden plank, then pushed the vessel into the water. He leaped on board and let the current drag them down river toward the waterfall. He'd need to figure out a way to steer them near the bank once they got within distance of the waterfall. Going under it seemed a bad option. He'd not come all this way to rescue them to drown due to stupidity.

A large splash hit the water behind them. A wave rolled toward them and crested. They bobbed in the wake. The second section of bridge had finally reached the bottom to unleash a host of the most horrible creatures Mikhail had ever seen. Gruesome with their empty eye sockets, decayed flesh, and festering sores, he'd never witnessed anything quite like them before—not even while studying various disease states. He questioned their ability to know where they moved or how they hunted without eyes, but in the fae realm, eyes might not be a requirement of sight.

The hellish beasts jumped from the bridge and charged the raft.

He had no way to make them go any faster, nor did he possess weapons to defend.

"I'll be damned if I'll let you get us." Mikhail shifted over a few steps and worked on breaking a loose board free. It might not be the weapon of choice, but it would make one hell of a club.

He pulled and tugged. The piece wouldn't come loose.

Mr. Alexandre started over to him. "What are you trying to do?"

"Stay where you are. You'll unbalance us." Last thing they needed was to get tipped into the river. Trampled. Drowned. He didn't know which demise was worse.

They went over a rapids. The raft picked up speed.

They were heading toward the falls.

The raft shot around the bend. Behind them the creatures snarled and clacked razor-like fangs.

A roar of water filled the gorge.

"We're heading right for the falls!" Mr. Alexandre yelled.

Another rumble rocked the ground. The raft jerked to the side and nearly capsized.

"Turn Mr. Cetanni prone and lay across his back. I can't steer us."

Mr. Alexandre did as instructed. Mikhail stood as the first of the creatures were upon them.

He balled up his fist and swung with all his might, knocking the creature square in the jaw. The shock of the hit drove the thing's head up and back. It stumbled, causing a chain reaction behind it.

Waters parted. Warriors stepped from behind the grotto, bows raised and arrows nocked.

"Get down!"

Mikhail hit the deck as the raft sailed through the falls and hit solid rock. He wasted no time pulling Mr. Cetanni from the raft. "Follow me. The rift is up ahead."

Light—that beautiful beacon of gold—shone the way, even in the darkness of the cave. Soon they were within the protective barrier of the fountain waters. The rope Mikhail had abandon lay on the ground.

"Dr. Stanslovich?"

Mikhail turned his attention to Mr. Alexandre whose voice held a decided tremor. "What is it?"

Mr. Alexandre's gaze was fixed not on Mikhail, but in Mr. Cetanni. Alarmed, Mikhail brought the man down off his shoulder, only to realize the problem—Mr. Cetanni had begun to fade.

"I'm sorry. I don't know if this is happening because we are close to the portal, or for the fact he cannot leave the fae realm." Mikhail took Mr. Cetanni back into his arms. He seemed lighter now, less substantial. Why hadn't he noticed it before?

"We can't leave him here."

"I have no intention of leaving him." Not after he'd gone through all the trouble to rescue them. They walked to the entrance. Each step lightened Mikhail's load. His arms moved through where Mr. Cetanni's hips should be.

As he came back through the breach, Mr. Cetanni faded completely. Gone from existence as if that part had never been.

Dante stood at the opening, his eyes wide. "You found them."

"For all the good it did." Mikhail took off for the surgery, determined to see if carrying Mr. Cetanni's subconscious to the breach had any impact.

Dante put his arm around Mr. Alexandre and helped him along. Mr. King and Henri stayed behind to close the breach.

A horrible rumbling filled the garden. The fountain began to tremble.

"Get away from there!" Mikhail yelled to Henri and Mr. King. "It's going to blow."

No sooner had the words left his mouth than the entire fountain exploded in a shower of water and stone. When the debris cleared, there was nothing left but the fountain's motor, whirring pointlessly.

Mikhail took in the destruction. With luck, they'd not have need of the particular means of travel anytime soon.

Roman woke to a familiar face, but not the one he'd expected.

Valentine stood over him, looking down into his eyes with concern. "Welcome back."

"Thank you, I think." His voice was scratchy and cracked from disuse. His eyes burned as if his lids had been lifted and sand poured in them. The ache in his ribs went all the way to his backbone. He'd never been so happy to hurt in his life.

The resurrection tank began to oscillate. An ominous whine accompanied the sloshing of fluid over the top.

Valentine hurried to help Roman off the exam table. "We need to get to safety."

Roman agreed. "Should we try to turn it off?"

Even as he said the words, he noted the motor was not engaged.

"Run!"

Roman's legs didn't comply with the order from his brain. He slipped on the floor and went down hard. The tank combusted with all the elegance of a battlefield cannon. Glass, metal, and fluid shot out in a three-hundred-sixty-degree arc. He and Valentine lay on the floor, covering their heads with their arms.

A commotion sounded at the door, but he was too dizzy, stiff, and winded from his run to turn his head and look who made it, or to even raise as much as a care. As long as Azgarth didn't lift his head to finish what he'd started, he was perfectly content to lie there on the hard slab of the floor and rest.

Then Nicholas was there, turning Roman over. "It worked. It worked."

Love moved warm and sweet through his veins. "If you mean your killing strike to the palace heart, then mad dash through Azgarth's house of ruin, yes. I believe it did."

Nicholas ran his free hand over Roman's brow. "We...we...lost you at the rift. Then the fountain exploded."

Roman started to shake his head, but pain shot through his skull. He took a deep breath and let it out slowly. After a few beats of quiet, he said, "We had a similar experience in here." And the ruined tank was proof.

Nicholas helped him to a sitting position.

"I was never truly lost, Nicco, though a bit disoriented. I had my feet in both worlds. I heard every word, felt every pain."

"You're safe now."

Roman gave what he hoped passed for a reassuring smile.

"What aren't you telling me, Roman?"

"Nothing."

Nicholas narrowed his eyes. "Did you see something in the fae realm we need to know?"

A rusty laugh fell from his lips. "Everything about the fae realm you need to know, but it's always in flux. Even more so now."

"But it appears Azgarth may very well be defeated."

"And Oiredon was not able to shield me from Azgarth's attacks." Roman put out shaky arms to steady himself. "How long do you think it will be before he rallies and rebuilds?"

"You're saying we aren't free. We never were." Nicholas's expression fell. "Even by shattering the heart?"

Roman rubbed a hand over his face. He felt as if something had gone horribly wrong, above and beyond nearly being killed by Azgarth. Deep in his soul, a tether pulled taut. Connecting him to the fae as if he'd never been apart from them. "If Oiredon chooses not to make good on his promise, we're never going to be free."

After a moment of sitting in silence, a horrible expression morphed Nicholas's face. He stood, taking his hand from Roman's.

"What is it?" Roman tried to reach for him, but Nicholas had already moved out of range. "Tell me."

Nicholas's eyes blazed with fury. "You've turned your soul over in keeping with another fae and still we've gained no ground. When does it stop?"

Roman shook his head. "I don't know. We've been freed from Azgarth, but whatever is going on between he and his brother, I'm sure is far from finished."

Air shimmered around them and Oiredon appeared, looking tired and a bit worse for wear. Whatever the toll of the feud with Azgarth, the conflict wore heavily on Oiredon.

"A most industrious way to aid me. Your assistance is most appreciated." A smile lingered on his lips. "Though I most heartily give you your freedom from fae control, I warn you, Azgarth will return and his rage will be great."

Roman exchanged glances with Nicholas.

Oiredon waved his hand. "I will shield you the best I can, for his influence is no greater than my own in the world of man. However, I fear your friends may not fare as well."

Roman followed Oiredon's gaze to where Drs. Savoy and Stanslovich cleaned the remains of the shattered tank.

"You will watch out for them?"

"As much as I am able."

Roman gave a nod.

A tiny tendril of unease uncurled inside, leaving behind a well where his soul felt new and clean. Heat seeped into his veins, chasing away the lingering cold. Nicholas squatted where Roman remained on the floor and slid his hand into Roman's once again. Tears stood in his eyes.

"We'll render them aid if needed," Nicholas assured. "I'd not leave them exposed to Azgarth."

Roman's heart swelled with love. He squeezed Nicholas's hand. "Together."

"Together."

About the Author

Cassie Sweet lives and writes from the beautiful white sand beaches of Florida's Gulf Coast. She loves to hear from fans and encourages emails and contacting her on social media.

Email: MysticKat1965@yahoo.com

Facebook: www.facebook.com/cassiesweetauthor or www.facebook.com/kat.mancos

Twitter: @MKMancosKScott

Website: www.MysticKat.com

Also Available from NineStar Press

Connect with NineStar Press

www.ninestarpress.com

www.facebook.com/ninestarpress

www.facebook.com/groups/NineStarNiche

www.twitter.com/ninestarpress

www.tumblr.com/blog/ninestarpress